The Mummy's Foot and Other Fantastic Tales

The Hippocampus Press Classics of Gothic Horror Series

Edited by S. T. Joshi

Johnson Looked Back: The Collected Weird Stories of Thomas Burke
The Harbor-Master: Best Weird Stories of Robert W. Chambers
Lost Ghosts: The Complete Weird Stories of Mary E. Wilkins Freeman
Back There in the Grass: The Horror Tales of
Irvin S. Cobb and Gouverneur Morris
The Mummy's Foot and Other Fantastic Tales, Théophile Gautier
Twin Spirits: The Complete Weird Stories of W. W. Jacobs
From the Dead: The Complete Weird Stories of E. Nesbit
Frankenstein and Others: The Complete Weird Fiction of Mary Shelley

THE MUMMY'S FOOT

AND OTHER FANTASTIC TALES

Théophile Gautier

Edited, with an Introduction, by S. T. Joshi

Hippocampus Press

New York

Contents

Introduction, *by S. T. Joshi* 7

Omphale: A Rococo Story 21

Clarimonde 31

One of Cleopatra's Nights 63

The Mummy's Foot 97

Arria Marcella: A Souvenir of Pompeii 109

Avatar 139

Jettatura 217

Spirite: A Fantastic Tale 299

Introduction

The tradition of French weird fiction is rich and deep, and needs to be more widely appreciated by Anglophone readers. There are fantastic elements in the work of such classic writers as Rabelais and Voltaire, although not much of it is weird or horrific in the strictest sense. Relatively few French writers contributed to the Gothic novel during its heyday (1764–1820), but it was not long thereafter that Victor Hugo, Charles Nodier, and others began writing novels, tales, and poems that placed them among the forefront of the weird fiction of their era. Among the most notable of these was Théophile Gautier (1811–1872), whose weird work extends far beyond the one or two anthology chestnuts for which he has hitherto been known in the English-speaking world.

Pierre-Jules-Théophile Gautier was born on August 30, 1811, to Pierre and Antoinette-Adélaide Gautier at Tarbes, a French city near the border with Spain. This remoteness from the nation's dominant cultural center, Paris, perhaps signaled Gautier's self-perception as both a Frenchman and a citizen of the world: he became one of the most widely traveled men of his generation. In 1815 the family moved to Paris, as Gautier's father became a minor functionary in the government. After a brief and unhappy few months at the Collège Royal de Louis-le-Grand in 1822, Gautier enjoyed his years spent at the Collège Charlemagne, where the young poet Gérard de Nerval became a lifelong friend. Gautier was fascinated with Latin and Greek but also relished reading the Gothic novels of Radcliffe, Maturin, and "Monk" Lewis—a fusion of classicism and Romanticism that dominated the rest of his life and his literary work. Gautier also studied painting, and he remained extraordinarily sensitive to the pictorial and plastic arts.

In 1829 he met Victor Hugo (1802–1885), whose post-Gothic novel *Han d'Icelande* (1823; Han of Iceland) focused on a diabolical figure in the wilds of Norway. It was in 1830 that Gautier himself published a slim volume of his *Poésies* (it was paid for by his father) and also attended the premiere of Hugo's revolutionary play *Hernani,* which officially launched the Romantic movement in France. In 1832 he published a long poem, *Albertus,* described by his biographer as "the tale of a witch turned woman who persuades her lover to sell his soul to the devil."[1] Shortly thereafter Gautier began writing articles on painting for *Le France Littéraire,* the first of many magazines and newspapers for which he would write thousands of pieces of journalism over the next forty years.

In 1834 Gautier wrote what became his manifesto for the credo of "art for art's sake." It was published as the preface to his novel *Mademoiselle de Maupin* (1835), a fascinating account of a woman who disguises herself as a man and thereby attracts the love of both a man and a woman. The novel remains Gautier's most celebrated work, but it is the preface that attracted the greatest attention at the time for its uncompromising stance on the independence of art from conventional morality and its provocative declaration that art is, and must be, "useless":

> Nothing that is beautiful is indispensable to life. You might suppress flowers, and the world would not suffer materially; yet who would wish that there were no more flowers? I would rather give up potatoes than roses, and I think that there is none but an utilitarian in the world capable of pulling up a bed of tulips in order to plant cabbages therein.
>
> What is the use of women's beauty? Provided that a woman be medically well formed, and in condition to bear children, she will always be good enough for economists.
>
> What is the good of music? of painting? Who would be foolish enough to prefer Mozart to Monsieur Carrel, and Michael Angelo to the inventor of white mustard?
>
> There is truly nothing beautiful but that which can never be of any use whatsoever; everything useful is ugly, for it is the expression of some need, and man's needs are ignoble and disgusting like his own poor and infirm nature. The most useful place in a house is the water-closet.[2]

---

1. Joanna Richardson, *Théophile Gautier: His Life and Times* (New York: Coward-McCann, 1959), 23.

2. "Preface" to *Mademoiselle de Maupin* (New York: Boni & Liveright, n.d.), xxv.

That comment on "women's beauty" is significant, for Gautier came to believe that the human female constituted the most exalted form of beauty in all creation, and much of his work—and, for that matter, his life—was devoted to seeking it out.

The young novelist Honoré de Balzac (1799–1850) read *Mademoiselle de Maupin* and sought out Gautier, urging him to write for his paper, *Le Chronique de Paris.* But Gautier also seized the opportunity to write for Emile de Girardin's paper *La Presse,* and over the next several decades he contributed enormous quantities of dramatic criticism to it, becoming perhaps the leading drama critic in France during that period. Around this time he met Eugénie Fort, and she became the first of his several mistresses. She bore him a child, Théophile Gautier *fils,* on November 27, 1836, and remained in close touch with him (although their relationship later became platonic) for the rest of his life.

Gautier's first voyage outside of France was a modest trip to Belgium in 1836, accompanied by Gérard de Nerval. But in 1840 he undertook a more extensive trip to Spain. A travelogue he later wrote, *Voyage en Espagne,* was published posthumously in 1881. (This is not to be confused with his 1843 play *Voyage en Espagne.*) In 1841 he wrote the hugely successful ballet *Giselle.* It was written largely with the celebrated ballerina Carlotta Grisi in mind; he had fallen in love with Carlotta, but for various reasons she was not available to him. A few years later he initiated a liaison with her sister, Ernesta, who gave birth to two daughters, Judith (1845–1917) and Estelle (b. 1848). Judith would later become a poet and novelist in her own right.

The year 1842 saw Gautier's first trip to England, a country he would visit repeatedly over the next several decades. A voyage to Algeria occurred in 1845, followed by another trip to Spain the next year. But Gautier's life was disrupted by the Revolution of 1848; his contract with *La Presse* was cancelled (although he later resumed writing for the paper on a freelance basis), and for the next decade or more he suffered considerably from financial difficulties. In 1849, on another trip to England, he met Maria Mattei, who briefly became his mistress; but she broke from him because she could not endure his continuing involvement with Ernesta and other women. In 1850 Gautier made an extensive trip to Italy, visiting Venice, Florence, Rome, Naples, and Pompeii;

that last locale led directly to his weird tale "Arria Marcella: A Souvenir of Pompeii" (1852). The year 1852 also saw Gautier undertaking a two-month visit to Constantinople (Istanbul); on his return to France, he stopped off in Greece and absorbed the ancient monuments that had been a source of wonder and fascination for him since childhood.

The year 1852 was also notable for the publication of a slim poetry volume *Emaux et Camées* (Enamels and Cameos), initially containing only eighteen poems but augmented in several succeeding editions. It was hailed as an impeccable fusion of classical precision and Romantic sensibility. A few years later Gautier gave up writing for *La Presse* and turned his attention to another paper, *Le Moniteur Universel.* By this time he was hobnobbing with the leading literary figures of France, including Flaubert, Hugo, the Goncourt brothers, and the critic C. A. Sainte-Beuve, as well as painters such as Gustave Doré and the composers Georges Bizet, Giuseppe Verdi, and Hector Berlioz. The deaths of Balzac in 1850 and of Gérard de Nerval (by suicide) in 1855 affected him deeply, but he was gratified to receive the dedication of the first edition of Charles Baudelaire's *Les Fleurs du mal:*

AU POÈTE IMPECCABLE
au perfait magician ès lettres françaises
à mon très-cher et très-vénéré maître et ami
THÉOPHILE GAUTIER
avec les sentiments de la plus profonde
humilité
je dédie ces fleurs maladives
C. B.

[To the impeccable poet, the perfect magician of French literature, to my dearest and most venerated master and friend, Théophile Gautier, with feelings of the deepest humility, I dedicate these sickly flowers. C. B.]

In the fall of 1856 Gautier began writing *Le Roman de la momie* (1857; The Romance of a Mummy), a novel about an English explorer who unearths a lovely female mummy. There are no weird elements here, as the novel is a straight historical novel in which a scroll found in the mummy's sarcophagus narrates her life and loves in ancient Egypt. In late 1856 Gautier became editor of *L'Artiste,* where he devoted himself to art criticism. He championed many of the revolutionary French painters of his day, including Delacroix, Ingres, Millet, Corot, and Manet. He spent several months, from the fall of 1858 to the spring of 1859, in Russia, as he was commissioned to write a book about Russian art. Another trip to Russia followed in 1861.

The year 1863 saw the appearance of a novel that Gautier had long worked on, *Le Capitaine Fracasse.* Although highly melodramatic (with many tropes derived from the Gothic novels), it is full of lush and vivid imagery. It proved to be a critical and financial success; Gautier boasted in a letter: "*Le Capitaine Fracasse* is more successful than [Hugo's] *Les Misérables* [which had appeared in 1862], and the success grows daily."[3] The fantastic novel *Spirite,* inspired by Carlotta Grisi, began appearing in the *Moniteur Universel* on November 17, 1865.

Although his financial situation was now more secure, Gautier was at this time plagued by various illnesses: "rheumatism, haemorrhoids, excessive sweating, frequent colds, depression, lethargy," as his biographer notes.[4] His personal life was also in turmoil. His daughter Judith had fallen in love with the poet Catulle Mendès. For various reasons Gautier considered him an unsuitable husband for Judith, but she married him anyway. And because Ernesta Grisi had encouraged the marriage, Gautier broke off relations with her.

In 1868 Gautier gained a sinecure by becoming the librarian (and sometime lover) of Princess Mathilde. The next year he undertook his long-deferred trip to Egypt. The man who had written "One of Cleopatra's Nights" and "The Mummy's Foot" decades before he had ever seen Egypt would now finally set foot on the soil of the ancient land. But the journey began inauspiciously—he broke his arm on board the ship that took him there—and the trip itself featured numerous other disappointments and irritants. Nevertheless, he did see Cairo, Alexandria, and the Suez Canal.

---

3. Quoted in Richardson, 185.

4. Richardson, 201.

But with the onset of the Franco-Prussian War on July 15, 1870, Gautier's life took a sudden turn for the worse. Although he arranged for his daughter Estelle to stay with Carlotta Grisi in Switzerland, he himself returned to Paris in early September, where he endured appalling conditions during the siege of Paris:

> We are eating horse, donkey, macaroni without butter or cheese; we shall soon be down to rats and mice. The horse is excellent, but the donkey is a real delicacy. There is nothing less true than the phrase: "Tough as a donkey." . . . We're rationed for gas as we are for meat. We only light one jet in four and the sight of these black streets, where a rare passer-by brushes against the walls and we do not hear the sound of a single carriage, is really not calculated to enliven us. But either we bury ourselves beneath the ruins of Paris or we die of hunger if we cannot fight our way out.[5]

Later on Gautier actually did say that "I regaled myself with a rat *pâté* which wasn't bad at all." He managed to write *Tableaux de Siège* (1871), but it provided little material comfort. The war finally ended on May 10, 1871, with France's humiliating defeat; but at least the siege was over.

Gautier's health, however, was permanently shattered. For the remaining seventeen months of his life, he went from bad to worse, suffering several heart attacks and strokes in June and July 1872. He somehow continued writing, working on an ambitious *Histoire du romanticisme,* an account of literary and artistic movements from the epochal date of 1830 to 1868; although not fully complete, it was published posthumously in 1880. Gautier, largely bedridden for the final months of his life, died quietly on October 23, 1872.

Gautier's influence on French—and English—literature should not be underestimated. He may well have been the key transitional figure leading from the fiery Romanticism of the early nineteenth century to the realism and naturalism (ultimately embodied in the novels of Émile Zola) in the later nineteenth and early twentieth centuries. Joanna Richardson speaks eloquently of Gautier's influence on Flaubert:

---

5. Letter dated 31 October 1870; cited in Richardson, 252.

It was probably in Gautier that Flaubert discovered his pessimism, his descriptive vocation, his passion for colour, his doctrine of Art for Art's Sake, his exclusive cult of form, his hatred of the *bourgeois*. It was Gautier, it is said, who inspired *Salammbô*. No one could be the friend of Gautier without becoming the friend of Flaubert, too. "He was," wrote Flaubert to [Ernest] Feydeau, after Gautier's death, "a great man of letters and a great poet."[6]

Later Richardson writes: "There is much indeed to confirm the contention that if Gautier had not existed, Baudelaire and the Parnassians, Flaubert and the Goncourts, Anatole France and Pierre Louÿs would probably have written their work; but certainly they would not have written it as we know it."[7] And Gautier's influence on the preeminent British advocate of art for art's sake, Oscar Wilde, is patent. Was it not he who stated satirically, in the preface to *The Picture of Dorian Gray,* that "all art is quite useless"?

Specifically in terms of Gautier's weird work, we can state that he initiated or broached a number of themes and motifs that numerous other writers would take up in the decades that followed. Several of his weird tales were written early in his career, among them "Omphale: A Rococo Story" (1834), "Clarimonde" (1836), "One of Cleopatra's Nights" (1838), and "The Mummy's Foot" (1840). "Clarimonde" is a pioneering story of a vampire, written less than two decades after John Polidori's *The Vampyre* (1819) and anticipating some of the details of J. Sheridan Le Fanu's "Carmilla" (1871–72), with its lustful female vampire. The figure of Clarimonde, who seeks to corrupt a hapless priest both physically and spiritually, is unforgettable. And Gautier was one of the earliest to find horror in the appalling antiquity of Egypt. While—as Albert B. Smith, the most exhaustive commentator in English on Gautier's weird work, rightly contends[8]—it is an exaggeration to say that "One of Cleopatra's Nights" is in the strictest sense weird, it may well have contribut-

---

6. Richardson, 205.

7. Richardson, 281.

8 See Albert B. Smith, *Théophile Gautier and the Fantastic* (University, MS: Romance Monographs, 1977), 56.

ed its mite to subsequent writers' focus on Egypt as a locus of aeon-old horror. Certainly, a passage like the following—

> [Egypt] is only a vast covering for a tomb—the dome of a necropolis; a sky dead and dried up like the mummies it hangs over; it weighs upon my shoulders like an over-heavy mantle; it constrains and terrifies me; it seems to me that I could not stand up erect without striking my forehead against it . . . whithersoever one turns, only frightful monsters are visible—dogs with the heads of men; men with the heads of dogs; chimeras begotten of hideous couplings in the shadowy depths of the labyrinths . . .

—anticipates what H. P. Lovecraft wrote in "Under the Pyramids" (1924), where the protagonist (Harry Houdini) cries out at one point:

> I saw the horror and unwholesome antiquity of Egypt, and the grisly alliance it has always had with the tombs and temples of the dead. I saw phantom processions of priests with the heads of bulls, falcons, cats, and ibises; phantom processions marching interminably through subterraneous labyrinths and avenues of titanic propylaea beside which a man is as a fly, and offering unnamable sacrifices to indescribable gods. . . . *Hippopotami should not have human hands and carry torches . . . men should not have the heads of crocodiles. . . .*[9]

And a story like "Arria Marcella" is a relatively rare instance of an author attempting to evoke weirdness from Greco-Roman antiquity.

The dominant thread of Gautier's weird work—in line with his Romanticism and his devotion to female beauty—is the union of supernaturalism and romance. The evil Clarimonde is an anomaly in Gautier's weird fiction; in nearly every other tale in this volume, women are either the pursuers or the pursued in love affairs that at times transcend death and the centuries. "Omphale" is a Pygmalion-type tale wherein a beautiful woman emerges from a tapestry to make love to the astounded protagonist. The essence of "One of Cleopatra's Nights" is the nearly blasphemous quest of an Egyptian peasant to spend a night of love and

---

9. H. P. Lovecraft, "Under the Pyramids," in *Collected Fiction: A Variorum Edition,* ed. S. T. Joshi (New York: Hippocampus Press, 2015), 1.434, 446.

feasting with the unapproachable queen; her insuperable boredom causes her to acquiesce to the man's outrageous desires before having him summarily executed.

It is in the three longer works that conclude this volume that the romance element truly comes to the fore. The fetching Princess Prascovie Labinska is the focal point of the innovative "Avatar" (1856), where a hopeless lover, Octave de Saville, cajoles a physician to transfer his soul or personality into the body of Prascovie's husband, Count Labinski. (The physician has picked up this neat trick from Brahmins in India.) But evidently the transference of the soul does not allow the soul to have access to the mind or intellect of the body it now occupies, for Octave is unable to reply in Polish when the countess speaks to him in that language; as a result, she instantly suspects that something is amiss and refuses his overtures. The novella takes a striking turn when Labinski (in Octave's body) challenges Octave to a duel. Gautier relishes the thought of what one's sensations would be in such a situation: could one have the fortitude to kill the body that one had previously occupied for decades? "Avatar" deftly treated the issue of personality exchange decades before Barry Pain's *An Exchange of Souls* (1911) or H. P. Lovecraft's "The Thing on the Doorstep" (1933) did so.

"Jettatura" (1856) also has a love story at its core; but here the focus is not on Paul d'Aspremont's love for and pending marriage to the lovely young Englishwoman Alicia Ward, but on Paul's increasing psychological disturbance over the possibility that he is a *jettatore* (a person with the evil eye). Throughout the course of the tale we are informed in no uncertain terms that Alicia herself regards the whole notion as superstitious nonsense; but the numerous instances where Paul is involved in peculiar and tragic events make her, her father, and Paul's rival, Count d'Altavilla, pause in uncertainty. Ultimately we are probably to interpret this tale as one of psychological terror—but the supernatural is never fully ruled out.

Spirite (1865) is definitely supernatural, for the female ghost of the title—a young woman who wasted away and died in a convent out of a hopeless love for the protagonist, the dashing man-about-town Guy de Malivert—is seen by numerous persons aside from Guy himself. The delicacy of the supernatural manifestations in this short novel—as in the portrayal of Spirite herself—is a triumph of subtlety, and the work remains compelling in spite, or perhaps even because, of the paucity of overt weirdness.

Théophile Gautier's immense literary output—he himself estimated that his journalism, written over a period of four decades, would fill 300 volumes—is even today not appreciated as it deserves to be. *Mademoiselle de Maupin* remains a classic that can take its place with Hugo's *Les Misérables* and Flaubert's *Madame Bovary,* but the great bulk of his other writing has fallen into obscurity. But, like so many other writers, his weird work continues to find new readers and helps to keep alive a writer whose melding of classic precision, Romantic sensibility, and diversity of setting derived from his wide-ranging travels renders his weird tales eternally compelling. His effective use of such motifs as the revivification of mummies, the endurance of love after death, and the transference of souls provided models that many later weird writers adapted for their own tales; but his own work remains unmatched for its uniquely French devotion to the religion of art and to the imperishable beauty of the human female.

—S. T. JOSHI

A Note on This Edition

The first five tales in this volume appeared in a notable English translation by Lafcadio Hearn, under the title *One of Cleopatra's Nights and Other Fantastic Romances* (New York: Worthington, 1882). "Avatar" was translated by Edgar Saltus (under the pseudonym Myndart Verelst) along with Prosper Mérimée's "The Venus of Ille" in the volume *Tales Before Supper* (New York: Brentano's, 1887). I have made only some minor revisions in punctuation and other small details in these translations. I have taken greater liberties in the translation of "Jettatura" and *Spirite* by F. C. de Sumichrast, appearing as part of *The Works of Théophile Gautier* (Boston: C. T. Brainard, 1900–03).

Information on the first publication in French of the tales is as follows:

"Omphale: A Rococo Story": "Omphale," *Journal des Gens du Monde* (7 February 1834).

"Clarimonde": "La Morte amoureuse," *Chronique de Paris* (23 & 26 June 1836).

"One of Cleopatra's Nights": "Une Nuit de Cléopâtre," *La Presse* (29 November–6 December 1838).

"The Mummy's Foot": "Le Pied de la momie," *Musée des Familles* (September 1840).

"Arria Marcella: A Souvenir of Pompeii": "Arria Marcella," *Revue de Paris* (1 March 1852).

"Avatar": *Moniteur Universel* (29 February–3 April 1856; Paris: Lévy, 1857).

"Jettatura": *Moniteur Universel* (25 June–23 July 1856; Paris: Lévy, 1857).

Spirite: Moniteur Universel (17 November–6 December 1865; Paris: Charpentier, 1866).

Hearn also translated "King Candaules" ("Le Roi Candaule," *La Presse,* 1–5 October 1844), but this story is a purely historical tale of ancient Persia derived from an anecdote in Herodotus.

THE MUMMY'S FOOT AND OTHER FANTASTIC TALES

Omphale: A Rococo Story

My uncle, the Chevalier de ——, resided in a small mansion which looked out upon the dismal Rue de Tournelles on one side, and the equally dismal Boulevard St. Antoine upon the other. Between the Boulevard and the house itself a few ancient elm-trees, eaten alive by mosses and insects, piteously extended their skeleton arms from the depth of a species of sink surrounded by high black walls. Some emaciated flowers hung their heads languidly, like young girls in consumption, waiting for a ray of sunshine to dry their half-rotten leaves. Weeds had invaded the walks, which were almost undistinguishable, owing to the length of time that had elapsed since they were last raked. One or two goldfish floated rather than swam in a basin covered with duckweed and half-choked by water plants.

My uncle called that his garden!

Besides all the fine things above described in my uncle's garden, there was also a rather unpleasant pavilion, which he had entitled the *Délices,* doubtless by antiphrasis. It was in a state of extreme dilapidation. The walls were bulging outwardly. Great masses of detached plaster still lay among the nettles and wild oats where they had fallen. The lower portions of the wall surfaces were green with putrid mould. The woodwork of the window-shutters and doors had been badly sprung, and they closed only partially or not at all. A species of decoration, strongly suggestive of an immense kitchen-pot with various effluvia radiating from it, ornamented the main entrance, for in the time of Louis XV., when it was the custom to build *Délices,* there were always two entrances to such pleasure houses for precaution's sake. The cornice, overburdened with ovulos, foliated arabesques, and volutes, had been badly dismantled by the infiltration of rain-water. In short, the *Délices* of my uncle, the Chevalier de ——, presented a rather lamentable aspect.

21

This poor ruin, dating only from yesterday, although wearing the dilapidated look of a thousand years' decay—a ruin of plaster, not of stone, all cracked and warped, covered with a leprosy of lichen growth, moss-eaten and mouldy—seemed to resemble one of those precociously old men worn out by filthy debauches. It inspired no feeling of respect, for there is nothing in the world so ugly and so wretched as either an old gauze robe or an old plaster wall, two things which ought not to endure, yet which do.

It was in this pavilion that my uncle had lodged me.

The interior was not less rococo than the exterior, although remaining in a somewhat better state of preservation. The bed was hung with yellow lampas, spotted over with large white flowers. An ornamental shellwork clock ticked away upon a pedestal inlaid with ivory and mother-of-pearl. A wreath of ornamental roses coquettishly twined around a Venetian glass. Above the door the Four Seasons were painted in cameo. A fair lady with thickly powdered hair, a sky-blue corset, and an array of ribbons of the same hue, who had a bow in her right hand, a partridge in her left, a crescent upon her forehead, and a leverette at her feet, strutted and smiled with ineffable graciousness from within a large oval frame. This was one of my uncle's mistresses of old, whom he had had painted as Diana. It will scarcely be necessary to observe that the furniture itself was not of the most modern style. There was, in fact, nothing to prevent one from fancying himself living at the time of the Regency, and the mythological tapestry with which the walls were hung rendered the illusion complete.

The tapestry represented Hercules spinning at the feet of Omphale. The design was tormented after the fashion of Vanloo, and in the most Pompadour style possible to imagine. Hercules had a spindle decorated with rose-colored favors. He elevated his little finger with a peculiar and special grace, like a marquis in the act of taking a pinch of snuff, while turning a white flake of flax between his thumb and index finger. His muscular neck was burdened with bows of ribbons, rosettes, strings of pearls, and a thousand other feminine gew-gaws, and a large *gorge-de-pigeon* colored petticoat, with two very large panniers, lent quite a gallant air to the monster-conquering hero.

Omphale's white shoulders were half covered by the skin of the

Nemean lion. Her slender hand leaned upon her lover's knotty club. Her lovely blonde hair, powdered to ash-color, fell loosely over her neck—a neck as supple and undulating in its outlines as the neck of a dove. Her little feet, true realizations of the typical Andalusian or Chinese foot, and which would have been lost in Cinderella's glass slippers, were shod with half-antique buskins of a tender lilac color, sprinkled with pearls. In truth, she was a charming creature. Her head was thrown back with an adorable little mock swagger, her dimpled mouth wore a delicious little pout, her nostrils were slightly expanded, her cheeks had a delicate glow—an *assassin** cunningly placed there relieved their beauty in a wonderful way; she only needed a little mustache to make her a first-class mousquetaire.

There were many other personages also represented in the tapestry—the kindly female attendant, the indispensable little Cupid—but they did not leave a sufficiently distinct outline in my memory to enable me to describe them.

In those days I was quite young—not that I wish to be understood as saying that I am now very old; but I was fresh from college, and was to remain in my uncle's care until I could choose a profession. If the good man had been able to foresee that I should embrace that of a fantastic story-writer, he would certainly have turned me out of doors forthwith and irrevocably disinherited me, for he always entertained the most aristocratic contempt for literature in general and authors in particular. Like the fine gentleman that he was, it would have pleased him to have had all those petty scribblers who busy themselves in disfiguring paper, and speaking irreverentially about people of quality, hung or beaten to death by his attendants. Lord have mercy on my poor uncle! He really esteemed nothing in the world except the epistle to Zetulba.

Well, then, I had only just left college. I was full of dreams and illusions. I was as naive as a *rosière* of Salency, perhaps more so. Delighted at having no more pensums to make, everything seemed to me for the best in the best of all possible worlds. I believed in an infinity of things. I believed in M. de Florian's shepherdess with her combed and powdered sheep. I never for a moment doubted the reality of Madame

---

*Beauty-spot.—[Trans.]

Deshoulière's flock. I believed that there were actually nine muses, as stated in Father Jouvency's *Appendix de Diis et Heroïbus.* My recollections of Berquin and of Gessner had created a little world for me in which everything was rose-colored, sky-blue, and apple-green. Oh, holy innocence!—*sancta simplicitas!* as Mephistopheles says.

When I found myself alone in this fine room—my own room, all to myself!—I felt superlatively overjoyed. I made a careful inventory of everything, even the smallest article of furniture. I rummaged every corner, and explored the chamber in the fullest sense of the word. I was in the fourth heaven, as happy as a king, or rather as two kings. After supper (for we used to sup at my uncle's—a charming custom, now obsolete, together with many other equally charming customs which I mourn for with all the heart I have left), I took my candle and retired forthwith, so impatient did I feel to enjoy my new dwelling-place.

While I was undressing I fancied that Omphale's eyes had moved. I looked more attentively in that direction, not without a slight sensation of fear, for the room was very large, and the feeble luminous penumbra which floated about the candle only served to render the darkness still more visible. I thought I saw her turning her head toward me. I became frightened in earnest, and blew out the light. I turned my face to the wall, pulled the bedclothes over my head, drew my nightcap down to my chin, and finally went to sleep.

I did not dare to look at the accursed tapestry again for several days.

It may be well here, for the sake of imparting something of verisimilitude to the very unlikely story I am about to relate, to inform my fair readers that in those days I was really a very pretty boy. I had the handsomest eyes in the world, at least they used to tell me so; a much fairer complexion than I have now, a true carnation tint; curly brown hair, which I still have, and seventeen years, which I have no longer. I needed only a pretty stepmother to be a very tolerable cherub. Unfortunately mine was fifty-seven years of age, and had only three teeth, which was too much of one thing and too little of the other.

One evening, however, I finally plucked up courage enough to take a peep at the fair mistress of Hercules. She was looking at me with the saddest and most languishing expression possible. This time I pulled my nightcap down to my very shoulders, and buried my head in the coverlets.

I had a strange dream that night, if indeed it was a dream.

I heard the rings of my bed-curtains sliding with a sharp squeak upon their curtain-rods, as if the curtains had been suddenly pulled back. I awoke, at least in my dream it seemed to me that I awoke. I saw no one.

The moon shone full upon the window-panes, and projected her wan bluish light into the room. Vast shadows, fantastic forms, were defined upon the floor and the walls. The clock chimed a quarter, and the vibration of the sound took a long time to die away. It seemed like a sigh. The plainly audible strokes of the pendulum seemed like the pulsations of a young heart, throbbing with passion.

I felt anything but comfortable, and a very bewilderment of fear took possession of me.

A furious gust of wind banged the shutters and made the window-sashes tremble. The woodwork cracked, the tapestry undulated. I ventured to glance in the direction of Omphale, with a vague suspicion that she was instrumental in all this unpleasantness, for some secret purpose of her own. I was not mistaken.

The tapestry became violently agitated. Omphale detached herself from the wall and leaped lightly to the carpet. She came straight toward my bed, after having first turned herself carefully in my direction. I fancy it will hardly be necessary to describe my stupefaction. The most intrepid old soldier would not have felt very comfortable under similar circumstances, and I was neither old nor a soldier. I awaited the end of the adventure in terrified silence.

A flute-toned, pearly little voice sounded softly in my ears, with that pretty lisp affected during the Regency by marchionesses and people of high degree:

"Do I really frighten you, my child? It is true that you are only a child, but it is not nice to be afraid of ladies, especially when they are young ladies and only wish you well. It is uncivil and unworthy of a French gentleman. You must be cured of such silly fears. Come, little savage, leave off these foolish airs, and cease hiding your head under the bedclothes. Your education is by no means complete yet, my pretty page, and you have not learned so very much. In my time cherubs were more courageous."

"But, lady, it is because—"

"Because it seems strange to you to find me here instead of there," she said, biting her ruddy lip with her white teeth, and pointing toward the wall with her long taper finger. "Well, in fact, the thing does not look very natural, but were I to explain it all to you, you would be none the wiser. Let it be sufficient for you to know that you are not in any danger."

"I am afraid you may be the—the—"

"The devil—out with the word!—is it not? That is what you wanted to say. Well, at least you will grant that I am not black enough for a devil, and that if hell were peopled with devils shaped as I am, one might have quite as pleasant a time there as in Paradise."

And to prove that she was not flattering herself, Omphale threw back her lion's skin and allowed me to behold her exquisitely moulded shoulders and bosom, dazzling in their white beauty.

"Well, what do you think of me?" she exclaimed, with a pretty little air of satisfied coquetry.

"I think that even were you the devil himself I should not feel afraid of you any more, Madame Omphale."

"Ah, now you talk sensibly, but do not call me madame, or Omphale, I do not wish you to look upon me as a madame, and I am no more Omphale than I am the devil."

"Then who are you?"

"I am the Marchioness de T——. A short time after I was married the marquis had this tapestry made for my apartments, and had me represented on it in the character of Omphale. He himself figures there as Hercules. That was a queer notion he took, for God knows there never was anybody in the world who bore less resemblance to Hercules than the poor marquis! It has been a long time since this chamber was occupied. I naturally love company, and I almost died of *ennui* in consequence. It gave me the headache. To be only with one's husband is the same thing as being alone. When you came I was overjoyed. This dead room became reanimated. I had found some one to feel interested in. I watched you come in and go out, I heard you murmuring in your sleep, I watched you reading, and my eyes followed the pages. I found you were nicely behaved, and had a fresh, innocent way about you that pleased me. In short, I fell in love with you. I tried to make you understand. I sighed. You thought it was only the sighing of the wind. I made signs to you. I looked at you with languishing eyes, and only succeeded in frightening you terribly. So at last in despair I resolved upon this rather improper course which I have taken, to tell you frankly what you could not take a hint about. Now that you know I love you, I hope that—"

The conversation was interrupted at this juncture by the grating of a key in the lock of the chamber door.

Omphale started and blushed to the very whites of her eyes.

"Adieu," she whispered, "till to-morrow." And she returned to her place on the wall, walking backward, for fear that I should see her reverse side, doubtless.

It was Baptiste, who came to brush my clothes.

"You ought not to sleep with your bed-curtains open, sir," he remarked. "You might catch a bad cold. This room is so chilly."

The curtains were actually open, and as I had been under the impression that I was only dreaming, I felt very much astonished, for I was certain that they had been closed when I went to bed.

As soon as Baptiste left the room, I ran to the tapestry. I felt it all over. It was indeed a real woollen tapestry, rough to the touch like any other tapestry. Omphale resembled the charming phantom of the night only as a dead body resembles a living one. I lifted the hangings. The wall was solid throughout. There were no masked panels or secret doors. I only noticed that a few threads were broken in the groundwork of the tapestry where the feet of Omphale rested. This afforded me food for reflection.

All that day I remained buried in the deepest brown study imaginable. I longed for evening with a mingled feeling of anxiety and impatience. I retired early, resolved on learning how this mystery was going to end. I got into bed. The marchioness did not keep me waiting long. She leaped down from the tapestry in front of the pier-glass, and dropped right by my bed. She seated herself by my pillow, and the conversation commenced.

I asked her questions as I had done the evening before, and demanded explanations. She eluded the former, and replied in an evasive manner to the latter, yet always after so witty a fashion that within a quarter of an hour I felt no scruples whatever in regard to my liaison with her.

While conversing she passed her fingers through my hair, tapped me gently on the cheeks, and softly kissed my forehead.

She chatted and chatted in a pretty mocking way, in a style at once elegantly polished and yet familiar and altogether like a great lady, such as I have never since heard from the lips of any human being.

She was then seated upon the easy-chair beside the bed. In a little while she slipped one of her arms around my neck, and I felt her heart beating passionately against me. It was indeed a charming and handsome real woman, a veritable marchioness whom I found beside me, poor student of seventeen! There was more than enough to make one lose his head, so I lost mine. I did not know very well what was going to happen, but I felt a vague presentiment that it would displease the marquis.

"And Monsieur le Marquis, on the wall up there—what will he say?"

The lion's skin had fallen to the floor, and the soft lilac-colored buskins, filigreed with silver, were lying beside my shoes.

"He will not say anything," replied the marchioness, laughing heartily. "Do you suppose he ever sees anything? Besides, even should he see, he is the most philosophical and inoffensive husband in the world. He is used to such things. Do you love me, little one?"

"Indeed I do, ever so much!—ever so much!"

Morning dawned. My mistress stole away.

The day seemed to me frightfully long. At last evening came. The same things happened as on the evening before, and the second night left no regrets for the first. The marchioness became more and more adorable, and this state of affairs continued for a long time. As I never slept at night, I wore a somnolent expression in the daytime which did not augur well for me with my uncle. He suspected something. He probably listened at the door and heard everything, for one fine morning he entered my room so brusquely that Antoinette had scarcely time to get back to her place on the tapestry.

He was followed by a tapestry-hanger with pincers and a ladder.

He looked at me with a shrewd and severe expression which convinced me that he knew all.

"This Marchioness de T—— is certainly crazy. What the devil could have put it into her head to fall in love with a brat like that?" muttered my uncle between his teeth. "She promised to behave herself.

"Jean, take that tapestry down, roll it up, and put it in the garret."

Every word my uncle spoke went through my heart like a poniard-thrust.

Jean rolled up my sweetheart Omphale, otherwise the Marchioness Antoinette de T——, together with Hercules, or the Marquis de T——, and carried the whole thing off to the garret. I could not restrain my tears.

Next day my uncle sent me back in the B—— diligence to my respectable parents, to whom, you may feel assured, I never breathed a word of my adventure.

My uncle died; his house and furniture were sold; probably the tapestry was sold with the rest.

But a long time afterward, while foraging the shop of a bric-à-brac merchant in search of oddities, I stumbled over a great dusty roll of something covered with cobwebs.

"What is that?" I said to the Auvergnat.

"That is a rococo tapestry representing the amours of Madame Omphale and Monsieur Hercule. It is genuine Beauvais, worked in silk, and in an excellent state of preservation. Buy this from me for your study. I will not charge you dear for it, since it is you."

At the name of Omphale all my blood rushed to my heart.

"Unroll that tapestry," I said to the merchant in a hurried, gasping voice, like one in a fever.

It was indeed she! I fancied that her mouth smiled graciously at me, and that her eye lighted up on meeting mine.

"How much do you ask?"

"Well, I could not possibly let you have it for any less than five hundred francs."

"I have not that much with me now. I will get it and be back in an hour."

I returned with the money, but the tapestry was no longer there. An Englishman had bargained for it during my absence, offered six hundred francs for it, and taken it away with him.

After all, perhaps it was best that it should have been thus, and that I should preserve this delicious souvenir intact. They say one should never return to a first love, or look at the rose which one admired the evening before.

And then I am no longer so young or so pretty that tapestries should come down from their walls to honor me.

Clarimonde

Brother, you ask me if I have ever loved. Yes. My story is a strange and terrible one; and though I am sixty-six years of age, I scarcely dare even now to disturb the ashes of that memory. To you I can refuse nothing; but I should not relate such a tale to any less experienced mind. So strange were the circumstances of my story, that I can scarcely believe myself to have ever actually been a party to them. For more than three years I remained the victim of a most singular and diabolical illusion. Poor country priest though I was, I led every night in a dream—would to God it had been all a dream!—a most worldly life, a damning life, a life of Sardanapalus. One single look too freely cast upon a woman well-nigh caused me to lose my soul; but finally by the grace of God and the assistance of my patron saint, I succeeded in casting out the evil spirit that possessed me. My daily life was long interwoven with a nocturnal life of a totally different character. By day I was a priest of the Lord, occupied with prayer and sacred things; by night, from the instant that I closed my eyes I became a young nobleman, a fine connoisseur in women, dogs, and horses; gambling, drinking, and blaspheming, and when I awoke at early daybreak, it seemed to me, on the other hand, that I had been sleeping, and had only dreamed that I was a priest. Of this somnambulistic life there now remains to me only the recollection of certain scenes and words which I cannot banish from my memory; but although I never actually left the walls of my presbytery, one would think to hear me speak that I were a man who, weary of all worldly pleasures, had become a religious, seeking to end a tempestuous life in the service of God, rather than an humble seminarist who has grown old in this obscure curacy, situated in the depths of the woods and even isolated from the life of the century.

Yes, I have loved as none in the world ever loved—with an insensate and furious passion—so violent that I am astonished it did not cause my heart to burst asunder. Ah, what nights—what nights!

From my earliest childhood I had felt a vocation to the priesthood, so that all my studies were directed with that idea in view. Up to the age of twenty-four my life had been only a prolonged novitiate. Having completed my course of theology I successively received all the minor orders, and my superiors judged me worthy, despite my youth, to pass the last awful degree. My ordination was fixed for Easter week.

I had never gone into the world. My world was confined by the walls of the college and the seminary. I knew in a vague sort of a way that there was something called Woman, but I never permitted my thoughts to dwell on such a subject, and I lived in a state of perfect innocence. Twice a year only I saw my infirm and aged mother, and in those visits were comprised my sole relations with the outer world.

I regretted nothing; I felt not the least hesitation at taking the last irrevocable step; I was filled with joy and impatience. Never did a betrothed lover count the slow hours with more feverish ardor; I slept only to dream that I was saying mass; I believed there could be nothing in the world more delightful than to be a priest; I would have refused to be a king or a poet in preference. My ambition could conceive of no loftier aim.

I tell you this in order to show you that what happened to me could not have happened in the natural order of things, and to enable you to understand that I was the victim of an inexplicable fascination.

At last the great day came. I walked to the church with a step so light that I fancied myself sustained in air, or that I had wings upon my shoulders. I believed myself an angel, and wondered at the sombre and thoughtful faces of my companions, for there were several of us. I had passed all the night in prayer, and was in a condition wellnigh bordering on ecstasy. The bishop, a venerable old man, seemed to me God the Father leaning over his Eternity, and I beheld Heaven through the vault of the temple.

You well know the details of that ceremony—the benediction, the communion under both forms, the anointing of the palms of the hands with the Oil of Catechumens, and then the holy sacrifice offered in concert with the bishop.

Ah, truly spake Job when he declared that the imprudent man is one who hath not made a covenant with his eyes! I accidentally lifted my head, which until then I had kept down, and beheld before me, so close that it seemed that I could have touched her—although she was actually a considerable distance from me and on the further side of the sanctuary railing—a young woman of extraordinary beauty, and attired with royal magnificence. It seemed as though scales had suddenly fallen from my eyes. I felt like a blind man who unexpectedly recovers his sight. The bishop, so radiantly glorious but an instant before, suddenly vanished away, the tapers paled upon their golden candlesticks like stars in the dawn, and a vast darkness seemed to fill the whole church. The charming creature appeared in bright relief against the background of that darkness, like some angelic revelation. She seemed herself radiant, and radiating light rather than receiving it.

I lowered my eyelids, firmly resolved not to open them again, that I might not be influenced by external objects, for distraction had gradually taken possession of me until I hardly knew what I was doing.

In another minute, nevertheless, I reopened my eyes, for through my eyelashes I still beheld her, all sparkling with prismatic colors, and surrounded with such a purple penumbra as one beholds in gazing at the sun.

Oh, how beautiful she was! The greatest painters, who followed ideal beauty into heaven itself, and thence brought back to earth the true portrait of the Madonna, never in their delineations even approached that wildly beautiful reality which I saw before me. Neither the verses of the poet nor the palette of the artist could convey any conception of her. She was rather tall, with a form and bearing of a goddess. Her hair, of a soft blonde hue, was parted in the midst and flowed back over her temples in two rivers of rippling gold; she seemed a diademed queen. Her forehead, bluish-white in its transparency, extended its calm breadth above the arches of her eyebrows, which by a strange singularity were almost black, and admirably relieved the effect of sea-green eyes of unsustainable vivacity and brilliancy. What eyes! With a single flash they could have decided a man's destiny. They had a life, a limpidity, an ardor, a humid light which I have never seen in human eyes; they shot forth rays like arrows, which I could distinctly *see* enter my heart. I know not if the fire which illumined them came from heaven or from hell, but assuredly it came from one or the other. That woman was either an angel or a demon, perhaps both. Assuredly she never sprang from the flank of Eve, our common mother. Teeth of the most lustrous pearl gleamed in her ruddy smile, and at every inflection of her lips little dimples appeared in the satiny rose of her adorable cheeks. There was a delicacy and pride in the regal outline of her nostrils bespeaking noble blood. Agate gleams played over the smooth lustrous skin of her half-bare shoulders, and strings of great blonde pearls—almost equal to her neck in beauty of color—descended upon her bosom. From time to time she elevated her head with the undulating grace of a startled serpent or peacock, thereby imparting a quivering motion to the high lace ruff which surrounded it like a silver trellis-work.

She wore a robe of orange-red velvet, and from her wide ermine-lined sleeves there peeped forth patrician hands of infinite delicacy, and so ideally transparent that, like the fingers of Aurora, they permitted the light to shine through them.

All these details I can recollect at this moment as plainly as though they were of yesterday, for notwithstanding I was greatly troubled at the time, nothing escaped me; the faintest touch of shading, the little dark speck at the point of the chin, the imperceptible down at the corners of the lips, the velvety floss upon the brow, the quivering shadows of the eyelashes upon the cheeks, I could notice everything with astonishing lucidity of perception.

And gazing I felt opening within me gates that had until then remained closed; vents long obstructed became all clear, permitting glimpses of unfamiliar perspectives within; life suddenly made itself visible to me under a totally novel aspect. I felt as though I had just been born into a new world and a new order of things. A frightful anguish commenced to torture my heart as with red-hot pincers. Every successive minute seemed to me at once but a second and yet a century. Meanwhile the ceremony was proceeding, and I shortly found myself transported far from that world of which my newly-born desires were furiously besieging the entrance. Nevertheless I answered "Yes" when I wished to say "No," though all within me protested against the violence done to my soul by my tongue. Some occult power seemed to force the words from my throat against my will. Thus it is, perhaps, that so many young girls walk to the altar firmly resolved to refuse in a startling manner the husband imposed upon them, and that yet not one ever fulfils her intention. Thus it is, doubtless, that so many poor novices take the veil, though they have resolved to tear it into shreds at the moment when called upon to utter the vows. One dares not thus cause so great a scandal to all present, nor deceive the expectation of so many people. All those eyes, all those wills seem to weigh down upon you like a cope of lead; and, moreover, measures have been so well taken, everything has been so thoroughly arranged beforehand and after a fashion so evidently irrevocable, that the will yields to the weight of circumstances and utterly breaks down.

As the ceremony proceeded the features of the fair unknown changed their expression. Her look had at first been one of caressing tenderness; it changed to an air of disdain and of mortification, as though at not having been able to make itself understood.

With an effort of will sufficient to have uprooted a mountain, I strove to cry out that I would not be a priest, but I could not speak; my tongue seemed nailed to my palate, and I found it impossible to express my will by the least syllable of negation. Though fully awake, I felt like one under the influence of a nightmare, who vainly strives to shriek out the one word upon which life depends.

She seemed conscious of the martyrdom I was undergoing, and, as though to encourage me, she gave me a look replete with divinest promise. Her eyes were a poem; their every glance was a song.

She said to me:

"If thou wilt be mine, I shall make thee happier than God Himself in His paradise. The angels themselves will be jealous of thee. Tear off that funeral shroud in which thou art about to wrap thyself. I am Beauty, I am Youth, I am Life. Come to me! Together we shall be Love. Can Jehovah offer thee aught in exchange? Our lives will flow on like a dream, in one eternal kiss.

"Fling forth the wine of that chalice, and thou art free. I will conduct thee to the Unknown Isles. Thou shalt sleep in my bosom upon a bed of massy gold under a silver pavilion, for I love thee and would take thee away from thy God, before whom so many noble hearts pour forth floods of love which never reach even the steps of His throne!"

These words seemed to float to my ears in a rhythm of infinite sweetness, for her look was actually sonorous, and the utterances of her eyes were reëchoed in the depths of my heart as though living lips had breathed them into my life. I felt myself willing to renounce God, and yet my tongue mechanically fulfilled all the formalities of the ceremony. The fair one gave me another look, so beseeching, so despairing that keen blades seemed to pierce my heart, and I felt my bosom transfixed by more swords than those of Our Lady of Sorrows.

All was consummated; I had become a priest.

Never was deeper anguish painted on human face than upon hers. The maiden who beholds her affianced lover suddenly fall dead at her side, the mother bending over the empty cradle of her child, Eve seated at the threshold of the gate of Paradise, the miser who finds a stone substituted for his stolen treasure, the poet who accidentally permits the only manuscript of his finest work to fall into the fire, could not wear a look so despairing, so inconsolable. All the blood had abandoned her charming face, leaving it whiter than marble; her beautiful arms hung lifelessly on either side of her body as though their muscles had suddenly relaxed, and she sought the support of a pillar, for her yielding limbs almost betrayed her. As for myself, I staggered toward the door of the church, livid as death, my forehead bathed with a sweat bloodier than that of Calvary; I felt as though I were being strangled; the vault seemed to have flattened down upon my shoulders, and it seemed to me that my head alone sustained the whole weight of the dome.

As I was about to cross the threshold a hand suddenly caught mine—a woman's hand! I had never till then touched the hand of any woman. It was cold as a serpent's skin, and yet its impress remained upon my wrist, burnt there as though branded by a glowing iron. It was she. "Unhappy man! Unhappy man! What hast thou done?" she exclaimed in a low voice, and immediately disappeared in the crowd.

The aged bishop passed by. He cast a severe and scrutinizing look upon me. My face presented the wildest aspect imaginable; I blushed and turned pale alternately; dazzling lights flashed before my eyes. A companion took pity on me. He seized my arm and led me out. I could not possibly have found my way back to the seminary unassisted. At the corner of a street, while the young priest's attention was momentarily turned in another direction, a negro page, fantastically garbed, approached me, and without pausing on his way slipped into my hand a little pocket-book with gold-embroidered corners, at the same time giving me a sign to hide it. I concealed it in my sleeve, and there kept it until I found myself alone in my cell. Then I opened the clasp. There were only two leaves within, bearing the words, "Clarimonde. At the Concini Palace." So little acquainted was I at that time with the things of this world that I had never heard of Clarimonde, celebrated as she was, and I had no idea as to where the Concini Palace was situated. I hazarded a thousand conjectures, each more extravagant than the last; but, in truth, I cared little whether she were a great lady or a courtesan, so that I could but see her once more.

My love, although the growth of a single hour, had taken imperishable root. I did not even dream of attempting to tear it up, so fully was I convinced such a thing would be impossible. That woman had completely taken possession of me. One look from her had sufficed to change my very nature. She had breathed her will into my life, and I no longer lived in myself, but in her and for her. I gave myself up to a thousand extravagancies. I kissed the place upon my hand which she had touched, and I repeated her name over and over again for hours in succession. I only needed to close my eyes in order to see her distinctly as though she were actually present; and I reiterated to myself the words she had uttered in my ear at the church porch: "Unhappy man! Unhappy man! What hast thou done?" I comprehended at last the full horror of my situation, and the funereal and awful restraints of the state into which I had just entered became clearly revealed to me. To be a priest!—that is, to be chaste, never to love, to observe no distinction of sex or age, to turn from the sight of all beauty, to put out one's own eyes, to hide forever crouching in the chill shadows of some church or cloister, to visit none but the dying, to watch by unknown corpses, and ever to bear about with one the black soutane as a garb of mourning for one's self, so that your very dress might serve as a pall for your coffin.

And I felt life rising within me like a subterranean lake, expanding and overflowing; my blood leaped fiercely through my arteries; my long-restrained youth suddenly burst into active being, like the aloe which blooms but once in a hundred years, and then bursts into blossom with a clap of thunder.

What could I do in order to see Clarimonde once more? I had no pretext to offer for desiring to leave the seminary, not knowing any person in the city. I would not even be able to remain there but a short time, and was only waiting my assignment to the curacy which I must thereafter occupy. I tried to remove the bars of the window; but it was at a fearful height from the ground, and I found that as I had no ladder it would be useless to think of escaping thus. And, furthermore, I could descend thence only by night in any event, and afterward how should I be able to find my way through the inextricable labyrinth of streets? All these difficulties, which to many would have appeared altogether insignificant, were gigantic to me, a poor seminarist who had fallen in love only the day before for the first time, without experience, without money, without attire.

"Ah!" cried I to myself in my blindness, "were I not a priest I could have seen her every day; I might have been her lover, her spouse. Instead of being wrapped in this dismal shroud of mine I would have had garments of silk and velvet, golden chains, a sword, and fair plumes like other handsome young cavaliers. My hair, instead of being dishonored by the tonsure, would flow down upon my neck in waving curls; I would have a fine waxed mustache; I would be a gallant " But one hour passed before an altar, a few hastily articulated words, had forever cut me off from the number of the living, and I had myself sealed down the stone of my own tomb; I had with my own hand bolted the gate of my prison!

I went to the window. The sky was beautifully blue; the trees had donned their spring robes; nature seemed to be making parade of an ironical joy. The *Place* was filled with people, some going, others coming; young beaux and young beauties were sauntering in couples toward the groves and gardens; merry youths passed by, cheerily trolling refrains of drinking songs—it was all a picture of vivacity, life, animation, gayety, which formed a bitter contrast with my mourning and my solitude. On the steps of the gate sat a young mother playing with her child. She kissed its little rosy mouth still impearled with drops of milk, and performed, in order to amuse it, a thousand divine little puerilities such as only mothers know how to invent. The father standing at a little distance smiled gently upon the charming group, and with folded arms seemed to hug his joy to his heart. I could not endure that spectacle. I closed the window with violence, and flung myself on my bed, my heart filled with frightful hate and jealousy, and gnawed my fingers and my bedcovers like a tiger that has passed ten days without food.

I know not how long I remained in this condition, but at last, while writhing on the bed in a fit of spasmodic fury, I suddenly perceived the Abbé Sérapion, who was standing erect in the centre of the room, watching me attentively. Filled with shame of myself, I let my head fall upon my breast and covered my face with my hands.

"Romuald, my friend, something very extraordinary is transpiring within you," observed Sérapion, after a few moments' silence; "your conduct is altogether inexplicable. You—always so quiet, so pious, so gentle—you to rage in your cell like a wild beast! Take heed, brother—do not listen to the suggestions of the devil. The Evil Spirit, furious that you have consecrated yourself forever to the Lord, is prowling around you like a ravening wolf and making a last effort to obtain possession of you. Instead of allowing yourself to be conquered, my dear Romuald, make to yourself a cuirass of prayers, a buckler of mortifications, and combat the enemy like a valiant man; you will then assuredly overcome him. Virtue must be proved by temptation, and gold comes forth purer from the hands of the assayer. Fear not. Never allow yourself to become discouraged. The most watchful and steadfast souls are at moments liable to such temptation. Pray, fast, meditate, and the Evil Spirit will depart from you."

The words of the Abbé Sérapion restored me to myself, and I became a little more calm. "I came," he continued, "to tell you that you have been appointed to the curacy of C——. The priest who had charge of it has just died, and Monseigneur the Bishop has ordered me to have you installed there at once. Be ready, therefore, to start to-morrow." I responded with an inclination of the head, and the Abbé retired. I opened my missal and commenced reading some prayers, but the letters became confused and blurred under my eyes, the thread of the ideas entangled itself hopelessly in my brain, and the volume at last fell from my hands without my being aware of it.

To leave to-morrow without having been able to see her again, to add yet another barrier to the many already interposed between us, to lose forever all hope of being able to meet her, except, indeed, through a miracle! Even to write her, alas! would be impossible, for by whom could I despatch my letter? With my sacred character of priest, to whom could I dare unbosom myself, in whom could I confide? I became a prey to the bitterest anxiety.

Then suddenly recurred to me the words of the Abbé Sérapion regarding the artifices of the devil; and the strange character of the adventure, the supernatural beauty of Clarimonde, the phosphoric light of her eyes, the burning imprint of her hand, the agony into which she had thrown me, the sudden change wrought within me when all my piety vanished in a single instant—these and other things clearly testified to the work of the Evil One, and perhaps that satiny hand was but the glove which concealed his claws. Filled with terror at these fancies, I again picked up the missal which had slipped from my knees and fallen upon the floor, and once more gave myself up to prayer.

Next morning Sérapion came to take me away. Two mules freighted with our miserable valises awaited us at the gate. He mounted one, and I the other as well as I knew how.

As we passed along the streets of the city, I gazed attentively at all the windows and balconies in the hope of seeing Clarimonde, but it was yet early in the morning, and the city had hardly opened its eyes. Mine sought to penetrate the blinds and window curtains of all the palaces before which we were passing. Sérapion doubtless attributed this curiosity to my admiration of the architecture, for he slackened the pace of his animal in order to give me time to look around me. At last we passed the city gates and commenced to mount the hill beyond. When we arrived at its summit I turned to take a last look at the place where Clarimonde dwelt. The shadow of a great cloud hung over all the city; the contrasting colors of its blue and red roofs were lost in the uniform half-tint, through which here and there floated upward, like white flakes of foam, the smoke of freshly kindled fires. By a singular optical effect one edifice, which surpassed in height all the neighboring buildings that were still dimly veiled by the vapors, towered up, fair and lustrous with the gilding of a solitary beam of sunlight—although actually more than a league away it seemed quite near. The smallest details of its architecture were plainly distinguishable—the turrets, the platforms, the window-casements, and even the swallow-tailed weather vanes.

"What is that palace I see over there, all lighted up by the sun?" I asked Sérapion.

He shaded his eyes with his hand, and having looked in the direction indicated, replied: "It is the ancient palace which the Prince Concini has given to the courtesan Clarimonde. Awful things are done there!"

At that instant, I know not yet whether it was a reality or an illusion, I fancied I saw gliding along the terrace a shapely white figure, which gleamed for a moment in passing and as quickly vanished. It was Clarimonde.

Oh, did she know that at that very hour, all feverish and restless—from the height of the rugged road which separated me from her and which, alas! I could never more descend—I was directing my eyes upon the palace where she dwelt, and which a mocking beam of sunlight seemed to bring nigh to me, as though inviting me to enter therein as its lord? Undoubtedly she must have known it, for her soul was too sympathetically united with mine not to have felt its least emotional thrill, and that subtle sympathy it must have been which prompted her to climb—although clad only in her night-dress—to the summit of the terrace, amid the icy dews of the morning.

The shadow gained the palace, and the scene became to the eye only a motionless ocean of roofs and gables, amid which one mountainous undulation was distinctly visible. Sérapion urged his mule forward, my own at once followed at the same gait, and a sharp angle in the road at last hid the city of S—— forever from my eyes, as I was destined never to return thither. At the close of a weary three days' journey through dismal country fields, we caught sight of the cock upon the steeple of the church which I was to take charge of, peeping above the trees, and after having followed some winding roads fringed with thatched cottages and little gardens, we found ourselves in front of the façade, which certainly possessed few features of magnificence. A porch ornamented with some mouldings, and two or three pillars rudely hewn from sandstone; a tiled roof with counterforts of the same sandstone as the pillars, that was all. To the left lay the cemetery, overgrown with high weeds, and having a great iron cross rising up in its centre; to the right stood the presbytery, under the shadow of the church. It was a house of the most extreme simplicity and frigid cleanliness. We entered the enclosure. A few chickens were picking up some oats scattered upon the ground; accustomed, seemingly, to the black habit of ecclesiastics, they showed no fear of our presence and scarcely troubled themselves to get out of our way. A hoarse, wheezy barking fell upon our ears, and we saw an aged dog running toward us.

It was my predecessor's dog. He had dull bleared eyes, grizzled hair, and every mark of the greatest age to which a dog can possibly attain. I patted him gently, and he proceeded at once to march along beside me with an air of satisfaction unspeakable. A very old woman, who had been the housekeeper of the former curé, also came to meet us, and after having invited me into a little back parlor, asked whether I intended to retain her. I replied that I would take care of her, and the dog, and the chickens, and all the furniture her master had bequeathed her at his death. At this she became fairly transported with joy, and the Abbé Sérapion at once paid her the price which she asked for her little property.

As soon as my installation was over, the Abbé Sérapion returned to the seminary. I was, therefore, left alone, with no one but myself to look to for aid or counsel. The thought of Clarimonde again began to haunt me, and in spite of all my endeavors to banish it, I always found it present in my meditations. One evening, while promenading in my little garden along the walks bordered with box-plants, I fancied that I saw through the elm-trees the figure of a woman, who followed my every movement, and that I beheld two sea-green eyes gleaming through the foliage; but it was only an illusion, and on going round to the other side of the garden, I could find nothing except a footprint on the sanded walk—a footprint so small that it seemed to have been made by the foot of a child. The garden was enclosed by very high walls. I searched every nook and corner of it, but could discover no one there. I have never succeeded in fully accounting for this circumstance, which, after all, was nothing compared with the strange things which happened to me afterward.

For a whole year I lived thus, filling all the duties of my calling with the most scrupulous exactitude, praying and fasting, exhorting and lending ghostly aid to the sick, and bestowing alms even to the extent of frequently depriving myself of the very necessaries of life. But I felt a great aridness within me, and the sources of grace seemed closed against me. I never found that happiness which should spring from the fulfilment of a holy mission; my thoughts were far away, and the words of Clarimonde were ever upon my lips like an involuntary refrain. Oh, brother, meditate well on this! Through having but once lifted my eyes to look upon a woman, through one fault apparently so venial, I have for years remained a victim to the most miserable agonies, and the happiness of my life has been destroyed forever.

I will not longer dwell upon those defeats, or on those inward victories invariably followed by yet more terrible falls, but will at once proceed to the facts of my story. One night my door-bell was long and violently rung. The aged housekeeper arose and opened to the stranger, and the figure of a man, whose complexion was deeply bronzed, and who was richly clad in a foreign costume, with a poniard at his girdle, appeared under the rays of Barbara's lantern. Her first impulse was one of terror, but the stranger reassured her, and stated that he desired to see me at once on matters relating to my holy calling. Barbara invited him upstairs, where I was on the point of retiring. The stranger told me that his mistress, a very noble lady, was lying at the point of death, and desired to see a priest. I replied that I was prepared to follow him, took with me the sacred articles necessary for extreme unction, and descended in all haste. Two horses black as the night itself stood without the gate, pawing the ground with impatience, and veiling their chests with long streams of smoky vapor exhaled from their nostrils. He held the stirrup and aided me to mount upon one; then, merely laying his hand upon the pummel of the saddle, he vaulted on the other, pressed the animal's sides with his knees, and loosened rein. The horse bounded forward with the velocity of an arrow. Mine, of which the stranger held the bridle, also started off at a swift gallop, keeping up with his companion. We devoured the road. The ground flowed backward beneath us in a long streaked line of pale gray, and the black silhouettes of the trees seemed fleeing by us on either side like an army in rout. We passed through a forest so profoundly gloomy that I felt my flesh creep in the chill darkness with superstitious fear. The showers of bright sparks which flew from the stony road under the ironshod feet of our horses remained glowing in our wake like a fiery trail; and had any one at that hour of the night beheld us both—my guide and myself—he must have taken us for two spectres riding upon nightmares. Witch-fires ever and anon flitted across the road before us, and the night-birds shrieked fear-somely in the depth of the woods beyond, where we beheld at intervals the phosphorescent eyes of wildcats. The manes of the horses became more and more dishevelled, the sweat streamed over their flanks, and their breath came through their nostrils hard and fast. But when he found them slacking pace, the guide reanimated them by uttering a strange, guttural, unearthly cry, and the gallop recommenced with fury. At last the whirlwind race ceased; a huge black mass pierced through with many bright points of light suddenly rose before us, the hoofs of our horses echoed louder upon a strong wooden drawbridge, and we rode under a great vaulted archway which darkly yawned between two enormous towers. Some great excitement evidently reigned in the castle. Servants with torches were crossing the courtyard in every direction, and above lights were ascending and descending from landing to landing. I obtained a confused glimpse of vast masses of architecture—columns, arcades, flights of steps, stairways—a royal voluptuousness and elfin magnificence of construction worthy of fairyland. A negro page—the same who had before brought me the tablet from Clarimonde, and whom I instantly recognized—approached to aid me in dismounting, and the major-domo, attired in black velvet with a gold chain about his neck, advanced to meet me, supporting himself upon an ivory cane. Large tears were falling from his eyes and streaming over his cheeks and white beard. "Too late!" he cried, sorrowfully shaking his venerable head. "Too late, sir priest! But if you have not been able to save the soul, come at least to watch by the poor body."

He took my arm and conducted me to the death chamber. I wept not less bitterly than he, for I had learned that the dead one was none other than that Clarimonde whom I had so deeply and so wildly loved. A *prie-dieu* stood at the foot of the bed; a bluish flame flickering in a bronze patera filled all the room with a wan, deceptive light, here and there bringing out in the darkness at intervals some projection of furni-ture or cornice. In a chiselled urn upon the table there was a faded white rose, whose leaves—excepting one that still held—had all fallen, like odorous tears, to the foot of the vase. A broken black mask, a fan, and disguises of every variety, which were lying on the armchairs, bore witness that death had entered suddenly and unannounced into that sumptuous dwelling. Without daring to cast my eyes upon the bed, I knelt down and commenced to repeat the Psalms for the Dead, with exceeding fervor, thanking God that he had placed the tomb between me and the memory of this woman, so that I might thereafter be able to utter her name in my prayers as a name forever sanctified by death. But my fervor gradually weakened, and I fell insensibly into a reverie. That chamber bore no semblance to a chamber of death. In lieu of the foetid and cadaverous odors which I had been accustomed to breathe during such funereal vigils, a languorous vapor of Oriental perfume—I know not what amorous odor of woman—softly floated through the tepid air. That pale light seemed rather a twilight gloom contrived for voluptuous pleasure than a substitute for the yellow-flickering watch-tapers which shine by the side of corpses. I thought upon the strange destiny which enabled me to meet Clarimonde again at the very moment when she was lost to me forever, and a sigh of regretful anguish escaped from my breast. Then it seemed to me that some one behind me had also sighed, and I turned round to look. It was only an echo. But in that moment my eyes fell upon the bed of death which they had till then avoided. The red damask curtains, decorated with large flowers worked in embroidery, and looped up with gold bullion, permitted me to behold the fair dead, lying at full length, with hands joined upon her bosom. She was covered with a linen wrapping of dazzling whiteness, which formed a strong contrast with the gloomy purple of the hangings, and was of so fine a texture that it concealed nothing of her body's charming form, and allowed the eye to follow those beautiful outlines—undulating like the neck of a swan—which even death had not robbed of their supple grace. She seemed an alabaster statue executed by some skilful sculptor to place upon the tomb of a queen, or rather, perhaps, like a slumbering maiden over whom the silent snow had woven a spotless veil.

I could no longer maintain my constrained attitude of prayer. The air of the alcove intoxicated me, that febrile perfume of half-faded roses penetrated my very brain, and I commenced to pace restlessly up and down the chamber, pausing at each turn before the bier to contemplate the graceful corpse lying beneath the transparency of its shroud. Wild fancies came thronging to my brain. I thought to myself that she might not, perhaps, be really dead; that she might only have feigned death for the purpose of bringing me to her castle, and then declaring her love. At one time I even thought I saw her foot move under the whiteness of the coverings, and slightly disarrange the long, straight folds of the winding sheet.

And then I asked myself: "Is this indeed Clarimonde? What proof have I that it is she? Might not that black page have passed into the service of some other lady? Surely, I must be going mad to torture and afflict myself thus!" But my heart answered with a fierce throbbing: "It is she; it is she indeed!" I approached the bed again, and fixed my eyes with redoubled attention upon the object of my incertitude. Ah, must I confess it? That exquisite perfection of bodily form, although purified and made sacred by the shadow of death, affected me more voluptuously than it should have done, and that repose so closely resembled slumber that one might well have mistaken it for such. I forgot that I had come there to perform a funeral ceremony; I fancied myself a young bridegroom entering the chamber of the bride, who all modestly hides her fair face, and through coyness seeks to keep herself wholly veiled. Heartbroken with grief, yet wild with hope, shuddering at once with fear and pleasure, I bent over her and grasped the corner of the sheet. I lifted it back, holding my breath all the while through fear of waking her. My arteries throbbed with such violence that I felt them hiss through my temples, and the sweat poured from my forehead in streams, as though I had lifted a mighty slab of marble. There, indeed, lay Clarimonde, even as I had seen her at the church on the day of my ordination. She was not less charming than then. With her, death seemed but a last coquetry. The pallor of her cheeks, the less brilliant carnation of her lips, her long eyelashes lowered and relieving their dark fringe against that white skin, lent her an unspeakably seductive aspect of melancholy chastity and mental suffering; her long loose hair, still intertwined with some little blue flowers, made a shining pillow for her head, and veiled the nudity of her shoulders with its thick ringlets; her beautiful hands, purer, more diaphanous than the Host, were crossed on her bosom in an attitude of pious rest and silent prayer, which served to counteract all that might have proven otherwise too alluring—even after death—in the exquisite roundness and ivory polish of her bare arms from which the pearl bracelets had not yet been removed. I remained long in mute contemplation, and the more I gazed, the less could I persuade myself that life had really abandoned that beautiful body forever. I do not know whether it was an illusion or a reflection of the lamplight, but it seemed to me that the blood was again commencing to circulate under that lifeless pallor, although she remained all motionless. I laid my hand lightly on her arm; it was cold, but not colder than her hand on the day when it touched mine at the portals of the church. I resumed my position, bending my face above her, and bathing her cheeks with the warm dew of my tears. Ah, what bitter feelings of despair and helplessness, what agonies unutterable did I endure in that long watch! Vainly did I wish that I could have gathered all my life into one mass that I might give it all to her, and breathe into her chill remains the flame which devoured me. The night advanced, and feeling the moment of eternal separation approach, I could not deny myself the last sad sweet pleasure of imprinting a kiss upon the dead lips of her who had been my only love. . . . Oh, miracle! A faint breath mingled itself with my breath, and the mouth of Clarimonde responded to the passionate pressure of mine. Her eyes unclosed, and lighted up with something of their former brilliancy; she uttered a long sigh, and uncrossing her arms, passed them around my neck with a look of ineffable delight. "Ah, it is thou, Romuald!" she murmured in a voice languishingly sweet as the last vibrations of a harp. "What ailed thee, dearest? I waited so long for thee that I am dead; but we are now betrothed; I can see thee and visit thee. Adieu, Romuald, adieu! I love thee. That is all I wished to tell thee, and I give thee back the life which thy kiss for a moment recalled. We shall soon meet again."

Her head fell back, but her arms yet encircled me, as though to retain me still. A furious whirlwind suddenly burst in the window and entered the chamber. The last remaining leaf of the white rose for a moment palpitated at the extremity of the stalk like a butterfly's wing, then it detached itself and flew forth through the open casement, bearing with it the soul of Clarimonde. The lamp was extinguished, and I fell insensible upon the bosom of the beautiful dead.

When I came to myself again I was lying on the bed in my little room at the presbytery, and the old dog of the former curé was licking my hand which had been hanging down outside of the covers. Barbara, all trembling with age and anxiety, was busying herself about the room, opening and shutting drawers, and emptying powders into glasses. On seeing me open my eyes, the old woman uttered a cry of joy, the dog yelped and wagged his tail, but I was still so weak that I could not speak a single word or make the slightest motion. Afterward I learned that I had lain thus for three days, giving no evidence of life beyond the faintest respiration. Those three days do not reckon in my life, nor could I ever imagine whither my spirit had departed during those three days; I have no recollection of aught relating to them. Barbara told me that the same coppery-complexioned man who came to seek me on the night of my departure from the presbytery had brought me back the next morning in a close litter, and departed immediately afterward. When I became able to collect my scattered thoughts, I reviewed within my mind all the circumstances of that fateful night. At first I thought I had been the victim of some magical illusion, but ere long the recollection of other circumstances, real and palpable in themselves, came to forbid that supposition. I could not believe that I had been dreaming, since Barbara as well as myself had seen the strange man with his two black horses, and described with exactness every detail of his figure and apparel. Nevertheless it appeared that none knew of any castle in the neighborhood answering to the description of that in which I had again found Clarimonde.

One morning I found the Abbé Sérapion in my room. Barbara had advised him that I was ill, and he had come with all speed to see me. Although this haste on his part testified to an affectionate interest in me, yet his visit did not cause me the pleasure which it should have done. The Abbé Sérapion had something penetrating and inquisitorial in his gaze which made me feel very ill at ease. His presence filled me with embarrassment and a sense of guilt. At the first glance he divined my interior trouble, and I hated him for his clairvoyance.

While he inquired after my health in hypocritically honeyed accents, he constantly kept his two great yellow lion-eyes fixed upon me, and plunged his look into my soul like a sounding lead. Then he asked me how I directed my parish, if I was happy in it, how I passed the leisure hours allowed me in the intervals of pastoral duty, whether I had become acquainted with many of the inhabitants of the place, what was my favorite reading, and a thousand other such questions. I answered these inquiries as briefly as possible, and he, without ever waiting for my answers, passed rapidly from one subject of query to another. That conversation had evidently no connection with what he actually wished to say. At last, without any premonition, but as though repeating a piece of news which he had recalled on the instant and feared might otherwise be forgotten subsequently, he suddenly said, in a clear vibrant voice, which rang in my ears like the trumpets of the Last Judgment:

"The great courtesan Clarimonde died a few days ago, at the close of an orgie which lasted eight days and eight nights. It was something infernally splendid. The abominations of the banquets of Belshazzar and Cleopatra were reënacted there. Good God, what age are we living in? The guests were served by swarthy slaves who spoke an unknown tongue, and who seemed to me to be veritable demons. The livery of the very least among them would have served for the gala-dress of an emperor. There have always been very strange stories told of this Clarimonde, and all her lovers came to a violent or miserable end. They used to say that she was a ghoul, a female vampire; but I believe she was none other than Beelzebub himself."

He ceased to speak and commenced to regard me more attentively than ever, as though to observe the effect of his words on me. I could not refrain from starting when I heard him utter the name of Clarimonde, and this news of her death, in addition to the pain it caused me by reason of its coincidence with the nocturnal scenes I had witnessed, filled me with an agony and terror which my face betrayed, despite my utmost endeavors to appear composed. Sérapion fixed an anxious and severe look upon me, and then observed: "My son, I must warn you that you are standing with foot raised upon the brink of an abyss; take heed lest you fall therein. Satan's claws are long, and tombs are not always true to their trust. The tombstone of Clarimonde should be sealed down with a triple seal, for, if report be true, it is not the first time she has died. May God watch over you, Romuald!"

And with these words the Abbé walked slowly to the door. I did not see him again at that time, for he left for S—— almost immediately.

I became completely restored to health and resumed my accustomed duties. The memory of Clarimonde and the words of the old Abbé were constantly in my mind; nevertheless no extraordinary event had occurred to verify the funereal predictions of Sérapion, and I had commenced to believe that his fears and my own terrors were over-exaggerated, when one night I had a strange dream. I had hardly fallen asleep when I heard my bed-curtains drawn apart, as their rings slided back upon the curtain rod with a sharp sound. I rose up quickly upon my elbow, and beheld the shadow of a woman standing erect before me. I recognized Clarimonde immediately. She bore in her hand a little lamp, shaped like those which are placed in tombs, and its light lent her fingers a rosy transparency, which extended itself by lessening degrees even to the opaque and milky whiteness of her bare arm. Her only gar-ment was the linen winding-sheet which had shrouded her when lying upon the bed of death. She sought to gather its folds over her bosom as though ashamed of being so scantily clad, but her little hand was not equal to the task. She was so white that the color of the drapery blended with that of her flesh under the pallid rays of the lamp. Enveloped with this subtle tissue which betrayed all the contour of her body, she seemed rather the marble statue of some fair antique bather than a woman endowed with life. But dead or living, statue or woman, shadow or body, her beauty was still the same, only that the green light of her eyes was less brilliant, and her mouth, once so warmly crimson, was on-ly tinted with a faint tender rosiness, like that of her cheeks. The little blue flowers which I had noticed entwined in her hair were withered and dry, and had lost nearly all their leaves, but this did not prevent her from being charming—so charming that notwithstanding the strange character of the adventure, and the unexplainable manner in which she had entered my room, I felt not even for a moment the least fear.

She placed the lamp on the table and seated herself at the foot of my bed; then bending toward me, she said, in that voice at once silvery clear and yet velvety in its sweet softness, such as I never heard from any lips save hers:

"I have kept thee long in waiting, dear Romuald, and it must have seemed to thee that I had forgotten thee. But I come from afar off, very far off, and from a land whence no other has ever yet returned. There is neither sun nor moon in that land whence I come: all is but space and shadow; there is neither road nor pathway: no earth for the foot, no air for the wing; and nevertheless behold me here, for Love is stronger than

Death and must conquer him in the end. Oh what sad faces and fearful things I have seen on my way hither! What difficulty my soul, returned to earth through the power of will alone, has had in finding its body and reinstating itself therein! What terrible efforts I had to make ere I could lift the ponderous slab with which they had covered me! See, the palms of my poor hands are all bruised! Kiss them, sweet love, that they may be healed!" She laid the cold palms of her hands upon my mouth, one after the other. I kissed them, indeed, many times, and she the while watched me with a smile of ineffable affection.

I confess to my shame that I had entirely forgotten the advice of the Abbé Sérapion and the sacred office wherewith I had been invested. I had fallen without resistance, and at the first assault. I had not even made the least effort to repel the tempter. The fresh coolness of Clarimonde's skin penetrated my own, and I felt voluptuous tremors pass over my whole body. Poor child! in spite of all I saw afterward, I can hardly yet believe she was a demon; at least she had no appearance of being such, and never did Satan so skilfully conceal his claws and horns. She had drawn her feet up beneath her, and squatted down on the edge of the couch in an attitude full of negligent coquetry. From time to time she passed her little hand through my hair and twisted it into curls, as though trying how a new style of wearing it would become my face. I abandoned myself to her hands with the most guilty pleasure, while she accompanied her gentle play with the prettiest prattle. The most remarkable fact was that I felt no astonishment whatever at so extraordinary an adventure, and as in dreams one finds no difficulty in accepting the most fantastic events as simple facts, so all these circumstances seemed to me perfectly natural in themselves.

"I loved thee long ere I saw thee, dear Romuald, and sought thee everywhere. Thou wast my dream, and I first saw thee in the church at the fatal moment. I said at once, 'It is he!' I gave thee a look into which I threw all the love I ever had, all the love I now have, all the love I shall ever have for thee—a look that would have damned a cardinal or brought a king to his knees at my feet in view of all his court. Thou remainedst unmoved, preferring thy God to me!

"Ah, how jealous I am of that God whom thou didst love and still lovest more than me!

"Woe is me, unhappy one that I am! I can never have thy heart all to myself, I whom thou didst recall to life with a kiss—dead Clarimonde, who for thy sake bursts asunder the gates of the tomb, and comes to consecrate to thee a life which she has resumed only to make thee happy!"

All her words were accompanied with the most impassioned caresses, which bewildered my sense and my reason to such an extent that I did not fear to utter a frightful blasphemy for the sake of consoling her, and to declare that I loved her as much as God.

Her eyes rekindled and shone like chrysoprases. "In truth?—in very truth?—as much as God!" she cried, flinging her beautiful arms around me. "Since it is so, thou wilt come with me; thou wilt follow me whithersoever I desire. Thou wilt cast away thy ugly black habit. Thou shalt be the proudest and most envied of cavaliers; thou shalt be my lover! To be the acknowledged lover of Clarimonde, who has refused even a Pope, that will be something to feel proud of! Ah, the fair, unspeakably happy existence, the beautiful golden life we shall live together! And when shall we depart, my fair sir?"

"To-morrow! To-morrow!" I cried in my delirium.

"To-morrow, then, so let it be!" she answered. "In the meanwhile I shall have opportunity to change my toilet, for this is a little too light and in nowise suited for a voyage. I must also forthwith notify all my friends who believe me dead, and mourn for me as deeply as they are capable of doing. The money, the dresses, the carriages—all will be ready. I shall call for thee at this same hour. Adieu, dear heart!" And she lightly touched my forehead with her lips. The lamp went out, the curtains closed again, and all became dark; a leaden, dreamless sleep fell on me and held me unconscious until the morning following.

I awoke later than usual, and the recollection of this singular adventure troubled me during the whole day. I finally persuaded myself that it was a mere vapor of my heated imagination. Nevertheless its sensations had been so vivid that it was difficult to persuade myself that they were not real, and it was not without some presentiment of what was going to happen that I got into bed at last, after having prayed God to drive far from me all thoughts of evil, and to protect the chastity of my slumber.

I soon fell into a deep sleep, and my dream was continued. The curtains again parted, and I beheld Clarimonde, not as on the former occasion, pale in her pale winding-sheet, with the violets of death upon her cheeks, but gay, sprightly, jaunty, in a superb travelling dress of green velvet, trimmed with gold lace, and looped up on either side to allow a glimpse of satin petticoat. Her blond hair escaped in thick ringlets from beneath a broad black felt hat, decorated with white feathers whimsically twisted into various shapes. In one hand she held a little riding whip terminated by a golden whistle. She tapped me lightly with it and exclaimed: "Well, my fine sleeper, is this the way you make your preparations? I thought I would find you up and dressed. Arise quickly, we have no time to lose."

I leaped out of bed at once.

"Come, dress yourself, and let us go," she continued, pointing to a little package she had brought with her. "The horses are becoming impatient of delay and champing their bits at the door. We ought to have been by this time at least ten leagues distant from here."

I dressed myself hurriedly, and she handed me the articles of apparel herself one by one, bursting into laughter from time to time at my awkwardness, as she explained to me the use of a garment when I had made a mistake. She hurriedly arranged my hair, and this done, held up before me a little pocket mirror of Venetian crystal, rimmed with silver filigree-work, and playfully asked: "How dost find thyself now? Wilt engage me for thy valet de chambre?"

I was no longer the same person, and I could not even recognize myself. I resembled my former self no more than a finished statue resembles a block of stone. My old face seemed but a coarse daub of the one reflected in the mirror. I was handsome, and my vanity was sensibly tickled by the metamorphosis. That elegant apparel, that richly embroidered vest had made of me a totally different personage, and I marvelled at the power of transformation owned by a few yards of cloth cut after a certain pattern. The spirit of my costume penetrated my very skin, and within ten minutes more I had become something of a coxcomb.

In order to feel more at ease in my new attire, I took several turns up and down the room. Clarimonde watched me with an air of maternal pleasure, and appeared well satisfied with her work. "Come, enough of this child's-play! Let us start, Romuald, dear. We have far to go, and we may not get there in time." She took my hand and led me forth. All the doors opened before her at a touch, and we passed by the dog without awaking him.

At the gate we found Margheritone waiting, the same swarthy groom who had once before been my escort. He held the bridles of three horses, all black like those which bore us to the castle—one for me, one for him, one for Clarimonde. Those horses must have been Spanish genets born of mares fecundated by a zephyr, for they were fleet as the wind itself, and the moon, which had just risen at our departure to light us on the way, rolled over the sky like a wheel detached from her own chariot. We beheld her on the right leaping from tree to tree, and putting herself out of breath in the effort to keep up with us. Soon we came upon a level plain where, hard by a clump of trees, a carriage with four vigorous horses awaited us. We entered it, and the postilions urged their animals into a mad gallop. I had one arm around Clarimonde's waist, and one of her hands clasped in mine; her head leaned upon my shoulder, and I felt her bosom, half bare, lightly pressing against my arm. I had never known such intense happiness. In that hour I had forgotten everything, and I no more remembered having ever been a priest than I remembered what I had been doing in my mother's womb, so great was the fascination which the evil spirit exerted upon me. From that night my nature seemed in some sort to have become halved, and there were two men within me, neither of whom knew the other. At one moment I believed myself a priest who dreamed nightly that he was a gentleman, at another that I was a gentleman who dreamed he was a priest. I could no longer distinguish the dream from the reality, nor could I discover where the reality began or where ended the dream. The exquisite young lord and libertine railed at the priest, the priest loathed the dissolute habits of the young lord. Two spirals entangled and confounded the one with the other, yet never touching, would afford a fair representation of this bicephalic life which I lived. Despite the strange character of my condition, I do not believe that I ever inclined, even for a moment, to madness. I always retained with extreme vividness all the perceptions of my two lives. Only there was one absurd fact which I could not explain to myself—namely, that the consciousness of the same individuality existed in two men so opposite in character. It was an anomaly for which I could not account—whether I believed myself to be the curé of the little village of C——, or *Il Signor Romualdo,* the titled lover of Clarimonde.

Be that as it may, I lived, at least I believed that I lived, in Venice. I have never been able to discover rightly how much of illusion and how much of reality there was in this fantastic adventure. We dwelt in a great palace on the Canaleio, filled with frescoes and statues, and containing two Titians in the noblest style of the great master, which were hung in Clarimonde's chamber. It was a palace well worthy of a king. We had each our gondola, our *barcarolli* in family livery, our music hall, and our special poet. Clarimonde always lived upon a magnificent scale; there was something of Cleopatra in her nature. As for me, I had the retinue of a prince's son, and I was regarded with as much reverential respect as though I had been of the family of one of the twelve Apostles or the four Evangelists of the Most Serene Republic. I would not have turned aside to allow even the Doge to pass, and I do not believe that since Satan fell from heaven, any creature was ever prouder or more insolent than I. I went to the Ridotto, and played with a luck which seemed absolutely infernal. I received the best of all society—the sons of ruined families, women of the theatre, shrewd knaves, parasites, hectoring swashbucklers. But notwithstanding the dissipation of such a life, I always remained faithful to Clarimonde. I loved her wildly. She would have excited satiety itself, and chained inconstancy. To have Clarimonde was to have twenty mistresses; aye, to possess all women: so mobile, so varied of aspect, so fresh in new charms was she all in herself—a very chameleon of a woman, in sooth. She made you commit with her the infidelity you would have committed with another, by donning to perfection the character, the attraction, the style of beauty of the woman who appeared to please you. She returned my love a hundredfold, and it was in vain that the young patricians and even the Ancients of the Council of Ten made her the most magnificent proposals. A Foscari even went so far as to offer to espouse her. She rejected all his overtures. Of gold she had enough. She wished no longer for anything but love—a love youthful, pure, evoked by herself, and which should be a first and last passion. I would have been perfectly happy but for a cursed nightmare which recurred every night, and in which I believed myself to be a poor village curé, practising mortification and penance for my excesses during the day. Reassured by my constant association with her, I never thought further of the strange manner in which I had become acquainted with Clarimonde. But the words of the Abbé Sérapion concerning her recurred often to my memory, and never ceased to cause me uneasiness.

For some time the health of Clarimonde had not been so good as usual; her complexion grew paler day by day. The physicians who were summoned could not comprehend the nature of her malady and knew not how to treat it. They all prescribed some insignificant remedies, and never called a second time. Her paleness, nevertheless, visibly increased, and she became colder and colder, until she seemed almost as white and dead as upon that memorable night in the unknown castle. I grieved with anguish unspeakable to behold her thus slowly perishing; and she, touched by my agony, smiled upon me sweetly and sadly with the fateful smile of those who feel that they must die.

One morning I was seated at her bedside, and breakfasting from a little table placed close at hand, so that I might not be obliged to leave her for a single instant. In the act of cutting some fruit I accidentally inflicted rather a deep gash on my finger. The blood immediately gushed forth in a little purple jet, and a few drops spurted upon Clarimonde. Her eyes flashed, her face suddenly assumed an expression of savage and ferocious joy such as I had never before observed in her. She leaped out of her bed with animal agility—the agility, as it were, of an ape or a cat—and sprang upon my wound, which she commenced to suck with an air of unutterable pleasure. She swallowed the blood in little mouthfuls, slowly and carefully, like a connoisseur tasting a wine from Xeres or Syracuse. Gradually her eyelids half closed, and the pupils of her green eyes became oblong instead of round. From time to time she paused in order to kiss my hand, then she would recommence to press her lips to the lips of the wound in order to coax forth a few more ruddy drops. When she found that the blood would no longer come, she arose with eyes liquid and brilliant, rosier than a May dawn; her face full and fresh, her hand warm and moist—in fine, more beautiful than ever, and in the most perfect health.

"I shall not die! I shall not die!" she cried, clinging to my neck, half mad with joy. "I can love thee yet for a long time. My life is thine, and all that is of me comes from thee. A few drops of thy rich and noble blood, more precious and more potent than all the elixirs of the earth, have given me back life."

This scene long haunted my memory, and inspired me with strange doubts in regard to Clarimonde; and the same evening, when slumber had transported me to my presbytery, I beheld the Abbé Sérapion, graver and more anxious of aspect than ever. He gazed attentively at me, and sorrowfully exclaimed: "Not content with losing your soul, you now desire also to lose your body. Wretched young man, into how terrible a plight have you fallen!" The tone in which he uttered these words powerfully affected me, but in spite of its vividness even that impression was soon dissipated, and a thousand other cares erased it from my mind. At last one evening, while looking into a mirror whose traitorous position she had not taken into account, I saw Clarimonde in the act of emptying a powder into the cup of spiced wine which she had long been in the habit of preparing after our repasts. I took the cup, feigned to carry it to my lips, and then placed it on the nearest article of furniture as though intending to finish it at my leisure. Taking advantage of a moment when the fair one's back was turned, I threw the contents under the table, after which I retired to my chamber and went to bed, fully resolved not to sleep, but to watch and discover what should come of all this mystery. I did not have to wait long. Clarimonde entered in her night-dress, and having removed her apparel, crept into bed and lay down beside me. When she felt assured that I was asleep, she bared my arm, and drawing a gold pin from her hair, commenced to murmur in a low voice:

"One drop, only one drop! One ruby at the end of my needle. . . . Since thou lovest me yet, I must not die! . . . Ah, poor love! His beautiful blood, so brightly purple, I must drink it. Sleep, my only treasure! Sleep, my god, my child! I will do thee no harm; I will only take of thy life what I must to keep my own from being forever extinguished. But that I love thee so much, I could well resolve to have other lovers whose veins I could drain; but since I have known thee all other men have become hateful to me. . . . Ah, the beautiful arm! How round it is! How white it is! How shall I ever dare to prick this pretty blue vein!" And while thus murmuring to herself she wept, and I felt her tears raining on my arm as she clasped it with her hands. At last she took the resolve, slightly punctured me with her pin, and commenced to suck up the blood which oozed from the place. Although she swallowed only a few drops, the fear of weakening me soon seized her, and she carefully tied a little band around my arm, afterward rubbing the wound with an unguent which immediately cicatrized it.

Further doubts were impossible. The Abbé Sérapion was right. Notwithstanding this positive knowledge, however, I could not cease to love Clarimonde, and I would gladly of my own accord have given her all the blood she required to sustain her factitious life. Moreover, I felt but little fear of her. The woman seemed to plead with me for the vampire, and what I had already heard and seen sufficed to reassure me completely. In those days I had plenteous veins, which would not have been so easily exhausted as at present; and I would not have thought of bargaining for my blood, drop by drop. I would rather have opened myself the veins of my arm and said to her: "Drink, and may my love infiltrate itself throughout thy body together with my blood!" I carefully avoided ever making the least reference to the narcotic drink she had prepared for me, or to the incident of the pin, and we lived in the most perfect harmony.

Yet my priestly scruples commenced to torment me more than ever, and I was at a loss to imagine what new penance I could invent in order to mortify and subdue my flesh. Although these visions were involuntary, and though I did not actually participate in anything relating to them, I could not dare to touch the body of Christ with hands so impure and a mind defiled by such debauches whether real or imaginary. In the effort to avoid falling under the influence of these wearisome hallucinations, I strove to prevent myself from being overcome by sleep. I held my eyelids open with my fingers, and stood for hours together leaning upright against the wall, fighting sleep with all my might; but the dust of drowsiness invariably gathered upon my eyes at last, and finding all resistance useless, I would have to let my arms fall in the extremity of despairing weariness, and the current of slumber would again bear me away to the perfidious shores. Sérapion addressed me with the most vehement exhortations, severely reproaching me for my softness and want of fervor. Finally, one day when I was more wretched than usual, he said to me: "There is but one way by which you can obtain relief from this continual torment, and though it is an extreme measure it must be made use of; violent diseases require violent remedies. I know where Clarimonde is buried. It is necessary that we shall disinter her remains, and that you shall behold in how pitiable a state the object of your love is. Then you will no longer be tempted to lose your soul for the sake of an unclean corpse devoured by worms, and ready to crumble into dust. That will assuredly restore you to yourself." For my part, I was so tired of this double life that I at once consented, desiring to ascertain beyond a doubt whether a priest or a gentleman had been the victim of delusion. I had become fully resolved either to kill one of the two men within me for the benefit of the other, or else to kill both, for so terrible an existence could not last long and be endured. The Abbé Sérapion provided himself with a mattock, a lever, and a lantern, and at midnight we wended our way to the cemetery of ——, the location and place of which were perfectly familiar to him. After having directed the rays of the dark lantern upon the inscriptions of several tombs, we came at last upon a great slab, half concealed by huge weeds and devoured by mosses and parasitic plants, whereupon we deciphered the opening lines of the epitaph:

> Here lies Clarimonde
> Who was famed in her lifetime
> As the fairest of women.*

"It is here without a doubt," muttered Sérapion, and placing his lantern on the ground, he forced the point of the lever under the edge of the stone and commenced to raise it. The stone yielded, and he proceeded to work with the mattock. Darker and more silent than the night itself, I stood by and watched him do it, while he, bending over his dismal toil, streamed with sweat, panted, and his hard-coming breath seemed to have the harsh tone of a death rattle. It was a weird scene, and had any persons from without beheld us, they would assuredly have taken us rather for profane wretches and shroud-stealers than for priests

---

* Ici gît Clarimonde
Qui fut de son vivant
La plus belle du monde.
The broken beauty of the lines is unavoidably lost in the translation.—[Trans.]

of God. There was something grim and fierce in Sérapion's zeal which lent him the air of a demon rather than of an apostle or an angel, and his great aquiline face, with all its stern features brought out in strong relief by the lantern-light, had something fearsome in it which enhanced the unpleasant fancy. I felt an icy sweat come out upon my forehead in huge beads, and my hair stood up with a hideous fear. Within the depths of my own heart I felt that the act of the austere Sérapion was an abominable sacrilege; and I could have prayed that a triangle of fire would issue from the entrails of the dark clouds, heavily rolling above us, to reduce him to cinders. The owls which had been nestling in the cypress-trees, startled by the gleam of the lantern, flew against it from time to time, striking their dusty wings against its panes, and uttering plaintive cries of lamentation; wild foxes yelped in the far darkness, and a thousand sinister noises detached themselves from the silence. At last Sérapion's mattock struck the coffin itself, making its planks reëcho with a deep sonorous sound, with that terrible sound nothingness utters when stricken. He wrenched apart and tore up the lid, and I beheld Clarimonde, pallid as a figure of marble, with hands joined; her white winding-sheet made but one fold from her head to her feet. A little crimson drop sparkled like a speck of dew at one corner of her colorless mouth. Sérapion, at this spectacle, burst into fury: "Ah, thou art here, demon! Impure courtesan! Drinker of blood and gold!" And he flung holy water upon the corpse and the coffin, over which he traced the sign of the cross with his sprinkler. Poor Clarimonde had no sooner been touched by the blessed spray than her beautiful body crumbled into dust, and became only a shapeless and frightful mass of cinders and half-calcined bones.

"Behold your mistress, my Lord Romuald!" cried the inexorable priest, as he pointed to these sad remains. "Will you be easily tempted after this to promenade on the Lido or at Fusina with your beauty?" I covered my face with my hands, a vast ruin had taken place within me. I returned to my presbytery, and the noble Lord Romuald, the lover of Clarimonde, separated himself from the poor priest with whom he had kept such strange company so long. But once only, the following night, I saw Clarimonde. She said to me, as she had said the first time at the portals of the church: "Unhappy man! Unhappy man! What hast thou

done? Wherefore have hearkened to that imbecile priest? Wert thou
not happy? And what harm had I ever done thee that thou shouldst vio-
late my poor tomb, and lay bare the miseries of my nothingness? All
communication between our souls and our bodies is henceforth forever
broken. Adieu! Thou wilt yet regret me!" She vanished in air as smoke,
and I never saw her more.

Alas! she spoke truly indeed. I have regretted her more than once,
and I regret her still. My soul's peace has been very dearly bought. The
love of God was not too much to replace such a love as hers. And this,
brother, is the story of my youth. Never gaze upon a woman, and walk
abroad only with eyes ever fixed upon the ground; for however chaste
and watchful one may be, the error of a single moment is enough to
make one lose eternity.

One of Cleopatra's Nights

I

Nineteen hundred years ago from the date of this writing, a magnificently gilded and painted cangia was descending the Nile as rapidly as fifty long, flat oars, which seemed to crawl over the furrowed water like the legs of a gigantic scarabaeus, could impel it.

This cangia was narrow, long, elevated at both ends in the form of a new moon, elegantly proportioned, and admirably built for speed; the figure of a ram's head, surmounted by a golden globe, armed the point of the prow, showing that the vessel belonged to some personage of royal blood.

In the centre of the vessel arose a flat-roofed cabin—a sort of *naos,* or tent of honor—colored and gilded, ornamented with palm-leaf mouldings, and lighted by four little square windows.

Two chambers, both decorated with hieroglyphic paintings, occupied the horns of the crescent. One of them, the larger, had a second story of lesser height built upon it, like the *chateaux gaillards* of those fantastic galleys of the sixteenth century drawn by Della-Bella; the other and smaller chamber, which also served as a pilot-house, was surmounted with a triangular pediment.

In lieu of a rudder, two immense oars, adjusted upon stakes decorated with stripes of paint, which served in place of our modern rowlocks, extended into the water in rear of the vessel like the webbed feet of a swan; heads crowned with *pshents,* and bearing the allegorical horn upon their chins, were sculptured upon the handles of these huge oars, which were manoeuvred by the pilot as he stood upon the deck of the cabin above.

He was a swarthy man, tawny as new bronze, with bluish surface gleams playing over his dark skin; long oblique eyes, hair deeply black

63

and all plaited into little cords, full lips, high cheek-bones, ears standing out from the skull—the Egyptian type in all its purity. A narrow strip of cotton about his loins, together with five or six strings of glass beads and a few amulets, comprised his whole costume.

He appeared to be the only one on board the cangia; for the rowers bending over their oars, and concealed from view by the gunwales, made their presence known only through the symmetrical movements of the oars themselves, which spread open alternately on either side of the vessel, like the ribs of a fan, and fell regularly back into the water after a short pause.

Not a breath of air was stirring; and the great triangular sail of the cangia, tied up and bound to the lowered mast with a silken cord, testified that all hope of the wind rising had been abandoned.

The noonday sun shot his arrows perpendicularly from above; the ashen-hued slime of the river banks reflected the fiery glow; a raw light, glaring and blinding in its intensity, poured down in torrents of flame; the azure of the sky whitened in the heat as a metal whitens in the furnace; an ardent and lurid fog smoked in the horizon. Not a cloud appeared in the sky—a sky mournful and changeless as Eternity

The water of the Nile, sluggish and wan, seemed to slumber in its course, and slowly extend itself in sheets of molten tin. No breath of air wrinkled its surface, or bowed down upon their stalks the cups of the lotus-flowers, as rigidly motionless as though sculptured; at long intervals the leap of a bechir or fabaka expanding its belly scarcely caused a silvery gleam upon the current; and the oars of the cangia seemed with difficulty to tear their way through the fuliginous film of that curdled water. The banks were desolate, a solemn and mighty sadness weighed upon this land, which was never aught else than a vast tomb, and in which the living appeared to be solely occupied in the work of burying the dead. It was an arid sadness, dry as pumice stone, without melancholy, without reverie, without one pearly gray cloud to follow toward the horizon, one secret spring wherein to lave one's dusty feet; the sadness of a sphinx weary of eternally gazing upon the desert, and unable to detach herself from the granite socle upon which she has sharpened her claws for twenty centuries.

So profound was the silence that it seemed as though the world had become dumb, or that the air had lost all power of conveying sound. The only noises which could be heard at intervals were the whisperings and stifled "chuckling" of the crocodiles, which, enfeebled by the heat, were wallowing among the bulrushes by the river banks; or the sound made by some ibis, which, tired of standing with one leg doubled up against its stomach, and its head sunk between its shoulders, suddenly abandoned its motionless attitude and, brusquely whipping the blue air with its white wings, flew off to perch upon an obelisk or a palm-tree.

The cangia flew like an arrow over the smooth river-water, leaving behind it a silvery wake which soon disappeared; and only a few foam-bubbles rising to break at the surface of the stream bore testimony to the passage of the vessel, then already out of sight.

The ochre-hued or salmon-colored banks unrolled themselves rap-idly, like scrolls of papyrus, between the double azure of water and sky so similar in tint that the slender tongue of earth which separated them seemed like a causeway stretching over an immense lake, and that it would have been difficult to determine whether the Nile reflected the sky, or whether the sky reflected the Nile.

The scene continually changed. At one moment were visible gigan-tic propylaea, whose sloping walls, painted with large panels of fantastic figures, were mirrored in the river; pylons with broad-bulging capitals; stairways guarded by huge crouching sphinxes, wearing caps with lappets of many folds, and crossing their paws of black basalt below their sharp-ly projecting breasts; palaces, immeasurably vast, projecting against the horizon the severe horizontal lines of their entablatures, where the em-blematic globe unfolded its mysterious wings like an eagle's vast-extending pinions; temples with enormous columns thick as towers, on which were limned processions of hieroglyphic figures against a back-ground of brilliant white—all the monstrosities of that Titanic architec-ture. Again the eye beheld only landscapes of desolate aridity—hills formed of stony fragments from excavations and building works, crumbs of that gigantic debauch of granite which lasted for more than thirty centuries; mountains exfoliated by heat, and mangled and striped with black lines which seemed like the cauterizations of a conflagration; hillocks humped and deformed, squatting like the criocephalus of the tombs, and projecting the outlines of their misshapen attitude against the sky-line; expanses of greenish clay, reddle, flour-white tufa; and from time to time some steep cliff of dry, rose-colored granite, where yawned the black mouths of the stone quarries.

This aridity was wholly unrelieved; no oasis of foliage refreshed the eye; green seemed to be a color unknown to that nature; only some meagre palm-tree, like a vegetable crab, appeared from time to time in the horizon; or a thorny fig-tree brandished its tempered leaves like sword blades of bronze; or a carthamus-plant, which had found a little moisture to live upon in the shadow of some fragment of a broken column, relieved the general uniformity with a speck of crimson.

After this rapid glance at the aspect of the landscape, let us return to the cangia with its fifty rowers, and, without announcing ourselves, enter boldly into the *naos* of honor.

The interior was painted white with green arabesques, bands of vermilion, and gilt flowers fantastically shaped; an exceedingly fine rush matting covered the floor; at the further end stood a little bed, supported upon griffin's feet, having a back resembling that of a modern lounge or sofa; a stool with four steps to enable one to climb into bed; and (rather an odd luxury according to our ideas of comfort) a sort of hemicycle of cedar wood, supported upon a single leg, and designed to fit the nape of the neck so as to support the head of the person reclining.

Upon this strange pillow reposed a most charming head, one look of which once caused the loss of half a world; an adorable, a divine head; the head of the most perfect woman that ever lived; the most womanly and most queenly of all women; an admirable type of beauty which the imagination of poets could never invest with any new grace, and which dreamers will find forever in the depths of their dreams—it is not necessary to name Cleopatra.

Beside her stood her favorite slave Charmion, waving a large fan of ibis feathers; and a young girl was moistening with scented water the little reed blinds attached to the windows of the *naos,* so that the air might only enter impregnated with fresh odors.

Near the bed of repose, in a striped vase of alabaster with a slender neck and a peculiarly elegant, tapering shape, vaguely recalling the form of a heron, was placed a bouquet of lotus-flowers, some of a celestial blue, others of a tender rose-color, like the finger-tips of Isis the great goddess.

Either from caprice or policy, Cleopatra did not wear the Greek dress that day. She had just attended a panegyris,* and was returning to her summer palace still clad in the Egyptian costume she had worn at the festival.

Perhaps our fair readers will feel curious to know how Queen Cleopatra was attired on her return from the Mammisi of Hermonthis whereat were worshipped the holy triad of the god Mandou, the goddess Ritho, and their son, Harphra; luckily we are able to satisfy them in this regard.

For head-dress Queen Cleopatra wore a kind of very light helmet of beaten gold, fashioned in the form of the body and wings of the sacred partridge. The wings, opening downward like fans, covered the temples, and extending below, almost to the neck, left exposed on either side, through a small aperture, an ear rosier and more delicately curled than the shell whence arose that Venus whom the Egyptians named Athor; the tail of the bird occupied that place where our women wear their chignons; its body, covered with imbricated feathers, and painted in variegated enamel, concealed the upper part of the head; and its neck, gracefully curving forward over the forehead of the wearer, formed together with its little head a kind of horn-shaped ornament, all sparkling with precious stones; a symbolic crest, designed like a tower, completed this odd but elegant head-dress. Hair dark as a starless night flowed from beneath this helmet, and streamed in long tresses over the fair shoulders whereof the commencement only, alas! was left exposed by a collarette, or gorget, adorned with many rows of serpentine stones, azodrachs, and chrysoberyls; a linen robe diagonally cut—a mist of material, of woven air, *ventus textilis* as Petronius says, undulated in vapory whiteness about a lovely body whose outlines it scarcely shaded with the softest shading. This robe had half-sleeves, tight at the shoulder, but widening toward the elbows like our *manches-à-sabot,* and permitting a glimpse of an adorable arm and a perfect hand, the arm being clasped

---

* *Panegyris;* pl., *panegyreis*—from the Greek πανήγυρις—signifies the meeting of a whole people to worship at a common sanctuary or participate in a national religious festival. The assemblies at the Olympic, Pythian, Nemean, or Isthmian games were in this sense *panegyreis.* See Smith's Dict. Antiq.—[Trans.]

by six golden bracelets, and the hand adorned with a ring representing the sacred scarabaeus. A girdle, whose knotted ends hung down in front, confined this free-floating tunic at the waist; a short cloak adorned with fringing completed the costume; and, if a few barbarous words will not frighten Parisian ears, we might add that the robe was called *schenti,* and the short cloak, *calisiris.*

Finally, we may observe that Queen Cleopatra wore very thin, light sandals, turned up at the toes, and fastened over the instep, like the *souliers-à-la-poulaine* of the mediaeval *chatelaines.*

But Queen Cleopatra did not wear that air of satisfaction which becomes a woman conscious of being perfectly beautiful and perfectly well dressed. She tossed and turned in her little bed, and her sudden movements momentarily disarranged the folds of her gauzy *conopeum,* which Charmion as often rearranged with inexhaustible patience, and without ceasing to wave her fan.

"This room is stifling," said Cleopatra; "even if Pthah the God of Fire established his forges in here, he could not make it hotter; the air is like the breath of a furnace!" And she moistened her lips with the tip of her little tongue, and stretched out her hand like a feverish patient seeking an absent cup.

Charmion, ever attentive, at once clapped her hands. A black slave clothed in a short tunic hanging in folds like an Albanian petticoat, and a panther-skin thrown over his shoulders, entered with the suddenness of an apparition; with his left hand balancing a tray laden with cups, and slices of watermelon, and carrying in his right a long vase with a spout like a modern teapot.

The slave filled one of these cups, pouring the liquor into it from a considerable height with marvellous dexterity, and placed it before the queen. Cleopatra merely touched the beverage with her lips, laid the cup down beside her, and turning upon Charmion her beautiful liquid black eyes, lustrous with living light, exclaimed:

"O Charmion, I am weary unto death!"

II

Charmion, at once anticipating a confidence, assumed a look of pained sympathy, and drew nearer to her mistress.

"I am horribly weary!" continued Cleopatra, letting her arms fall like one utterly discouraged. "This Egypt crushes, annihilates me; this sky with its implacable azure is sadder than the deep night of Erebus; never a cloud, never a shadow, and always that red, sanguine sun, which glares down upon you like the eye of a Cyclops. Ah, Charmion, I would give a pearl for one drop of rain! From the inflamed pupil of that sky of bronze no tear has ever yet fallen upon the desolation of this land; it is only a vast covering for a tomb—the dome of a necropolis; a sky dead and dried up like the mummies it hangs over; it weighs upon my shoulders like an over-heavy mantle; it constrains and terrifies me; it seems to me that I could not stand up erect without striking my forehead against it. And, moreover, this land is truly an awful land; all things in it are gloomy, enigmatic, incomprehensible. Imagination has produced in it only monstrous chimeras and monuments immeasurable; this architecture and this art fill me with fear; those colossi, whose stone-entangled limbs compel them to remain eternally sitting with their hands upon their knees, weary me with their stupid immobility; they trouble my eyes and my horizon. When, indeed, shall the giant come who is to take them by the hand and relieve them from their long watch of twenty centuries? For even granite itself must grow weary at last! Of what master, then, do they await the coming, to leave their mountain-seats and rise in token of respect? Of what invisible flock are those huge sphinxes the guardians, crouching like dogs on the watch, that they never close their eyelids, and forever extend their claws in readiness to seize? Why are their stony eyes so obstinately fixed upon eternity and infinity? What weird secret do their firmly locked lips retain within their breasts? On the right hand, on the left, whithersoever one turns, only frightful monsters are visible—dogs with the heads of men; men with the heads of dogs; chimeras begotten of hideous couplings in the shadowy depths of the labyrinths; figures of Anubis, Typhon, Osiris; partridges with great yellow eyes that seem to pierce through you with their inquisitorial gaze, and see beyond and behind you things which one dare not speak of—a family of animals and horrible gods with scaly wings, hooked beaks, trenchant claws, ever ready to seize and devour you should you venture to cross the threshold of the temple, or lift a corner of the veil.

"Upon the walls, upon the columns, on the ceilings, on the floors, upon palaces and temples, in the long passages and the deepest pits of the necropoli, even within the bowels of the earth where light never comes, and where the flames of the torches die for want of air, forever and everywhere are sculptured and painted interminable hieroglyphics, telling in language unintelligible of things which are no longer known, and which belong, doubtless, to the vanished creations of the past—prodigious buried works wherein a whole nation was sacrificed to write the epitaph of one king! Mystery and granite—this is Egypt! Truly a fair land for a young woman, and a young queen.

"Menacing and funereal symbols alone meet the eye—the emblems of the *pedum,* the *tau,* allegorical globes, coiling serpents, and the scales in which souls are weighed—the Unknown, death, nothingness. In the place of any vegetation only *stelae* limned with weird characters; instead of avenues of trees, avenues of granite obelisks; in lieu of soil, vast pavements of granite for which whole mountains could each furnish but one slab; in place of a sky, ceilings of granite—eternity made palpable, a bitter and everlasting sarcasm upon the frailty and brevity of life—stairways built only for the limbs of Titans, which the human foot cannot ascend save by the aid of ladders; columns that a hundred arms cannot encircle; labyrinths in which one might travel for years without discovering the termination—the vertigo of enormity, the drunkenness of the gigantic, the reckless efforts of that pride which would at any cost engrave its name deeply upon the face of the world.

"And, moreover, Charmion, I tell you a thought haunts me which terrifies me. In other lands of the earth, corpses are burned, and their ashes soon mingle with the soil. Here, it is said that the living have no other occupation than that of preserving the dead. Potent balms save them from destruction; the remains endure after the soul has evaporated. Beneath this people lie twenty peoples; each city stands upon twenty layers of necropoli; each generation which passes away leaves a population of mummies to a shadowy city. Beneath the father you find the grandfather and the great-grandfather in their gilded and painted boxes, even as they were during life; and should you dig down forever, forever you would still find the underlying dead.

"When I think upon those bandage-swathed myriads—those multitudes of parched spectres who fill the sepulchral pits, and who have been there for two thousand years face to face in their own silence, which nothing ever breaks, not even the noise which the graveworms make in crawling, and who will be found intact after yet another two thousand years, with their crocodiles, their cats, their ibises, and all things that lived in their lifetime—then terrors seize me, and I feel my flesh creep. What do they mutter to each other? For they still have lips, and every ghost would find its body in the same state as when it quitted it, if they should all take the fancy to return.

"Ah, truly is Egypt a sinister kingdom and little suited to me, the laughter-loving and merry one. Everything in it encloses a mummy; that is the heart and the kernel of all things. After a thousand turns you must always end there; the Pyramids themselves hide sarcophagi. What nothingness and madness is this! Disembowel the sky with gigantic triangles of stone—you cannot thereby lengthen your corpse an inch. How can one rejoice and live in a land like this, where the only perfume you can respire is the acrid odor of the naphtha and bitumen which boil in the caldrons of the embalmers, where the very flooring of your chamber sounds hollow because the corridors of the hypogea and the mortuary pits extend even under your alcove? To be the queen of mummies, to have none to converse with but statues in constrained and rigid attitudes—this is, in truth, a cheerful lot. Again, if I only had some heartfelt passion to relieve this melancholy, some interest in life; if I could but love somebody or something; if I were even loved; but I am not.

"This is why I am weary, Charmion. With love, this grim and arid Egypt would seem to me fairer than even Greece with her ivory gods, her temples of snowy marble, her groves of laurel, and fountains of living water. There I should never dream of the weird face of Anubis and the ghastly terrors of the cities underground."

Charmion smiled incredulously. "That ought not, surely, to be a source of much grief to you, O queen; for every glance of your eyes transpierces hearts, like the golden arrows of Eros himself."

"Can a queen," answered Cleopatra, "ever know whether it is her face or her diadem that is loved? The rays of her starry crown dazzle the eyes and the heart. Were I to descend from the height of my throne, would I even have the celebrity or the popularity of Bacchis or Archianassa, of the first courtesan from Athens or Miletus? A queen is something so far removed from men, so elevated, so widely separated from them, so impossible for them to reach! What presumption dare flatter itself in such an enterprise? It is not simply a woman, it is an august and sacred being that has no sex, and that is worshipped kneeling without being loved. Who was ever really enamoured of Hera the snowy-armed or Pallas of the sea-green eyes? Who ever sought to kiss the silver feet of Thetis or the rosy fingers of Aurora? What lover of the divine beauties ever took unto himself wings that he might soar to the golden palaces of heaven? Respect and fear chill hearts in our presence, and in order to obtain the love of our equals, one must descend into those necropoli of which I have just been speaking."

Although she offered no further objection to the arguments of her mistress, a vague smile which played about the lips of the handsome Greek slave showed that she had little faith in the inviolability of the royal person.

"Ah," continued Cleopatra, "I wish that something would happen to me, some strange, unexpected adventure. The songs of the poets; the dances of the Syrian slaves; the banquets, rose garlanded, and prolonged into the dawn; the nocturnal races; the Laconian dogs; the tame lions; the humpbacked dwarfs; the brotherhood of the Inimitables; the combats of the arena; the new dresses; the byssus robes; the clusters of pearls; the perfumes from Asia; the most exquisite of luxuries; the wildest of splendors—nothing any longer gives me pleasure. Everything has become indifferent to me, everything is insupportable to me."

"It is easily to be seen," muttered Charmion to herself, "that the queen has not had a lover nor had any one killed for a whole month."

Fatigued with so lengthy a tirade, Cleopatra once more took the cup placed beside her, moistened her lips with it, and putting her head beneath her arm, like a dove putting its head under its wing, composed herself for slumber as best she could. Charmion unfastened her sandals and commenced to gently tickle the soles of her feet with a peacock's feather, and Sleep soon sprinkled his golden dust upon the beautiful eyes of Ptolemy's sister.

While Cleopatra sleeps, let us ascend upon deck and enjoy the glorious sunset view. A broad band of violet color, warmed deeply with ruddy tints toward the west, occupies all the lower portion of the sky; encountering the zone of azure above, the violet shade melts into a clear lilac, and fades off through half-rosy tints into the blue beyond; afar, where the sun, red as a buckler fallen from the furnace of Vulcan, casts his burning reflection, the deeper shades turn to pale citron hues, and glow with turquoise tints. The water, rippling under an oblique beam of light, shines with the dull gleam of the quicksilvered side of a mirror, or like a damascened blade. The sinuosities of the bank, the reeds, and all objects along the shore are brought out in sharp black relief against the bright glow. By the aid of this crepuscular light you may perceive afar off, like a grain of dust floating upon quicksilver, a little brown speck trembling in the network of luminous ripples. Is it a teal diving, a tortoise lazily drifting with the current, a crocodile raising the tip of his scaly snout above the water to breathe the cooler air of evening, the belly of a hippopotamus gleaming amidstream, or perhaps a rock left bare by the falling of the river? For the ancient Opi-Mou, Father of Waters, sadly needs to replenish his dry urn from the solstitial rains of the Mountains of the Moon.

It is none of these. By the atoms of Osiris so deftly resewn together, it is a man, who seems to walk, to skate, upon the water! Now the frail bark which sustains him becomes visible, a very nutshell of a boat, a hollow fish; three strips of bark fitted together (one for the bottom and two for the sides), and strongly fastened at either end by cord well smeared with bitumen. The man stands erect, with one foot on either side of this fragile vessel, which he impels with a single oar that also serves the purpose of a rudder; and although the royal cangia moves rapidly under the efforts of the fifty rowers, the little black bark visibly gains upon it.

Cleopatra desired some strange adventure, something wholly unexpected. This little bark which moves so mysteriously seems to us to be conveying an adventure, or, at least, an adventurer. Perhaps it contains the hero of our story; the thing is not impossible.

At any rate he was a handsome youth of twenty, with hair so black that it seemed to own a tinge of blue, a skin blond as gold, and a form so perfectly proportioned that he might have been taken for a bronze statue by Lysippus. Although he had been rowing for a very long time he betrayed no sign of fatigue, and not a single drop of sweat bedewed his forehead.

The sun half sank below the horizon, and against his broken disk figured the dark silhouette of a far distant city, which the eye could not have distinguished but for this accidental effect of light. His radiance soon faded altogether away, and the stars, fair night-flowers of heaven, opened their chalices of gold in the azure of the firmament. The royal cangia, closely followed by the little bark, stopped before a huge marble stairway, whereof each step supported one of those sphinxes that Cleopatra so much detested. This was the landing-place of the summer palace.

Cleopatra, leaning upon Charmion, passed swiftly, like a gleaming vision, between a double line of lantern-bearing slaves.

The youth took from the bottom of his little boat a great lion-skin, threw it across his shoulders, drew the tiny shell upon the beach, and wended his way toward the palace.

III

Who is this young man, balancing himself upon a fragment of bark, who dares follow the royal cangia, and is able to contend in a race of speed against fifty strong rowers from the land of Kush, all naked to the waist, and anointed with palm-oil? What secret motive urges him to this swift pursuit? That, indeed, is one of the many things we are obliged to know in our character of the intuition-gifted poet, for whose benefit all men, and even all women (a much more difficult matter), must have in their breasts that little window which Momus of old demanded.

It is not a very easy thing to find out precisely what a young man from the land of Kemi, who followed the barge of Cleopatra, queen and goddess Evergetes, on her return from the Mammisi of Hermonthis two thousand years ago, was then thinking of. But we shall make the effort notwithstanding.

Meïamoun, son of Mandouschopsh, was a youth of strange character; nothing by which ordinary minds are affected made any impression
upon him. He seemed to belong to some loftier race, and might well
have been regarded as the offspring of some divine adultery. His glance
had the steady brilliancy of a falcon's gaze, and a serene majesty sat on
his brow as upon a pedestal of marble; a noble pride curled his upper
lip, and expanded his nostrils like those of a fiery horse. Although owning a grace of form almost maidenly in its delicacy, and though the bosom of the fair and effeminate god Dionysos was not more softly
rounded or smoother than his, yet beneath this soft exterior were hidden sinews of steel and the strength of Hercules—a strange privilege of
certain antique natures to unite in themselves the beauty of woman with
the strength of man.

As for his complexion, we must acknowledge that it was of a tawny
orange color, a hue little in accordance with our white-and-rose ideas of
beauty; but which did not prevent him from being a very charming
young man, much sought after by all kinds of women—yellow, red, copper-colored, sooty-black, or golden-skinned, and even by one fair, white
Greek.

Do not suppose from this that Meïamoun's lot was altogether enviable. The ashes of aged Priam, the very snows of Hippolytus, were not
more insensible or more frigid; the young white-robed neophyte preparing for the initiation into the mysteries of Isis led no chaster life; the
young maiden benumbed by the icy shadow of her mother was not
more shyly pure.

Nevertheless, for so coy a youth, the pleasures of Meïamoun were
certainly of a singular nature. He would go forth quietly some morning
with his little buckler of hippopotamus hide, his *harpe* or curved sword,
a triangular bow, and a snake-skin quiver filled with barbed arrows; then
he would ride at a gallop far into the desert, upon his slender-limbed,
small-headed, wild-maned mare, until he could find some lion-tracks.
He especially delighted in taking the little lion-cubs from underneath
the belly of their mother. In all things he loved the perilous or the
unachievable. He preferred to walk where it seemed impossible for any
human being to obtain a foothold, or to swim in a raging torrent, and he

had accordingly chosen the neighborhood of the cataracts for his bathing place in the Nile. The Abyss called him!

Such was Meïamoun, son of Mandouschopsh.

For some time his humors had been growing more savage than ever. During whole months he buried himself in the Ocean of Sands, returning only at long intervals. Vainly would his uneasy mother lean from her terrace and gaze anxiously down the long road with tireless eyes. At last, after weary waiting, a little whirling cloud of dust would become visible in the horizon, and finally the cloud would open to allow a full view of Meïamoun, all covered with dust, riding upon a mare gaunt as a wolf, with red and bloodshot eyes, nostrils trembling, and huge scars along her flanks—scars which certainly were not made by spurs.

After having hung up in his room some hyena or lion skin, he would start off again.

And yet no one might have been happier than Meïamoun. He was beloved by Nephthe, daughter of the priest Afomouthis, and the loveliest woman of the Nome Arsinoites. Only such a being as Meïamoun could have failed to see that Nephthe had the most charmingly oblique and indescribably voluptuous eyes, a mouth sweetly illuminated by ruddy smiles, little teeth of wondrous whiteness and transparency, arms exquisitely round, and feet more perfect than the jasper feet of the statue of Isis. Assuredly there was not a smaller hand nor longer hair than hers in all Egypt. The charms of Nephthe could have been eclipsed only by those of Cleopatra. But who could dare to dream of loving Cleopatra? Ixion, enamoured of Juno, strained only a cloud to his bosom, and must forever roll the wheel of his punishment in hell.

It was Cleopatra whom Meïamoun loved.

He had at first striven to tame this wild passion; he had wrestled fiercely with it; but love cannot be strangled even as a lion is strangled, and the strong skill of the mightiest athlete avails nothing in such a contest. The arrow had remained in the wound, and he carried it with him everywhere. The radiant and splendid image of Cleopatra, with her golden-pointed diadem and her imperial purple, standing above a nation on their knees, illumined his nightly dreams and his waking thoughts. Like some imprudent man who has dared to look at the sun and forever thereafter beholds an impalpable blot floating before his eyes, so Meïamoun ever beheld Cleopatra. Eagles may gaze undazzled at the sun, but what diamond eye can with impunity fix itself upon a beautiful woman, a beautiful queen?

He commenced at last to spend his life in wandering about the neighborhood of the royal dwelling, that he might at least breathe the same air as Cleopatra, that he might sometimes kiss the almost imperceptible print of her foot upon the sand (a happiness, alas! rare indeed). He attended the sacred festivals and *panegyreis,* striving to obtain one beaming glance of her eyes, to catch in passing one stealthy glimpse of her loveliness in some of its thousand varied aspects. At other moments, filled with sudden shame of this mad life, he gave himself up to the chase with redoubled ardor, and sought by fatigue to tame the ardor of his blood and the impetuosity of his desires.

He had gone to the panegyris of Hermonthis, and, in the vague hope of beholding the queen again for an instant as she disembarked at the summer palace, had followed her cangia in his boat—little heeding the sharp stings of the sun—through a heat intense enough to make the panting sphinxes melt in lava-sweat upon their reddened pedestals.

And then he felt that the supreme moment was nigh, that the decisive instant of his life was at hand, and that he could not die with his secret in his breast.

It is a strange situation truly to find oneself enamoured of a queen. It is as though one loved a star; yet she, the star, comes forth nightly to sparkle in her place in heaven. It is a kind of mysterious rendezvous. You may find her again, you may see her; she is not offended at your gaze. Oh, misery! to be poor, unknown, obscure, seated at the very foot of the ladder, and to feel one's heart breaking with love for something glittering, solemn, and magnificent—for a woman whose meanest female attendant would scorn you!—to gaze fixedly and fatefully upon one who never sees you, who never will see you; one to whom you are no more than a ripple on the sea of humanity, in nowise differing from the other ripples, and who might a hundred times encounter you without once recognizing you; to have no reason to offer should an opportunity for addressing her present itself in excuse for such mad audacity—neither poetical talent, nor great genius, nor any superhuman qualification— nothing but love; and to be able to offer in exchange for beauty, nobility, power, and all imaginable splendor only one's passion and one's youth—rare offerings, forsooth!

Such were the thoughts which overwhelmed Meïamoun. Lying upon the sand, supporting his chin on his palms, he permitted himself to be lifted and borne away by the inexhaustible current of reverie; he sketched out a thousand projects, each madder than the last. He felt convinced that he was seeking after the unattainable, but he lacked the courage to frankly renounce his undertaking, and a perfidious hope came to whisper some lying promises in his ear.

"Athor, mighty goddess," he murmured in a deep voice, "what evil have I done against thee that I should be made thus miserable? Art thou avenging thyself for my disdain of Nephthe, daughter of the priest Afomouthis? Hast thou afflicted me thus for having rejected the love of Lamia, the Athenian hetaira, or of Flora, the Roman courtesan? Is it my fault that my heart should be sensible only to the matchless beauty of thy rival, Cleopatra? Why hast thou wounded my soul with the envenomed arrow of unattainable love? What sacrifice, what offerings dost thou desire? Must I erect to thee a chapel of the rosy marble of Syene with columns crowned by gilded capitals, a ceiling all of one block, and hieroglyphics deeply sculptured by the best workmen of Memphis and of Thebes? Answer me."

Like all gods or goddesses thus invoked, Athor answered not a word, and Meïamoun resolved upon a desperate expedient.

Cleopatra, on her part, likewise invoked the goddess Athor. She prayed for a new pleasure, for some fresh sensation. As she languidly reclined upon her couch she thought to herself that the number of the senses was sadly limited, that the most exquisite refinements of delight soon yielded to satiety, and that it was really no small task for a queen to find means of occupying her time. To test new poisons upon slaves; to make men fight with tigers, or gladiators with each other; to drink pearls dissolved; to swallow the wealth of a whole province—all these things had become commonplace and insipid.

Charmion was fairly at her wit's end, and knew not what to do for her mistress.

Suddenly a whistling sound was heard, and an arrow buried itself, quivering, in the cedar wainscoting of the wall.

Cleopatra well-nigh fainted with terror. Charmion ran to the window, leaned out, and beheld only a flake of foam on the surface of the river. A scroll of papyrus encircled the wood of the arrow. It bore only these words, written in Phoenician characters, "I love you!"

IV

"I love you," repeated Cleopatra, making the serpent-coiling strip of papyrus writhe between her delicate white fingers. "Those are the words I longed for. What intelligent spirit, what invisible genius has thus so fully comprehended my desire?"

And thoroughly aroused from her languid torpor, she sprang out of bed with the agility of a cat which has scented a mouse, placed her little ivory feet in her embroidered *tatbebs,* threw a byssus tunic over her shoulders, and ran to the window from which Charmion was still gazing.

The night was clear and calm. The risen moon outlined with huge angles of light and shadow the architectural masses of the palace, which stood out in strong relief against a background of bluish transparency; and the waters of the river, wherein her reflection lengthened into a shining column, were frosted with silvery ripples. A gentle breeze, such as might have been mistaken for the respiration of the slumbering sphinxes, quivered among the reeds and shook the azure bells of the lotus flowers; the cables of the vessels moored to the Nile's banks groaned feebly, and the rippling tide moaned upon the shore like a dove lamenting for its mate. A vague perfume of vegetation, sweeter than that of the aromatics burned in the *anschir* of the priests of Anubis, floated into the chamber. It was one of those enchanted nights of the Orient, which are more splendid than our fairest days; for our sun can ill compare with that Oriental moon.

"Do you not see far over there, almost in the middle of the river, the head of a man swimming? See, he crosses that track of light, and passes into the shadow beyond! He is already out of sight!" And, supporting herself upon Charmion's shoulder, she leaned out, with half of her fair body beyond the sill of the window, in the effort to catch another glimpse of the mysterious swimmer; but a grove of Nile acacias, dhoum-palms, and sayals flung its deep shadow upon the river in that direction, and protected the flight of the daring fugitive. If Meïamoun had but had the courtesy to look back, he might have beheld Cleopatra, the sidereal queen, eagerly seeking him through the night gloom—he, the poor obscure Egyptian, the miserable lion-hunter.

"Charmion, Charmion, send hither Phrehipephbour, the chief of the rowers, and have two boats despatched in pursuit of that man!" cried Cleopatra, whose curiosity was excited to the highest pitch.

Phrehipephbour appeared, a man of the race of Nahasi, with large hands and muscular arms, wearing a red cap not unlike a Phrygian helmet in form, and clad only in a pair of narrow drawers diagonally striped with white and blue. His huge torso, entirely nude, black and polished like a globe of jet, shone under the lamplight. He received the commands of the queen and instantly retired to execute them.

Two long, narrow boats, so light that the least inattention to equilibrium would capsize them, were soon cleaving the waters of the Nile with hissing rapidity under the efforts of the twenty vigorous rowers, but the pursuit was all in vain. After searching the river banks in every direction, and carefully exploring every patch of reeds, Phrehipephbour returned to the palace, having only succeeded in putting to flight some solitary heron which had been sleeping on one leg, or in troubling the digestion of some terrified crocodile.

So intense was the vexation of Cleopatra at being thus foiled that she felt a strong inclination to condemn Phrehipephbour either to the wild beasts or to the hardest labor at the grindstone. Happily, Charmion interceded for the trembling unfortunate, who turned pale with fear, despite his black skin. It was the first time in Cleopatra's life that one of her desires had not been gratified as soon as expressed, and she experienced, in consequence, a kind of uneasy surprise; a first doubt, as it were, of her own omnipotence.

She, Cleopatra, wife and sister of Ptolemy—she who had been proclaimed goddess Evergetes, living queen of the regions Above and Below, Eye of Light, Chosen of the Sun (as may still be read within the cartouches sculptured on the walls of the temples)—she to find an obstacle in her path, to have wished aught that failed of accomplishment, to have spoken and not been obeyed! As well be the wife of some wretched Paraschistes, some corpse-cutter, and melt natron in a caldron! It was monstrous, preposterous! and none but the most gentle and clement of queens could have refrained from crucifying that miserable Phrehipephbour.

You wished for some adventure, something strange and unexpected. Your wish has been gratified. You find that your kingdom is not so dead as you deemed it. It was not the stony arm of a statue which shot that arrow; it was not from a mummy's heart that came those three words which have moved even you—you who smilingly watched your poisoned slaves dashing their heads and beating their feet upon your beautiful mosaic and porphyry pavements in the convulsions of death-agony; you who even applauded the tiger which boldly buried its muzzle in the flank of some vanquished gladiator.

You could obtain all else you might wish for—chariots of silver, starred with emeralds; griffin-quadrigerae; tunics of purple thrice-dyed; mirrors of molten steel, so clear that you might find the charms of your loveliness faithfully copied in them; robes from the land of Serica, so fine and subtly light that they could be drawn through the ring worn upon your little finger; Orient pearls of wondrous color; cups wrought by Myron or Lysippus; Indian paroquets that speak like poets—all things else you could obtain, even should you ask for the Cestus of Venus or the *pshent* of Isis, but most certainly you cannot this night capture the man who shot the arrow which still quivers in the cedar wood of your couch.

The task of the slaves who must dress you to-morrow will not be a grateful one. They will hardly escape with blows. The bosom of the unskilful waiting-maid will be apt to prove a cushion for the golden pins of the toilette, and the poor hairdresser will run great risk of being suspended by her feet from the ceiling.

"Who could have had the audacity to send me this avowal upon the shaft of an arrow? Could it have been the Nomarch Amoun-Ra who fancies himself handsomer than the Apollo of the Greeks? What think you, Charmion? Or perhaps Cheâpsiro, commander of Hermothybia, who is so boastful of his conquests in the land of Kush? Or is it not more likely to have been young Sextus, that Roman debauchee who paints his face, lisps in speaking, and wears sleeves in the fashion of the Persians?"

"Queen, it was none of those. Though you are indeed the fairest of women, those men only flatter you; they do not love you. The Nomarch

Amoun-Ra has chosen himself an idol to which he will be forever faithful, and that is his own person. The warrior Cheâpsiro thinks of nothing save the pleasure of recounting his victories. As for Sextus, he is so seriously occupied with the preparation of a new cosmetic that he cannot dream of anything else. Besides, he had just purchased some Laconian dresses, a number of yellow tunics embroidered with gold, and some Asiatic children which absorb all his time. Not one of those fine lords would risk his head in so daring and dangerous an undertaking; they do not love you well enough for that.

"Yesterday, in your cangia, you said that men dared not fix their dazzled eyes upon you; that they knew only how to turn pale in your presence, to fall at your feet and supplicate your mercy; and that your sole remaining resource would be to awake some ancient, bitumen-perfumed Pharaoh from his gilded coffin. Now here is an ardent and youthful heart that loves you. What will you do with it?"

Cleopatra that night sought slumber in vain. She tossed feverishly upon her couch, and long and vainly invoked Morpheus, the brother of Death. She incessantly repeated that she was the most unhappy of queens, that every one sought to persecute her, and that her life had become insupportable; woeful lamentations which had little effect upon Charmion, although she pretended to sympathize with them.

Let us for a while leave Cleopatra to seek fugitive sleep, and direct her suspicions successively upon each noble of the court. Let us return to Meïamoun, and as we are much more sagacious than Phrehipephbour, chief of the rowers, we shall have no difficulty in finding him.

Terrified at his own hardihood, Meïamoun had thrown himself into the Nile, and had succeeded in swimming the current and gaining the little grove of dhoum-palms before Phrehipephbour had even launched the two boats in pursuit of him.

When he had recovered breath and brushed back his long black locks, all damp with river foam, behind his ears, he began to feel more at ease, more inwardly calm. Cleopatra possessed something which had come from him; some sort of communication was now established between them. Cleopatra was thinking of him, Meïamoun. Perhaps that thought might be one of wrath; but then he had at least been able to awake some feeling within her, whether of fear, anger, or pity. He had forced her to the consciousness of his existence. It was true that he had forgotten to inscribe his name upon the papyrus scroll, but what more of him could the queen have learned from the inscription, *Meïamoun, Son of Mandouschopsh?* In her eyes the slave and the monarch were equal. A goddess in choosing a peasant for her lover stoops no lower than in choosing a patrician or a king. The Immortals from a height so lofty can behold only love in the man of their choice.

The thought which had weighed upon his breast like the knee of a colossus of brass had at last departed. It had traversed the air; it had even reached the queen herself, the apex of the triangle, the inaccessible summit. It had aroused curiosity in that impassive heart; a prodigious advance, truly, toward success.

Meïamoun, indeed, never suspected that he had so thoroughly succeeded in this wise, but he felt more tranquil; for he had sworn unto himself by that mystic Bari who guides the souls of the dead to Amenthi, by the sacred birds Bermou and Ghenghen, by Typhon and by Osiris, and by all things awful in Egyptian mythology, that he should be the accepted lover of Cleopatra, though it were but for a single night, though for only a single hour, though it should cost him his life and even his very soul.

If we must explain how he had fallen so deeply in love with a woman whom he had beheld only from afar off, and to whom he had hardly dared to raise his eyes—even he who was wont to gaze fearlessly into the yellow eyes of the lion—or how the tiny seed of love, chance-fallen upon his heart, had grown there so rapidly and extended its roots so deeply, we can answer only that it is a mystery which we are unable to explain. We have already said of Meïamoun—The Abyss called him.

Once assured that Phrehipephbour had returned with his rowers, he again threw himself into the current and once more swam toward the palace of Cleopatra, whose lamp still shone through the window curtains like a painted star. Never did Leander swim with more courage and vigor toward the tower of Sestos; yet for Meïamoun no Hero was waiting, ready to pour vials of perfume upon his head to dissipate the briny odors of the sea and banish the sharp kisses of the storm.

A strong blow from some keen lance or *harpe* was certainly the worst he had to fear, and in truth he had but little fear of such things.

He swam close under the walls of the palace, which bathed its marble feet in the river's depths, and paused an instant before a submerged archway into which the water rushed downward in eddying whirls. Twice, thrice he plunged into the vortex unsuccessfully. At last, with better luck, he found the opening and disappeared.

This archway was the opening to a vaulted canal which conducted the waters of the Nile into the baths of Cleopatra.

V

Cleopatra found no rest until morning, at the hour when wandering dreams reënter the Ivory Gate. Amid the illusions of sleep she beheld all kinds of lovers swimming rivers and scaling walls in order to come to her, and, through the vague souvenirs of the night before, her dreams appeared fairly riddled with arrows bearing declarations of love. Starting nervously from time to time in her troubled slumbers, she struck her little feet unconsciously against the bosom of Charmion, who lay across the foot of the bed to serve her as a cushion.

When she awoke, a merry sunbeam was playing through the window curtain, whose woof it penetrated with a thousand tiny points of light, and thence came familiarly to the bed, flitting like a golden butterfly over her lovely shoulders, which it lightly touched in passing by with a luminous kiss. Happy sunbeam, which the gods might well have envied.

In a faint voice, like that of a sick child, Cleopatra asked to be lifted out of bed. Two of her women raised her in their arms and gently laid her on a tiger-skin stretched upon the floor, of which the eyes were formed of carbuncles and the claws of gold. Charmion wrapped her in a *calasiris* of linen whiter than milk, confined her hair in a net of woven silver threads, tied to her little feet cork *tatbebs* upon the soles of which were painted, in token of contempt, two grotesque figures, representing two men of the races of Nahasi and Nahmou, bound hand and foot, so that Cleopatra literally deserved the epithet, "Conculcatrix of Nations,"* which the royal cartouche inscriptions bestow upon her.

---

*Conculcatrice des peuples. From the Latin conculcare, to trample under foot: therefore, the epithet literally signifies the "Trampler of nations."—[Trans.]

It was the hour for the bath. Cleopatra went to bathe, accompanied by her women.

The baths of Cleopatra were built in the midst of immense gardens filled with mimosas, aloes, carob-trees, citron-trees, and Persian apple-trees, whose luxuriant freshness afforded a delicious contrast to the arid appearance of the neighboring vegetation. There, too, vast terraces up-lifted masses of verdant foliage, and enabled flowers to climb almost to the very sky upon gigantic stairways of rose-colored granite; vases of Pentelic marble bloomed at the end of each step like huge lily-flowers, and the plants they contained seemed only their pistils; chimeras caressed into form by the chisels of the most skilful Greek sculptors, and less stern of aspect than the Egyptian sphinxes, with their grim mien and moody attitudes, softly extended their limbs upon the flower-strewn turf, like shapely white leverettes upon a drawing-room carpet. These were charming feminine figures, with finely chiselled nostrils, smooth brows, small mouths, delicately dimpled arms, breasts fair-rounded and daintily formed; wearing earrings, necklaces, and all the trinkets suggested by adorable caprice; whose bodies terminated in bifurcated fishes' tails, like the women described by Horace, or extended into birds' wings, or rounded into lions' haunches, or blended into volutes of foliage, according to the fancies of the artist or in conformity to the architectural position chosen. A double row of these delightful monsters lined the alley which led from the palace to the bathing halls.

At the end of this alley was a huge fountain-basin, approached by four porphyry stairways. Through the transparent depths of the diamond-clear water the steps could be seen descending to the bottom of the basin, which was strewn with gold-dust in lieu of sand. Here figures of women terminating in pedestals like Caryatides* spurted from their breasts slender jets of perfumed water, which fell into the basin in silvery dew, pitting the clear watery mirror with wrinkle-creating drops. In addition to this task these Caryatides had likewise that of supporting upon their heads an entablature decorated with Nereids and Tritons in bas-relief, and furnished with rings of bronze to which the silken cords of a

---

*The Greeks and Romans usually termed such figures Hermae or Termini. Caryatides were, strictly, entire figures of women.—[Trans.]

velarium might be attached. From the portico was visible an extending expanse of freshly humid, bluish-green verdure and cool shade, a fragment of the Vale of Tempe transported to Egypt. The famous gardens of Semiramis would not have borne comparison with these.

We will not pause to describe the seven or eight other halls of various temperature, with their hot and cold vapors, perfume boxes, cosmetics, oils, pumice stone, gloves of woven horsehair, and all the refinements of the antique balneatory art brought to the highest pitch of voluptuous perfection.

Hither came Cleopatra, leaning with one hand upon the shoulder of Charmion. She had taken at least thirty steps all by herself. Mighty effort, enormous fatigue! A tender tint of rose commenced to suffuse the transparent skin of her cheeks, refreshing their passionate pallor; a blue network of veins relieved the amber blondness of her temples; her marble forehead, low like the antique foreheads, but full and perfect in form, united by one faultless line with a straight nose, finely chiselled as a cameo, with rosy nostrils which the least emotion made palpitate like the nostrils of an amorous tigress; the lips of her small, rounded mouth, slightly separated from the nose, wore a disdainful curve; but an unbridled voluptuousness, an indescribable vital warmth, glowed in the brilliant crimson and humid lustre of the under lip. Her eyes were shaded by level eyelids, and eyebrows slightly arched and delicately outlined. We cannot attempt by description to convey an idea of their brilliancy. It was a fire, a languor, a sparkling limpidity which might have made even the dog-headed Anubis giddy. Every glance of her eyes was in itself a poem richer than aught of Homer or Mimnermus. An imperial chin, replete with force and power to command, worthily completed this charming profile.

She stood erect upon the upper step of the basin, in an attitude full of proud grace; her figure slightly thrown back, and one foot in suspense, like a goddess about to leave her pedestal, whose eyes still linger on heaven. Her robe fell in two superb folds from the peaks of her bosom to her feet in unbroken lines. Had Cleomenes been her contemporary and enjoyed the happiness of beholding her thus, he would have broken his Venus in despair.

Before entering the water she bade Charmion, for a new caprice, to change her silver hair-net; she preferred to be crowned with reeds and lotos-flowers, like a water divinity. Charmion obeyed, and her liberated hair fell in black cascades over her shoulders, and shadowed her beautiful cheeks in rich bunches, like ripening grapes.

Then the linen tunic, which had been confined only by one golden clasp, glided down over her marble body, and fell in a white cloud at her feet, like the swan at the feet of Leda. . . .

And Meïamoun, where was he?

Oh cruel lot, that so many insensible objects should enjoy the favors which would ravish a lover with delight! The wind which toys with a wealth of perfumed hair, or kisses beautiful lips with kisses which it is unable to appreciate; the water which envelops an adorably beautiful body in one universal kiss, and is yet, notwithstanding, indifferent to that exquisite pleasure; the mirror which reflects so many charming images; the buskin or *tatbeb* which clasps a divine little foot—oh, what happiness lost!

Cleopatra dipped her pink heel in the water and descended a few steps. The quivering flood made a silver belt about her waist, and silver bracelets about her arms, and rolled in pearls like a broken necklace over her bosom and shoulders; her wealth of hair, lifted by the water, extended behind her like a royal mantle; even in the bath she was a queen. She swam to and fro, dived, and brought up handfuls of gold-dust with which she laughingly pelted some of her women. Again, she clung suspended to the balustrade of the basin, concealing or exposing her treasures of loveliness—now permitting only her lustrous and polished back to be seen, now showing her whole figure, like Venus Anadyomene, and incessantly varying the aspects of her beauty.

Suddenly she uttered a cry as shrill as that of Diana surprised by Actaeon. She had seen gleaming through the neighboring foliage a burning eye, yellow and phosphoric as the eye of a crocodile or lion.

It was Meïamoun, who, crouching behind a tuft of leaves, and trembling like a fawn in a field of wheat, was intoxicating himself with the dangerous pleasure of beholding the queen in her bath. Though brave even to temerity, the cry of Cleopatra passed through his heart, coldly piercing as the blade of a sword. A death-like sweat covered his whole body; his arteries hissed through his temples with a sharp sound; the iron hand of anxious fear had seized him by the throat and was strangling him.

The eunuchs rushed forward, lance in hand. Cleopatra pointed out to them the group of trees, where they found Meïamoun crouching in concealment. Defence was out of the question. He attempted none, and suffered himself to be captured. They prepared to kill him with that cruel and stupid impassibility characteristic of eunuchs; but Cleopatra, who, in the interim, had covered herself with her *calasiris,* made signs to them to stop, and bring the prisoner before her.

Meïamoun could only fall upon his knees and stretch forth suppliant hands to her, as to the altars of the gods.

"Are you some assassin bribed by Rome, or for what purpose have you entered these sacred precincts from which all men are excluded?" demanded Cleopatra with an imperious gesture of interrogation.

"May my soul be found light in the balance of Amenti, and may Tmeï, daughter of the Sun and goddess of Truth, punish me if I have ever entertained a thought of evil against you, O queen!" answered Meïamoun, still upon his knees.

Sincerity and loyalty were written upon his countenance in characters so transparent that Cleopatra immediately banished her suspicions, and looked upon the young Egyptian with a look less stern and wrathful. She saw that he was beautiful.

"Then what motive could have prompted you to enter a place where you could only expect to meet death?"

"I love you!" murmured Meïamoun in a low, but distinct voice; for his courage had returned, as in every desperate situation when the odds against him could be no worse.

"Ah!" cried Cleopatra, bending toward him, and seizing his arm with a sudden brusque movement, "so, then, it was you who shot that arrow with the papyrus scroll! By Oms, the Dog of Hell, you are a very foolhardy wretch! . . . I now recognize you. I long observed you wandering like a complaining Shade about the places where I dwell. . . . You were at the Procession of Isis, at the Panegyris of Hermonthis. You followed the royal cangia. Ah! you must have a queen? . . . You have no mean ambitions. You expect, without doubt, to be well paid in return. . . . Assuredly I am going to love you. . . . Why not?"

"Queen," returned Meïamoun with a look of deep melancholy, "do not rail. I am mad, it is true. I have deserved death; that is also true. Be humane; bid them kill me."

"No; I have taken the whim to be clement to-day. I will give you your life."

"What would you that I should do with life? I love you!"

"Well, then, you shall be satisfied; you shall die," answered Cleopatra. "You have indulged yourself in wild and extravagant dreams; in fancy your desires have crossed an impassable threshold. You imagined yourself to be Caesar or Mark Antony. You loved the queen. In some moment of delirium you have been able to believe that, under some condition of things which takes place but once in a thousand years, Cleopatra might some day love you. Well, what you thought impossible is actually about to happen. I will transform your dream into a reality. It pleases me, for once, to secure the accomplishment of a mad hope. I am willing to inundate you with glories and splendors and lightnings. I intend that your good fortune shall be dazzling in its brilliancy. You were at the bottom of the ladder. I am about to lift you to the summit, abruptly, suddenly, without a transition. I take you out of nothingness, I make you the equal of a god, and I plunge you back again into nothingness; that is all. But do not presume to call me cruel or to invoke my pity; do not weaken when the hour comes. I am good to you. I lend myself to your folly. I have the right to order you to be killed at once; but since you tell me that you love me, I will have you killed to-morrow instead. Your life belongs to me for one night. I am generous. I will buy it from you; I could take it from you. But what are you doing on your knees at my feet? Rise, and give me your arm, that we may return to the palace."

VI

Our world of to-day is puny indeed beside the antique world. Our banquets are mean, niggardly, compared with the appalling sumptuousness of the Roman patricians and the princes of ancient Asia. Their ordinary repasts would in these days be regarded as frenzied orgies, and a whole modern city could subsist for eight days upon the leavings of one supper given by Lucullus to a few intimate friends. With our miserable habits we find it difficult to conceive of those enormous existences, realizing everything vast, strange, and most monstrously impossible that imagination could devise. Our palaces are mere stables, in which Caligula would not quarter his horse. The retinue of our wealthiest constitutional king is as nothing compared with that of a petty satrap or a Roman proconsul. The radiant suns which once shone upon the earth are forever extinguished in the nothingness of uniformity. Above the dark swarm of men no longer tower those Titanic colossi who bestrode the world in three paces, like the steeds of Homer; no more towers of Lylacq; no giant Babel scaling the sky with its infinity of spirals; no temples immeasurable, builded with the fragments of quarried mountains; no kingly terraces for which successive ages and generations could each erect but one step, and from whence some dreamfully reclining prince might gaze on the face of the world as upon a map unfolded; no more of those extravagantly vast cities of cyclopaean edifices, inextricably piled upon one another, with their mighty circumvallations, their circuses roaring night and day, their reservoirs filled with ocean brine and peopled with whales and leviathans, their colossal stairways, their super-imposition of terraces, their tower-summits bathed in clouds, their giant palaces, their aqueducts, their multitude-vomiting gates, their shadowy necropoli. Alas! henceforth only plaster hives upon chessboard pavements.

One marvels that men did not revolt against such confiscation of all riches and all living forces for the benefit of a few privileged ones, and that such exorbitant fantasies should not have encountered any opposition on their bloody way. It was because those prodigious lives were the realizations by day of the dreams which haunted each man by night, the personifications of the common ideal which the nations beheld living symbolized under one of those meteoric names that flame inextinguishably through the night of ages. To-day, deprived of such dazzling spectacles of omnipotent will, of the lofty contemplation of some human mind whose least wish makes itself visible in actions unparalleled, in enormities of granite and brass, the world becomes irredeemably and hopelessly dull. Man is no longer represented in the realization of his imperial fancy.

The story which we are writing, and the great name of Cleopatra which appears in it, have prompted us to these reflections, so ill-sounding, doubtless, to modern ears. But the spectacle of the antique world is something so crushingly discouraging, even to those imaginations which deem themselves exhaustless, and those minds which fancy themselves to have conceived the utmost limits of fairy magnificence, that we cannot here forbear recording our regret and lamentation that we were not contemporaries of Sardanapalus; of Teglathphalazar; of Cleopatra, queen of Egypt; or even of Elagabalus, emperor of Rome and priest of the Sun.

It is our task to describe a supreme orgie—a banquet compared with which the splendors of Belshazzar's feast must pale—one of Cleopatra's nights. How can we picture forth in this French tongue, so chaste, so icily prudish, that unbounded transport of passions, that huge and mighty debauch which feared not to mingle the double purple of wine and blood, those furious outbursts of insatiate pleasure, madly leaping toward the Impossible with all the wild ardor of senses as yet untamed by the long fast of Christianity?

The promised night should well have been a splendid one, for all the joys and pleasures possible in a human lifetime were to be concentrated into the space of a few hours. It was necessary that the life of Meïamoun should be converted into a powerful elixir which he could imbibe at a single draught. Cleopatra desired to dazzle her voluntary victim, and plunge him into a whirlpool of dizzy pleasures; to intoxicate and madden him with the wine of orgie, so that death, though freely accepted, might come invisibly and unawares.

Let us transport our readers to the banquet-hall.

Our existing architecture offers few points for comparison with those vast edifices whose very ruins resemble the crumblings of mountains rather than the remains of buildings. It needed all the exaggeration of the antique life to animate and fill those prodigious palaces, whose halls were too lofty and vast to allow of any ceiling save the sky itself—a magnificent ceiling, and well worthy of such mighty architecture.

The banquet-hall was of enormous and Babylonian dimensions; the eye could not penetrate its immeasurable depth. Monstrous columns—short, thick, and solid enough to sustain the pole itself—heavily expanded their broad-swelling shafts upon socles variegated with hieroglyphics, and sustained upon their bulging capitals gigantic arcades of granite rising by successive tiers, like vast stairways reversed. Between each two pillars a colossal sphinx of basalt, crowned with the *pshent,* bent forward her oblique-eyed face and horned chin, and gazed into the hall with a fixed and mysterious look. The columns of the second tier, receding from the first, were more elegantly formed, and crowned in lieu of capitals with four female heads addorsed, wearing caps of many folds and all the intricacies of the Egyptian head-dress. Instead of sphinxes, bull-headed idols—impassive spectators of nocturnal frenzy and the furies of orgie—were seated upon thrones of stone, like patient hosts awaiting the opening of the banquet.

A third story, constructed in a yet different style of architecture, with elephants of bronze spouting perfume from their trunks, crowned the edifice; above, the sky yawned like a blue gulf, and the curious stars leaned over the frieze.*

Prodigious stairways of porphyry, so highly polished that they reflected the human body like a mirror, ascended and descended on every hand, and bound together these huge masses of architecture.

We can only make a very rapid sketch here, in order to convey some idea of this awful structure, proportioned out of all human measurements. It would require the pencil of Martin,† the great painter of enormities passed away, and we can present only a weak pen-picture in lieu of the Apocalyptic depth of his gloomy style; but imagination may supply our deficiencies. Less fortunate than the painter and the musician, we can only present objects and ideas separately in slow succession. We have as yet spoken of the banquet-hall only, without referring

---

*Does not this suggest the lines which De Quincey so much admired?—

"A wilderness of building, sinking far, And self-withdrawn into a wondrous depth Far sinking into splendor, without end. Fabric it seemed of diamond, and of gold, With alabaster domes and silver spires, And blazing terrace upon terrace, high Uplifted. Here serene pavilions bright. In avenues disposed; their towers begirt With *battlements that on their restless fronts Bore stars.*"—[Trans.]

† John Martin, the English painter, whose creations were unparalleled in breadth and depth of composition. His pictures seem to have made a powerful impression upon the highly imaginative author of these Romances. There is something in these descriptions of antique architecture that suggests the influence of such pictured fantasies as Martin's "Seventh Plague"; "The Heavenly City"; and perhaps, especially, the famous "Pandemonium," with its infernal splendor, in Martin's illustrations to *Paradise Lost.*—[Trans.]

to the guests, and yet we have but barely indicated its character. Cleopatra and Meïamoun are waiting for us. We see them drawing near. . . .

Meïamoun was clad in a linen tunic constellated with stars, and a purple mantle, and wore a fillet about his locks, like an Oriental king. Cleopatra was apparelled in a robe of pale green, open at either side, and clasped with golden bees. Two bracelets of immense pearls gleamed around her naked arms; upon her head glimmered the golden-pointed diadem. Despite the smile on her lips, a slight cloud of preoccupation shadowed her fair forehead, and from time to time her brows became knitted in a feverish manner. What thoughts could trouble the great queen? As for Meïamoun, his face wore the ardent and luminous look of one in ecstasy or vision; light beamed and radiated from his brow and temples, surrounding his head with a golden nimbus, like one of the twelve great gods of Olympus.

A deep, heartfelt joy illumined his every feature. He had embraced his restless-winged chimera, and it had not flown from him; he had reached the goal of his life. Though he were to live to the age of Nestor or Priam, though he should behold his veined temples hoary with locks whiter than those of the high priest of Ammon, he could never know another new experience, never feel another new pleasure. His maddest hopes had been so much more than realized that there was nothing in the world left for him to desire.

Cleopatra seated him beside her upon a throne with golden griffins on either side, and clapped her little hands together. Instantly lines of fire, bands of sparkling light, outlined all the projections of the architecture—the eyes of the sphinxes flamed with phosphoric lightnings; the bull-headed idols breathed flame; the elephants, in lieu of perfumed water, spouted aloft bright columns of crimson fire; arms of bronze, each bearing a torch, started from the walls, and blazing aigrettes bloomed in the sculptured hearts of the lotos flowers.

Huge blue flames palpitated in tripods of brass; giant candelabras shook their dishevelled light in the midst of ardent vapors; everything sparkled, glittered, beamed. Prismatic irises crossed and shattered each other in the air. The facets of the cups, the angles of the marbles and jaspers, the chiselling of the vases—all caught a sparkle, a gleam, or a flash as of lightning. Radiance streamed in torrents and leaped from step to step like a cascade, over the porphyry stairways. It seemed the reflection of a conflagration on some broad river. Had the Queen of Sheba ascended thither she would have caught up the folds of her robe, and believed herself walking in water, as when she stepped upon the crystal pavements of Solomon. Viewed through that burning haze, the monstrous figures of the colossi, the animals, the hieroglyphics, seemed to become animated and to live with a factitious life; the black marble rams bleated ironically, and clashed their gilded horns; the idols breathed harshly through their panting nostrils.

The orgie was at its height: the dishes of phenicopters' tongues, and the livers of scarus fish; the eels fattened upon human flesh, and cooked in brine; the dishes of peacock's brains; the boars stuffed with living birds; and all the marvels of the antique banquets were heaped upon the three table-surfaces of the gigantic triclinium. The wines of Crete, of Massicus, and of Falernus foamed up in cratera wreathed with roses, and filled by Asiatic pages whose beautiful flowing hair served the guests to wipe their hands upon. Musicians playing upon the sistrum, the tympanum, the sambuke, and the harp with one-and-twenty strings filled all the upper galleries, and mingled their harmonies with the tempest of sound that hovered over the feast. Even the deep-voiced thunder could not have made itself heard there.

Meïamoun, whose head was lying on Cleopatra's shoulder, felt as though his reason were leaving him. The banquet-hall whirled around him like a vast architectural nightmare; through the dizzy glare he beheld perspectives and colonnades without end; new zones of porticoes seemed to uprear themselves upon the real fabric, and bury their summits in heights of sky to which Babel never rose. Had he not felt within his hand the soft, cool hand of Cleopatra, he would have believed himself transported into an enchanted world by some witch of Thessaly or Magian of Persia.

Toward the close of the repast humpbacked dwarfs and mummers engaged in grotesque dances and combats; then young Egyptian and Greek maidens, representing the black and white Hours, danced with inimitable grace a voluptuous dance after the Ionian manner.

Cleopatra herself arose from her throne, threw aside her royal mantle, replaced her starry diadem with a garland of flowers, attached gold-

en *crotali** to her alabaster hands, and began to dance before Meïamoun, who was ravished with delight. Her beautiful arms, rounded like
the handles of an alabaster vase, shook out bunches of sparkling notes,
and her *crotali* prattled with ever-increasing volubility. Poised on the
pink tips of her little feet, she approached swiftly to graze the forehead
of Meïamoun with a kiss; then she recommenced her wondrous art, and
flitted around him, now backward-leaning, with head reversed, eyes half
closed, arms lifelessly relaxed, locks uncurled and loose-hanging like a
Bacchante of Mount Maenalus; now again, active, animated, laughing,
fluttering, more tireless and capricious in her movements than the pil-
fering bee. Heart-consuming love, sensual pleasure, burning passion,
youth inexhaustible and ever-fresh, the promise of bliss to come—she
expressed all. . . .

The modest stars had ceased to contemplate the scene; their golden
eyes could not endure such a spectacle; the heaven itself was blotted
out, and a dome of flaming vapor covered the hall.

Cleopatra seated herself once more by Meïamoun. Night advanced;
the last of the black Hours was about to take flight; a faint blue glow entered with bewildered aspect into the tumult of ruddy light as a moonbeam falls into a furnace; the upper arcades became suffused with pale
azure tints—day was breaking.

Meïamoun took the horn vase which an Ethiopian slave of sinister
countenance presented to him, and which contained a poison so violent
that it would have caused any other vase to burst asunder. Flinging his
whole life to his mistress in one last look, he lifted to his lips the fatal
cup in which the envenomed liquor boiled up, hissing.

Cleopatra turned pale, and laid her hand on Meïamoun's arm to
stay the act. His courage touched her. She was about to say, "Live to
love me yet, I desire it! . . ." when the sound of a clarion was heard.
Four heralds-at-arms entered the banquet-hall on horseback; they were
officers of Mark Antony, and rode but a short distance in advance of
their master. Cleopatra silently loosened the arm of Meïamoun. A long
ray of sunlight suddenly played upon her forehead, as though trying to
replace her absent diadem.

---

* Antique castanets.—[Trans.]

"You see the moment has come; it is daybreak, it is the hour when happy dreams take flight," said Meïamoun. Then he, emptied the fatal vessel at a draught, and fell as though struck by lightning. Cleopatra bent her head, and one burning tear—the only one she had ever shed—fell into her cup to mingle with the molten pearl.

"By Hercules, my fair queen! I made all speed in vain. I see I have come too late," cried Mark Antony, entering the banquet-hall, "the supper is over. But what signifies this corpse upon the pavement?"

"Oh, nothing!" returned Cleopatra, with a smile; "only a poison I was testing with the idea of using it upon myself should Augustus take me prisoner. My dear Lord, will you not please to take a seat beside me, and watch those Greek buffoons dance?"

The Mummy's Foot

I had entered, in an idle mood, the shop of one of those curiosity venders who are called *marchands de bric-à-brac* in that Parisian *argot* which is so perfectly unintelligible elsewhere in France.

You have doubtless glanced occasionally through the windows of some of these shops, which have become so numerous now that it is fashionable to buy antiquated furniture, and that every petty stockbroker thinks he must have his *chambre au moyen âge.*

There is one thing there which clings alike to the shop of the dealer in old iron, the ware-room of the tapestry maker, the laboratory of the chemist, and the studio of the painter: in all those gloomy dens where a furtive daylight filters in through the window-shutters the most manifestly ancient thing is dust. The cobwebs are more authentic than the guimp laces, and the old pear-tree furniture on exhibition is actually younger than the mahogany which arrived but yesterday from America.

The warehouse of my bric-à-brac dealer was a veritable Capharnaum. All ages and all nations seemed to have made their rendezvous there. An Etruscan lamp of red clay stood upon a Boule cabinet, with ebony panels, brightly striped by lines of inlaid brass; a duchess of the court of Louis XV. nonchalantly extended her fawn-like feet under a massive table of the time of Louis XIII., with heavy spiral supports of oak, and carven designs of chimeras and foliage intermingled.

Upon the denticulated shelves of several sideboards glittered immense Japanese dishes with red and blue designs relieved by gilded hatching, side by side with enamelled works by Bernard Palissy, representing serpents, frogs, and lizards in relief.

From disembowelled cabinets escaped cascades of silver-lustrous Chinese silks and waves of tinsel, which an oblique sunbeam shot through with luminous beads, while portraits of every era, in frames more or less tarnished, smiled through their yellow varnish.

The striped breastplate of a damascened suit of Milanese armor glittered in one corner; loves and nymphs of porcelain, Chinese grotesques, vases of *céladon* and crackleware, Saxon and old Sèvres cups encumbered the shelves and nooks of the apartment.

The dealer followed me closely through the tortuous way contrived between the piles of furniture, warding off with his hand the hazardous sweep of my coat-skirts, watching my elbows with the uneasy attention of an antiquarian and a usurer.

It was a singular face, that of the merchant; an immense skull, polished like a knee, and surrounded by a thin aureole of white hair, which brought out the clear salmon tint of his complexion all the more strikingly, lent him a false aspect of patriarchal *bonhomie,* counteracted, however, by the scintillation of two little yellow eyes which trembled in their orbits like two louis-d'or upon quicksilver. The curve of his nose presented an aquiline silhouette, which suggested the Oriental or Jewish type. His hands—thin, slender, full of nerves which projected like strings upon the finger-board of a violin, and armed with claws like those on the terminations of bats' wings—shook with senile trembling; but those convulsively agitated hands became firmer than steel pincers or lobsters' claws when they lifted any precious article—an onyx cup, a Venetian glass, or a dish of Bohemian crystal. This strange old man had an aspect so thoroughly rabbinical and cabalistic that he would have been burnt on the mere testimony of his face three centuries ago.

"Will you not buy something from me to-day, sir? Here is a Malay kreese with a blade undulating like flame. Look at those grooves contrived for the blood to run along, those teeth set backward so as to tear out the entrails in withdrawing the weapon. It is a fine character of ferocious arm, and will look well in your collection. This two-handed sword is very beautiful. It is the work of Josepe de la Hera; and this *colichemarde,* with its fenestrated guard—what a superb specimen of handicraft!"

"No; I have quite enough weapons and instruments of carnage. I want a small figure, something which will suit me as a paper-weight, for I cannot endure those trumpery bronzes which the stationers sell, and which may be found on everybody's desk."

The old gnome foraged among his ancient wares, and finally arranged before me some antique bronzes, so-called at least; fragments of malachite, little Hindoo or Chinese idols, a kind of poussah-toys in jade-stone, representing the incarnations of Brahma or Vishnoo, and wonderfully appropriate to the very undivine office of holding papers and letters in place.

I was hesitating between a porcelain dragon, all constellated with warts, its mouth formidable with bristling tusks and ranges of teeth, and an abominable little Mexican fetich, representing the god Vitziliputzili *au naturel,* when I caught sight of a charming foot, which I at first took for a fragment of some antique Venus.

It had those beautiful ruddy and tawny tints that lend to Florentine bronze that warm living look so much preferable to the gray-green aspect of common bronzes, which might easily be mistaken for statues in a state of putrefaction. Satiny gleams played over its rounded forms, doubtless polished by the amorous kisses of twenty centuries, for it seemed a Corinthian bronze, a work of the best era of art, perhaps moulded by Lysippus himself.

"That foot will be my choice," I said to the merchant, who regarded me with an ironical and saturnine air, and held out the object desired that I might examine it more fully.

I was surprised at its lightness. It was not a foot of metal, but in sooth a foot of flesh, an embalmed foot, a mummy's foot. On examining it still more closely the very grain of the skin, and the almost imperceptible lines impressed upon it by the texture of the bandages, became perceptible. The toes were slender and delicate, and terminated by perfectly formed nails, pure and transparent as agates. The great toe, slightly separated from the rest, afforded a happy contrast, in the antique style, to the position of the other toes, and lent it an aërial lightness—the grace of a bird's foot. The sole, scarcely streaked by a few almost imperceptible cross lines, afforded evidence that it had never touched the bare ground, and had only come in contact with the finest matting of Nile rushes and the softest carpets of panther skin.

"Ha, ha, you want the foot of the Princess Hermonthis!" exclaimed the merchant, with a strange giggle, fixing his owlish eyes upon me. "Ha, ha, ha! For a paper-weight! An original idea!—artistic idea! Old Pharaoh would certainly have been surprised had some one told him that the foot of his adored daughter would be used for a paper-weight after he had had a mountain of granite hollowed out as a receptacle for the triple coffin, painted and gilded, covered with hieroglyphics and beautiful paintings of the Judgment of Souls," continued the queer little merchant, half audibly, as though talking to himself.

"How much will you charge me for this mummy fragment?"

"Ah, the highest price I can get, for it is a superb piece. If I had the match of it you could not have it for less than five hundred francs. The daughter of a Pharaoh! Nothing is more rare."

"Assuredly that is not a common article, but still, how much do you want? In the first place let me warn you that all my wealth consists of just five louis. I can buy anything that costs five louis, but nothing dearer. You might search my vest pockets and most secret drawers without even finding one poor five-franc piece more."

"Five louis for the foot of the Princess Hermonthis! That is very little, very little indeed. 'Tis an authentic foot," muttered the merchant, shaking his head, and imparting a peculiar rotary motion to his eyes. "Well, take it, and I will give you the bandages into the bargain," he added, wrapping the foot in an ancient damask rag. "Very fine! Real damask—Indian damask which has never been re-dyed. It is strong, and yet it is soft," he mumbled, stroking the frayed tissue with his fingers, through the trade-acquired habit which moved him to praise even an object of such little value that he himself deemed it only worth the giving away.

He poured the gold coins into a sort of mediaeval alms-purse hanging at his belt, repeating:

"The foot of the Princess Hermonthis to be used for a paperweight!"

Then turning his phosphorescent eyes upon me, he exclaimed in a voice strident as the crying of a cat which has swallowed a fish-bone:

"Old Pharaoh will not be well pleased. He loved his daughter, the dear man!"

"You speak as if you were a contemporary of his. You are old enough, goodness knows! but you do not date back to the Pyramids of Egypt," I answered, laughingly, from the threshold.

I went home, delighted with my acquisition.

With the idea of putting it to profitable use as soon as possible, I placed the foot of the divine Princess Hermonthis upon a heap of papers scribbled over with verses, in themselves an undecipherable mosaic work of erasures; articles freshly begun; letters forgotten, and posted in the table drawer instead of the letter-box, an error to which absent-minded people are peculiarly liable. The effect was charming, bizarre, and romantic.

Well satisfied with this embellishment, I went out with the gravity and pride becoming one who feels that he has the ineffable advantage over all the passers-by whom he elbows, of possessing a piece of the Princess Hermonthis, daughter of Pharaoh.

I looked upon all who did not possess, like myself, a paper-weight so authentically Egyptian as very ridiculous people, and it seemed to me that the proper occupation of every sensible man should consist in the mere fact of having a mummy's foot upon his desk.

Happily I met some friends, whose presence distracted me in my infatuation with this new acquisition. I went to dinner with them, for I could not very well have dined with myself.

When I came back that evening, with my brain slightly confused by a few glasses of wine, a vague whiff of Oriental perfume delicately titillated my olfactory nerves. The heat of the room had warmed the natron, bitumen, and myrrh in which the *paraschistes,* who cut open the bodies of the dead, had bathed the corpse of the princess. It was a perfume at once sweet and penetrating, a perfume that four thousand years had not been able to dissipate.

The Dream of Egypt was Eternity. Her odors have the solidity of granite and endure as long.

I soon drank deeply from the black cup of sleep. For a few hours all remained opaque to me. Oblivion and nothingness inundated me with their sombre waves.

Yet light gradually dawned upon the darkness of my mind. Dreams commenced to touch me softly in their silent flight.

The eyes of my soul were opened, and I beheld my chamber as it actually was. I might have believed myself awake but for a vague consciousness which assured me that I slept, and that something fantastic was about to take place.

The odor of the myrrh had augmented in intensity, and I felt a slight headache, which I very naturally attributed to several glasses of champagne that we had drunk to the unknown gods and our future fortunes.

I peered through my room with a feeling of expectation which I saw nothing to justify. Every article of furniture was in its proper place. The lamp, softly shaded by its globe of ground crystal, burned upon its bracket; the water-color sketches shone under their Bohemian glass; the curtains hung down languidly; everything wore an aspect of tranquil slumber.

After a few moments, however, all this calm interior appeared to become disturbed. The woodwork cracked stealthily, the ash-covered log suddenly emitted a jet of blue flame, and the disks of the pateras seemed like great metallic eyes, watching, like myself, for the things which were about to happen.

My eyes accidentally fell upon the desk where I had placed the foot of the Princess Hermonthis.

Instead of remaining quiet, as behooved a foot which had been embalmed for four thousand years, it commenced to act in a nervous manner, contracted itself, and leaped over the papers like a startled frog. One would have imagined that it had suddenly been brought into contact with a galvanic battery. I could distinctly hear the dry sound made by its little heel, hard as the hoof of a gazelle.

I became rather discontented with my acquisition, inasmuch as I wished my paper-weights to be of a sedentary disposition, and thought it very unnatural that feet should walk about without legs, and I commenced to experience a feeling closely akin to fear.

Suddenly I saw the folds of my bed-curtain stir, and heard a bumping sound, like that caused by some person hopping on one foot across the floor. I must confess I became alternately hot and cold, that I felt a strange wind chill my back, and that my suddenly rising hair caused my nightcap to execute a leap of several yards.

The bed-curtains opened and I beheld the strangest figure imaginable before me.

It was a young girl of a very deep coffee-brown complexion, like the bayadere Amani, and possessing the purest Egyptian type of perfect beauty. Her eyes were almond-shaped and oblique, with eyebrows so black that they seemed blue; her nose was exquisitely chiselled, almost

Greek in its delicacy of outline; and she might indeed have been taken for a Corinthian statue of bronze but for the prominence of her cheekbones and the slightly African fulness of her lips, which compelled one to recognize her as belonging beyond all doubt to the hieroglyphic race which dwelt upon the banks of the Nile.

Her arms, slender and spindle-shaped like those of very young girls, were encircled by a peculiar kind of metal bands and bracelets of glass beads; her hair was all twisted into little cords, and she wore upon her bosom a little idol-figure of green paste, bearing a whip with seven lashes, which proved it to be an image of Isis; her brow was adorned with a shining plate of gold, and a few traces of paint relieved the coppery tint of her cheeks.

As for her costume, it was very odd indeed.

Fancy a *pagne,* or skirt, all formed of little strips of material bedizened with red and black hieroglyphics, stiffened with bitumen, and apparently belonging to a freshly unbandaged mummy.

In one of those sudden flights of thought so common in dreams I heard the hoarse falsetto of the bric-à-brac dealer, repeating like a monotonous refrain the phrase he had uttered in his shop with so enigmatical an intonation:

"Old Pharaoh will not be well pleased. He loved his daughter, the dear man!"

One strange circumstance, which was not at all calculated to restore my equanimity, was that the apparition had but one foot; the other was broken off at the ankle!

She approached the table where the foot was starting and fidgeting about more than ever, and there supported herself upon the edge of the desk. I saw her eyes fill with pearly gleaming tears.

Although she had not as yet spoken, I fully comprehended the thoughts which agitated her. She looked at her foot—for it was indeed her own—with an exquisitely graceful expression of coquettish sadness, but the foot leaped and ran hither and thither, as though impelled on steel springs.

Twice or thrice she extended her hand to seize it, but could not succeed.

Then commenced between the Princess Hermonthis and her foot—

which appeared to be endowed with a special life of its own—a very fantastic dialogue in a most ancient Coptic tongue, such as might have been spoken thirty centuries ago in the syrinxes of the land of Ser. Luckily I understood Coptic perfectly well that night.

The Princess Hermonthis cried, in a voice sweet and vibrant as the tones of a crystal bell:

"Well, my dear little foot, you always flee from me, yet I always took good care of you. I bathed you with perfumed water in a bowl of alabaster; I smoothed your heel with pumice-stone mixed with palm oil; your nails were cut with golden scissors and polished with a hippopotamus tooth; I was careful to select *tatbebs* for you, painted and embroidered and turned up at the toes, which were the envy of all the young girls in Egypt. You wore on your great toe rings bearing the device of the sacred Scarabaeus, and you supported one of the lightest bodies that a lazy foot could sustain."

The foot replied in a pouting and chagrined tone:

"You know well that I do not belong to myself any longer. I have been bought and paid for. The old merchant knew what he was about. He bore you a grudge for having refused to espouse him. This is an ill turn which he has done you. The Arab who violated your royal coffin in the subterranean pits of the necropolis of Thebes was sent thither by him. He desired to prevent you from being present at the reunion of the shadowy nations in the cities below. Have you five pieces of gold for my ransom?"

"Alas, no! My jewels, my rings, my purses of gold and silver were all stolen from me," answered the Princess Hermonthis, with a sob.

"Princess," I then exclaimed, "I never retained anybody's foot unjustly. Even though you have not got the five louis which it cost me, I present it to you gladly. I should feel unutterably wretched to think that I were the cause of so amiable a person as the Princess Hermonthis being lame."

I delivered this discourse in a royally gallant, troubadour tone which must have astonished the beautiful Egyptian girl.

She turned a look of deepest gratitude upon me, and her eyes shone with bluish gleams of light.

She took her foot, which surrendered itself willingly this time, like a woman about to put on her little shoe, and adjusted it to her leg with much skill.

This operation over, she took a few steps about the room, as though to assure herself that she was really no longer lame.

"Ah, how pleased my father will be! He who was so unhappy because of my mutilation, and who from the moment of my birth set a whole nation at work to hollow me out a tomb so deep that he might preserve me intact until that last day, when souls must be weighed in the balance of Amenthi! Come with me to my father. He will receive you kindly, for you have given me back my foot."

I thought this proposition natural enough. I arrayed myself in a dressing-gown of large-flowered pattern, which lent me a very Pharaonic aspect, hurriedly put on a pair of Turkish slippers, and informed the Princess Hermonthis that I was ready to follow her.

Before starting, Hermonthis took from her neck the little idol of green paste, and laid it on the scattered sheets of paper which covered the table.

"It is only fair," she observed, smilingly, "that I should replace your paper-weight."

She gave me her hand, which felt soft and cold, like the skin of a serpent, and we departed.

We passed for some time with the velocity of an arrow through a fluid and grayish expanse, in which half-formed silhouettes flitted swiftly by us, to right and left.

For an instant we saw only sky and sea.

A few moments later obelisks commenced to tower in the distance; pylons and vast flights of steps guarded by sphinxes became clearly outlined against the horizon.

We had reached our destination.

The princess conducted me to a mountain of rose-colored granite, in the face of which appeared an opening so narrow and low that it would have been difficult to distinguish it from the fissures in the rock, had not its location been marked by two stelae wrought with sculptures.

Hermonthis kindled a torch and led the way before me.

We traversed corridors hewn through the living rock. Their walls, covered with hieroglyphics and paintings of allegorical processions, might well have occupied thousands of arms for thousands of years in their formation. These corridors of interminable length opened into square chambers, in the midst of which pits had been contrived, through which we descended by cramp-irons or spiral stairways. These pits again conducted us into other chambers, opening into other corridors, likewise decorated with painted sparrow-hawks, serpents coiled in circles, the symbols of the *tau* and *pedum*—prodigious works of art which no living eye can ever examine—interminable legends of granite which only the dead have time to read through all eternity.

At last we found ourselves in a hall so vast, so enormous, so immeasurable, that the eye could not reach its limits. Files of monstrous columns stretched far out of sight on every side, between which twinkled livid stars of yellowish flame; points of light which revealed further depths incalculable in the darkness beyond.

The Princess Hermonthis still held my hand, and graciously saluted the mummies of her acquaintance.

My eyes became accustomed to the dim twilight, and objects became discernible.

I beheld the kings of the subterranean races seated upon thrones—grand old men, though dry, withered, wrinkled like parchment, and blackened with naphtha and bitumen—all wearing *pshents* of gold, and breastplates and gorgets glittering with precious stones, their eyes immovably fixed like the eyes of sphinxes, and their long beards whitened by the snow of centuries. Behind them stood their peoples, in the stiff and constrained posture enjoined by Egyptian art, all eternally preserving the attitude prescribed by the hieratic code. Behind these nations, the cats, ibixes, and crocodiles contemporary with them—rendered monstrous of aspect by their swathing bands—mewed, flapped their wings, or extended their jaws in a saurian giggle.

All the Pharaohs were there—Cheops, Chephrenes, Psammetichus, Sesostris, Amenotaph—all the dark rulers of the pyramids and syrinxes. On yet higher thrones sat Chronos and Xixouthros, who was contemporary with the deluge, and Tubal Cain, who reigned before it.

The beard of King Xixouthros had grown seven times around the granite table, upon which he leaned, lost in deep reverie, and buried in dreams.

Farther back, through a dusty cloud, I beheld dimly the seventy-two preadamite kings, with their seventy-two peoples, forever passed away.

After permitting me to gaze upon this bewildering spectacle a few moments, the Princess Hermonthis presented me to her father Pharaoh, who favored me with a most gracious nod.

"I have found my foot again! I have found my foot!" cried the princess, clapping her little hands together with every sign of frantic joy. "It was this gentleman who restored it to me."

The races of Kemi, the races of Nahasi—all the black, bronzed, and copper-colored nations repeated in chorus:

"The Princess Hermonthis has found her foot again!"

Even Xixouthros himself was visibly affected.

He raised his heavy eyelids, stroked his mustache with his fingers, and turned upon me a glance weighty with centuries.

"By Oms, the Dog of Hell, and Tmeï, daughter of the Sun and of Truth, this is a brave and worthy lad!" exclaimed Pharaoh, pointing to me with his sceptre, which was terminated with a lotus-flower.

"What recompense do you desire?"

Filled with that daring inspired by dreams in which nothing seems impossible, I asked him for the hand of the Princess Hermonthis. The hand seemed to me a very proper antithetic recompense for the foot.

Pharaoh opened wide his great eyes of glass in astonishment at my witty request.

"What country do you come from, and what is your age?"

"I am a Frenchman, and I am twenty-seven years old, venerable Pharaoh."

"Twenty-seven years old, and he wishes to espouse the Princess Hermonthis who is thirty centuries old!" cried out at once all the Thrones and all the Circles of Nations.

Only Hermonthis herself did not seem to think my request unreasonable.

"If you were even only two thousand years old," replied the ancient king, "I would willingly give you the princess, but the disproportion is too great; and, besides, we must give our daughters husbands who will last well. You do not know how to preserve yourselves any longer. Even those who died only fifteen centuries ago are already no more than a handful of dust. Behold, my flesh is solid as basalt, my bones are bars of steel!

"I will be present on the last day of the world with the same body and the same features which I had during my lifetime. My daughter Hermonthis will last longer than a statue of bronze.

"Then the last particles of your dust will have been scattered abroad by the winds, and even Isis herself, who was able to find the atoms of Osiris, would scarce be able to recompose your being.

"See how vigorous I yet remain, and how mighty is my grasp," he added, shaking my hand in the English fashion with a strength that buried my rings in the flesh of my fingers.

He squeezed me so hard that I awoke, and found my friend Alfred shaking me by the arm to make me get up.

"Oh, you everlasting sleeper! Must I have you carried out into the middle of the street, and fireworks exploded in your ears? It is afternoon. Don't you recollect your promise to take me with you to see M. Aguado's Spanish pictures?"

"God! I forgot all, all about it," I answered, dressing myself hurriedly. "We will go there at once. I have the permit lying there on my desk."

I started to find it, but fancy my astonishment when I beheld, instead of the mummy's foot I had purchased the evening before, the little green paste idol left in its place by the Princess Hermonthis!

Arria Marcella:
A Souvenir of Pompeii

Three young friends, who had undertaken an Italian tour together last year, visited the Studii Museum at Naples, where the various antique objects exhumed from the ashes of Pompeii and Herculaneum have been collected.

They scattered through the halls, inspecting the mosaics, the bronzes, the frescoes detached from the walls of the dead city, each following the promptings of his own particular taste in such matters; and whenever one of the party encountered something especially curious, he summoned his comrades with cries of delight, much to the scandal of the taciturn English visitors, and the staid *bourgeois* who studiously thumbed their catalogues.

But the youngest of the three, who had paused before a glass case, appeared wholly deaf to the exclamations of his comrades, so deeply had he become absorbed in contemplation. The object that he seemed to be examining with so much interest was a black mass of coagulated cinders, bearing a hollow imprint. One might easily have mistaken it for the fragment of some statue-mould, broken in the casting. The trained eye of an artist would have readily therein recognized the impression of a perfect bosom and a flank as faultless in its outlines as a Greek statue. It is well known, indeed the commonest traveller's guide will tell you, that this lava, in cooling about the body of a woman, preserved its charming contours. Thanks to the caprice of the eruption that destroyed four cities, that noble form, though crumbled to dust nearly two thousand years ago, has come down to us; the rounded loveliness of a throat has lived through the centuries in which so many empires perished without even leaving the traces of their existence; chance-imprinted upon the volcanic scoriae, that seal of beauty remains unobliterated.

Finding that he still remained absorbed in contemplation, Octavian's friends returned to where he stood; and Max, touching his shoulder, caused him to start like one surprised in a secret. Evidently Octavian had not been aware of the approach of Max or Fabio.

"Come, Octavian," exclaimed Max, "do not stay lingering whole hours before every cabinet, else we shall get late for the train and miss seeing Pompeii to-day."

"What is our comrade looking at?" asked Fabio, drawing near. "Ah, the imprint found in the house of Arrius Diomedes!" And he turned a peculiar, quick glance upon Octavian.

Octavian slightly blushed, took Max's arm, and the visit terminated without further incident. On leaving the Studii Museum, the three friends entered a *corricolo,* and were driven to the railway station. The *corricolo,* with its great red wheels, its tracket seat studded with brass nails, and its thin, spirited horse harnessed like a Spanish mule, and galloping at full speed over the great slabs of lava pavement, is too familiar to need description here, especially as we are not recording impressions of a trip to Naples, but the simple narrative of an adventure which, although true, may seem both fantastic and incredible in the extreme.

The railroad by which Pompeii is reached runs for almost its entire length by the sea, whose long volutes of foam advance to unroll themselves upon a beach of blackish sand resembling sifted charcoal. This beach has actually been formed by lava-streams and volcanic cinders, and its deep tone forms a strong contrast with the blue of the sky and the blue of the waters. The earth alone, in that sunny brightness, seems able to retain a shadow.

The villages bordered or traversed by the railway—Portici, celebrated in one of Auber's operas; Resina, Torre del Graeco, Torre dell' Annunziata, whose dwellings with their arcades and terraced roofs attract the traveller's gaze—have, notwithstanding the intensity of the sunlight and the southern love for whitewashing, something of a Plutonian and ferruginous character like Birmingham or Manchester. The very dust is black there. An impalpable soot clings to everything. One feels that the mighty forge of Vesuvius is panting and smoking only a few paces off.

The three friends left the station at Pompeii, laughing among themselves at the odd commingling of antique and modern ideas suggested by the sign, "Pompeii Station"—a Graeco-Roman city and a railway depot!

They crossed the cotton-field, with its fluttering white bolls, between the railway and the disinterred city, and at the inn which has been built just without the ancient rampart they took a guide, or, more correctly speaking, the guide took them, a calamity which is not easily avoided in Italy.

It was one of those delightful days so common in Naples, when the brilliancy of the sunlight and the transparency of the air cause objects to take such hues as in the North would be deemed fabulous, and appear indeed to belong to the world of dreams rather than to that of realities. The Northern visitor who has once looked upon that glow of azure and gold is apt to carry back with him into the depths of his native fogs an incurable nostalgia.

Having shaken off a corner of her cinder shroud, the resurrected city again rose with her thousand details under a dazzling day. The cone of Vesuvius, furrowed with striae of blue, rosy, and violet-hued lavas, ruddily bronzed by the sun, towered sharply defined in the background. A thin haze, almost imperceptible in the sunlight, hooded the blunt crest of the mountain. At first sight it might have been taken for one of those clouds which shadow the brows of lofty peaks on the fairest days. Upon a nearer view, slender threads of white vapor could be perceived rising from the mountain-summit, as from the orifices of a perfuming pan, to reunite above in a light cloud. The volcano, being that day in a good humor, smoked his pipe very peacefully; and but for the example of Pompeii, buried at his feet, no one would ever have suspected him of being by nature any more ferocious than Montmartre. On the other side fair hills, with outlines voluptuously undulating like the hips of a woman, barred the horizon; and, further yet, the sea, that in other days bore biremes and triremes under the ramparts of the city, extended its azure boundary.

Of all spectacles, the sight of Pompeii is one of the most surprising. This sudden backward leap of nineteen centuries astonishes even the least comprehensive and most prosaic natures. Two paces lead you from the antique life to the life of to-day, and from Christianity to paganism. Thus, when the three friends beheld those streets wherein the forms of a vanished past are preserved yet intact, they were strangely and profoundly affected, however well prepared by the study of books and drawings they might have been. Octavian, above all, seemed stricken with stupefaction, and like a man walking in his sleep, mechanically followed the guide, without hearing the monotonous nomenclature that the varlet had learned by heart and recited like a lesson.

He gazed wildly on those ruts hollowed out in the cyclopean pavements of the streets by the chariot wheels, and which seem to be of yesterday, so fresh do they appear; those inscriptions in red letters skilfully traced upon the surfaces of the walls by rapid strokes of the brush (theatrical advertisements, notices of houses to let, votive formulas, signs, announcements of all descriptions, not less curious than a freshly discovered fragment of the walls of Paris, with advertising bills and placards attached, would prove a thousand years hence for the unknown people of the future); those houses, whose shattered roofs permit one to penetrate at a glance into all those interior mysteries, all those domestic details which historians invariably neglect, and whereof the secrets die with dying civilizations; those fountains that even now seem scarcely dried up; that forum whose restoration was interrupted by the great catastrophe, and whose architraves and columns, all ready cut and sculptured, still seem waiting in their purity of angle to be lifted into place; those temples, consecrated, in that mythologic age when atheists were yet unknown, to gods that have long ceased to be; those shops wherein the merchant only is missing; that public tavern where may still be seen the circular stain of the drinking cups upon the marble; that barracks with its ochre and minium-painted columns, on which the soldiers scratched grotesque caricatures of battle, and those juxtaposed double theatres of song and drama which might even now resume their entertainments, were not the companies who performed in them turned long since to clay, and at present occupied perchance in closing the bunghole of a cask or stopping a crevice in the wall, after the fashion of Alexander's ashes or Caesar's dust, according to the melancholy reflections of Hamlet!

Fabio mounted upon the thymele of the tragic theatre while Max and Octavian climbed to the upper benches; and there, with extravagant gestures, he commenced to recite whatever poetical fragments came to his memory, much to the terror of the lizards, who fled, vibrating their tails, and hid themselves in the joints of the ruined stonework. Although the brazen or earthen vessels formerly used to reverberate sounds no longer existed, Fabio's voice sounded none the less full and vibrant.

The guide then conducted them across the open fields which over-lie those portions of Pompeii still buried, to the amphitheatre situated at the other end of the city. They passed under those trees whose roots plunge down through the roofs of the edifices interred, displacing tiles, cleaving ceilings asunder, and disjointing columns; and they traversed the farms where vulgar vegetables sprout above wonders of art—material images of that oblivion wherewith time covers all things.

The amphitheatre caused them little surprise. They had seen that of Verona, vaster and equally well preserved; besides, the arrangement of such antique arenas was as familiar to them as that of those in which bull-fights are held in Spain, and which they much resemble save in so-lidity of construction and beauty of material.

Accordingly they soon retraced their footsteps and gained the Street of Fortune by a cross-path, listening half-distractedly to the *cicerone,* who named each house they passed by the name which had been given it immediately upon its discovery, owing to some characteristic peculiari-ty—the House of the Brazen Bull, the House of the Faun, the House of the Ship, the Temple of Fortune, the House of Meleager, the Tavern of Fortune, at the angle of the Consular Road (Via Consularia), the Acad-emy of Music, the Public Market, the Pharmacy, the Surgeon's Shop, the Custom House, the House of the Vestals, the Inn of Albinus, the Thermopolium, and so on—until they came to that gate which leads to the Street of the Tombs.

Within the interior arch of this brick-built gate, once adorned with statues which have long since disappeared, may be noticed two deep grooves designed to receive a sliding portcullis, after the style of a medi-aeval donjon, to which era, indeed, one might have supposed such a de-fence peculiar.

"Who," exclaimed Max to his friends, "could have dreamed of find-ing in Pompeii, the Graeco-Latin city, a gate so romantically Gothic? Fancy some belated Roman knight blowing his horn before this en-trance, summoning them to raise the portcullis, like a page of the fif-teenth century!"

"There is nothing new under the sun," replied Fabio; "and the aph-orism itself is not new, inasmuch as it was formulated by Solomon."

"Perhaps there may be something new under the moon," observed Octavian, with a smile of melancholy irony.

"My dear Octavian," cried Max, who during this little conversation had paused before an inscription traced in rubric upon the outer wall, "wilt behold the combats of the gladiators? See the advertisement! Combat and chase on the 5th day of the nones of April; the masts of the velarium will be rigged; twenty pairs of gladiators will fight during the nones; if you fear for the delicacy of your complexion, be assured that the awnings will be spread; and as you might in any case prefer to visit the amphitheatre early, these men will cut each other's throats in the morning—*matutini erunt.* Nothing could be more considerate."

Thus chatting, the three friends followed that sepulchre-fringed road which, according to our modern ideas, would be a lugubrious avenue for any city, but which had no sad significations for the ancients, whose tombs contained in lieu of hideous corpses only a pinch of dust— abstract idea of death! Art beautified these last resting-places, and, as Goethe says, the pagan decorated sarcophagi and funeral urns with the images of life.

It was therefore, doubtless, that Fabio and Max could visit, with a lively curiosity and a joyous sense of being, such as they could not have felt in any Christian cemetery, those funeral monuments, all gayly gilded by the sun, which, as they stood by the wayside, seemed still trying to cling to life, and inspired none of those chill feelings of repulsion, none of those fantastic terrors evoked by our modern dismal places of sepulture. They paused before the tomb of Mammia, the public priestess, near which a tree (either a cypress or a willow) is growing; they seated themselves in the hemicycle of the triclinium, where the funeral feasts were held, laughing like fortunate heirs; they read with mock solemnity the epitaphs of Navoleia, Labeon, and the Arria family, silently followed by Octavian, who seemed more deeply touched than his careless companions by the fate of those dead of two thousand years ago.

Thus they came to the villa of Arrius Diomedes, one of the finest residences in Pompeii. It is approached by a flight of brick steps, and after entering the door-way, which is flanked by two small lateral columns, one finds himself in a court resembling the *patio* which occupies the centre of Spanish and Moorish dwellings, and which the ancients termed *impluvium* or *cavaedium.* Fourteen columns of brick, overlaid with stucco, once supported on four sides a portico or covered peristyle, not unlike a convent cloister, and beneath which one could walk secure from the rain. This courtyard is paved in mosaic with brick and white marble, which presents a subdued and pleasing effect of color. In its centre a quadrilateral marble basin, which still exists, formerly caught the rain-water that dripped from the roof of the portico. It was a strange experience, entering thus into the life of the antique world, and treading with well-blacked boots upon the marbles worn smooth by the sandals and buskins of the contemporaries of Augustus and Tiberius.

The cicerone led them through the *exedra* or summer parlor, which opened to the sea, to receive its cooling breezes. It was there that the family received company, and took their siesta during those burning hours when prevailed the mighty zephyr of Africa, laden with languors and storms. He brought them into the basilica, a long open gallery which lighted the various apartments, and in which clients and visitors erst awaited the call of the Nomenclator. Then he conducted them to the white marble terrace, whence extended a broad view of verdant gardens and blue sea. Then he showed them the *Nymphaeum,* or Hall of Baths, with its yellow-painted walls, its stucco columns, its mosaic pavement, and its marble bathing-basin which had contained so many of the lovely bodies that have long since passed away like shadows; the *cubiculum,* where flitted so many dreams from the Ivory Gate, and whose alcoves contrived in the wall were once closed by a *conopeum* or curtain, of which the bronze rings still lie upon the floor; the *tetrastyle,* or Hall of Recreation; the Chapel of the Lares; the Cabinet of Archives; the Library; the Museum of Paintings; the *gynaeceum* or women's apartment, comprising a suite of small chambers, now half fallen into ruin, but whose walls yet bear traces of paintings and arabesques, like fair cheeks from which the rouge has been but half wiped off.

Having fully inspected all these, they descended to the lower floor, for the ground is much lower on the garden side than it is on the side of the Street of the Tombs. They traversed eight halls painted in antique red, whereof one has its walls hollowed with architectural niches, after that style of which we have to-day a good example in the vestibule of the Hall of the Ambassadors at the Alhambra, and finally they came to a sort of cave or cellar, whose purpose was clearly indicated by eight earthen amphorae propped up against the wall, and once perfumed, doubtless, like the odes of Horace with the wines of Crete, Falernia, or Massica.

One solitary bright ray of sunshine streamed through a narrow aperture above, half choked by nettles, whose light-traversed leaves it transformed into emeralds and topazes, and this gay natural detail seemed to smile opportunely through the sadness of the place.

"It was here," observed the cicerone, in his customary indifferent tone, "that among seventeen others was found the skeleton of the lady whose mould is exhibited at the Naples Museum. She wore gold rings, and the shreds of her fine tunic still clung to the mass of cinders which have preserved her shape."

The guide's commonplace phrases deeply affected Octavian. He made the man point out to him the exact spot where the precious remains had been discovered, and had it not been for the restraining presence of his friends, he would have abandoned himself to some extravagant lyrism. His chest heaved, his eyes glistened with a furtive moisture. Though blotted out by twenty centuries of oblivion, that catastrophe touched him like a recent misfortune. Not even the death of a mistress or a friend could have affected him more profoundly; and while Max and Fabio had their backs turned, a tear, two thousand years late, fell upon the spot where that woman, with whom he felt he had fallen retrospectively in love, had perished, suffocated by the hot cinders of the volcano.

"Enough of this archaeology," cried Fabio. "We do not propose to write dissertations upon an ancient jug or a tile of the age of Julius Caesar in order to obtain memberships in some provincial academy. These classic souvenirs give me the stomachache. Let us go to dinner—if such a thing be possible—in that picturesque hostelry, where I fear we shall be served with fossil beefsteaks and fresh eggs laid prior to the death of Pliny."

"I will not exclaim with Boileau:

'Un sot, quelquefois, ouvre un avis important,'"

exclaimed Max, with a laugh. "That would be ill-mannered, but your idea is a good one. Still, I think it would have been pleasant to banquet here, on some triclinium, reclining after the antique fashion, and waited upon by slaves according to the style of Lucullus or Trimalchio. It is true that I see no oysters from Lake Lucrinus, the turbots and mullets from the Adriatic are wanting, the Apuleian boar cannot be had in market, and the loaves and honey-cakes on exhibition in the Naples Museum lie, hard as stones, beside their green-gray moulds. Even raw macaroni sprinkled with *cacciacavallo,* detestable as it may be, is certainly better than nothing. What does friend Octavian think about it?"

Octavian, who was deeply regretting that he had not happened to be in Pompeii on the day of the eruption, so that he might have saved the lady of the gold rings, and thereby merited her love, had not heard a syllable of this gastronomic conversation. Only the last two words uttered by Max had fallen upon his ears, and feeling no desire to broach a discussion, he gave a random nod of assent, upon which the amicable party retraced the road along the ramparts to the inn.

The table was placed under a sort of open porch which served as a vestibule to the hostelry, whose rough cast walls were decorated with various daubs that the host entitled "Salvator Rosa," "Espagnolet," "Cavalier Massimo," and other celebrated names of the Neapolitan School, which he deemed himself bound to extol.

"Venerable host," cried Fabio, "do not waste your eloquence to no purpose. We are not Englishmen, and we prefer young women to old canvases. Better send us your wine-list by that handsome brunette with the velvety eyes whom I just now perceived on the stairway."

Finding that his guests did not belong to the mystifiable class of Philistines and *bourgeois,* the *palforio* ceased to vaunt his gallery in order to glorify his cellar. To begin with, he had all the best vintages: Château Margaux, Grand Lafitte which had been twice to the Indies, Sillery de Moët, Hochmeyer, scarlet wine, port and porter, ale and ginger beer, white and red Lachryma Christi, Caprian, and Falernian.

"What, you have Falernian wine, *animal!* And put it at the end of your list! And you dare to subject us to an unendurable œnological litany!" cried Max, leaping at the inn-keeper's throat with burlesque fury. "Why, you have no sentiment of local color. You are unworthy to live in this antique neighborhood. Is it even good, this Falernian wine of yours? Was it put in amphorae under the Consul Plancus—*Consule Planco?*"

"I know nothing about the Consul Plancus, and my wine is not put in amphorae, but it is good, and worth ten carlins a bottle," answered the inn-keeper.

Day had faded away and the night came, a serene, transparent night, clearer, assuredly, than full midday in London. The earth had tints of azure, and the sky silvery reflections of inconceivable sweetness. The air was so still that the flames of the candles on the table did not oscillate.

A young boy, playing a flute, approached the table, and standing there, with his eyes fixed upon the three guests, performed upon his sweet and melodious instrument one of those popular airs in a minor key which have a penetrating charm.

Perhaps that lad was a direct descendant of the flute-player who marched before Duilius.

"Our repast is assuming quite an antique aspect. We only need some Gaditanian dancing women and ivy garlands," exclaimed Max, as he helped himself to a great bumper of Falernian wine.

"I feel myself in the humor for making Latin quotations like a *feuilleton* in the *Débats.* Stanzas of odes come back to my memory," added Max.

"Keep them to yourself!" cried Fabio and Octavian, justly alarmed. "Nothing is so indigestible as Latin at dinner."

Among young men with cigars in their mouths and elbows on the table, who find themselves contemplating a certain number of empty flagons, especially when the wine has been capitally good, conversation never fails to turn upon women. Each explained his own system, whereof the following is a fair summary:

Fabio cared only for youth and beauty. Voluptuous and positive, he found no pleasure in illusions, and had no preferences in love. A peasant girl would have pleased his fancy as well as a princess, provided she were beautiful. The body rather than its apparel attracted him. He laughed much at certain of his friends who were enamored of so many yards of lace and silk, and he declared it were more rational to fall in love with the stock of a fashionable *marchand des nouveautés.* These opinions, which were rational enough in the main, and which he made no attempt to conceal, caused him to pass for an eccentric.

Max, less of an artist than Fabio, cared only for difficult undertakings, complicated intrigues. He sought resistances to vanquish, virtues to seduce, and played at love as at a game of chess, with long-premeditated moves, reserved ambuscades, and stratagems worthy of Polybius. In a drawing-room he would always choose the woman who seemed least in sympathy with him for the object of attack. To make her pass by skilful transition from aversion to love afforded him delicious pleasure. To impose himself upon characters which strove to repel him, and master wills that rebelled against his influence, seemed to him the sweetest of all triumphs. Like those hunters who, through rain, sunshine, or snow, through fields and woods, and over plains, pursue with excessive fatigue and unconquerable ardor some miserable quarry which in three cases out of four they would not deign to eat, so Max, having once captured his prey, troubled himself no further about it, and at once started off on another chase.

As for Octavian, he confessed that reality itself had little charm for him, not because he indulged in student-dreams, all moulded of lilies and roses like one of Demoustier's madrigals, but because there were too many prosaic and repulsive details surrounding all beauty, too many doting and decorated fathers, coquettish mothers who wore natural flowers in false hair, ruddy-faced cousins meditating proposals, ridiculous aunts in love with little dogs. An acquatinta engraving after Horace Vernet or Delaroche, hung up in a woman's room, would have been sufficient to check a growing passion within him. More poetical even than amorous, he wanted a terrace on Isola-Bella, in Lake Maggiore, under the light of a full moon to frame a rendezvous. He would have wished to elevate his love above the midst of common life, and transport its scenes to the stars. Thus he had by turns fallen fruitlessly and madly in love with all the grand feminine types preserved by history or art. Like Faust, he had loved Helen, and would have wished that the undulations of the ages might bear to him one of those sublime personifications of human desires and dreams, whose forms, to mortal eyes invisible, live immortally beyond Space and Time. He had created for himself an ideal seraglio, with Semiramis, Aspasia, Cleopatra, Diana of

Poitiers, Jane of Arragon. At times also he had fallen in love with statues, and one day, passing before the Venus of Milo in the Museum, he
cried out passionately: "Oh, who will restore thy arms that thou may'st
crush me upon thy marble bosom!" At Rome, the sight of a matted
mass of long thick human hair, exhumed from an antique tomb, had
thrown him into a fantastic delirium. He had attempted, through the
medium of a few of those hairs, obtained by a golden bribe from the
custodian, and placed in the hands of a clairvoyant of great power, to
evoke the shade and form of the dead; but the conducting fluid—the
subtle odyle—had evaporated during the lapse of so many years, and the
apparition could no more come forth out of the eternal night.

As Fabio had divined before the glass cabinet in the Studii Museum,
the imprint discovered in the cellar at the villa of Arrius Diomedes had
excited in Octavian wild impulses toward a retrospective ideal. He
longed to soar beyond Life and Time and transport himself in spirit to
the age of Titus.

Max and Fabio retired to their room, and being somewhat heavy-
headed from the classic fumes of the Falernian, were soon sound asleep.
Octavian, who had more than once suffered the full glass to remain before him untasted, not wishing to disturb by a grosser intoxication the poetic drunkenness which boiled in his brain, felt from the agitation of his
nerves that sleep would not come to him, and left the hostelry on tiptoe
that he might cool his brow and calm his thoughts in the night air.

His feet bore him unawares to the entrance which leads into the
dead city. He removed the wooden bar that closed it, and wandered into the ruins beyond.

The moon illuminated the pale houses with her white beams, dividing the streets into double-edged lines of silvery white and bluish shadow.
This nocturnal day, with its subdued tints, disguised the degradation of
the buildings. The mutilated columns, the façades streaked with fugitive
lizards, the roofs crumbled in by the eruption, were less noticeable than
when beheld under the clear, raw light of the sun. The lost parts were
completed by the half-tint of shadow, and here and there one brusque
beam of light, like a touch of sentiment in a picture-sketch, marked where
a whole edifice had crumbled away. The silent genii of the night seemed
to have repaired the fossil city for some representation of fantastic life.

At times Octavian fancied that he saw vague human forms in the shadow, but they vanished the moment they approached the edge of the lighted portion of the street. A low whispering, an indefinite hum, floated through the silence. Our promenader at first attributed them to a fluttering in his eyes, to a buzzing in his ears; it might even, he thought, be merely an optical delusion, coupled with the sighing of the sea-breezes, or the flight of some snake or lizard through the nettles, for in nature all things live, even death; all things make themselves heard, even silence. Nevertheless he felt a kind of involuntary terror, a slight trembling, that might have been caused by the cold night air, but which made his flesh creep. Could it be that his comrades, actuated by the same impulses as himself, were seeking him among the ruins? Those dimly seen forms and those indistinct sounds of footsteps! Might it not have been only Max and Fabio walking and chatting together, who had just disappeared round the corner of a crossroad? But Octavian felt to his dismay that this very natural explanation could not be true, and the arguments which he made to himself in favor of it were the reverse of convincing. The solitude and the shadow were peopled with invisible beings whom he was disturbing. He had fallen into the midst of a mystery, and it seemed that they were awaiting his departure in order to commence again. Such were the extravagant ideas that floated through his brain, and obtained no little verisimilitude from the hour, the place, and the thousand alarming details which those can well understand who have ever found themselves alone by night in the midst of some vast ruin.

Passing before a house which he had attentively observed during the day, and which the moon shone fully upon, he beheld in perfect integrity a certain portico whereof he had vainly attempted to restore the design in fancy. Four Ionic columns—fluted for half their height and their shafts purple-robed with minium tints—sustained a cymatium adorned with polychromatic ornaments that the artist seemed only to have completed the day before. Upon one side wall of the entrance a Laconian molossus, painted in encaustic, and accompanied by the warning inscription *"Cave canem,"** barked at the moon and the visitor with pictured fury. On the mosaic threshold the word HAVE, in Oscan and

---

*["Beware of the dog."—S.T.J.]

Latin characters, saluted the guest with its friendly syllables. The outer surfaces of the walls, tinted with ochre and rubric, were unmarred by a single crack. The house had grown a story higher; and the tiled roof, now surmounted by a bronze acroterium, projected an intact outline against the light blue of the sky, where a few stars were growing pale.

This strange restoration effected between afternoon and evening by some unknown architect greatly puzzled Octavian, who felt certain of having the same day seen that very house in a lamentable state of ruin. The mysterious reconstructor had labored with great despatch, for all the neighboring dwellings had the same fresh, new look; all the pillars were coiffed with their capitals; not a single stone, a brick, a pellicle of stucco or a scale of paint was wanting upon the shining surfaces of the façades; and through the intervals of the peristyles surrounding the marble basin of the cavaedium one could catch glimpses of white laurels and bay-roses, myrtles and pomegranates. Surely all the historians were mistaken; the eruption had never taken place, or else the needle of Time had moved backward twenty secular hours upon the dial of Eternity!

In the climax of his astonishment, Octavian commenced to wonder whether he might not actually be sleeping upon his feet, and walking in a dream. He even seriously asked himself whether madness might not be parading its hallucinations before his eyes; but he soon felt himself compelled to admit that he was neither asleep nor mad.

A singular change had taken place in the atmosphere. Vague rose-tints were blending through brightening shades of violet with the faintly azure tints of moonlight; the sky commenced to glow brightly along its borders; daylight seemed about to dawn. Octavian took out his watch: it marked the hour of midnight. Fearing that it might have stopped, he pressed the spring of the repeating mechanism. It struck twelve times. It was midnight beyond a doubt, and yet the brightness ever increased. The moon sank through the azure which became momentarily more and more luminous. The sun rose!

Then Octavian, to whom all ideas of time had become hopelessly confused, was able to convince himself that he was walking, not through a dead Pompeii, the chill corpse of a city half-shrouded, but through a living, youthful, intact Pompeii over which the torrents of burning mud from Vesuvius had never flowed.

An inconceivable prodigy had transported him, a Frenchman of the nineteenth century, back to the age of Titus, not in spirit only, but in reality; or else had called up before him from the depths of the past a desolated city with its vanished inhabitants, for a man clothed in the antique fashion had just passed out of a neighboring house.

This man wore his hair short, and his face was closely shaven; he was dressed in a brown tunic and a grayish mantle, the ends of which were well tucked up so as not to impede his movements. He walked at a rapid gait, bordering upon a run, and passed by Octavian without perceiving him. He tarried on his arm a basket made of Spanish broom, and proceeded toward the Forum Nundinarium. He was evidently a slave, some Davus, going to market beyond a doubt.

The noise of wheels became audible, and an antique wagon, drawn by white oxen and loaded with vegetables, came along the street. Beside the team walked a peasant—with legs bare and sunburnt, and feet sandal-shod—who was clad in a sort of canvas shirt puffed out about the waist; a conical straw hat hanging at his shoulders, and depending from his neck by the chin-band, left his face exposed to view—a type of face unknown in these days—a forehead low and traversed by salient, knotty lines, hair black and curly, eyes tranquil as those of his oxen, and a neck like that of the rustic Hercules. As he gravely pricked his animals with the goad, his statuesque attitudes would have thrown Ingres into ecstasy.

The peasant perceived Octavian and appeared surprised, but he proceeded on his way without being able, doubtless, to find any explanation for the appearance of this strange-looking personage, and in his rustic simplicity willingly leaving the solution of the enigma to those wiser than himself.

Campanian peasants also appeared on the scene, driving before them asses laden with skins of wine, and ringing their brazen bells. Their physiognomies differed from those of the modern peasants as a medallion differs from a sou.

Gradually the city became peopled, like one of those panoramic pictures at first desolate, but which by a sudden change of light become animated with personages previously invisible.

Octavian's feelings had undergone a change. Only a short time before, amid the deceitful shadows of the night, he had fallen a prey to that uneasiness from which the bravest are not exempt amid such disquieting and fantastic surroundings as reason cannot explain. His vague terror had ultimately yielded to a profound stupefaction. The distinctness of his perceptions forbade him to doubt the testimony of his senses, yet what he beheld seemed altogether contrary to reason. Feeling still but half convinced, he sought by the authentication of minor actual details to assure himself that he was not the victim of hallucination. Those figures which passed before his eyes could not be phantoms, for the living sun shone upon them with unmistakable reality, and their shadows, elongated in the morning light, fell upon the pavement and the walls.

Without the faintest understanding of what had befallen him, Octavian, ravished with delight to find one of his most cherished dreams realized, no longer attempted to resist the fate of his adventure. He abandoned himself to the mystery of these marvels without any further attempt to explain them; he averred to himself that since he had been permitted, by virtue of some mysterious power, to live for a few hours in a vanished age, he would not waste time in efforts to solve an incomprehensible problem, and he proceeded fearlessly gazing to right and left upon this scene at once so old and yet so new to him. But to what epoch of Pompeiian life had he been transported? An aedile inscription engraved upon a wall showed him by the names of public personages there recorded, that it was about the commencement of the reign of Titus, or in the year 79 of our own era. A sudden thought flashed across Octavian's mind. The woman whose mould he had seen in the museum at Naples must be living, inasmuch as the eruption of Vesuvius by which she had perished took place on the 24th of August in this very year: he might therefore discover her, behold her, speak to her! . . . The mad longing which had seized him at the sight of that mass of cinders moulded upon a divinely perfect form was perhaps about to be fully satisfied, for surely naught could be impossible to a love which had had the strength to make Time itself recoil, and the same hour to pass twice through the sand-glass of Eternity!

While Octavian was abandoning himself to these reflections, beautiful young girls were passing by on their way to the fountains, all balancing urns upon their heads with their white finger-tips, and patricians clad in white togas bordered with purple bands were proceeding toward the

Forum, each followed by an escort of clients. The buyers commenced to throng about the booths, which were all designated by sculptured or pictured signs, and recalled by reason of their shape and small dimensions the moresque booths of Algiers. Over most of them a glorious phallus of baked and painted clay, together with the inscription, *Hic habitat Felicitas,** testified to superstitious precautions against the evil eye. Octavian also noticed an amulet shop, whose shelves were stocked with horns, bifurcated branches of coral, and little figures of Priapus in gold, like those worn in Naples even at this day as a safeguard against the *jettatura,* and he thought to himself that a superstition often outlives a religion.

Following the sidewalk which borders each street in Pompeii (and deprives the English of all claim to this invention), Octavian suddenly found himself face to face with a beautiful young man of about his own age, clad in a saffron-colored tunic, and a mantle of snowy linen as supple as cashmere. The sight of Octavian in his frightful modern hat, girthed about with a scanty black frockcoat, his legs confined in pantaloons, and his feet cramped in well-polished boots, seemed to surprise the young Pompeiian in much the same way as one of us would feel astonished to meet on the Boulevard de Gand some Iowa Indian or native of Butocudo, bedecked with his feathers, necklace of bear's claws, or whimsical tattooing. Nevertheless, being a well-bred young man, he did not burst out laughing in Octavian's face, and pitying the poor barbarian who had lost his way, no doubt, in that Graeco-Roman city, he said to him in a soft, clear voice:

"Advena, salve!"†

Nothing could be more natural than that an inhabitant of Pompeii, in the reign of the divine, most powerful, and most august Emperor Titus, should speak Latin, yet Octavian started at hearing this dead tongue in a living mouth. It was then, indeed, that he congratulated himself on having been proficient in his college studies, and taken the honors at the annual examinations. The Latin taught him by the University served

---

*["Happiness lives here."—S.T.J.]

†["Hello, stranger!"—S.T.J.]

him in good stead on that unique occasion, and calling back to mind some souvenirs of his college course, he returned the salutation of the Pompeiian after the style of *De viris illustribus* and *Selectae e profanis,* in a tolerably intelligible manner, but with a Parisian accent which forced the young man to smile despite himself,

"Perhaps it will be easier for you to converse in Greek," said the Pompeiian. "I am also acquainted with that language, for I studied at Athens."

"I am even less familiar with Greek than with Latin," replied Octavian. "I am from the land of Gaul—from Paris—from Lutetia."

"I know that country. My grandfather served under the great Julius Caesar in the Gallic wars. But what a strange dress you wear! The Gauls whom I saw at Rome were not thus attired."

Octavian attempted to explain to the young Pompeiian that twenty centuries had rolled by since the conquest of Gaul by Julius Caesar, and that the fashions had changed; but he forgot his Latin, and indeed, to tell the truth, he had but little to forget.

"My name is Rufus Holconius, and my house is at your service," said the young man, "unless, indeed, you prefer the freedom of the tavern. It is hard by the public-house of Albinus, near the gate of the suburb of Augustus Felix and the Inn of Sarinus, son of Publius, just at the second turn; but if you wish, I will be your guide through this city, in which you do not seem to be acquainted. Young barbarian, I like you, although you endeavored to impose upon my credulity by pretending that the Emperor Titus, who now reigns, died two thousand years ago, and that the Nazarean (whose infamous followers were plastered with pitch and burned to illuminate Nero's gardens) rules sole master of the deserted heavens whence the great gods have fallen! By Pollux!" he continued as his eyes fell upon a rubric inscription at a street-corner, "you have just come in good time. The *Casina* of Plautus, which has quite recently been put upon the stage, will be played today. It is a curious and laughable comedy which will amuse you, even if you only comprehend the pantomime of it. Come with me. It is nearly time for the play already. I will find you a place in the seat set apart for guests and strangers." And Rufus Holconius led the way toward the little comic theatre which the three friends had visited during the day.

The Frenchman and the citizen of Pompeii proceeded along the Street of the Fountains of Abundance and the Street of the Theatres, passing by the College, the Temple of Isis, and the Studio of the Sculptor, and entered the Odeon or Comic Theatre by a lateral vomitory. Through the recommendations of Holconius, Octavian obtained a seat near the proscenium in a part of the theatre corresponding to our private boxes which front upon the stage. All eyes were immediately turned upon him with good-natured curiosity, and a low whispering arose all through the amphitheatre.

The play had not yet commenced, and Octavian profited by the interval to examine the building. The semicircular seats, terminated at either end by a magnificent lion's paw sculptured in Vesuvian lava, receded, broadening as they rose, from an empty space corresponding to our *parterre,* but much narrower and paved in mosaic with Greek marble. The rows of seats widened above one another in regular gradation according to distance, and four stairways, corresponding with the vomitories, and sloping from the base to the summit of the amphitheatre, divided it into five *cunei* or wedge-shaped compartments, with the broad end uppermost. The spectators, all furnished with tickets consisting of little slips of ivory, upon which were indicated in numerical order the row, division, and seat, together with the name of the play and its author, took their places without confusion. The magistrates, nobility, married men, young folks, and the soldiers—who attracted attention by the gleaming of their bronze helmets—all occupied different rows of seats.

It was an admirable spectacle. Those beautiful togas and great white mantles displayed in the first row of seats, contrasting with the vari-colored garments of the women seated in the circle above, and the gray capes of the populace who were assigned to the upper benches near the columns which supported the roof, and between which were risible glimpses of a sky intensely blue as the azure background of the Panathenaea.

A fine spray aromatized with saffron fell from the friezes above in imperceptible mist, at once cooling and purifying the air. Octavian thought of the fetid emanations which vitiate the atmosphere of our modern theatres—theatres so uncomfortable that they may justly be considered places of torture rather than places of amusement, and he found that modern civilization had not, after all, made much progress.

The curtain, sustained by a transverse beam, sank into the depths of the orchestra; the musicians took their seats, and the Prologue appeared in grotesque attire, his face concealed by a frightful mask which fitted the head like a helmet.

Having saluted the audience and demanded applause, the Prologue commenced a merry argumentation. Old plays, he said, were like old wine which improves with age; and *Casina,* so dear to the old, should not be less so to the young: all could take pleasure in it, some because they were familiar with it, others because they were not. Moreover, the play had been carefully remounted, and should be heard with a cheerful mind, without thinking about one's debts or one's creditors, for people were not liable to be arrested at the theatre. It was a happy day, the weather was fair, and the halcyons hovered over the Forum.

Then he gave an analysis of the comedy about to be performed by the actors, with that minuteness of detail which shows how little the element of surprise entered into the theatrical pleasures of the ancient. He told how the aged Stalino, being enamored of his beautiful slave Casina, desired to marry her to his farmer Olympio, a complaisant spouse whose place he himself would fill on the nuptial night; and how Lycostrata, wife of Stalino, in order to thwart the luxury of her vicious husband, sought to unite Casina in marriage to the groom Chalinus with the further idea of favoring the amours of her son—in fine, how the deceived Stalino mistook a young slave in disguise for Casina, who, being discovered to be free, and of free birth, espouses the young master whom she loves and by whom she is beloved.

As in a reverie, the young Frenchman watched the actors with their bronze-mouthed masks, exerting themselves upon the stage; the slaves ran hither and thither, feigning great haste; the old man wagged his head and extended his trembling hand; the matron with high words and scornful mien strutted in her importance and quarrelled with her husband, to the great delight of the audience. All these personages made their entrances and exits through three doors contrived in the foundation-wall and communicating with the green-room of the actors. The house of Stalino occupied one corner of the stage, and that of his old friend Alcesimus faced it on the opposite side. These decorations, although very well painted, represented the idea of a place rather than the place itself, like most of the vague scenery of the classic theatres.

When the nuptial procession, pompously escorting the false Casina, entered upon the stage, a mighty burst of laughter, such as Homer attributes to the gods, rang through all the amphitheatre, and thunders of applause evoked the vibrating echoes of the enclosure, but Octavian heard no more and saw no more of the play.

In the circle of seats occupied by the women, he had just beheld a creature of marvellous beauty. From that moment all the other charming faces which had attracted his attention became eclipsed as the stars before the face of Phoebus—all vanished, all disappeared as in a dream; a mist clouded the circles of seats with their swarming multitudes, and the high-pitched voices of the actors seemed lost in infinite distance.

His heart received a sudden shock as of electricity, and it seemed to him that sparks flew from his breast when the eyes of that woman turned upon him.

She was dark and pale. Her locks, crisp-flowing and black as the tresses of Night, streamed backward over her temples after the fashion of the Greeks, and in her pallid face beamed soft, melancholy eyes, heavy with an indefinable expression of voluptuous sadness and passionate *ennui.* Her mouth, with its disdainful curves, protested by the living warmth of its burning crimson against the tranquil pallor of her cheeks, and the curves of her neck presented those pure and beautiful outlines now to be found only in statues. Her arms were naked to the shoulder, and from the peaks of her splendid bosom, which betrayed its superb curves beneath a mauve-rose tunic, fell two graceful folds of drapery that seemed to have been sculptured in marble by Phidias or Cleomenes.

The sight of that bosom, so faultless in contour, so pure in its outlines, magnetically affected Octavian. It seemed to him that those rich curves corresponded perfectly to that hollow mould in the museum at Naples which had thrown him into so ardent a reverie, and from the depths of his heart a voice cried out to him that this woman was indeed the same who had been suffocated in the villa of Arrius Diomedes by the cinders of Vesuvius. What prodigy, then, enabled him to behold her living, and witnessing the performance of the *Casina* of Plautus? But he forbore to seek an explanation of the problem. For that matter, how did he himself happen to be there? He accepted the fact of his presence as

in dreams we never question the intervention of persons actually long
dead, but who seem to act nevertheless like living people; besides, his
emotion forbade him to reason. For him the Wheel of Time had left its
track, and his all-conquering love had chosen its place among the ages
passed away. He found himself face to face with his chimera, one of the
most unattainable of all, a retrospective chimera. The cup of his whole
life had in a single instant been filled to overflowing.

While gazing upon that face, at once so calm and passionate, so
cold and yet so replete with warmth, so dead, yet so radiant with life, he
felt that he beheld before him his first and last love, his cup of supreme
intoxication; he felt all the memories of all the women whom he ever
believed that he had loved vanish like impalpable shadows, and his
heart became once more virginally pure of all anterior passion. The past
was dead within him.

Meanwhile the fair Pompeiian, resting her chin upon the palm of
her hand, turned upon Octavian, though feigning the while to be absorbed in the performance, the velvet gaze of her nocturnal eyes, and that
look fell upon him heavy and burning as a jet of molten lead. Then she
turned to whisper some words in the ear of a maid seated at her side.

The performance closed. The crowd poured out of the theatre
through the vomitories, and Octavian, disdaining the kindly offices of
his friend Holconius, rushed to the nearest doorway. He had scarcely
reached the entrance when a hand was lightly laid upon his arm, and a
feminine voice exclaimed in tones at once low yet so distinct that not a
syllable escaped him:

"I am Tyche Novaleia, entrusted with the pleasures of Arria Marcella, daughter of Arrius Diomedes. My mistress loves you. Follow me."

Arria Marcella had just entered her litter, borne by four strong Syrian slaves, naked to the waist, whose bronze torsos shone under the sunlight. The curtain of the litter was drawn aside, and a pale hand, starred
with brilliant rings, waved a friendly signal to Octavian, as though in confirmation of the attendant's words. Then the purple folds of the curtain
fell again, and the litter was borne away to the rhythmical sound of the
footsteps of the slaves.

Tyche conducted Octavian along winding byways, tripping lightly
across the streets over the stepping-stones which connected the foot-

paths, and between which the wheels of the chariots rolled, wending her way through the labyrinth with that certainty which bears witness to thorough familiarity with a city. Octavian noticed that he was traversing portions of Pompeii which had never been excavated, and which were in consequence totally unknown to him. Among so many other equally strange circumstances, this caused him no astonishment. He had made up his mind to be astonished at nothing. Amid all this archaic phantasmagory, which would have driven an antiquarian mad with joy, he no longer saw anything save the dark, deep eyes of Arria Marcella, and that superb bosom which had vanquished even Time, and which Destruction itself had sought to preserve.

They arrived at last before a private gate which opened to admit them, and closed again as soon as they had entered, and Octavian found himself in a court surrounded by Ionic columns of Greek marble, painted bright yellow for half their height and crowned with capitals relieved with blue and red ornaments. A wreath of aristolochia suspended its great green heart-shaped leaves from the projections of the architecture like a natural arabesque, and near a marble basin framed in plants one flaming rose towered on a single stalk—a plume-flower in the midst of natural flowers. The walls were adorned with panelled fresco-work, representing fanciful architecture or imaginary landscape views.

Octavian obtained only a hurried glance at all these details, for Tyche immediately placed him in the hands of the slaves who had charge of the bath, and who subjected him, notwithstanding his impatience, to all the refinements of the antique *thermae.* After having submitted to the several necessary degrees of vapor-heat, endured the scraper of the *strigillarius,* and felt cosmetics and perfumed oils poured over him in streams, he was reclothed with a white tunic, and again met Tyche at the opposite door, who took him by the hand and conducted him into another apartment gorgeously decorated.

Upon the ceiling were painted, with a purity of design, brilliancy of color, and freedom of touch which bespoke the hand of a great master rather than of the mere ordinary decorator, Mars, Venus, and Love. A frieze composed of deer, hares, and birds, disporting themselves amid rich foliage, ran around the apartment above a wainscoting of cipollino marble; the mosaic pavement, a marvellous work from the hand, perhaps, of Sosimus of Pergamos, represented banquet-scenes in relief, with a perfection of art which deluded the eye.

At the further end of the hall, upon a biclinium, or double couch, reclined Arria Marcella in an attitude which recalled the reclining woman of Phidias, upon the pediment of the Parthenon. Her pearl-embroidered shoes lay at the foot of the couch, and her beautiful bare foot, purer and whiter than marble, extended from beneath the light covering of byssus which had been thrown over her.

Two earrings, fashioned in the form of balance-scales, and bearing pearls in either scale, trembled in the light against her pale cheeks. A necklace of golden balls, with pear-shaped pendants attached, hung down upon her bosom, which the negligent folds of a straw-colored peplum, with a Greek border in black lines, had left half uncovered; a gold and black fillet passed and glittered here and there through her ebon tresses, for she had changed her dress upon returning from the theatre, and around her arm, like the asp about the arm of Cleopatra, a golden serpent with jewelled eyes entwined itself in many folds and sought to bite its own tail.

Close by the double couch had been placed a little table, supported upon griffins' paws, inlaid with mother-of-pearl, and freighted with different viands served upon dishes of silver and gold, or of earthenware enamelled with costly paintings. A Phasian bird, cooked in its plumage, was visible, and also various fruits which are seldom seen together in any one season.

Everything seemed to indicate that a guest was expected. The floor had been strewn with fresh flowers, and the amphorae of wine were plunged into urns filled with snow.

Arria Marcella made a sign to Octavian to lie down upon the biclinium beside her and share her repast. Half-maddened with astonishment and love, the young man took at random a few mouthfuls from the plates extended to him by little curly-haired Asiatic slaves, who wore short tunics. Arria did not eat, but she frequently raised to her lips an opal-tinted myrrhine vase filled with a wine darkly purple like thickened blood. As she drank an imperceptible rosy vapor mounted to her cheeks from her heart, the heart that had never throbbed for so many centuries; nevertheless, her bare arm, which Octavian lightly touched in the act of raising his cup, was cold as the skin of a serpent or the marble of a tomb.

"Ah, when you paused in the Studii Museum to contemplate the mass of hardened clay which still preserves my form," exclaimed Arria Marcella, turning her long, liquid eyes upon Octavian, "and your thoughts were ardently directed to me, my spirit felt it in that world where I float, invisible to vulgar eyes. Faith makes God, and love makes woman. One is truly dead only when one is no longer loved. Your desire has restored life to me. The mighty invocation of your heart overcame the dim distances that separated us."

The idea of amorous invocation which the young woman spoke of entered into the philosophic beliefs of Octavian, beliefs which we ourselves are not far from sharing.

In effect, nothing dies; all things are eternal. No power can annihilate that which once had being. Every action, every word, every thought which has fallen into the universal ocean of being therein creates circles which travel, and increase in travelling, even to the confines of eternity. To vulgar eyes only do natural forms disappear, and the spectres which have thence detached themselves people Infinity. Paris, in some unknown region of space, continues to carry off Helen. The galley of Cleopatra still floats down with swelling sails of silk upon the azure current of an ideal Cydnus. A few passionate and powerful minds have been able to recall before them ages apparently long passed away, and to restore to life personages dead to all the world beside. Faust has had for his mistress the daughter of Tyndarus, and conducted her to his Gothic castle in the depths of the mysterious abysses of Hades. Octavian had been able to live a day under the reign of Titus, and to make himself beloved of Arria Marcella, daughter of Arrius Diomedes, she who was at that moment lying upon an antique couch beside him in a city destroyed for all the rest of the world.

"From my disgust with other women," replied Octavian, "from the unconquerable reverie which attracted me toward its radiant shapes as to stars that lure on, I knew that I could never love save beyond the confines of Time and Space. It was you that I awaited; and that frail vestige of your being, preserved by the curiosity of men, has by its secret magnetism placed me in communication with your spirit. I know not if you be a dream or a reality, a phantom or a woman; if, like Ixion, I press but a cloud to my cheated breast; if I am only the victim of some vile spell of sorcery—but what I do truly know is that you will be my first and my last love."

"May Eros, son of Aphrodite, hear your promise," returned Arria Marcella, dropping her head upon the shoulder of her lover, who lifted her in a passionate embrace. "Oh, press me to your young breast! Envelop me with your warm breath. I am cold through having remained so long without love." And against his heart Octavian felt that beautiful bosom rise and fall, whose mould he had that very morning admired through the glass of a cabinet in the museum. The coolness of that beautiful flesh penetrated him through his tunic and made him burn. The gold and black fillet had become detached from Arria's head, passionately thrown back, and her hair streamed like a black river over the purple pillow.

The slaves had removed the table. A confused sound of sighs and kisses was alone audible. The pet quails, indifferent to this amorous scene, plundered the crumbs of the banquet upon the mosaic pavement, uttering sharp little cries.

Suddenly the brazen rings of the curtain which closed the entrance to the apartment slid back upon the curtain-rod, and an aged man of stern demeanor and wrapped in a great brown mantle appeared upon the threshold. His gray beard was divided into two points after the manner of the Nazareans. His face seemed furrowed by the suffering of ascetic mortifications, and a little cross of black wood was suspended from his neck, leaving no doubt as to his faith. He belonged to the sect, then new, of the Disciples of Christ.

On perceiving him, Arria Marcella, overwhelmed with confusion, hid her face in the folds of her mantle, like a bird which puts its head under its wing at the approach of an enemy from whom it cannot escape, to save itself at least from the horror of seeing him, while Octavian, rising on his elbow, stared fixedly at the provoking being who had thus abruptly interrupted his happiness.

"Arria, Arria!" exclaimed the austere personage in a voice of reproach, "did not your lifetime suffice for your misconduct, and must your infamous amours encroach upon centuries to which they do not belong? Can you not leave the living in their sphere? Have not your ashes cooled since the day when you perished unrepentant beneath the rain of volcanic fire? So, then, even two thousand years have not sufficed to calm your passion, and your voracious arms still draw to your heartless breast of marble the poor madmen whom your philters have intoxicated!"

"Arrius, father, mercy! Do not crush me in the name of that morose religion which was never mine! I believed in our ancient gods, who loved life and youth and beauty and pleasure. Do not hurl me back into pale nothingness! Let me enjoy this life that love has given back to me!"

"Silence, impious woman! Speak not to me of your gods, which are demons. Let this man, whom you have fettered with your impure seductions, depart hence. Draw him no more beyond the circle of that life which God measured out for him. Return to the Limbo of paganism with your Asiatic, Roman, or Greek lovers. Young Christian, forsake that larva, who would seem to you more hideous than Empousa or Phorkyas, could you but see her as she is!"

Pale and frozen with horror, Octavian tried to speak, but his voice clung to his throat, according to the expression of Virgil.

"Will you obey me, Arria?" imperiously cried the tall old man.

"No, never!" responded Arria, with flashing eyes, dilated nostrils, and passion-trembling lips, as she suddenly encircled the body of Octavian with her beautiful statuesque arms, cold, hard, and rigid as marble. Her furious beauty, enhanced by the struggle, shone forth at that supreme moment with supernatural brightness, as though to leave its imperishable souvenir with her young lover.

"Then, unhappy woman," exclaimed the old man, "I must needs employ extreme measures, and render your nothingness palpable and visible to this fascinated child." And in a voice of command he pronounced a formula of exorcism that banished from Arria's cheeks the purple tints with which the black wine from the myrrhine vase had suffused them.

At the same moment the distant bell of one of those hamlets which border the seacoast, or lie hidden in the mountain hollows, rang out the first peal of the angelus.

A sob of agony burst from the broken heart of the young woman at that sound. Octavian felt her encircling arms untwine, the draperies which covered her sank fold on fold, as though the contours which sustained them had suddenly given way, and the wretched night-walker beheld on the banquet-couch beside him only a handful of cinders mingled with a few fragments of calcined bones, among which gold bracelets and jewelry glittered, together with such other shapeless remains as were found in excavating the villa of Arrius Diomedes.

He uttered one fearful cry and became insensible.

The old man had disappeared, the sun rose, and the hall, so brilliantly decorated but a short time before, became only a dismantled ruin.

After a heavy slumber, inspired by the libations of the previous evening, Max and Fabio started from their sleep and at once called their comrade, whose room adjoined their own, with one of those burlesque rallying cries which are so commonly made use of by travellers. Octavian, for the best of reasons, returned no answer. Fabio and Max, hearing no response, entered their friend's chamber and perceived that the bed had not been disturbed.

"He must have fallen asleep in some chair," said Fabio, "without being able to get to bed, for our good Octavian cannot bear much liquor; and most likely he is taking an early walk to dissipate the fumes of the wine in the fresh morning air."

"But he did not drink much," returned Max, in a thoughtful manner. "All this seems very strange to me. Let us go and find him!"

Accompanied by the cicerone, the two friends searched all the streets, squares, crossroads, and alleys of Pompeii, entering every curious building where they thought Octavian might be occupied in copying a painting or taking down an inscription, and finally discovered him lying insensible upon the disjointed mosaic pavement of a small ruined chamber. They had much difficulty in restoring him to consciousness, and on reviving, his only explanation of the circumstance was that he had taken a fancy to see Pompeii by moonlight, and had been seized with a sudden faintness, which would doubtless result in nothing serious.

The little party returned by rail to Naples, as they had come, and the same evening, from their private box at the San Carlo, Max and Fabio watched through their opera glasses a troupe of nymphs dancing in a ballet, under the leadership of Amalia Ferraris, the *danseuse* then in vogue, all wearing under their gauzy skirts frightful green drawers, which made them look like so many frogs stung by a tarantula. Pale, with woeful eyes, and the general air of one crushed by suffering, Octavian seemed to doubt the reality of what transpired upon the stage, so difficult did he find it to resume the sentiments of real life after the marvellous adventures of the night.

From the time of that visit to Pompeii Octavian fell into a dismal melancholy, which the good-humored pleasantry of his companions rather aggravated than soothed. The image of Arria Marcella haunted him incessantly, and the sad termination of his fantastic good fortune had never destroyed its charm.

Unable to contain his misery, he returned secretly to Pompeii, and once again wandered among the ruins by moonlight as before, his heart palpitating with maddening hope; but the hallucination never returned. He saw only the lizards fleeing over the stones, he heard only the screams of the startled night-birds. He met his friend Rufus Holconius no more, Tyche came not to lay her supple hand upon his arm, Arria Marcella obstinately slumbered in her dust.

Abandoning all hope, Octavian finally married a charming young English girl, who is madly in love with him. He is perfectly well behaved to his wife, yet Ellen, with that subtle instinct of the heart which nothing can deceive, feels that her husband is enamored of another. But of whom? That is a mystery which the most unflagging watchfulness cannot enable her to unravel. Octavian never entertains actresses. In society he addresses to women only the most commonplace gallantries. He even returned with the greatest coldness the marked advances of a certain Russian princess celebrated for her beauty and her coquetry. A secret drawer, opened during her husband's absence, afforded no confirmation of infidelity to Ellen's suspicions. But how could she permit herself to be jealous of Arria Marcella, daughter of Arrius Diomedes, the freedman of Tiberius?

Avatar

I

No one could understand the malady which was slowly undermining Octave de Saville. He was not confined to his bed; his ordinary existence was unchanged; no complaint fell from his lips; and yet it was none the less evident that he was fading away. Questioned by the physicians whom the solicitations of his friends and relations forced him to consult, he could mention no definite suffering, nor could science discover an alarming symptom: the auscultation of the chest gave out a favorable sound, and the ear applied to the heart detected scarcely an irregular pulsation; he had neither cough nor fever, but life ebbed from him through one of those invisible rents of which, Terence says, man is full.

Sometimes a strange faintness made him white as marble, for a few moments he appeared lifeless, then the pendulum, no longer stopped by the mysterious finger which had held it, resumed its sway, and Octave awakened as from a dream.

He had been sent to a water-cure, but the thermal nymphs proved powerless to help him, and a journey to Naples produced no better result. The radiant sun, of which he had heard so much, was to him as black as Albert Dürer has engraved it; the bat with Melancholia written on its wing beat the dazzling sky with its dusky web, and flew between him and the light; on the quay of Mergellina, where the half-clad lazzaroni sun themselves till their skins take on the hue of bronze, he had felt chilled to the heart. So returning to his small apartment in the Rue Saint-Lazare, he had apparently resumed his former habits.

This apartment was for a bachelor most comfortably furnished. But as in time an interior becomes impressed with the look and even the very thought of its inhabitant, Octave's home had little by little grown dull and mournful; the damask curtains had faded and admitted but a gray light; the large bunches of flowers were withering on the dingy white of the carpet; the gilt frames of a few choice water-colors and sketches had slowly reddened under a relentless dust; a discouraged fire smoked and died out under its own ashes; the antique buhl clock, inlaid with brass and tortoise shell, withheld the noise of its tick-tack, and the voice of the dreary hours spoke low as one does in a sick-room; the doors closed silently, and the footfalls of rare visitors died away on the thick carpet; laughter ceased on penetrating these cold, sombre rooms, wherein modern luxury was omnipresent. Octave's servant, Jean, a duster under his arm, a tray in his hand, glided about like a shadow, for, unconsciously affected by the surrounding gloom, he had ended by losing his natural loquacity. Trophies, such as boxing gloves, masks, and foils, hung on the walls, but it was easy to see that they had long been untouched; books were tossed carelessly about, as if Octave had tried to lull some fixed idea by mechanical reading. An unfinished letter, yellowed with age, seemed to have been waiting its conclusion for months, and spread itself out on the table in silent reproach. Though inhabited, the apartment appeared deserted. Life was absent, and on entering one encountered the chill which issues from a tomb. In this lugubrious dwelling, where no woman ever set her foot, Octave was more at his ease than elsewhere; the silence, the sadness, and the neglect suited him; the joyous tumult of life disgusted him, though he made frequent efforts to join in it; but as he returned from the masquerades, the balls, or the suppers to which his friends dragged him, gloomier than before, he struggled no longer against his mysterious pain, and let the days slip by with the indifference of a man who expects nothing from the morrow. As he had lost faith in the future he made no plans, and having tacitly sent in his resignation to life, he was awaiting its acceptance. Nevertheless, if you imagined him thin of face, with an earthy complexion, attenuated limbs, and a wasted appearance, you would be much mistaken; a dark bruise under the eyelids, an orange shade around the orbits, a hollowing of the temples veined with blue, were alone observable. Yet his eyes were soulless, without trace of will, hope, or desire. This lifeless gaze in such a young face formed a strange contrast, and produced a more painful effect than the emaciated features and fevered expression of the ordinary invalid. Before his health was affected in this way Octave had been called a good-looking fellow, and he was so still; thick, wavy black hair clustered in silky, lustrous masses at his temples; his eyes were large, velvety, and deeply blue, fringed with curved lashes, and at times luminous with a liquid fire; in repose, and when unanimated by passion, they had the serene look which the eyes of Orientals wear when, after smoking their nargileh, they take their *kief* at the café doors of Smyrna or Constantinople. His skin, always pale, had that southern tint of olive white which is most effective by gaslight; his hand was slender and delicate; his foot narrow and arched. He dressed well, without being in advance of the fashion or behind it, and knew perfectly how to set off his natural attractions to their best advantage. Though without the pretensions of an exquisite or a sportsman, had he been put up at the Jockey Club he would not have been blackballed.

How was it, then, that a man, young, handsome, rich, with every incentive to happiness, should be thus miserably consuming himself? The reader will imagine that Octave was blasé, that the novels of the day had filled his brain with morbid ideas, that he had no beliefs, that of his youth and fortune squandered in dissipation nothing remained to him but debts. All these suppositions would be erroneous. Octave had seen too little of dissipation to be tired of it: neither splenetic, romantic, atheistic, nor libertine, his life had been that of the average young man, a commingling of study and relaxation. In the morning, lectures at the Sorbonne claimed his attention, and in the evening, he might be seen stationed on the staircase of the Opéra watching the tide of beauty disperse. He was not known to take interest in either actress or duchess, and he spent his income without encroaching on the principal—his lawyer respected him! In brief, he was of an equable temperament, incapable of jumping off a precipice, or setting a river on fire. The cause of his condition, which baffled the skill of the entire faculty, was so incredible in nineteenth-century Paris that we must leave its narration to our hero.

As the ordinary scientists could make nothing of this strange illness (at the amphitheatres of anatomy a soul has yet to be dissected), an eccentric physician recently returned from India, and reputed to effect marvelous cures, was consulted as a last resource.

Octave, foreseeing a superior discernment capable of penetrating

his secret, seemed to dread the doctor's visit, and it was only after repeated entreaties from his mother that he consented to receive M. Balthazar Cherbonneau. When the physician entered, Octave was
stretched on a sofa; his head was propped up by a cushion, another
supported his elbow, and a third covered his feet: wrapped in the soft
and supple folds of a Turkish gown, he was reading; or rather holding, a
book, for his eyes, though fixed on a page, saw nothing. His face was
colorless, but, as has been hinted, showed no marked alteration. A superficial examination would not have disclosed dangerous symptoms in
this young invalid, on whose table, instead of the pills, vials, potions, and
other drugs usual in such cases, stood a box of cigars. Though slightly
drawn, his clear-cut features had lost little of their natural charm, and
but for his extreme debility and the irremediable despondency of his
eye Octave would have appeared in a normal state of health.

In spite of his apathy Octave was struck by the physician's fantastic
appearance. M. Balthazar Cherbonneau seemed as though he had escaped from one of Hoffmann's Tales, and was wandering about
astounded at the reality of his own grotesqueness. His sunburnt face was
overhung by an enormous skull, which loss of hair made appear even
larger than it really was. The bald cranium, polished as ivory, had remained white, while the face, exposed to the rays of the sun, had taken
on the color of old oak or a smoky portrait. Its cavities and projecting
bones were thrown in such bold relief that their slight covering of wrinkled flesh resembled damp parchment stretched on a death's-head. The
infrequent gray hairs which still lingered on the back of the head were
gathered in three thin locks—two drawn up over the ears, and the third,
starting from the nape of the neck and ending abruptly at the beginning
of the forehead, crowned this nut-cracker countenance, and evoked unconscious regrets for the ancient peruque or the modern wig. But the
most extraordinary thing about him was his eyes. His face, wrinkled with
age, calcinated by incandescent skies, worn with vigils, marked in lines
more closely pressed than the pages of a book, with the wearisome fa-
tigues of life and of study, was illuminated by two orbs of turquoise blue,
inconceivably limpid, fresh, and youthful. Sunken in sombre sockets,
whose concentric membranes and pink edges vaguely recalled the dilat-
ing and contracting pupils of an owl, they gleamed like two blue stars,

and made one suspect that, aided by some witchery of the Brahmans, the physician had stolen the eyes of a child, and transplanted them to his own cadaverous visage. Octave's eyes were those of an octogenarian, but Cherbonneau's blazed with the fire of youth. He was dressed in the physician's ordinary garb, a suit of black with silk waistcoat of the same color, while his shirt-front was ornamented with a large diamond, the present of some rajah or nabob. But, as if suspended from a peg, his clothes hung on him in perpendicular folds, broken, when he was seated, into sharp angles by his limbs. India's devouring sun could hardly have been the only cause of the phenomenal emaciation which he exhibited. It may be that in view of some initiation he had undergone the prolonged fasts of the fakirs, and had been extended by the yogis between four glowing braziers on the skin of a gazelle. His attenuation, however, was not the outcome of debility. His fleshless knuckles moved noiselessly, as were they held together by strong ligaments stretched on the hands like the strings of a violin.

With a stiff movement of the elbows which resembled the folding of a yard-measure, the physician seated himself in the chair by the sofa to which Octave motioned him, betraying, as he did so, an inveterate habit of squatting on a mat. So placed, M. Cherbonneau's back was turned to the light which fell directly on the face of his patient, a situation most favorable to examination, and one usually chosen by observers more desirous of seeing than of being seen. Though the physician's face was hidden in shadow, and the top of his cranium, round and polished as a gigantic ostrich-egg, alone caught a ray of light, Octave discerned the scintillation of his singular blue pupils, which appeared endowed with the glimmer peculiar to phosphorescent bodies, and emitted a clear, sharp beam which penetrated the invalid's chest with the hot, pricking sensation which an emetic causes.

"Well, sir," said the physician after a moment's silence, during which he seemed to sum up the symptoms noted in his rapid inspection, "I see already that yours is not a case of everyday pathology. You have none of the well-known signs of catalogued maladies which the physician cures or aggravates; and I shall not ask you for paper, or write from the codex a soothing prescription with a hieroglyphical signature for tail-piece, or trouble your servant to go to the corner drug-shop."

Octave smiled faintly as if to thank M. Cherbonneau for sparing him useless and disagreeable remedies.

"But," resumed the physician, "do not rejoice too quickly; because you have neither heart-disease, consumption, spinal complaint, softening of the brain, typhoid or nervous fever, it does not follow that you are in good health. Give me your hand."

Thinking M. Cherbonneau wished to count his pulse, and expecting to see him take out his watch for that purpose, Octave drew back the sleeve of his dressing-gown, and baring his wrist extended it mechanically. Into his yellow paw, of which the bony fingers resembled the claws of a crab, M. Cherbonneau took the young man's moist, veined hand, but instead of feeling with his thumb for that uneven pulsation which indicates that the machinery of man is out of order, he pressed and kneaded it as if to put himself in magnetic communication with his subject.

Though a skeptic in medicine, Octave could not restrain a sort of anxious emotion. The blood receded from his temples, and it seemed to him as if the physician's pressure was subtracting his very soul.

"My dear sir," M. Cherbonneau said, as he dropped Octave's hand, "your condition is far graver than you think; the old-fashioned treatments that are in vogue in Europe cannot aid you in the least. You have lost the will to live; insensibly, your soul is slipping from your body; yet there is no trace of hypochondria, lymphomania, nor yet of melancholy and suicidal preoccupation. No! There is nothing of that. Strange as it may appear, you might, did I not prevent you, succumb suddenly, without a single noticeable rupture internal or external. It is high time that I was summoned, for your spirit holds on to your body merely by a thread; we will make a good strong knot of it, however." And therewith the doctor rubbed his hands blithesomely together, and smiled in a manner that sent the wrinkles eddying through the thousand lines of his weather-worn face.

"Monsieur Cherbonneau," Octave answered, "I do not know whether you will succeed, and as to that I care very little; but I must admit that you have gauged the cause of my mysterious affliction in the exactest and most penetrating manner. I feel as though I had become permeable, as though I were losing my ego as water runs through a sieve. I am melting away into the universal essence, and it is with difficulty that I distinguish my own identity from the surroundings into which it is being fused. Life, of which, as well as may be, I perform the daily pantomime to avoid grieving my relatives and friends, seems so far from me that there are moments when I feel as if I had already left this mortal sphere. Actuated by habitual motives whose mechanical impulse still lingers, I come and go, but without participating in my own actions. At the usual hours I seat myself at table, and appear to eat and drink; but the most highly seasoned dishes and the strongest wines have no flavor to me. The sunshine is pale as moonlight, and candle-flames are dark. I shiver in midsummer. Often an intense silence oppresses me, much as though my heart had ceased beating, and the wheelwork was clogged by some unknown cause. If the dead are sentient, my condition must resemble theirs."

"You have," replied the physician, "a chronic inability to live, an entirely moral disease, and one more frequent than is supposed. Thought is a force which can kill as surely as electricity or prussic acid, though the signs of its ravages cannot be grasped by the means of such analysis as is at the disposal of vulgar science. What sorrow has set its fangs in your heart? From what secretly ambitious height have you fallen crushed and broken? On what despair do you muse in your immobility? Is it the thirst for power which torments you? Have you voluntarily renounced an aim placed too high for human attainment? You are very young for that. May it be that a woman has betrayed you?"

"No, doctor," continued Octave; "I have not even enjoyed that happiness."

"And yet," continued M. Balthazar Cherbonneau, "in your dull eyes, in the listless attitude of your body, in the lifeless tones of your voice, I read, as plainly as if it were stamped in gold letters on a morocco binding, the title of one of Shakespeare's plays."

"And what is this play which I unconsciously translate?" asked Octave, whose curiosity was aroused in spite of himself.

"Love's Labor's Lost," continued the doctor, with a purity of accent which betrayed a long residence in the English colonies of India.

Octave did not answer; a slight blush reddened his cheeks, and to cover his embarrassment he toyed with the tassel of his girdle. The physician crossed one leg over the other, producing the effect of the crossbones carved on tombs, and clasped his foot in his hand in Oriental fashion. His blue eyes gazed into Octave's with a look at once soft and imperious.

"Come, come," said M. Balthazar Cherbonneau, "confide in me; souls are my specialty; you are my patient; and, like the Catholic priest to the penitent, I ask for a complete confession, and you can make it without kneeling."

"What good would it do? Supposing that you have divined correctly, the telling of my affliction would not relieve it. My sorrow is dumb. No earthly power, not even yours, can cure me."

"Perhaps," said the physician, settling himself more comfortably in his armchair, as if preparing to listen to a long confidence.

"I do not wish you," continued Octave, "to accuse me of a puerile obstinacy, nor to give you by my silence a pretext for washing your hands of my death; so, since you ask it, I will tell you my history: you have guessed the main point, I need not spare the details. Do not expect anything singular or romantic. It is a very simple adventure, very commonplace, very threadbare; but, as sings Henri Heine, whoso meets it finds it ever new, though the heart be broken every time. Really, I am ashamed to relate such an ordinary tale to a man who has lived in the most fabulous and chimerical countries."

"Do not fear," said the physician, smiling, "it is only the commonplace which can be extraordinary to me."

"Well, doctor, love is killing me."

II

"Towards the end of the summer of 184– I found myself in Florence, at the best season for seeing that city. I had time, money, excellent letters of introduction, and I was a good-humored youth, only too ready to be amused. I installed myself on the Lung'Arno, hired a trap, and drifted into that easy Florentine life which is so full of charm to the stranger. In the morning I visited some church, palace, or gallery, quite leisurely, without hurry, as I did not wish to give myself that indigestion of masterpieces which disgusts the too hasty tourist with art. One morning I examined the bronze doors of the Baptistery; another, the Perseus of Benvenuto under the Loggia dei Lanzi, the portrait of Fornarina, or

Canova's Venus in the Pitti Palace, but never more than one object at a time. Then I breakfasted off a cup of iced coffee at the Café Doney, smoked a cigar or two, glanced at the papers, and, my buttonhole decorated, willingly or not, by one of the pretty flower-girls who in their huge straw hats stand before the café, I returned home for a siesta. At three o'clock the carriage came to take me to the Cascine. The Cascine is to Florence what the Bois de Boulogne is to Paris, with this difference, that every one is acquainted, and the square is an open-air drawing-room, where chairs are replaced by the half circle of carriages. The women, in full dress, recline on the cushions, and receive the visits of lovers, friends, exquisites, and attachés, who pose, hat in hand, at the carriage-steps. But you know all this as well as I. There plans for the evening are made, meetings are arranged, answers are given, invitations accepted; it is like a Pleasure Exchange open from three to five in the shade of beautiful trees, under the world's fairest sky. It is incumbent on every one of the least consequence to be seen there daily, and I was careful not to miss it. In the evening I made a visit or two, or if the prima donna was an attraction I went to the Pergola.

"In this way I spent one of the happiest months of my life; but my good fortune was not destined to last. One day a magnificent open carriage made its first appearance at the Cascine. It was one of Laurenzi's *chef-d'oeuvres,* and a superb example of Viennese manufacture; glittering with varnish, and blazoned with an almost royal coat-of-arms, there was harnessed to it as handsome a pair of horses as ever paraded in Hyde Park, or drew up before Saint James' Palace during a drawing-room; added to this, it was driven à la Daumont in the correctest style by a youthful postilion in green livery and white knee-breeches. The brass on the harness, the boxes of the wheels, the door-handles, all shone like gold and sparkled in the sun; every eye followed this splendid equipage, which, after making a curve as regular as if traced by a compass, drew up near the other vehicles. The carriage, you may be sure, was not empty; but in the speed with which it passed nothing had been distinguished but the tip of a slipper extended on a cushion, a large fold of shawl, and the disk of a parasol fringed with white silk. The parasol was now closed, and a woman of incomparable beauty was revealed. Being on horseback, I was able to approach near enough to lose no detail of this poem in flesh. The fair stranger, with the assurance of a perfect blonde, wore a gown of that silvery Nile green which makes any woman whose skin is not irreproachable look as dark as that of a mole. A beautiful shawl of white crêpe de Chine, thick with embroidery of the same color, enveloped her like a Phidian statue in its clinging, rumpled drapery, while a bonnet of fine Florentine straw, covered with forget-me-nots and delicate aquatic plants of slender glaucous leaves, formed an aureole about her face. Her only ornament was a gold lizard studded with turquoises, which encircled the arm that held the parasol.

"Forgive me, doctor, this fashion-plate description. To a lover these trivialities are of enormous importance. Thick, rippling golden hair lay like undulations of light in luxuriant waves upon her brow, which itself was smooth and white as the new-fallen snow on the highest Alpine peak; long lashes, fine as the threads of gold radiating from the angel heads in the miniatures of the Middle Ages, veiled her eyes, whose pupils had the bluish-green light of a sun-pierced glacier. Her divinely modeled mouth glowed with the carmine of a sea-shell, and her cheeks resembled white roses flushed by the wooing of the nightingale or the kiss of the butterfly; no mortal brush could copy the suavity, the fairness, and the immaterial transparency of this complexion, of which the tints seemed hardly due to the blood which colors our coarser skins; the first blush of morn on the ridge of the Sierra Nevada, the rose-tipped petals of a camellia, Parian marble seen through a pink gauze veil, can alone give of it a vague idea. The creamy iridescence of the neck, visible between the shawl and the bonnet strings, gleamed with opalescent reflections. It was the Venetian coloring, and not the features, that arrested attention, though the latter were as clear cut and exquisite as the profile of an antique cameo. When I saw her, I forgot my past loves, as Romeo at sight of Juliet forgot Rosalind. The pages of my heart became blank: every name, every memory, was obliterated. I wondered how the commonplace love affairs which few young men escape had ever had any attraction for me, and I reproached myself for them as if they had been culpable infidelities. A new life dated for me from this fatal encounter.

"Presently the carriage left the Cascine and took the road back to town. When the dazzling vision had vanished I brought my horse alongside that of an amiable young Russian, a great lover of watering places, a man who had frequented all the cosmopolitan drawing-rooms of Europe, and who was thoroughly conversant with the traveling contingent of high life; I turned the conversation on the fair stranger, and learned that she was known as the Countess Prascovie Labinska, a Lithuanian of illustrious birth and great fortune, whose husband had been fighting for two years in the Caucasian war.

"It is needless to tell you what diplomacy I used to be received by the countess, who, in view of her husband's absence, was necessarily circumspect in her receptions. At last, however, I was admitted; two dowager princesses and four aged baronesses answering for me on their ancient virtue.

"The Countess Labinska had taken, a mile or so from Florence, a magnificent villa, a former belonging of the Salviati family, and in a short space of time had filled the mediaeval manor with every modern comfort without in the least disturbing its severe beauty and serious elegance. Heavy blazoned portières were in fit keeping with the vaulted arches from which they fell; the easy-chairs and other furniture of quaint and curious shapes harmonized with the sombre wainscoted walls and the frescoes dulled and faded to the hues of old tapestry; and through it all there was not a note that jarred. The present did not clash with the past. The countess was so naturally the chatelaine that the old palace seemed built as her appropriate setting.

"Fascinated as I had been by the countess' radiant beauty, at the end of several visits I was yet more charmed by her brilliant and subtle mind. When the conversation was of interest, her soul shone luminous in her eyes, the pallor of her cheek glowed with an inner flame as does a lamp of alabaster: the phosphorescent scintillations, the quivering of light of which Dante speaks in his description of the splendors of Paradise, were illustrated in her appearance, as who should say an angel thrown in bright relief against a sun. I stood bewildered, stupefied, and ecstatic. Lost in contemplation of her beauty, enchanted by the celestial tones of her voice, which made of every sentence ineffable music, I stammered, when obliged to speak, a few incoherent words, which must have given her a poor idea of my intelligence, and sometimes at certain phrases which denoted on my part either great embarrassment or incurable imbecility an imperceptible smile of friendly irony danced like a rose-colored ripple over her charming lips.

"Still I had not told my love, for in her presence I was without thought, strength, or courage; only my heart throbbed as would it break its bonds and fling itself at the knees of its sovereign. Twenty times I had determined to explain myself, but an insurmountable timidity restrained me; the least look of coldness or reserve from the countess threw me into a deathly trance comparable to that of the condemned who, bowed on the block, await the stroke of the axe that is to sever the head from the body. I was strangled by nervous contractions; I was bathed in an icy perspiration. I reddened, I grew pale, and without having dared to speak I came away, finding the door with difficulty, and staggering down the steps of the house like a drunkard. Once outside I came to my senses, and threw to the wind the most inflamed dithyrambs. I addressed to my absent idol a thousand declarations of an irresistible eloquence. In these mute apostrophes I equaled Love's greatest poets. The vertiginous perfume of the Orient, the poetry of Solomon's Song of Songs, hallucinated with hashish, the platonic subtleties and ethereal delicacy of Petrarch's sonnets, the nervous and delirious sensibility of Heine's 'Intermezzo,' could not compare with the exhaustless effusions of the soul in which my life wasted itself away. At the end of each monologue it seemed to me that the countess, vanquished at last, must descend from the heavens to my heart, and frequently I clasped my arms to my bosom, thinking to enfold her in them.

"I was so completely possessed that I spent hours in murmuring like a litany of love the two words—Prascovie Labinska; and in these syllables, dropped slowly like pearls, or repeated with the feverish volubility of a devotee exalted by prayer, I found an indefinable charm. Then again, I wrote the adored name on the finest parchment, illuminating it like a mediaeval manuscript with flowered designs and traceries of azure and gold. In this work of pathetic minuteness and puerile perfection I passed the long hours which separated my visits to the countess. I could not read or otherwise occupy myself. Nothing but Prascovie interested me, and even my letters from France lay unopened. I made repeated efforts to overcome this condition; I tried to recall the axioms of seduction accepted by young men, the stratagems used by the Valmonts of the

Café de Paris and the Don Juans of the Jockey Club; but to execute them my heart failed me, and I regretted that I had not, like Stendhal's Julien Sorel, a package of progressive epistles which I could copy and send to the countess. Unfortunately, I could only surrender myself, without the power to ask a return, without even a hope in the future; indeed, in my most audacious dreams I hardly dared touch with my lips the tips of Prascovie's rosy fingers. A fifteenth-century novice prostrate on the steps of an altar, a chevalier kneeling in his rigid armor, could not have had a more self-annihilating adoration for the Virgin."

M. Balthazar Cherbonneau had listened to Octave with profound attention; for to him the young man's story was not merely a tale of romance, and he murmured, during a pause in the narrative, as if to himself, "Yes, that is certainly a diagnostic of love, a curious malady which I have encountered but once—at Chandernagore—in a young Pariah in love with a Brahman; it killed her, poor girl, but she was a savage; you, M. Octave, you are a civilized being, and we will cure you." This parenthesis concluded, he motioned M. de Saville to continue; and, doubling back his leg to the thigh, like the articulated limb of a grasshopper, so as to support his chin on his knee, he settled himself in this position, impossible to any one else, but which to him appeared very restful.

"I do not want to bore you with the details of my secret martyrdom," resumed Octave; "I will hasten to a decisive scene. One day, unable to restrain my imperious desire to see the countess, I went to her before the hour at which she was accustomed to receive. The weather was heavy and overcast. Mme. Labinska was not in the salon. She was seated under a portico, which was supported by graceful columns, and opened on a terrace, from which one descended to the garden; she had had her piano, a wicker lounge, and a few chairs brought out, and jardinières filled with splendid flowers (nowhere are they so fresh and odorous as in Florence) stood between the columns, and impregnated with their perfume the infrequent breezes which came from the Apennines. In front, through the openings of the arcades, one could see the well-pruned yew and box trees, peopled with mythological statues in the labored style of Baccia Bandinelli or of Ammanato, and here and there a tall centenary cypress. In the dim distance rose the dome of Santa Maria del Fiore, and the square belfry of Palazza Vecchio jutted above the silhouette of the town.

"The countess was alone, and reclining on her lounge; never had I thought her so beautiful; in indolent languor she lay like a water nymph, billowed in the foamy whiteness of an ample India-muslin gown that was bordered with a frothy trimming which resembled the silvery edge of a wave, and clasped at the throat by an exquisitely chased Khorassan brooch. In brief, her costume was as airy as the drapery which floats about the figure of Victory. Her arms, fairer than the alabaster in which Florentine sculptors copy antique statues, issued from wide sleeves open to the shoulder like pistils from a flower chalice; a broad black sash knotted at the waist with falling ends contrasted sharply with all this whiteness; but the melancholy effect which these shades ascribed to mourning might have given was enlivened by the point of a tiny Circassian slipper of blue morocco figured with yellow arabesques, which peeped from beneath her skirt.

"The countess' blond hair, slightly raised as if by a passing zephyr, revealed her smooth forehead and transparent temples, and formed a nimbus, through which the light glittered in a shower of gold.

"On a chair near by, a large hat of rice straw, trimmed with long black ribbons, similar to those on her dress, fluttered in the breeze, and by it was a pair of unworn gloves of Swedish kid. On my arrival Prascovie closed the book she was reading—the poems of Mickiewicz—and gave me a kindly nod; she was alone, a circumstance as uncommon as it was favorable. I seated myself opposite her on the chair she designated, and for some minutes one of those silences fell upon us which are so painful if prolonged. None of the commonplaces of conversation came to my aid; my thoughts were confused, waves of flame rose from my heart to my eyes, and my passion cried, 'Do not lose this opportunity.'

"I do not know what I might have done if the countess, divining the cause of my emotion, had not partly risen, and extended her beautiful hand as though to close my mouth.

"'Not a word, Octave. You love me, I know, I feel, I believe it; nor does it anger me, for love is involuntary. Stricter women than I would be offended, but I pity you because I cannot return it, and it pains me to be the cause of your unhappiness. I regret that we should have met, and blame the whim which made me leave Venice for Florence. At first I hoped that my persistent coldness would weary and estrange you, but nothing rebuffs true love, of which I see all the signs in your eyes. Do not let my sympathy arouse in you either dreams or illusions; nor must you take it as an encouragement. An angel with diamond shield and flaming sword protects me more surely than religion, duty, or virtue against every seduction; and this angel is my love: I adore the Count Labinski. I have had the good fortune to make a love-match.'"

"A flood of tears burst from my eyes at this frank, loyal, yet modest avowal, and I felt the spring of life break within me.

"Prascovie rose in extreme agitation, and, with a motion of gracious feminine pity, pressed her delicate handkerchief to my eyes.

"'There, do not weep,' she said; 'I forbid it. Try to divert your thoughts; imagine that I have forever disappeared, that I am dead; forget me. Travel, work, do good; mingle actively in the tide of life; console yourself with art or love' . . . At this I interrupted her with a gesture.

"'Do you think,' she asked, 'you would suffer less in continuing to see me? If so, come. I will always receive you. God says we must pardon our enemies; why, then, should we ill-treat those who love us? Nevertheless, absence seems to me a more certain remedy. In two years we can shake hands without danger—for you,' she added, attempting a smile.

"The next day I left Florence; but neither study, travel, nor time has diminished my suffering. I am dying: do not prevent it, doctor!"

"Have you seen the countess since?" asked the physician, with an odd sparkle in his blue eyes.

"No," answered Octave, "but she is in Paris," and he extended a card on which was engraved:

The Countess Prascovie Labinska. And in a corner, *Thursdays.*

III

Among the infrequent passers who follow the Avenue Gabriel from the Turkish Embassy to the Elysée Bourbon, and prefer the silence, solitude, and fragrant calm of this avenue to the dusty whirl and noisy elegance of the Champs-Elysées, there are few who would not pause with mingled feelings of admiration and envy before a poetic and mysterious dwelling where for once felicity seemed to be lodged by wealth.

Who is there who has not halted at the railing of a park and gazed attentively through the green foliage at some white villa, and then passed on with heavy heart, as if the dream of his life lay hidden behind the walls? Then, again, other dwellings seen thus from the outside cause an indefinable melancholy. The gray gloom of desertion and despair has settled upon them and blighted the tops of the surrounding trees; the statues are moss-stained, the flowers droop, the water stagnates in the fountain; in spite of the rake, the paths are overrun with weeds, and if there are birds they are dumb.

The gardens on the Avenue Gabriel are separated from the sidewalk by a hedge, and extend in strips of varying size to the houses which face the Faubourg Saint-Honoré. The one alluded to ended at the street in an embankment supporting a wall of rocks chosen for the curious irregularity of their shape. The sides of this wall, being much higher than the centre, formed a rough, dark frame for the radiant landscape set between. The crevices of the rocks held soil enough to nourish the roots of rich plants and flowers, whose variegated verdure was thrown into relief against the sombre hue of the stone. No artist could have created a more effective foreground.

The walls that inclosed the sides of this miniature paradise disappeared under a curtain of climbing plants, of which the stalks, shoots, and tendrils formed a trellis of green. Thanks to this arrangement, the garden resembled an opening in a forest rather than a narrow grass-plot shut in the limits of civilization.

Just behind the rock-work stood several groups of slender trees, whose thick foliage contrasted picturesquely. Beyond them spread a plot of turf, without an uneven spear of grass. Finer, softer than the velvet of a queen's mantle, it was of that ideal green rarely obtained, except before the steps of a feudal English manor; a natural carpet on which the eye loves to rest, and the foot fears to crush; an emerald rug where, during the day, the pet gazelle frolics in the sun with the lace-frocked scion of an hundred earls, and where by moonlight a Titania of the West End glides hand in hand with an Oberon inscribed in the peerage. A path of sand, sifted through a sieve that no bit of shell or edge of flint should fret the aristocratic foot, circled like a yellow ribbon around this thick, smooth lawn, which, leveled by the roller, was moistened even in the dryest days of summer with the artificial rain of the sprinkler. At the end of the grass-plot blazed a bed of geraniums, a display of flowery fireworks, whose scarlet stars flamed against a dark mass of heath.

The charming façade of the house closed the perspective. Slim Ionic pillars, and a classical roof surmounted at each corner by graceful marble statues, gave it the appearance of a Greek temple transported by the fancy of a millionaire, and subdued, by a suggestion of art and poetry, all that might otherwise have seemed ostentatious luxury; between the pillars awnings slashed with crimson were usually lowered, shading and defining the windows which opened, at full length, like glass doors, under the portico.

When the capricious sky of Paris deigned to stretch a bit of blue behind this dainty palace it looked so lovely in its thicket of verdure that it might easily have been taken for the abode of a fairy queen, or for one of Baron's pictures enlarged.

Extending into the garden from each side of the house were two conservatories, whose crystal panes, set in gilt, sparkled in the sun, and gave to a world of the rarest exotic plants the illusion of their native air.

A matutinal poet strolling in the Avenue Gabriel at dawn would have heard the nightingale trilling the last notes of his nocturne, and seen the blackbird in his yellow slippers quite at home in the garden walks. At night, in the silence of the sleeping city, when the roll of carriages returning from the Opéra has ceased, the same poet might have dimly distinguished a white-robed form clinging to the arm of a young and handsome man, and he would certainly have returned to his solitary attic sad and depressed.

The reader, doubtless, divines that here lived the Countess Prascovie Labinska and her husband. Count Olaf Labinski had returned from the Caucasian war after a glorious campaign, in which, if he had not fought face to face with the mystical and intangible Schamyl, at least he had attacked the most devout and fanatic Mourides of the illustrious Sheik. He avoided bullets, as only the brave can, by rushing to meet them, and the curved scimitars of the warlike barbarians had broken on his chest without so much as scratching him. Courage is a flawless cuirass. The Count Labinski possessed the mad valor of the Slav races, who love danger for its own sake, and to whom can be applied the refrain of an old Scandinavian song: "They kill, die, and laugh!"

The rapture with which husband and wife, to whom marriage was a passion sanctioned by God and man, were reunited could only be described by Thomas Moore in the style of the "Loves of the Angels"! To portray it, each drop of ink would have to be transformed to a drop of light, and each word evaporate on the paper with the flame and the perfume of a grain of incense. What picture is possible of souls melted in one like two dew-drops which, dissolving on a lily petal, meet, blend, absorb one another, and form but a single gem?

Happiness is so rare in this world that man has not thought to invent words to depict it, while on the other hand the vocabulary of suffering, moral and physical, fills innumerable columns in the dictionaries of all languages.

Lovers, even in childhood, the hearts of Olaf and Prascovie had never throbbed to other names. In fact, knowing almost from the cradle that they were destined for each other, the rest of the world was but landscape to them. One might have said that they were the twin halves of Plato's Androgyne, which, seeking each other since the primeval divorce, were at last united and joined together. In short, they formed that duality in unity which is known as perfect harmony; and, side by side, they marched, or rather sped, through life with an equal impulse, sustained and impelled, as Dante has it, "like two doves beckoned by the same desire."

That nothing might disturb this felicity, a colossal fortune enveloped it in an atmosphere of gold. When this radiant couple appeared, Misery, consoled, shed its rags, and dried its tears; for Olaf and Prascovie had the noble egotism of happiness, and could not endure affliction amid their own delight.

Since polytheism has disappeared, and with it the young gods, the smiling genii, the celestial youths whose forms were absolute in perfection, harmonious in rhythm, and perfect in idealism, and since ancient Greece no longer chants the hymn to beauty in Parian strophes, man has cruelly abused his permission to be ill-favored. Although fashioned in God's image, he is but a poor likeness of him.

The Count Labinski, however, had not profited by this license. His face was an elongated oval; his nose was clearly and boldly cut; his mouth firmly outlined and accentuated by a pointed blond mustache;

his chin, cleft by a dimple, was ever raised; while his black eyes, through a striking and pleasing singularity, caused him to look like one of the warrior angels, St. Michael or Raphael, who, mailed in gold, combated the devil. In fact, he would have been too handsome were it not for the virile light which shone from the dark iris of his eyes, and the shade of bronze that the sun of Asia had spread over his features.

The count was of middle height, slight, graceful, nervous, concealing, beneath an apparent delicacy, muscles of steel. When for some embassy ball he donned a magnate's costume, that was embossed with gold, glittered with diamonds, and embroidered with pearls, he passed through the throng like a shining apparition, exciting the jealousy of the men and the admiration of the women, to whom, be it said, Prascovie rendered him indifferent. We need not add that the count was as intelligent as he was handsome; the good fairies had visited his cradle, and the evil witch who spoils everything was in a good humor that day.

It is easy to understand that with such a rival Octave de Saville stood a poor chance, and also, that he was sensible in allowing himself to expire quietly on the cushions of his sofa, and that, too, despite the hope with which the fantastic physician Balthazar Cherbonneau attempted to revivify his heart. The only way was to forget Prascovie, and that was impossible. To see her was evidently useless. Octave felt that the countess' resolution would never weaken in its gentle implacability and compassionate coldness. He was afraid that in the presence of his innocent and beloved assassin his wounds might reopen and bleed, and he did not wish to accuse her.

IV

Two years had passed since the day when the Countess Labinska had prevented Octave from making the declaration of love to which she had no right to listen. Awakened from his dream, Octave had taken his departure a prey to the blackest despair, and had not since communicated with her. The one word he would have wished to write was forbidden. Surprised at his silence, the countess' thoughts had frequently and sorrowfully turned to her unfortunate admirer: had he forgotten her? The simplicity of her nature made her hope that he had, without being able to believe that he had really done so, for the light of inextinguishable passion which blazed in Octave's eyes was not of a character to be misinterpreted. Love and the gods are recognized at first sight. The limpid azure of her content was slightly clouded by this knowledge, and it inspired her with the tender melancholy of the angels who, in heaven, have yet a thought for earth. Her gentle spirit suffered that she should be the cause of pain; but what can the golden star shining on high do for the obscure shepherd holding up his mortal arms? In mythological times it is true Diana descended in silvery rays upon the sleeping Endymion, but then Diana was not married to a Polish count.

The Countess Labinska, upon her arrival in Paris, had sent Octave the commonplace invitation which Dr. Balthazar Cherbonneau was twirling abstractedly between his fingers. Though she had wished him to come and see her, yet when he failed to do so she said to herself with a feeling of involuntary joy, "He loves me still!" She was a woman of angelic purity, and chaste as the uppermost snow of the Himalayas; but God himself in the depth of the infinite has to distract him from the monotony of eternity only the pleasure of hearing the beating heart of some poor, perishable creature on a puny globe that is itself lost in the immensities of space. Prascovie was not sterner than God, and Count Olaf could not have censured this delicate voluptuousness of the soul.

"Your story, to which I have listened attentively," said the physician to Octave, "proves to me that all hope on your part would be chimerical. The countess will never share your love."

"You see, Monsieur Cherbonneau, that I was right in not trying to retain my ebbing life."

"I said," the physician continued, "that ordinary remedies were useless. But, in lands which the stupidity of civilization regards as barbarous there are occult powers, of which contemporary science is absolutely ignorant. In those lands primitive man in his first contact with the vivifying forces of nature acquired a knowledge which is believed to have since been lost, a knowledge which the migrating tribes, the founders of races, were unable to preserve. This knowledge, handed down from initiate to initiate in the dumb recesses of temples, was subsequently confided to hieroglyphics paneled across the walls of the Elloran crypt in sacred idioms, unintelligible to the vulgar. But on the summit of Meru—the cradle

of the Ganges, at the foot of the marble stairs of the holy city of Bena-
res, in depths of the ruined pagodas of Ceylon—aged Brahmans are to
be seen deciphering forgotten manuscripts, yogis who, unconscious of
the birds that nest in their hair, pass their lives in repeating the ineffable
syllable Om, and fakirs whose shoulders still bear the cicatrices of the
Juggernaut's iron stamp. These are the ultimate depositaries of the lost
arcana, and it is they who, when they so deign, are able with their esoter-
ic lore to produce the most marvelous effects.

"The materialism of Europe has not the faintest conception of the
spirituality which the Hindus have reached: the protracted fasts, the self-
absorption, the impossible attitudes maintained for years together, attenu-
ate their bodies to such an extent that to see them crouched beneath a
molten sun, between glowing braziers, their long nails buried in the palms
of their hands, one might fancy they were Egyptian mummies withdrawn
from their tombs, and bent double in apelike positions. Their mortal envelope is but a chrysalis, which the immortal butterfly, the soul, can
abandon or resume at will. While their meagre form, inert and hideous,
lies like a night moth surprised by the dawn, their untrammeled spirit
rises on the wings of hallucination through incalculable distances to the
spheres of the supernatural. They are visited by dreams and visions;
from one ecstasy to another they follow the undulations that the ages
make as they sink and subside in the oceans of eternity. To them the
infinite delivers up its secrets; they assist at the creation of worlds, at the
genesis and metamorphosis of gods; they recall the sciences that have
been engulfed in plutonian and diluvian cataclysms, the unremembered
relations of man and of nature. When in this condition they mumble
words that no child of earth has lisped for aeons; they intercept the pri-
mordial tongue, the Logos which made light spring from the archaic
shadows. They are regarded as madmen; they are almost gods!"

This singular preamble aroused Octave's attention to the last degree. He was unable to understand what connection there could be between his love for the countess and the mummeries of the Hindus, and,
in consequence, his eyes bristled with interrogation points. His state of
mind was divined by the physician who, waving aside his questions with
a gesture as who should say, Be patient, you will see in a moment that I
am not digressing, continued as follows:—

"Outwearied of questioning, scalpel in hand, the dumb corpses in the amphitheatres, corpses that disclosed but death to me who sought life, I formed the project—and one, be it said, as audacious as that of Prometheus who scaled the heavens to rob them of fire—I formed the project of intercepting and surprising the soul, of analyzing and dissecting it, if I may so express myself. I passed over the effect; I looked for the cause; and therewith conceived an immense disdain for the self-evident nothingness of materialism.

"To work over a fortuitous combination of evanescent molecules seemed to me worthy only of a vulgar empiric. I attempted to undo with magnetism the bands that join mind and matter. In experiments that were certainly prodigious, but which failed to satisfy me, I surpassed Mesmer, Deslon, Maxwell, Puységur, and Deleuze: catalepsy, somnambulism, clairvoyance, soul projection, in fact, all the effects which are incomprehensible to the masses, though simple enough to me, I produced at will. Nay, I did more; from the ecstasies of Cardan and St. Thomas of Aquinas I ascended to the self-abstraction of the Pythians; I penetrated the mysteries of the Greeks; the arcana of the Hebrews; I pierced the innermost wisdom of Trophonius and Æsculapius, and therewithal, I found in their now traditional miracles that by a gesture, a word, a glance, by mere volition or some other unknown agent, the soul would shrink or expand. One by one I repeated all the miracles of Apollonius of Tyana. Yet still my ambition was unfulfilled; the soul escaped me; I could feel it, hear it, act upon it, but between it and myself there was a veil of flesh that I could not draw aside. Did I do so, the soul had vanished. I was like the bird-catcher who holds a bird beneath a net which he dare not raise lest his winged prey shall mount the sky and escape him.

"I went, therefore, to India. In that land of archaic wisdom I hoped to find the solution of the riddle. I learned Sanskrit and Prakrit, the idioms of the erudite, and the language of the people. I enabled myself to converse with Pundits and Brahmans. I crossed the tiger-haunted jungles. I skirted the sacred lakes possessed of crocodiles. I forced my way through impenetrable forests, scattering the bats and monkeys before my path, and at times, in a byway made by savage beasts, I halted abruptly face to face with an elephant. And all this to reach the hut of some far-famed yogi, one in communication with the Mahatmas; and near him I would sit for days sharing his gazelle skin, and noting the vague incantations that fell from his black, cracked lips. In this manner I caught the all-powerful words, the evoking formulas, the syllables of the creating Logos.

"In the interior recesses of pagodas that no eye save that of the initiate has seen, but which the garb of a Brahman permitted me to penetrate, I studied the symbolic sculptures. I read many of the cosmological mysteries, many of the legends of lost civilizations. I discovered the meaning of the emblems that the hybrid gods, profuse as Indian vegetation, clutch in their multiple hands. I meditated over Brahma's circle, Vishnu's lotus, the cobra de capello of the blue god Siro. Ganesa unrolling her pachyderm trunk, and winking her small eyes fringed with long lashes, seemed to smile at my efforts and encourage my researches. Each one of these monstrous figures appeared to whisper in their language of stone: 'We are but forms; it is the Spirit that stirs.'

"A priest of the Temple of Tirunamalay, to whom I disclosed my intentions, told me of a yogi who dwelt in one of the grottoes of the isle of Elephanta, and who had reached the highest degree of sanctity. I found him propped against the wall of the cavern. Robed in sackcloth, his knees drawn up to his chin, his fingers clasped around his legs, he crouched there motionless. His upturned pupils left visible only the whites of his eyes; his drawn lips exposed his teeth; his skin clung to his cheekbones; his hair, thrown back, hung in stiff locks like overhanging plants; his beard, divided in two floods, nearly touched the ground; and his nails curved inward like an eagle's claw.

"His skin, naturally brown, had been dried and darkened by the sun till it resembled basalt, and, thus seated, he looked, both in form and color, like a Canopic vase. At first I thought him dead. His arms, that were anchylosed in a cataleptic immobility, I shook in vain; in his ear I shouted the most powerful of the sacramental words which were to reveal me to him as initiate, but he heeded them not, nor did his eyelids quiver. In my despair of arousing him I was about to leave him, when suddenly I heard a singular rustle; swift as a lightning flash a bluish spark passed before my eyes, hovered for a second on the half-open lips of the penitent, and disappeared.

"Brahma-Logum (such was the name of this holy personage) seemed to awake from a lethargy; he opened his eyes, gazed at me in a natural manner, and answered my questions. 'Your wish is fulfilled,' he said; 'you have seen a soul. I have succeeded in freeing mine from my body whenever it so pleases me; it goes and returns like a luminous bee, perceptible only to the eyes of the adept. I have fasted, I have prayed, I have meditated so long, I have dominated the flesh so rigorously, that I have been able to loose the terrestrial bonds. Vishnu, the god of the tenfold incarnations, has revealed to me the mysterious syllable that guides the soul in its avatars. If, after making the consecrated gestures, I were to pronounce that word, your soul would fly away and animate whatever man or beast I might designate. I bequeath you this secret, which of the whole world I am now the sole possessor. I am glad you have come, for I long to disappear in the bosom of the Increate as does the drop of water that falls in the sea.' And therewith the penitent whispered in a voice as feeble as the last gasp of the moribund, but very distinctly, a few syllables which made a shudder, such as that which Job has mentioned, run down my back."

"Doctor," cried Octave, "what do you mean? I dare not fathom the awful profundities of your thought."

"I mean," M. Balthazar Cherbonneau tranquilly replied, "that I have not forgotten my friend Brahma-Logum's magic formula, and that the Countess Prascovie will be clever indeed if she recognizes the soul of Octave de Saville in the body of Olaf Labinski."

V

Dr. Balthazar Cherbonneau's reputation as physician and wonder-worker had begun to be noised through Paris. His eccentricities, affected or natural, had made him the fashion. But far from seeking to form what is called a practice, he rebuffed his patients by shutting the door in their faces, giving strange prescriptions, or ordering impossible regimens. The cases that he accepted were those that were hopeless; a vulgar consumption, a humdrum enterite, or a commonplace typhoid he disdainfully dismissed to the care of his brother practitioners. But on supreme occasions the cures he effected were simply inconceivable.

Standing at the bedside, he made magic gestures over a glass of water, and bodies already stiff and cold, prepared even for the coffin, after imbibing a few drops of the liquid recovered the flexibility of life, the colors of health, and sitting up again gazed about them with eyes that had become accustomed to the shadows of the tomb. In consequence, he was known as the resurrectionist, the physician of the dead. But it was not always that he consented to use his powers, and he often refused enormous sums from wealthy invalids. To decide him to undertake a struggle with destruction, he must needs be touched by the grief of some mother imploring the restoration of her only child; by the despair of some lover whose beloved was at the door of death; or else it was necessary for him to consider the patient as one whose life was valuable to poetry, science, or the progress of humanity. In this way he saved a delicious baby that was being throttled by croup's iron fingers, a charming maiden in the last stages of consumption, a poet in delirium tremens, an inventor attacked by cerebral congestion, and whose discovery would otherwise have been buried with him.

Elsewhere he declined to intervene, alleging that nature should not be interfered with, that certain deaths were necessary, and that in preventing them there was a risk of disturbing something in the order that is universal. You can see, therefore, that M. Balthazar Cherbonneau was the most paradoxical of physicians, and that he had brought with him from India a complete outfit of vagaries. His fame as a magnetizer was, however, even greater than his fame as a physician. In the presence of a select company he had given a séance or two, of which the marvels that were related disturbed every preconceived idea of the possible and the impossible and surpassed the prodigies of Cagliostro.

Dr. Cherbonneau lived on the ground floor of an old mansion in the Rue du Regard. The apartment which he occupied was strung out in the manner peculiar to former times. The high windows opened on a garden that was planted with great black-trunked trees topped with vibrant green. Although it was summer, powerful furnaces puffed from their brazen-grated mouths blasts of hot air that maintained throughout the vast chambers a temperature that exceeded a hundred degrees Fahrenheit, for the physician, accustomed to the incendiary climate of India, shivered beneath our pale sun very much as did that traveler who, returning from the equatorial sources of the Blue Nile, shook with cold in Cairo; as a consequence, Dr. Cherbonneau never left his house save in a closed carriage, and on such occasions he wrapped himself in a coat of Siberian fox, and rested his feet on a foot-warmer filled with boiling water.

His rooms were furnished with low couches covered with stuffs from Malabar, inworked with chimerical elephants and fabulous birds; there were detachable stands, colored and gilded by the Ceylonese with naïf barbarity; there were Japanese vases filled with exotic flowers; and on the floor from one end of the apartment to the other was spread one of those funereal carpets sprigged in black and white that the Thugs weave for punishment in prison, and of which the woof seems woven of the hemp from the ropes with which they strangle their victims. And therewith, in the corners, were a few Hindu idols of marble and bronze, the eyes long and almond-shaped, the nose hooped with rings, the lips thick and smiling, necklaced with pearls that descended to the waist, singular and mysterious in their attributes, the legs crossed on supporting pedestals. On the walls hung water-color miniatures by some Calcutta or Lucknow artist representing the Avatars which Vishnu has accomplished. his incarnation in a fish, in a tortoise, in a pig, in a lion with the head of man, in a Brahman dwarf, in Rama, in a hero combating the thousand-armed giant Cartasuciriargunen; in Krishna, the miraculous child in whom the dreamers see a Hindu Christ; in Buddha, adorer of the great god Mahadeva; and lastly, representing him asleep in the Milky Way on the five-headed serpent coiled in the form of a supporting dais, and there awaiting the hour when for final incarnation he shall assume the form of that winged white horse which in dropping its hoof upon the universe shall cause the world to cease to be.

In the last room, heated to an even greater degree than the others, M. Balthazar Cherbonneau was seated surrounded by Sanskrit volumes. In these volumes the letters had been made with a stylus on thin tablets of wood, which latter were pierced and strung together on a cord in a way which more closely resembled Venetian blinds than books, at least as European libraries understand them.

In the centre of the room an electric machine, its bottles filled with gold leaf and its glass plates revolved by cranks, raised its complicated and disquieting silhouette beside a mesmeric bucket spiked with numberless iron rods, and in which was plunged a metal lance. M. Cherbonneau was anything but a charlatan, and did not need a stage setting; but, nevertheless, it was difficult to enter this weird retreat without experiencing a little of the impression which, in olden times, the alchemic laboratories must have caused.

Count Olaf Labinski had heard of the miracles realized by the physician, and his half-credulous curiosity had been aroused. The Slav races have a natural leaning towards the marvelous, which the most careful education does not always correct, and, besides, witnesses worthy of belief who had assisted at these stances told things of them which could not be credited until seen, no matter how much confidence one had in the narrator. The count went, therefore, to call on the thaumaturgist.

When he entered Dr. Balthazar Cherbonneau's apartment he felt as if surrounded by imperceptible flames; the blood rushed to his head and seethed in the veins of his temples. He was suffocated by the excessive heat, and the lamps burning with aromatic oils, the huge Java flowers swaying their chalices like censers, intoxicated him with their vertiginous emanations and their asphyxiating perfumes. He staggered a few steps towards M. Cherbonneau, who was squatting on his divan in one of those strange fakir-like postures with which Prince Soltikoff has so picturesquely illustrated his book of Indian travels. One might have said, on seeing the angles formed by his joints beneath the folds of his garments, he was a human spider wrapped in his web, and crouching immovable before his prey. At sight of the count his turquoise pupils lighted up in their orbits, as yellow as the bistre of the liverwort, with a phosphorescent gleam, which as quickly died away, as if covered by a voluntary film.

Understanding Olaf's discomfort, the physician extended his hand towards him, and with two or three passes surrounded him with an atmosphere of spring, creating for him a cool paradise out of infernal heat.

"Do you feel better now?" he asked. "Your lungs, accustomed to the Baltic breezes, still icy from their contact with the perpetual snows of the pole, must pant like the bellows of a forge in this scorching air where, nevertheless, I shiver, I, baked, tempered, and, so to speak, calcinated in the furnaces of the sun."

Count Labinski made a sign to show that he no longer suffered from the high temperature of the apartment.

The physician continued in a good-humored tone—

"Well, you have heard my tricks of legerdemain spoken of, and you want a sample of my skill. Oh, I am cleverer than Comus, Comte, or Bosco."

"My curiosity is not so frivolous," replied the count, "and I have too much respect for one of the princes of science."

"I am not an erudite in the acceptation given to the word; but, on the other hand, in studying certain subjects disdained by science I have mastered some unemployed occult forces, and I produce effects which appear miraculous, though they are perfectly natural. By watching for it, I have sometimes surprised the soul; it has made me confidences by which I have profited, and repeated words which I have retained. The spirit is everything; matter exists only in appearance. The universe is, perhaps, but a dream of God, or an irradiation of the Logos in space. I rumple at will the garment of the body; I stop or quicken life, I remove the senses, I do away with distance; I rout pain without chloroform, ether, or other anaesthetic drug. Armed with the force of my will, that electricity of the intellect, I vivify or I annihilate. Nothing is opaque to my eyes; my gaze pierces everything; I discern the radiations of thought; and I can make them pass through my invisible prism and reflect themselves on the white curtain of my brain as the solar spectrums are projected on a screen. But all that is trifling beside the prodigies accomplished by certain yogis of India who have arrived at the sublimest height of asceticism. We Europeans are too superficial, too inattentive, too matter of fact, too much in love with our clay-prison, to open windows on the eternal and the infinite. Nevertheless, as you shall judge, I have obtained a few rather strange results."

Whereupon Dr. Balthazar Cherbonneau slid back on a rod the rings of a heavy portière which concealed a sort of alcove situate at the end of the room. By the light of an alcohol flame, which flickered on a bronze tripod, Count Olaf Labinski saw a spectacle, at which, notwithstanding his courage, he shuddered. On a black marble table was a young man, naked to the waist, and immobile as a corpse. Not a drop of blood flowed from his body, which bristled with arrows like that of St.

Sebastian. He might have been taken for the colored print of a martyr in which the vermilion tinting of the wounds had been forgotten.

"This eccentric physician," Olaf said to himself, "is perhaps a worshiper of Siva, and has sacrificed a victim to his god."

"Oh, he does not suffer at all; prick him without fear; not a muscle of his face will move," said the physician, drawing the arrows from the body as one takes pins from a cushion.

A few rapid motions of the hands released the patient from the web of emanations which imprisoned him, and he awoke, with an ecstatic smile on his lips, as if from a happy dream. M. Cherbonneau dismissed him with a gesture, and he withdrew by a small door cut in the woodwork with which the alcove was lined.

"I could have cut off a leg or an arm without his perceiving it," said the physician, moving his wrinkles by way of a smile; "I did not do it because as yet I cannot create, and man, in that respect inferior to the lizard, has not a sap sufficiently powerful to remake the members cut from him. But if I do not create, I at least rejuvenate." He raised a veil which covered an aged woman who, lost in a magnetic slumber, was seated in an armchair near the marble table. Her features, which might once have been beautiful, were withered, and the ravages of time could be read in the emaciated outlines of her arms, shoulders, and bust. The physician fixed his blue eyes on her with obstinate intensity for several minutes. Gradually the tremulous lines strengthened, the contour of the bust recovered its virginal purity, smooth white flesh filled the hollows of the throat, the cheeks rounded into the peach-like bloom and freshness of youth, the eyes opened sparkling in liquid vivacity, and the mask of age, lifted as by magic, disclosed a lovely young woman.

"Do you think the Fountain of Youth has somewhere poured forth its miraculous waters?" asked the physician of the count, who stood stupefied by this transformation. "I, at least, believe so, for man invents nothing, and each one of his dreams is a divination or a memory. But let us leave this figure, remodeled for an instant by my will, and consult the young girl tranquilly sleeping in this corner. Question her; she knows more than sages and sibyls. You can send her to one of your seven castles in Bohemia, and ask her what your most secret casket incloses; she will tell you, for it needs but a second for her soul to make the journey, which is not so surprising, after all, since electricity travels seventy thousand leagues in that space of time, and electricity is to thought what the cab is to the train. Give her your hand to put yourself in communication with her; you will not have to formulate your question, she will read it in your mind."

The young girl replied to the mental interrogation of the count in a voice as lifeless as that of a spectre.

"In the cedar casket there is a bit of clay on which can be seen the impress of a small foot."

"Has she guessed correctly?" asked the physician negligently, as though quite sure of the infallibility of his somnambulist.

The count's cheeks grew crimson. In the earliest days of his love he had taken the imprint of one of Prascovie's footsteps from an alley in a park, and he kept it, like a relic, in a box of the most costly workmanship inlaid with silver and enamel, whose microscopic key he wore hung at his neck on a Venetian chain.

M. Balthazar Cherbonneau, who was a well-bred man, seeing the count's embarrassment, did not insist, but led him to a table, on which was set some water that was crystal in its clarity.

"You have, of course, heard of the magic mirror in which Mephistopheles showed Faust the image of Helen; now, without having a hoof in my silk stocking or plumes in my hat, I am none the less able to entertain you with this innocent phenomenon. Lean over this bowl and think intently of the person you wish to see; living or dead, far or near, she will come at your call from the end of the world or the depths of history."

The count bent over the bowl. Soon the water grew troubled and took on opalescent tints, as if a drop of essence had been poured into it, and a rainbow-hued ring encircled the edge of the dish framing the picture which already sketched itself beneath the creamy cloud.

The mist faded. Through the now transparent water a young woman was revealed. Her loose gown was of lace, her eyes sea green, her hair wavy and golden. Over the ivory keys of a piano her lovely hands strayed like white butterflies. The picture was so marvelous in its perfection that at sight of it artists might have died of despair. It was Prascovie Labinska, who, unconsciously, obeyed the passionate invocation of the count.

"And now let us pass to something more curious," said the physician, grasping the count's hand and placing it on one of the rods belonging to the mesmeric bucket. Olaf had no sooner touched the metal charged with an overpowering magnetism than he fell stunned to the floor.

Taking him in his arms, the physician lifted him up, laid him on the divan, rang, and said to the servant who appeared at the door—

"Go find M. Octave de Saville."

VI

In a little while the wheels of a carriage resounded in the silent courtyard of the hotel, and almost simultaneously Octave was announced. When M. Cherbonneau showed him the Count Olaf Labinski stretched on a sofa, apparently lifeless, he was stupefied. At first he thought murder had been committed, and was struck dumb with horror; but, on a closer examination, he noticed that the chest of the sleeper rose and fell with an almost imperceptible respiration.

"There," said the physician, "there is your disguise already prepared. It is a little more difficult to put on than a domino; but Romeo, in climbing to the balcony at Verona, did not worry at the danger he ran of breaking his neck. He knew that Juliet awaited him in the silence of the night. The Countess Prascovie Labinska is well worth the daughter of the Capulets."

Perplexed by the weirdness of the situation, Octave did not answer. His eyes were fixed on the count, whose head slightly thrown back on a cushion gave him the appearance of one of those effigies of knights which, with their stiff necks resting on a carved marble pillow, lie above their tombs in Gothic cloisters. In spite of himself, this chivalrous figure, of which he was to take possession, smote him with remorse.

The physician mistook Octave's perplexity for hesitation. A vaguely disdainful smile flitted across his lips, and he said—

"If you are not decided I can awaken the count, who will depart as he came, astonished at my magnetic power. But, think it over; such a chance may never repeat itself. Still, however great my interest in your love may be, however much I desire to make an experiment which has never been attempted in Europe, I dare not hide from you that this exchange of souls is perilous. Question your heart. Will you risk your life in this supreme attempt? The Bible says Love is as strong as death."

"I am ready," Octave replied simply.

"Very good," cried the doctor, rubbing his shrunken, brown hands together with an extraordinary rapidity, as if he wished to strike fire in the manner of savages. "A passion which recoils at nothing pleases me. There are but two things in this world—passion and will. If you are not happy it will not be my fault. Ah, Brahma-Logum, from the depths of the sky of Indra, where the Apsaras surround you with their voluptuous choirs, you shall see if I have forgotten the irresistible formula which you gasped in my ear on abandoning your petrified carcass. Word and gestures, I have retained them all. To work! to work! We shall make in our caldron as strange a mess as the witches of Macbeth, without, however, the sorcery of the North. Take this armchair in front of me, and give yourself confidently into my power. Good! eye to eye, hand to hand. Already the charm works. The sense of time and space is lost, consciousness fades, the eyelids fall. The muscles, no longer commanded by the brain, relax; the mind is lulled, and all the delicate threads which hold the soul to the body are untied. Brahma in the golden egg, where he dreamed for ten thousand years, was not farther from external things. Now inundate him with electric currents, bathe him in psychic emanations."

While muttering these disjointed sentences, the physician did not for an instant discontinue his passes. Luminous rays flew from his distended hands and struck his patient on the brow and heart, while around him there gathered slowly a sort of visible atmosphere, phosphorescent like an aureole.

"That is perfect!" exclaimed M. Balthazar Cherbonneau, applauding himself for his success. "Now he is as I want him. But there," he cried, after a pause, as if he read through Octave's skull the last effort of his vanishing personality, "what is it that still resists? What is that mutinous idea which, driven from the circumvolutions of the brain, tries to escape my influence by crouching on the primal monad, in the sphericity of life? But I know how to reach and curb it."

To master this unconscious opposition the physician recharged the magnetic battery of his gaze, and caught the rebel thought between the base of the brain and the insertion of the spinal marrow, the most secret sanctuary, the most mysterious tabernacle of the soul. His triumph was complete.

He next prepared himself with a majestic solemnity for the surprising experiment he was to attempt. Robing himself in a linen gown like a Magus, he washed his hands in perfumed water. He took from different boxes powders, and smeared his brow and cheeks with hierarchic designs. He encircled his arm with the Brahman cord, and read two or three Slokas of the sacred poems, omitting none of the minute rites recommended by the Mahatmas of the isles of Elephanta.

These ceremonies terminated, he threw the doors of the furnaces wide open, and soon the room was filled with an incandescent atmosphere, which would have made tigers swoon in the jungle, cracked the cuirass of mud on the hides of buffaloes, and exploded aloes into bloom.

"The two sparks of divine fire which will now find themselves nude and divested for several seconds of their mortal envelope must not pale or waver in our icy air," said the physician, examining the thermometer, which marked 120 degrees Fahrenheit.

Between the inert bodies Dr. Balthazar Cherbonneau, garmented in white, looked like a priest of one of those sanguinary religions which throw the corpses of men on the altars of their gods. Indeed, he recalled that pontiff of Vitziliputzili, of whom Heine speaks in a ballad, though his intentions were necessarily more pacific.

Presently he approached the motionless count and pronounced the ineffable syllable, which he hastened to repeat to Octave, who lay in a profound slumber. M. Balthazar Cherbonneau's face, which under ordinary circumstances was simply fantastic, now assumed a singular majesty. The extent of the power which he wielded ennobled his irregular features, and if any one had witnessed the sacerdotal gravity with which he accomplished these mysterious rites he would not have recognized in him the Hoffmannesque physician who suggested, while defying the pencil of the caricaturist.

Strange things then came to pass: Octave de Saville and Count Olaf Labinski appeared to be simultaneously agitated by a convulsion of agony; their faces, which were of a deathly pallor, twitched nervously, and a slight froth rose to their lips. Two small blue flames scintillated hesitantly over their heads.

The physician made an imperious gesture, which seemed to trace the way for them through the air, and the two phosphorescent sparks began to move. They crossed to their new abodes, leaving a trail of light behind them. Octave's soul entered the body of Count Labinski, and the count's soul entered that of Octave. The avatar was accomplished.

A flush of red at the cheek-bones showed that life had reëntered the human clay, which, an instant soulless, would, without the physician's power, have become the prey of the angel of death.

Cherbonneau's blue eyes gleamed with joy at his triumph, and he said to himself, as he strode up and down the room, "I should like to see the most noted physicians do as much—they who are so proud of mending the human machine when it gets out of order: Hippocrates, Galen, Paracelsus, Van Helmont, Boerhaave, Tronchin, Hahnemann, Rasori, the most insignificant Indian fakir squatting on the steps of a pagoda knows a thousand times more than you! What matters the body when one can command the spirit?"

At the end of his sentence Dr. Balthazar Cherbonneau cut several capers of exultation, and danced like the hills in the Sir-Hasirim of Solomon; but, catching his foot in the hem of his Brahman gown, he almost fell on his nose, a trifling accident, which recalled him to his senses and calmed his excitement.

"Now to awake my sleeping friends," said he, after he had removed the smears of the colored powder with which he had streaked his face, and tossed aside his Brahman costume. Placing himself before the body of Count Labinski, which contained Octave's soul, he made the passes necessary to awaken him from his somnambulistic state, shaking from his fingers at each gesture the electric fluid withdrawn.

After a few minutes Octave-Labinski (hereafter we will so call him for the clearness of the story) rose on his elbow, rubbed his hands across his eyes, and cast around him a look of astonishment, not yet lighted by the consciousness of self. When a finer perception of objects returned to him the first thing he noticed was his own form placed quite away from him on a sofa. He saw himself, not reflected by a mirror, but in reality. He gave a cry—to his horror, this cry did not resound in his own tone of voice; the exchange of souls having occurred during the magnetic sleep, he had no recollection of it, and felt a strange sense of discomfort. His mind, served by new organs, was like a workman whose habitual tools had been taken away and replaced by others. Psyche, exiled, beat with restless wings the vault of this unfamiliar skull, and lost herself in the mazes of a brain in which still lingered traces of unfamiliar thoughts.

When the physician had sufficiently enjoyed Octave's surprise he said, "Well, how do you like your new habitation? Is your soul at home in the body of this handsome cavalier, hetman, hospodar, magnate, and husband of the most beautiful woman in the world? You no longer mean to let yourself die, as was your intention the first time I saw you in your gloomy apartment of the Rue Saint-Lazare now that the doors of the Labinski mansion are open to you, and you need not fear that Prascovie will close your mouth with her hand, as in the Villa Salviati, when you wish to speak of love. You see now that old Balthazar Cherbonneau, in spite of his hideous face—which, by the way, he can change when he wants to—has still rather good recipes in his box of tricks."

"Doctor," replied Octave-Labinski, "you have the power of a god, or at least of a demon."

"Oh, oh, do not fear; there is not the slightest deviltry in this! Your salvation is not in danger. I shall not make you sign a compact with a flourish. Nothing could be simpler than what has happened. The Logos which has created light can surely displace a soul. If men would but hearken to God across time and infinity they would see things even more surprising than that."

"With what gratitude, with what devotion, can I acknowledge this inestimable service?"

"You owe me nothing. You interest me; and to an old Lascar like myself, bronzed by every sun, hardened to every event, an emotion is a rare occurrence. You have revealed love to me, and you know we dreamers, who are more or less alchemists, magicians, and philosophers, all seek the absolute. But get up, move about, and see if your new skin is uncomfortable."

Octave-Labinski obeyed, and took a turn or two about the room. Already he was less awkward; though occupied by another soul, the body of the count retained the impulsion of its ordinary habits, and the new guest confided himself to these physical memories, for it was important for him to have the walk, the air, and the gestures of the former proprietor.

"Had I not myself but just operated the exchange of your souls," Dr. Balthazar Cherbonneau said, laughing, "I should think that nothing unusual had happened during the evening, and I should take you for the true, legitimate, and authentic Lithuanian Count Olaf Labinski, whose real self still sleeps there in the chrysalis which you have disdainfully discarded. But it will soon be midnight; and if you do not want Prascovie to scold you, or accuse you of preferring lansquenet or baccarat to her, you had now better go. You must not begin your married life with a quarrel; it would be a bad omen. In the mean time, I will busy myself in awakening your former envelope with all the care and respect it deserves."

Recognizing the importance of the physician's suggestion, Octave-Labinski hastened to leave. At the foot of the steps the count's magnificent bay horses snorted with impatience, and in champing their bits had flecked the pavement about them with froth. On Octave's appearance a superb green-garbed groom, of the lost race of heyduques, hurried to the carriage-step, which he lowered with a bang. Octave, who had first turned mechanically towards his modest brougham, installed himself in the splendid vehicle, and said to the chasseur, who flung the order to the coachman, "Home!" The door was hardly closed when the horses started, and the descendant of Almanzors and Azolans, aided by the large cords, swung himself up behind with a lightness one would not have expected of his immense size.

The distance between the Rue du Regard and the Faubourg Saint-Honoré is not long; it was covered in a few minutes; and presently the huge portals of the mansion opened and gave way for the carriage, which swept about a large graveled courtyard, and stopped with remarkable precision under a pink-and-white striped awning.

The courtyard was vast. Octave-Labinski took in the details with that rapidity of vision which the mind acquires on certain important occasions. Surrounded with symmetrical buildings, and lighted by bronze lamp-posts of which the gas darted white tongues of flame into crystal lanterns resembling those that in olden times ornamented the Bucentaur, the Labinski mansion looked more like a palace than a mere house. Boxes of orange trees, worthy of the terrace at Versailles, stood at equal distances along the edge of the asphalt, which framed, like a border, the carpet of turf forming the centre.

The transformed lover, on setting his foot on the threshold, was obliged to pause an instant and press his hand to his heart to still its beating. He had, indeed, the body of Count Olaf Labinski, but he possessed only its physical attributes; all the ideas belonging to the brain had flown with the soul of its first proprietor—this house, which was henceforth to be his, was strange to him; he was even ignorant of its interior arrangements. A staircase rose before him; he followed where it led, determined to attribute to abstraction any mistake he might make. The polished stone steps shone brilliantly, and threw into relief the opulent crimson of the broad strip of velvet carpet, which, held in place by rods of gilded brass, traced the way softly underfoot. Stands, filled with beautiful exotic plants, lined the stair. An immense windowed lantern, suspended by a heavy rope of knotted and tasseled purple silk, flashed golden shimmers over the stucco walls, smooth and white as marble, and threw a flood of light on a reproduction of one of Canova's most celebrated groups, Cupid embracing Psyche.

The landing of the first and only story was paved with mosaics of costly design, and on the walls, hung by silken cords, were four pictures, the work of Paris Bordone, Bonifazzio, Palma the elder, and Paul Veronese, whose architectural and pompous style harmonized with the magnificence of the staircase.

A high baize door, studded with gold nails, opened on the landing. Octave-Labinski pushed it, and found himself in a large antechamber, where drowsed several liveried footmen, who at his approach rose as if on springs, and ranged themselves along the walls with the impassibility of Oriental slaves. He passed on. A white-and-gold drawing-room succeeded the antechamber, but there was no one in it. Octave rang a bell. A maid appeared.

"Can madame receive me?"

"Her ladyship is undressing, but she will be visible presently."

VII

Left alone with the body of Octave de Saville, which the soul of Count Olaf Labinski inhabited, Dr. Balthazar Cherbonneau set himself to work to bring it back to every-day life. After a few passes Olaf-de Saville (we must now unite these two names to designate a double personage) came out of the profound slumber, or rather catalepsy, which had chained him, like a spectre from Hades, stiff and motionless, to the sofa. He rose with an automatic movement, undirected as yet by the will, and staggered from dizziness. Objects swayed about him; the incarnations of Vishnu on the walls danced a saraband. Dr. Cherbonneau, waving his arms like wings, and rolling his blue eyes in wrinkled, brown orbits which looked like the rims of spectacles, appeared to him as the Mahatma of Elephanta. The weird sights at which he had assisted before falling into the mesmeric trance reacted on his reason, and he grasped reality slowly. He resembled a sleeper suddenly awakened from a nightmare, who mistakes the clothes scattered over the furniture for vague, human shapes, and thinks the brass curtain knobs, shining with the reflection of the night-light, are the flaming eyes of cyclops.

Little by little this phantasmagoria evaporated, and things resumed their natural aspect; M. Balthazar Cherbonneau was no longer an Indian fakir, but a plain doctor of medicine, who smiled at his patient with commonplace good nature.

"Are you satisfied, sir," he said, in a tone of obsequious humility, in which could be discerned a shade of irony; "are you satisfied with the experiments which I have had the honor to make before you? I dare to hope that you will not much regret your evening, and that you will leave here convinced that all that is told of magnetism is not, as official science affirms, mere fable and jugglery."

Olaf-de Saville nodded assent, and left the apartment accompanied by Dr. Cherbonneau, who made him a low bow at each door.

The brougham drove up, grazing the steps, and the soul of the Countess Labinska's husband, which inhabited Octave de Saville's body, entered it without noticing that neither the livery nor the carriage was his.

The coachman asked where his master wished to go.

"Home," answered Olaf-de Saville, confusedly, astonished at not hearing the voice of the chasseur who usually asked him this question with a most pronounced Hungarian accent. The brougham in which he found himself was upholstered with dark-blue damask; his own coupé was lined with buttercup-colored satin, and the count, though surprised, accepted it all much as one does in a dream where ordinary objects present themselves under strange aspects without however ceasing to be recognizable. He felt smaller than usual; also, it seemed to him he had gone to the physician's in evening dress; yet, without remembrance of having changed his clothes, he saw that he wore a summer suit of thin material, which had never formed part of his wardrobe. His mind was confused, and his thoughts, so lucid in the morning, unraveled themselves laboriously. Attributing this singular state to the weird scenes of the evening, he thought no more of it; and leaning his head against the side of the carriage, he drifted into an undefined reverie, a vague dreaminess, which was neither waking nor sleeping.

The sudden halt of the horse, and the coachman's voice shouting "Gate!" recalled him to himself; he lowered the window, put out his head, and saw by the light of a lamp an unfamiliar street, and a house which was not his own.

"Where the devil have you brought me, fool?" he cried; "are we in the Faubourg Saint-Honoré—Hotel Labinski?"

"Excuse me, sir; I did not understand," muttered the coachman, turning his horse in the direction indicated.

During the transit the transformed count asked himself several questions which he was unable to answer. Why had his own carriage left without him, since he had ordered it to wait? Why did he find himself in some one else's. For the moment he fancied that the clearness of his perceptions must be obscured by fever, or perhaps that the thaumaturgistic doctor, to impress his credulity more keenly, had made him inhale in his sleep hashish or some other hallucinating drug, whose illusions would be dispelled by a night's rest.

The carriage reached the Labinski mansion. The Suisse, when

summoned, refused to open the door, saying it was not a reception evening, and adding that his master had returned an hour ago, and her ladyship had retired.

"Fool, are you drunk or crazy?" cried Olaf-de Saville, pushing aside the giant who rose colossal from the threshold of the half-open door, like one of those bronze statues which, in Arab tales, defend from wandering knights the entrance to enchanted castles.

"Drunk or crazy yourself, my little gentleman," answered the man, who from his natural crimson turned purple with anger.

"Scoundrel!" roared Olaf-de Saville, "did I not respect myself—"

"Be quiet, or I will break you across my knee and throw the pieces on the sidewalk," replied the giant, opening a hand larger than the huge plaster hand in the glove shop of the Rue Richelieu; "you must not be ugly with me, my little man, because you have drunk too much champagne."

Olaf-de Saville, exasperated, shoved the Suisse so fiercely that he got by under the porch. Several footmen who were still up ran forward at the noise of the altercation.

"I discharge you, stupid animal, wretch, villain! You shall not even spend the night in the house. Go, or I will kill you as I would a mad dog. Do not force me to spill the base blood of a lackey."

And the count, dispossessed of his body, with blood-shot eyes, foaming lips, and clinched hands, rushed at the enormous Suisse, who grasped his aggressor's hands in one of his own, and held them almost crushed in the vise of his short, thick fingers, fleshy and knotted like those of a mediaeval torturer.

"There now," said the giant, who, good-natured enough in the main, and fearing nothing more from his adversary, simply gave him a shake or two to keep him respectful. "There now, is there any sense in getting into such a state when one is dressed like a man of the world, and then come like a rowdy making a racket at night in respectable houses? One owes a certain consideration to wine, and that which has made you so drunk must be famous, that is why I do not knock you down, and I shall just put you gently out on the sidewalk, where the watchman will pick you up if you continue your uproar. A breath of prison air will sharpen your wits."

"Rascals," cried Olaf-de Saville to the assembled lackeys, "you allow this low varlet to insult your master, the noble Count Labinski!"

At this name the footmen with one accord gave a loud shout; a burst of laughter, Homeric and convulsive, lifted their galloon-covered chests.

"This little gentleman who thinks himself the Count Labinski! ha, ha, ha! the idea is good!"

An icy sweat broke out on Olaf-de Saville's temples. A sharp thought pierced his brain like a dagger, and he felt the marrow freeze in his bones. Was Smarra's knee on his chest, or was this real life? Had his reason foundered in the bottomless sea of magnetism, or was he the plaything of some diabolical machination? Not one of his servants, so trembling, so submissive, so prostrate before him, recognized their master. Had his body been changed as well as his clothing and carriage?

"That you may be very sure of not being the Count Labinski," said one of the most insolent of the group, "look, there he is, aroused by your clamor, descending the steps himself."

The Suisse's captive turned his eyes towards the end of the court, and saw, erect under the awning of the marquise, a slender, graceful young man, with oval face, black eyes, aquiline nose, and slight mustache, a young man who was none other than himself, or else his own ghost modeled by the devil with delusive cunning.

The Suisse dropped the hands which he held imprisoned. The lackeys ranged themselves respectfully against the wall, and with lowered eyes, hanging hands, in an absolute immobility, like pages at the approach of the Sultan, they rendered to this phantom the honors which the real count was denied.

Prascovie's husband, though brave as a Slav, a term which implies everything, felt an unspeakable terror at the approach of this Menaechmus, who in mingling with real life and making his double unrecognizable was far more terrible than on the stage. An ancient family legend came to his mind and increased his dread. Each time a Labinski was to die, he was warned by the appearance of a phantom exactly similar to himself. Among northern nations to see one's double, even in a dream, is always regarded as a fatal omen, and the intrepid warrior of the Caucasus, at the aspect of this external vision of his own self, was seized with an insurmountable superstitious horror. He who would have plunged his arm in the mouth of a loaded cannon recoiled at sight of himself.

Octave-Labinski advanced toward his former body, in which the count's indignant soul was struggling and shivering, and said, in a tone of cold and haughty politeness—

"Sir, do not compromise yourself with these servants. The Count Labinski, if you wish to speak to him, is visible from noon until two o'clock. The countess receives on Thursdays those who have had the honor to be presented to her."

Having uttered these sentences slowly, and emphasized each syllable, the pseudo-count quietly withdrew, and the doors closed behind him.

Olaf-de Saville was put in his carriage unconscious. When he came to his senses he was lying on a bed unlike his own in shape, in a room which he did not remember ever to have entered. At his side stood a strange servant, who raised his head and made him smell a bottle of salts. "Do you feel better, sir?" Jean asked the count, whom he took for his master.

"Yes," answered Olaf-de Saville; "it was nothing but a momentary faintness."

"Shall I leave you, sir, or had I better sit up?"

"No, leave me; but, before going, light the candelabra by the mirror."

"You are not afraid, sir, that the light will prevent your sleeping?"

"Not at all; besides, I am not yet sleepy."

"I shall not go to bed, sir," said Jean, inwardly alarmed at the count's pallor and drawn features, "and if you need anything I will come at the first sound of the bell."

When Jean, after lighting the candles, had gone, the count hurried to the mirror, and in the clear glass where the scintillations of the lights flickered he saw the face of a young man that was sad and gentle, he saw abundant black hair, eyes of a sombre azure, and pale cheeks covered with a dark, silky beard. In fact, a visage which was not his own, and which gazed at him from the depths of the mirror with an air of surprise. At first he tried to believe that some practical joker was framing his face in the brass and inlaid mother-of-pearl border of the Venetian mirror. He felt behind it; there was no one.

His hands, which he then examined, were longer, thinner, and more veined than his own. On the fourth finger projected a heavy gold ring with a seal, on which was engraved a coat-of-arms—a shield divided, gules and silver, surmounted by a baron's crown. This ring had never belonged to the count, who wore one that bore an eagle displayed in sable, and for crest a pearled coronet. He searched his pockets and drew out a small card-case containing visiting cards with the name: "Octave de Saville."

The laughter of the lackeys at the Hotel Labinski, the apparition of his double, the unknown physiognomy substituted for his own reflection in the mirror, all this might possibly be the illusions of a disordered brain; but these different clothes, the ring which he took from his finger, were material, palpable proofs, evidence not to be denied. A complete metamorphosis had taken place in him without his knowledge. A magician, without doubt, a devil perhaps, had stolen from him his form, his nobility, his name, his whole personality, leaving him only his soul without means to manifest it. The fantastic stories of Peter Schlemil and the Tale of Saint Sylvester's Night came to his mind. But La Motte-Fouqué and Hoffmann's characters had only lost the one his shadow, and the other his reflection, and if this strange loss of a projection which every one possesses inspired vexatious suspicions, at least no one denied that they were themselves.

The count's position was far worse. He could not claim his own title with the body in which he was now imprisoned. In the eyes of the world he would pass for an impudent impostor, or at least for a madman. In this deceitful envelope even his wife would disown him. How could he prove to her his identity? Yet surely there were a thousand familiar events, a thousand intimate details unknown to every one else, which, recalled to Prascovie, would make her recognize her husband's soul in this disguise; but of what use would her recognition be even if he obtained it, against the verdict of the world?

He was really and absolutely dispossessed of his self. And he had another anxiety. Was his transformation limited to the exterior change of figure and features, or did he really inhabit the body of another? In this case, what had been done with his own? Had a lime pit consumed it, or had it become the property of some bold marauder? The double seen at the Hotel Labinski could be a spectre, a vision perhaps, but it might also be a physical being, installed in the skin which that fakir-faced physician had stolen from him with infernal skill.

A frightful idea stung his heart like a viper's fang: "But this fictitious Count Labinski pressed into my shape by the devil's hands, this vampire who is now living in my house, whom my servants obey in spite of me, perhaps at this moment he is setting his cloven hoof on the threshold of that room where I have never entered less agitated than on the first night. And does Prascovie smile and, with a divine blush, lean her charming head on that shoulder marked by the devil's claw, taking for me that lying shell, that ghoul, that hideous son of night and hell? Shall I rush to the house, and setting it on fire, shout amid the flames to Prascovie: 'You are deceived; it is not your beloved Olaf whom you press to your heart! You are about to commit an abominable crime which my despairing soul will still remember when Time is weary of turning his hour-glass!'"

Waves of flame surged through the count's brain. He gave inarticulate cries of rage, gnawed his knuckles, and paced the room like a wild beast. Insanity was about to submerge the dim consciousness of self which remained to him. He ran to Octave's toilet table, filled a basin with water, and plunged his head into an icy bath.

His presence of mind returned. He told himself that the age of magic and sorcery was past; that death alone separated body and soul; that in the centre of Paris a Polish count accredited with several millions at Rothschilds, related to the best families, the beloved husband of a fashionable woman, and decorated with the Order of Saint-André, could not be juggled with in this way. All this was undoubtedly but a joke, in very bad taste, indeed, but still a joke of M. Balthazar Cherbonneau, a joke which could be explained as naturally as the bugbears of Ann Radcliffe's novels. As he was worn out with fatigue he threw himself on Octave's bed, and fell into a deep sleep, so heavy that it resembled death, and which lasted until Jean, thinking his master awake, came in to lay the letters and newspapers on the table.

VIII

The count opened his eyes and cast about him an investigating look. He saw a comfortable but simple bedroom. A carpet, spotted in imitation of a leopard skin, covered the floor, and tapestry curtains, which Jean had just drawn back, hung at the windows and hid the doors; on the walls was a green velvet paper simulating cloth. A clock cut from a block of black marble, with a metal dial, surmounted by the statuette of Diana in oxidized silver reduced by Barbedienne, and accompanied by two antique vases also in silver, decorated the mantel, which was of white marble veined with blue. The Venetian mirror in which the count had discovered the previous evening that he did not possess his usual face, and the portrait of an old lady painted by Flandrin, without doubt Octave's mother, were the only ornaments of this rather sad, sedate chamber.

A divan, an armchair near the fireplace, a study table covered with books and papers, furnished the room comfortably, but in no wise recalled the sumptuousness of the Hotel Labinski.

"Will you get up, sir?" said Jean in the careful voice which he had adopted during Octave's illness, as he handed the count the silk shirt, flannel trousers, and Algerian gandoura, which formed his master's morning costume. Though the count revolted at putting on a stranger's clothes, he was obliged to accept those Jean offered him or remain naked; so he put his feet down on the soft black bearskin rug at the side of the bed.

His toilet was soon finished, and Jean, without appearing to have the least doubt as to the identity of the false Octave de Saville whom he helped to dress, asked him, "At what hour will you breakfast, sir?"

"At the usual hour," replied the count, who had resolved to outwardly accept his incomprehensible transformation so as not to raise obstacles to the steps he intended to take to recover his personality.

Jean left the room, and Olaf-de Saville opened the two letters which had come with the newspapers, hoping to get from them some information. The first contained friendly reproaches, and complained that the old habits of comradeship were interrupted without motive; it was signed with a name unknown to him. The second was from Octave's lawyer, and urged him to come and draw a quarter's income long due him, or at least to designate an investment for this money which was lying unproductive.

"So it seems," the count said to himself, "that the Octave de Saville whose body I occupy much against my will really exists. He is not a fanciful being, a character of Achim Arnim or of Clément Brentano: he has an apartment, friends, a lawyer, an income greater than his wants, in fact everything which constitutes the legal status of a gentleman. Nevertheless, it seems to me I am the Count Olaf Labinski."

A glance in the mirror convinced him that this opinion would be shared by no one; the reflection was the same by the clear daylight as by the uncertain flicker of the candles.

In continuing the domiciliary visit he opened the drawers of the table: in one he found title deeds of property, two one-thousand franc notes, and fifty louis, which latter he appropriated without scruple for the needs of the campaign which he was about to begin; while in the other drawer he noticed a Russian leather portfolio closed by a patent lock.

Jean entered announcing M. Alfred Humbert, who rushed into the room with the familiarity of an old friend without waiting till the servant returned with his master's answer.

"Good morning, Octave," said the newcomer, a handsome young man with a frank, cordial manner; "what are you up to, what has become of you, are you dead or alive? No one sees you; I write, you do not answer. I should avoid you, but I have no false pride in matters of affection, and I come to see how you are. Good heavens! I cannot let a college friend die of melancholy in the depths of this apartment which is as lugubrious as one of Charles the Fifth's cells in the Yuste Monastery. You imagine you are ill, but you are bored, that is all. I shall force you to distract yourself, and I mean to play the despot and take you to a jolly breakfast in which Gustave Raimbaud buries his bachelor freedom."

Uttering this tirade in a half angry, half humorous tone, he took the count's hand in his and shook it vigorously.

"No," answered Prascovie's husband, entering into the spirit of his part, "I am even more indisposed to-day than usual; I am not in good condition; I should sadden and depress you."

"It is true you are pale and you look tired. I will wait for a more favorable occasion. I am off, for I am late for three dozen oysters and a bottle of Sauterne," said Alfred, going towards the door. "Raimbaud will be sorry not to see you."

This visit increased the count's depression. Jean took him for his master, Alfred for his friend. A last trial awaited him. The door opened, and a lady whose hair was streaked with gray, and who in the most striking manner resembled the portrait on the wall, entered the room, took a seat on the sofa, and said to the count—

"How are you, my poor Octave? Jean has told me that you came in late yesterday in a state of alarming weakness; do take care of yourself, my dear son, for you know how much I love you notwithstanding the grief caused me by this inexplicable melancholy, the secret of which you have never been willing to confide."

"Fear nothing, mother, it is not serious," replied Olaf-de Saville; "I am much better to-day."

Reassured, Mme. de Saville rose and departed, not wishing to annoy her son, who, she knew, disliked to be long disturbed in his solitude.

"Now I am decidedly Octave de Saville," cried the count when the old lady had gone; "his mother recognizes me, and does not divine a stranger under her son's epidermis. Perhaps I am then forever immured in this envelope. What a curious prison for a soul is the body of another! It is hard though to renounce being the Count Olaf Labinski, to lose his coat-of-arms, his wife, his fortune, and to be reduced to a miserable commonplace existence. Oh! to get out of it I would tear this skin of Nessus which clings to me, and I would return it to its owner in a thousand shreds. Shall I go back to the hotel? No!—I should make a terrible scandal, and the Suisse would throw me out, for I have no strength in this invalid's dressing-gown. I must think, and look about me, for I must know something about the life of this Octave de Saville who is at present myself."

He tried to open the portfolio. Touched by chance the spring yielded, and the count drew from the leather pockets first a number of sheets of paper blackened with fine, close writing, and then a square of vellum. On this an unskilled but faithful hand had drawn, with love's memory and a resemblance not always attained by great artists, a crayon portrait which it was impossible not to recognize at the first glance. It was the Countess Prascovie Labinska!

At this discovery the count was stupefied. A feeling of furious jealousy succeeded his surprise; how did the countess's portrait come to be in the private portfolio of this strange young man? how did he get it? who had made it? who had given it to him? Had the religiously adored Prascovie descended from her sky of love to a vulgar intrigue? What infernal jest incarnated him, the husband, in the body of the lover of this woman, till then believed so pure? After being the husband, he was to be the lover! Sarcastic metamorphosis, a reversal of position sufficient to turn one's brain, he might trick himself, be at the same time Clitandre and Georges Dandin! All these ideas buzzed tumultuously in his mind; he felt he was losing his reason, and he made a supreme effort of will to regain a little composure. Without hearing Jean announce that breakfast was ready, he continued with nervous trepidation the examination of the mysterious portfolio.

The leaves composed a sort of psychological journal, abandoned and resumed at different intervals. Here are several fragments devoured by the count with anxious curiosity.

"She will never love me, never, never! I have read in her soft eyes the cruel sentence than which Dante could find nothing more severe to inscribe on the bronze gates of the *Cité Dolente:* 'Lose all hope.' What have I done to God to be damned alive? To-morrow, after to-morrow, always, it will be the same. The planets may intercross their orbits, the stars in conjunction may knot, but nothing in my destiny will change. With a word she has dispelled the dream; with a gesture broken the chimera's wings. The fabulous combinations of the impossible offer me no chance; the numbers thrown a million times in fortune's wheel will never come up—there is no winning number for me!

"Fool that I am! I know that paradise is closed to me, and I sit stupidly on the threshold, with my back against the door which will not open, and I weep silently, without violence, without effort, as if my eyes were living springs. I have not the courage to rise and plunge into the immense desert or into the tumultuous Babel of men.

"When, sometimes, in the night I cannot sleep, I think of Prascovie; if I sleep I dream of her. Oh, how beautiful she was that day in the garden of the Villa Salviati, at Florence! That white dress with the black ribbons, it was charming and funereal! The white for her, the black for me! Now and then the ribbons stirred by the breeze formed a cross on the background of startling white, an invisible spirit was murmuring the death mass of my heart.

"Should some surprising catastrophe tiara my brow with the crown of an emperor or caliph, should the earth bleed for me her veins of gold, should the diamond mines of Golconda and of Visiapour allow me to dig in their sparkling galleries, should Byron's lyre resound under my fingers, should the most perfect works of antique and modern art lend me their charms, should I discover a new world, well, for all that I would not be further advanced!

"On what a thread hangs fate! If I had had the desire to go to Constantinople I should not have met her; I stay in Florence, I see her, and I die.

"I should have killed myself, but she breathes the air in which I live, and perhaps my covetous lip may seize—oh, ineffable joy!—a distant emanation of that perfumed breath. And, besides, my guilty soul would be assigned to an exile's planet, and I should lose the chance to make her love me in another life. To be separated there, she in paradise, I in hell: oh, maddening thought!

"Why must I love precisely the one woman who cannot love me! Others, called beautiful, who were free, smiled on me with their tenderest smiles, and seemed to invite an avowal which did not come. Oh, how happy is he! What sublimity of former life does God recompense in him by the magnificent gift of her love?"

It was unnecessary to read further. The suspicion which the count had conceived at sight of Prascovie's portrait had vanished at the first lines of this sad confession. He understood that the cherished image, recommenced a thousand times, had been drawn far from the model with the tender and indefatigable patience of an unhappy love, and that it was the madonna of a mystical shrine, before which kneeled a hopeless adoration.

"But perhaps this Octave has made a compact with the devil to divest me of my body, and then in my form to profit by Prascovie's unsuspecting love!"

Though it troubled him strangely, the improbability of such a supposition in these modern days made the count soon discard it.

Smiling to himself at his credulity, he ate the now cold breakfast which Jean had brought, then dressed, and ordered the carriage. When it was ready, he had himself driven to Dr. Balthazar Cherbonneau's, and crossed the rooms which he had entered the day before as the Count Olaf Labinski, and from which he had come out saluted by all the world with the name of Octave de Saville. The physician was seated, as usual, on the divan in the farthest room, holding his foot in his hand, and seemingly plunged in a profound meditation.

At the sound of the count's steps he raised his head.

"Ah! it is you, my dear Octave. I was about to go to you, but it is a good sign when the invalid comes to the physician."

"Always Octave! I think I shall go mad with rage," thought the count. Then crossing his arms, he stood in front of the physician, and fastening on him a terrible look, said—

"You know perfectly, M. Balthazar Cherbonneau, that I am not Octave, but Count Olaf Labinski, and you know it, because last evening, on this very spot you stole my skin by means of your foreign witchcraft."

At these words the doctor gave a shout of laughter, fell back on his cushions, and held his sides to restrain the convulsions of his gayety.

"Moderate this excessive mirth of which you may repent, doctor. I speak seriously."

"So much the worse! that proves that the anaesthesia and the hypochondria for which I have been treating you are turning into insanity. I must change the regimen, that is all."

"I do not know what keeps me from strangling you with my hands, you doctor of the devil," cried the count, advancing towards Cherbonneau.

The physician smiled at the count's menace, and touched him with the end of a little steel rod. Olaf-de Saville received a frightful shock, and thought his arm was broken.

"Oh! we have means to compel invalids when they resist," said Cherbonneau, turning on him the look, cold as a douche, which conquers madmen and subdues the lion. "Go home, take a bath, and this excitement will pass away."

Confused by the electric shock, Olaf-de Saville left Dr. Cherbonneau's, more upset and uncertain than ever. He had himself driven to Passy to consult Dr. B.

To this celebrated physician he said, "I am the prey of a strange hallucination; when I look in the glass my face does not appear to me with its usual features; the objects which surround me are changed; I do not recognize either the walls or the furniture of my room; it seems to me that I am not myself but some one else."

"Under what aspect do you see yourself?" asked the physician; "the delusion may come from the eyes or from the brain."

"I see myself with black hair, dark blue eyes, and a pale face framed by a beard."

"A passport description could not be more exact: you have neither mental hallucination nor perverted sight. You are, in fact, just as you describe."

"Oh, no! I have really fair hair, black eyes, tanned skin, and a slight mustache *à la hongroise.*"

"Here," replied the physician, "begins an alteration of the mental faculties."

"Nevertheless, doctor, I am not in the least insane."

"Quite true. It is only sane people who come to me of themselves. A little fatigue, some excess in study or pleasure, has caused this trouble. You are mistaken; the vision is real, the idea chimerical: instead of being fair and seeing yourself dark, you are dark and think yourself fair."

"Still, I am sure of being Count Olaf Labinski, but since yesterday every one calls me Octave de Saville."

"That is precisely what I said," answered the doctor. "You are M. de Saville, and you imagine yourself to be Count Labinski, whom I remember to have seen, and who, as you say, is fair. That explains perfectly why you see yourself in the mirror with another face; this face which is yours does not correspond with your idea and surprises you. Remember this, that every one calls you M. de Saville, and consequently does not share your belief. Come and spend a fortnight here; the baths, the rest, the walks under the large trees, will dissipate this annoying impression."

The count bowed and promised to come again. He no longer knew what to think. He returned to the apartment in the Rue Saint-Lazare, and by chance saw on the table the invitation of the Countess Labinska, which Octave had shown to M. Cherbonneau.

"With this talisman," he cried to himself, "I can see her to-morrow."

IX

When the real Count Labinski, chased from his terrestrial paradise by the false guardian angel who stood on the threshold, had been taken to his carriage by the servants, the transformed Octave went back to the little cream-and-gold salon to wait the countess' leisure.

Leaning against a white marble mantel of which the hearth was filled with flowers, he saw himself reflected in the depths of the glass placed on a gilt-legged console opposite. Though he was in the secret of his metamorphosis, or, to speak more exactly, of his transposition, he had some difficulty in persuading himself that this image, so different from his own, was the reflection of his present form, and he could not turn his eyes from the phantom stranger who yet had become himself. He gazed at himself and saw some one else. Involuntarily he looked to see if the Count Olaf were not leaning on the mantel beside him and thus throwing his reflection in the mirror. But he was quite alone. Dr. Cherbonneau had done the thing thoroughly.

After a few minutes, Octave-Labinski ceased to consider the marvelous avatar which had placed his soul in the body of Prascovie's husband; his thoughts took a turn more conformable to his situation. This incredible event, of which the wildest visionary would not in his delirium have dared to dream, had been brought about. He was to find himself in the presence of the beautiful and adored being, and she would not repulse him! The only combination which could unite his happiness with the immaculate virtue of the countess was achieved!

At the approach of this supreme moment his soul underwent the most dreadful agony and anxiety; the timidity of true love made it as weak as were it still in the despised body of Octave de Saville.

The entrance of the maid put an end to his combat with this tumult of thoughts. At sight of her he could not control a nervous start, and the blood surged to his heart when she said—

"Her ladyship can receive you now, sir."

Octave-Labinski followed the woman, for he was unfamiliar with the different parts of the house and did not wish to betray his ignorance by taking uncertain steps. The maid showed him into a good-sized room; it was a dressing-room ornamented with all the most delicate refinements of luxury. A set of wardrobes in precious wood carved by Knecht and Lienhart formed a sort of architectural wainscoting, a portico of capricious style, rare elegance, and finished execution. The doors were separated by columns around which heart-shaped leaves of convolvuli and bell-like flowers, cut with infinite skill, twined in ascending spirals. In these wardrobes were kept gowns of velvet and of silk, cashmeres, wraps, laces, cloaks of sable and blue fox, hats of a thousand shapes, and all the belongings of a pretty woman.

Opposite, the same idea was repeated with this difference, that the smooth panels were replaced by mirrors revolving on hinges like the leaves of a screen, so that it was possible to see the face, profile, or back, and to judge of the effect of a bodice or a head-dress. On the third side was a long toilet-table with an alabaster-onyx top, where the silver faucets spouted hot and cold water into huge Japanese bowls set in an open-work rim of the same metal; Bohemian glass bottles sparkling in the candlelight like diamonds and rubies, contained essences and perfumes.

The walls and ceiling were tufted with Nile green satin, like the inside of a jewel-case. A thick Smyrna rug, with softly blending colors, wadded the floor.

On a green velvet pedestal in the centre of the room was set a large chest of fantastic shape in Khorassan steel, chased, embossed, and engraved with arabesques amplificated enough to make the ornamentation of the Ambassadors' Hall in the Alhambra appear simplicity itself. Oriental art seemed to have done its best in this marvelous work, in which the fairy fingers of the Peris must surely have taken part. It was in this chest that the Countess Prascovie Labinska inclosed her ornaments, jewels fit for a queen, which she wore rarely, thinking, with reason, that they were not worth the place they covered. Her woman's instinct told her that she was too beautiful to need magnificence! In consequence, they only saw the light on solemn occasions when the hereditary pomp of the ancient Labinski family had to appear in all its splendor. Diamonds never lay more idle.

Near the window, whose ample curtains hung in heavy folds, the Countess Prascovie Labinska, radiantly fair and beautiful, was seated at a lace-covered dressing-table, before a mirror held toward her by two angels carved by Mlle. de Fauveau with the fragile elegance which characterizes that lady's talent; two candelabra, each with six candles, flooded her with light. An ideally fine Algerian burnous, with blue and white stripes in alternation opaque and transparent, enveloped her like a fleecy cloud; the thin material had slipped from the satiny tissue of the shoulders, and revealed the lines of a throat beside which the snow-white neck of a swan would have appeared gray indeed. The opening of the folds was filled by the laces of a batiste gown, a nocturnal attire without a restraining belt. The countess' hair was undone, and fell behind her in a mass as opulent as the mantle of an empress. The flowing golden locks, from which Venus Aphrodite kneeling in her mother-of-pearl shell wrung the drops when she rose like a flower from the blue Ionian Sea, were not more blonde or luxurious! Blend Titian's amber and Paul Veronese's silver with the golden varnish of Rembrandt, make the sun shine through a topaz, and yet you will not obtain the marvelous tint of her wonderful hair, which seemed to give out light instead of receiving it, and which would have merited more than did Berenice's to shine, a new constellation, among the ancient planets! Two women were dividing, smoothing, and rolling it in coils carefully arranged that the contact with the pillow should not rumple it.

During this delicate operation the countess balanced on the end of her foot a Turkish slipper of white velvet embroidered with gold, small enough to create jealousy in the hearts of the Sultan's khanouns and odalisques. Now and then, throwing back the silky folds of the burnous, she uncovered her white arm, and with a gently impatient motion pushed aside some stray lock of hair.

Reclining in this indolent posture she recalled the graceful figures in the Greek toilet scenes which decorate antique vases, and of which no artist has since been able to reproduce the pure and correct outlines or the youthful and slender beauty. She was a thousand times more seductive than in the garden of the Villa Salviati at Florence, and had Octave not been already wildly in love with her he would then have infallibly become so; but happily, nothing can be added to the infinite.

At sight of her Octave-Labinski acted as if he had seen the most terrible spectacle; his knees knocked together and almost gave way under him. His mouth grew parched. Distress seized him at the throat like the hand of a Thug, and flames danced before his eyes. Her loveliness magnetized him.

Reflecting, however, that this stupid and bewildered manner fit for a repulsed lover was perfectly ridiculous in a husband, no matter how much in love he might still be with his wife, he made a courageous effort, and stepped firmly enough toward the countess.

"Ah! it is you, Olaf! How late you are this evening!" said the countess without turning, for her head was held by the long braids which the maids were twisting. Freeing it from the folds of the burnous, she offered him one of her beautiful hands. Octave-Labinski grasped her soft, flower-like hand, carried it to his lips, and pressed it with a long, burning kiss—his whole soul concentrating itself on the little spot.

It is impossible to know what sensitiveness of the epidermis, what instinct of divine modesty, what unconscious intuition of the heart warned the countess; but a crimson flush spread swiftly over her face. Her throat and her arms took on the hue of the snow on the mountain-tops at the sun's earliest kiss. She started, and, half angry, half ashamed, slowly withdrew her hand. Octave's lips had given her the impression of a hot iron. She quickly recovered herself, however, and smiled at her childishness.

"You do not answer me, dear Olaf. Do you know that it is over six hours since I saw you? You neglect me," she added, in a reproachful tone; "formerly you would not have deserted me so for a whole long evening. Did you even think of me?"

"All the time," replied Octave-Labinski.

"Oh, no, not all the time. I know when you think of me even at a distance. This evening, for instance, I was alone, seated at the piano, playing a piece of Weber's to soothe my dullness with music; in the sonorous pulsations of the notes your spirit hovered about me for several minutes; but at the last chord it flew away I know not whither, and did not return. Do not contradict me, I am sure of what I say."

Prascovie in fact was not mistaken. It was the moment when Count Olaf Labinski, at Dr. Cherbonneau's, had leaned over the magical glass of water evoking with all the force of a fixed idea an adored image. From that instant, submerged in the fathomless ocean of a magnetic slumber, the count had been without thought, feeling, or volition.

Having finished the countess' toilet, the maids withdrew. Octave-Labinski remained standing, gazing at Prascovie with a look of passion.

Constrained and oppressed by his expression, the countess wrapped herself in her burnous like Polymnia in her draperies. Only her head appeared above the blue-and-white folds, uneasy but charming.

No human penetration could divine the mysterious displacement of souls performed by Dr. Cherbonneau by means of the Sannyâsi Brahma-Logum formula; still Prascovie did not recognize in the eyes of Octave-Labinski her husband's usual expression, that look of love, chaste, calm, equal, eternal as the love of angels. This look was kindled by an earthly passion which troubled her and made her blush. She did not understand what it was, but she knew something had happened. A thousand wild suppositions crossed her mind. Was she no longer for Olaf anything but a common woman, desired for her beauty like a courtesan? Had the sublime accord of their souls been broken by some dissonance of which she was ignorant? Did Olaf love another, or had the corruptions of Paris sullied the purity of his heart? She asked herself these questions rapidly without being able to answer them in a satisfactory manner, and she told herself she was foolish, but still she felt afraid. A secret terror invaded her as though she were in the presence of some danger, unknown, but divined by that second sight of the mind which it is always wrong to disobey.

Nervous and agitated, she arose and went toward the door of the bedroom. The pseudo count accompanied her as Othello leads away Desdemona at each exit in Shakespeare's play, with one arm around her waist; but when she was on the threshold she turned white and cold as a statue, stopped a second, gave a timorous glance at the young man, then entered, closed the door quickly, and shot the bolt.

"Octave's look!" she cried, and sank fainting on a sofa. As her senses came back she said to herself: "But how is it that this look which I have never forgotten shines to-night in Olaf's eyes? Why have I seen its gloomy and despairing flame sparkle in the pupils of my husband? Is Octave dead? Is it his soul which gleamed before me an instant to bid me farewell on leaving this world? Olaf! Olaf! If I was mistaken, if I foolishly yielded to empty fears, you will forgive me; but if I had welcomed you to-night I should have thought I was giving myself to another."

The countess assured herself that the door was well bolted, lighted a pendent lamp, and with a sensation of indefinable anguish like a timid child she hid herself in the bed. Towards morning she fell asleep; but strange and incoherent dreams tormented her restless slumber. Ardent eyes—Octave's eyes—stared at her from a mist, and darted at her forks of fire; while at the foot of her bed crouched a black and wrinkled figure, muttering syllables in an unknown tongue. Count Olaf also appeared in this absurd dream, but clothed in a form which was not his own.

We will not attempt to portray Octave's disappointment when he found himself facing a closed door and heard the bolt grating inside. His supreme hope had failed. He had had recourse to strange and terrible methods; he had surrendered himself to a magician, perhaps a demon, risking his life in this world, and his soul in the next, to conquer a woman who escaped him, though rendered defenseless by the sorcery of India. Repulsed as a lover, he was not more fortunate as a husband; Prascovie's invincible purity thwarted the most infernal plots. On the door-sill of the bedchamber she had seemed to him like one of Swedenborg's white angels anathematizing the Evil Spirit.

He could not stay all night in this ridiculous position, so he looked for the count's apartment. At the end of a suite of rooms he found one which contained an ebony columned bed with tapestry curtains, where amid the scrolls and flowers was embroidered a coat-of-arms. The panoplies of Oriental armor, knights' cuirasses and helmets, touched by the reflection of a lamp, threw vague glimmers into the shadow. Bohemian leather stamped with gold gleamed on the walls. Three or four huge carved armchairs and a heavy cabinet loaded with ornaments completed this mediaeval furniture, which would not have been out of place in the great hall of a Gothic manor. On the count's part this was not a frivolous imitation of the fashion, but a hallowed memory. The room exactly reproduced the one he had inhabited at his mother's, and though often laughed at about it—this fifth-act scenery—he had always refused to change its style.

Octave-Labinski, exhausted with fatigue and emotion, flung himself on the bed and fell asleep, cursing Dr. Balthazar Cherbonneau.

Fortunately, the morning brought with it serener thoughts; he promised himself to act hereafter in a more moderate fashion, to dull his glances, and to assume the manners of a husband. Aided by the count's valet, he dressed himself in a plain and simple costume, and went quietly down to the dining-room to breakfast with the countess.

X

Octave-Labinski walked in the footsteps of the valet, for in this house of which he was the apparent master he did not know where the dining-room was. It was a vast room on the ground floor, opening on the court, and in its noble and severe style recalled both an abbey and a manor. Dark oak wainscoting, arranged in symmetrical designs, reached to the ceiling, where plaster moulded in relief formed hexagonal panels painted blue and delicately arabesqued in gold. On the long panels of the wood-work Philippe Rousseau had painted the four seasons symbolically, not in mythological figures, but by trophies of still-life composed of the fruits appropriate to each season of the year. Game by Jadin corresponded to the fruits of Rousseau, and above each painting gleamed like the disk of a shield an immense plate by Bernard Palissy or Léonard de Limoges, of Japanese porcelain, Majolica or Arabian pottery, the glaze opalescent with all the colors of the prism. Stags' antlers and aurochs' horns alternated with the faience, and at each end of the room rose a large sideboard, as high as the altar-pieces in Spanish churches, of elaborate architecture and carved decoration, and rivaling the most beautiful works of Berruguete, Cornejo Duque, and Verbruggen. On their shelves glittered in confusion the antique silver of the Labinski family. Pitchers with fantastic handles, salt-cellars of ancient shape, large bowls, drinking-cups, centre pieces shaped by the quaint German fancy, all worthy of a place amid the treasures of the Dresden Green Vault. Opposite the antique plate shone the marvelous products of modern silverware. The masterpieces of Wagner, Duponchel, Rudolphi, and Froment-Meurice; enameled tea-sets with figures by Feuchère and Vechte; chased salvers, champagne coolers with vine-leaved handles, and bacchanals in bas-relief, chafing-dishes as graceful as the Pompeian tripods, not to mention the Bohemian crystal, the Venetian glass, and the services in old Saxe and old Sèvres.

Oak chairs covered with green morocco were ranged along the walls, and over a table of which the feet were carved like eagle's claws there fell a clear, equal light through the ground white glass set in the centre panel of the ceiling. A transparent wreath of vine-leaves framed this milky square with green foliage. On the table, set in Russian fashion, the fruit was already placed, surrounded by a garland of violets; and under silver covers that were polished like emirs' helmets, the viands awaited the knife and fork. A Moscow samovar hissed forth a jet of steam; and two footmen in knee-breeches and white cravats stood silent and immovable behind the two armchairs, facing each other like domestic statues.

Octave, in order not to be involuntarily preoccupied by the novelty of objects with which he ought to have been familiar, took in all these things at a glance.

A rustle on the marble slabs, a murmur of silk, made him turn his head. It was the Countess Prascovie Labinska who approached and seated herself, after making him an amicable little gesture. She wore a morning gown of pale green and white plaid silk trimmed with a pinked ruching of the same material. Her hair lay in thick waves on her temples, and was gathered at the nape of her neck in a golden coil resembling the scroll of an Ionian pillar, a style as simple as it was dignified, and which a Greek sculptor could not have wished to change. Her rose-tinted cheeks were delicately blanched by the evening's emotion and the agitated sleep of the night. An imperceptible aureole of shadow encircled her eyes, usually so clear and calm. She had a weary, languid air; but thus softened, her beauty was only the more penetrating; it acquired a human touch, the goddess became a woman, the angel, folding her wings, ceased to soar.

Octave, grown prudent, veiled the flame in his eyes with a look of indifference.

The countess, with a slight motion of the shoulders as if chilled by a remnant of fever, stretched out her small bronze-slippered foot to the silky wool of a rug that had been placed under the table to neutralize the cold contact of the mosaic of white and Veronese variegated marble which paved the dining-room. Fixing her blue eyes on her companion, whom she took for her husband, for with the daylight had vanished the presentiments, the fears, and the phantoms of the night, she spoke a sentence in Polish in a tender, melodious voice, rich with chaste caresses. In moments of affection and intimacy she often used the dear maternal language with the count, especially in the presence of French servants to whom this idiom was unfamiliar.

The Parisian Octave was well up in Latin, Italian, Spanish, and knew a few words of English; but, like all Gallo-Romans, he was entirely ignorant of the Slavic tongues. The bristling bastion of consonants which protects the rare vowels in Polish would have inhibited his access even had he wished to approach it. In Florence the countess had always spoken to him in French or Italian, and the idea of learning the language in which Mickiewicz has almost equaled Byron had not occurred to him. It is impossible to think of everything.

On hearing this phrase, there took place in the count's brain, inhabited by the mind of Octave, a very singular phenomenon. The sounds, so strange to the Parisian, following the folds of a Slav ear reached the usual place where Olaf's mind received and transferred them into thoughts, and evoked there a sort of physical remembrance. Octave had a confused idea of their meaning; words hidden in the cerebral circumvolutions, in the secret recesses of memory, arose buzzing, ready to reply; but these vague reminiscences, failing to communicate with the mind, soon dispersed, and all was again a blank. The poor lover's embarrassment was dreadful; in taking the form of Count Olaf Labinski, he had not dreamed of this complication, and he realized that in seizing his position he had exposed himself to severe disasters.

Astonished at Octave's silence, and fancying that through some momentary abstraction he had not heard her, Prascovie repeated her remark slowly and in a louder tone.

If he heard more plainly the sound of the words, the pseudo-count understood their signification none the better. He made desperate efforts to guess what it might be about, but for those who do not know them the dense languages of the North have no transparency, and if a Frenchman can surmise what an Italian says, he is deaf when listening to a Pole. In spite of himself, a violent blush covered his cheeks, he bit his lips, and to keep himself in countenance hacked furiously at the meat on his plate.

"One would certainly suppose, my sweet prince," said the countess this time in French, "that you do not hear, or that you do not understand me."

"Really," faltered Octave-Labinski, hardly knowing what he said, "that terrible language is so difficult!"

"Difficult! Yes! perhaps it is for strangers; but for those who have stammered it at their mother's knee it springs from the lips like the breath of life, and with the unconsciousness of thought."

"Yes, doubtless; but there are times when it seems to me as if I no longer know it."

"What are you saying, Olaf? What! you have forgotten the language of your ancestors, the language of the Fatherland, the language which enables you to recognize your brothers among men, and," added she in a lower voice, "the language in which you first told me you loved me!"

"The habit of using another tongue . . ." ventured Octave-Labinski, at the end of his arguments.

"Olaf," answered the countess reproachfully, "I see that Paris has spoiled you; I was right in not wishing to come here. Who could have told me that when the noble Count Labinski returned to his domains he would no longer know how to reply to the felicitations of his vassals?"

Prascovie's charming countenance assumed a doleful expression; for the first time sadness cast its shadow on her angelically smooth brow. This strange forgetfulness wounded her inmost soul, and seemed almost treasonable.

The rest of the breakfast passed in silence. Prascovie frowned on the man whom she thought the count. Octave was in torment, for he dreaded other questions which he would be compelled to leave unanswered. At last the countess rose and returned to her rooms.

Left alone, Octave played with the handle of a knife which he was tempted to thrust in his heart, for his situation was unbearable. He had counted on a surprise, and now he found himself involved in the to him issueless labyrinths of an unknown existence. In assuming the body of Count Olaf Labinski he should also have taken from him his previous ideas, the languages he knew, his childhood's memories, the thousand intimate details which compose a man's self, the links binding his existence to the existences of others. But for that, all Dr. Balthazar Cherbonneau's knowledge would not have sufficed. What a fate! actually to be in this paradise whose threshold he had hardly dared glance at from afar, to live under the same roof with Prascovie, see her, speak to her, kiss her hand with the very lips of her husband, and yet be unable to deceive her divine modesty, and to betray himself every instant by some inexplicable stupidity! "It was written above that Prascovie would never love me! And yet I have made the greatest sacrifice to which mortal pride can descend; I have renounced my *self,* I have consented to profit under a strange form by caresses destined for another!"

At this point in his monologue a groom bowed before him and asked, with every sign of the deepest respect, what horse he would ride. Seeing that the count did not answer, the man, much frightened at his own boldness, risked murmuring—

"Vultur or Rustem? they have not been out for a week."

"Rustem," replied Octave-Labinski, as he would have said Vultur had not the last name clung to his distraught mind.

He dressed for riding and started for the Bois de Boulogne, wishing to give his shaken nerves a bath of fresh air.

Rustem, a magnificent animal of the Nedji race, that carried on his breast, in an Oriental bag of gold-embroidered velvet, titles to a nobility extending back to the first years of the hegira, did not need to be roused. He seemed to understand his rider's thoughts, and as soon as he had left the pavements and struck the bridle-paths he started off, fleet as an arrow, before Octave had touched him with the spur. After two hours of hard riding the horseman and his beast returned to the hotel, the one quite calm, and the other fuming, with scarlet nostrils.

The pseudo-count joined the countess, whom he found in her drawing-room, dressed in a gown of white silk flounced to the waist, a knot of ribbon in her hair.

It was Thursday, the day on which she remained at home and received her visitors.

"Well," she said to him, with a gracious smile, for her beautiful lips could not pout for long, "have you regained your memory galloping in the alleys of the Bois?"

"No, my dear," replied Octave-Labinski, "but I have a confession to make."

"Do I not know in advance all your thoughts? Are we no longer transparent to each other?"

"Yesterday I went to see the physician who is so much talked about."

"Yes, Dr. Balthazar Cherbonneau, who made a long stay in India, and has, they say, learned from the Brahmans a lot of secrets, each more marvelous than the other. You even wished to take me, but I am not curious; for I know you love me, and that knowledge is all I require."

"He made such singular experiments before me, he produced such miraculous effects, that my mind is still disturbed by them. This eccentric fellow, who has an irresistible power at his disposal, threw me into a magnetic sleep so profound that on awakening I no longer had the same faculties. I had lost the remembrance of many things. The past floated in a mist of obscurity; my love for you alone remained intact."

"You were wrong, Olaf, to put yourself under the influence of this physician. God, who has created the soul, has the right to touch it," said the countess in a grave tone; "but man in attempting to do so commits an impious action. I hope that you will not go back there, and I hope, too, that when I say something agreeable to you—in Polish—you will understand me as you once did."

During his ride Octave had conceived this excuse of magnetism to palliate the errors which he could not fail to make in his new life. But his troubles were not ended. A servant opening the door announced a visitor.

"M. Octave de Saville."

Though he might have expected this meeting one day or another, at these simple words the real Octave trembled as if the trumpet of the last judgment had suddenly sounded in his ear. He had need to call up all his courage, and to tell himself that he had the best of the situation, to prevent himself from reeling. Instinctively he clutched the back of a chair, and thus managed to stand apparently firm and tranquil.

Count Olaf, clothed in the form of Octave, advanced towards the countess with a deep bow.

"The Count Labinski . . . M. Octave de Saville," said the countess, presenting the gentlemen.

The two men bowed coldly, and over the marble mask of worldly politeness which sometimes covers such evil passions shot savage glances at each other.

"You have grown formal since Florence days, Monsieur Octave," said the countess in a familiar and friendly tone, "and I was afraid I should leave Paris without seeing you. You were more assiduous at the Villa Salviati, and you were numbered among the faithful."

"Madam," the pseudo-Octave answered constrainedly, "I have traveled, I have been ailing, ill even, and on receiving your gracious invitation I asked myself whether I should profit by it, for one must not be an egotist and abuse the indulgence that people are good enough to have for a bore."

"Bored perhaps, but never a bore," replied the countess. "You have always been melancholy; yet does not one of your poets say of melancholy,

'After idleness, 't is the best of ills'?"

"It is a report which happy people spread to dispense themselves from pitying those who suffer," said Olaf-de Saville.

As if to beg his pardon for the love with which she had involuntarily inspired him, the countess cast a look of ineffable sweetness on the count, shut up in Octave's body.

"You think me more frivolous than I am; all real pain has my pity, and if I cannot relieve, I can at least commiserate. I would like to have had you happy, dear Monsieur Octave; but why have you immured yourself in sadness, why have you refused the life which came to you with its joys, its seductions, and its duties? Why have you refused my proffered friendship?"

These simple and sincere phrases impressed the two listeners differently. Octave heard in them the confirmation of the judgment pronounced in the Salviati garden by this perfect mouth unsoiled by lies; and Olaf, a proof of his wife's unalterable virtue, which nothing but diabolical cunning could overcome. And a sudden madness seized him on seeing his spectre animated by another soul installed in his own house. He sprang at the throat of the false count.

"Thief, brigand, rogue, give me back my body!"

At this most extraordinary action the countess rushed to the bell and the footmen carried out the count.

"That poor Octave has gone crazy!" said Prascovie while Olaf, struggling vainly, was being taken away.

"Yes," answered the real Octave, "crazy with love! Countess, you are decidedly too beautiful!"

XI

Two hours after this scene the false count received from the real one a letter bearing the seal of Octave de Saville—the unhappy dispossessed Olaf had no other at his disposal. It produced an odd effect on the usurper of Count Labinski's body to open a missive sealed with his own crest, but everything had to be peculiar in this abnormal position.

The letter contained the following lines, traced by a stiff hand, in a writing which looked like counterfeit, for Olaf was not accustomed to holding a pen with Octave's fingers:—

"Read by another than yourself, this letter would appear to be dated from a lunatic asylum, but you will understand it. An inexplicable combination of circumstances never before produced, perhaps, since the earth has turned about the sun forces me to act as no man has ever done. I write to myself and put on the address a name which is my own, a name which with my person you have stolen from me. I am ignorant of the plot of which I am the victim and of the circle of infernal illusions into which I have put my foot. You, of course, know all about it.

"If you are not a coward, the mouth of my pistol or the point of my sword will demand of you this secret on a ground where every man, honorable or infamous, answers the questions put to him. To-morrow one of us must have ceased to see the light of day. The universe is now too narrow for us both. I will kill my body filled with your lying spirit, or you will kill yours, wherein my soul rages at being imprisoned.

"Do not try to prove me crazy. I shall have the strength to be reasonable, and everywhere I meet you I will insult you with the politeness of a gentleman and the coolness of a diplomat. The Count Olaf Labinski's mustache may displease M. Octave de Saville, and, every day, feet are trodden on at the exit of the Opéra. I trust that my words, though obscure, will have no ambiguity for you, and that my seconds will come to a perfect understanding with yours as to the hour, the place, and the conditions of the duel."

This letter threw Octave into a quandary. He could not refuse the count's challenge, and yet it went against him to fight with himself, for he had kept a sort of tenderness for his old envelope. The idea of being forced into this duel by some open insult made him decide to accept it, though if necessary he could have put his adversary into a lunatic's strait-jacket and thus stayed his arm; but his delicacy revolted at such a method. If carried along by an overpowering passion he had committed a reprehensible action and hidden the lover under the disguise of the husband to triumph over a virtue above all seduction, he was still a man not without honor and courage. Besides, he had not taken this extreme step until, after three years of struggle and suffering, the moment had arrived when his life, consumed by love, was escaping him. He did not know the count; he was not his friend, he owed him nothing, and he had profited by the hazardous means which Dr. Balthazar Cherbonneau had offered to him.

Where find seconds? Of course among the count's friends; but Octave in the one day he had lived in the house had had no chance to meet them.

On the mantelpiece were two vases of china with gold dragons for handles. One held rings, pins, seals, and other trifling jewels—the other, visiting cards, on which, under the coronet of duke, marquis, or count, were inscribed by skilled engravers in Gothic, round, or English type a multitude of names, Polish, Russian, Hungarian, German, Italian, Spanish, and attesting the roving existence of the count, who had friends in every land.

Octave took two hap-hazard: Count Zamoieczki and the Marquis de Sepulveda. He ordered the carriage, and drove to their addresses. He found them both in. They did not appear surprised at the request of the man whom they thought Count Olaf Labinski. Totally devoid of the sensitiveness of middle-class seconds, they did not ask if the affair could be compromised, and like the perfect gentlemen they were maintained a silence full of good taste as to the motive of the quarrel.

On his side, the real count, or, if you like it better, the pseudo-Octave, was a prey to a similar embarrassment. He remembered Alfred Humbert and Gustave Raimbaud, whose breakfast he had refused to attend, and he requested them to help him in this encounter. The two young men showed considerable surprise at finding their friend involved in a duel, for he had hardly left his room in a year, and they knew his character was more pacific than quarrelsome. But when he had told them that it was a mortal combat, they made no further objections, and went to the Hotel Labinski.

The conditions were soon arranged. The adversaries having declared that sword or pistol suited them equally well, a gold coin thrown in the air decided the weapon. They were to meet in the Avenue des Poteaux of the Bois de Boulogne, near the rustic thatched summer-house, where the fine gravel offers a favorable arena for this sort of combat.

When all was settled it was nearly midnight, and Octave went to the door of Prascovie's apartment. As on the previous evening it was bolted, and the countess' mocking voice flung this sarcasm at him through the door—

"Come back when you know Polish; I am too patriotic to receive a foreigner."

Notified by Octave, Dr. Cherbonneau came in the morning, carrying a case of surgical instruments and a roll of bandages. They entered a carriage together, MM. Zamoieczki and de Sepulveda following in their coupé.

"Well, my dear Octave," said the physician; "so the adventure is already turning into tragedy? I ought to have let the count sleep in your body on my divan for a week. I have prolonged magnetic slumbers beyond that limit. But even when one has learned wisdom from the Brahmans, the Pandit, and the Sannyâsis of India, one always forgets something, and imperfections are found in the best combined plans. But how did Countess Prascovie welcome her Florence lover thus disguised?"

"I think," replied Octave, "that either she recognized me notwithstanding my metamorphosis, or else her guardian angel whispered in her ear to distrust me. I found her as chaste, as cold, as pure, as polar snow. Doubtless her exquisite nature divined a stranger under the beloved form of her husband. I told you truly that you could do nothing for me; indeed I am even more unhappy than when you paid me your first visit."

"Who can fix a boundary to the soul's power," said Dr. Balthazar

Cherbonneau thoughtfully, "especially when it is weakened by no earthly preoccupation, soiled by no human tie, and keeps itself in the glow and contemplation of love just as it left the Creator's hands? Yes, you are right; she recognized you, her heavenly modesty shrank at the look of desire, and instinctively veiled itself with its white wings. I pity you, my poor Octave! Your wound is indeed immedicable. Were we in the Middle Ages, I should say, Get thee to a monastery."

"I have often thought of it," replied Octave.

Presently they reached the meeting ground. The counterfeit Octave's brougham was already at the place designated.

At this early hour the Bois presented a really picturesque aspect, which later in the day fashion makes it lose. Summer was at that stage when the sun has not yet had time to darken the green of the foliage; fresh, translucent tints, washed by the night's dew, variegated the forest, and gave out an odor of tender vegetation. At this spot the trees are particularly fine; perhaps because they have encountered a more favorable soil, or because they are the only survivors of some old plantation. Their vigorous trunks, stained with moss or glossed with a silvery bark, clutch the earth with gnarled roots, and project oddly bent branches. They might have served as models for the studies of artists and decorators who go much further to seek less remarkable ones. A few birds, which later the day's noises silence, chirped gayly in the leafy retreat; a timid rabbit crossed the gravel of the alley in three bounds and ran to hide in the grass, frightened at the sound of the wheels.

These poems of nature surprised in undress occupied the two adversaries and their seconds very little, as you can imagine. The sight of Dr. Balthazar Cherbonneau made a disagreeable impression on Count Olaf Labinski, but he recovered himself quickly.

The swords were measured, their places assigned to the combatants, who after taking off their coats fell into position.

"Ready!" the seconds cried.

In every duel, no matter what the fury of the adversaries may be, there is a moment of solemn immobility: each combatant silently studies his enemy and makes his plan, reflecting on the attack and preparing to parry and thrust. Then the swords seek, provoke, and feel each other, so to speak, without separating; that lasts several seconds, which seem minutes, hours, to the anxiety of the assistants.

The conditions of this duel, apparently commonplace to the spectators, were so abnormal for the combatants that they remained thus on guard longer than is customary. Each had in front of him his own body, and must drive the steel into flesh which had belonged to himself two days before.

The fight was complicated by a sort of unforeseen suicide, and, though both were brave, yet Octave and the count felt an instinctive horror at standing, sword in hand, face to face with their own phantoms, and ready to fall on themselves. The impatient seconds were about to cry again, "Gentlemen, are you ready!" when at last the blades crossed.

Several attacks were parried with agility on each side.

Thanks to his military education, the count was a skillful fencer; he had pinked the plastron of the most famous masters. But if he still had the method he no longer possessed the muscular arm which had routed the Mourides of Schamyl; it was Octave's weak wrist which wielded his sword.

Octave on the contrary felt, in the count's body, an unaccustomed strength, and though less expert, he always parried the steel which sought his breast.

It was in vain that Olaf strove to touch his adversary and risked thrusts which exposed himself. Octave, cooler and more steady, baffled every feint.

The count began to get excited, and his play grew nervous and uneven. Though he would then have to remain Octave de Saville, he wanted to kill this deceptive body which might even deceive Prascovie—a thought which lashed him into an inexpressible rage.

At the risk of being run through, he tried a straight thrust to reach, through his own body, the life and heart of his rival; but Octave's sword wound round his with such a quick, sharp, irresistible movement that the steel was wrenched from his hand, and springing in the air fell several steps away.

Olaf's life was at Octave's disposal; he had only to thrust and run him through.

The count's face quivered; not that he feared death, but he thought that he was about to leave his wife to this body-thief whom nothing hereafter could unmask.

Far from profiting by his advantage, Octave threw down his sword, and motioning to the seconds not to interfere walked towards the stupefied count, whom he took by the arm and dragged into the depth of the wood.

"What do you want with me?" said the count. "Why not kill me when you have the chance? Why not continue the duel after letting me recover my sword if it revolts you to strike an unarmed man? You know that the sun should not cast the shadows of both of us on the ground, and that the earth must receive one or the other."

"Listen to me patiently," replied Octave. "Your happiness is in my hands. I can keep forever this body in which I dwell to-day and which in legitimate propriety belongs to you. It suits me to acknowledge this now that there are no witnesses near us, and only the wild birds, who never repeat, can hear. Count Olaf Labinski, whom I represent as well as I can, is a better fencer than Octave de Saville, whose form you now have, and which I, much to my regret, would be obliged to suppress. This death, though not real, as my soul would survive, would desolate my mother."

Recognizing the truth of these remarks, the count maintained an acquiescent silence.

"If I should oppose it," continued Octave, "you would never succeed in reintegrating your identity; you see in what your two attempts ended. Other trials would stamp you as a monomaniac. No one would believe a word of your allegations, and, as you have already been able to convince yourself, when you pretended to be Count Olaf Labinski every one would laugh in your face. You would be shut up, and you would pass the rest of your life protesting under the shower-bath that you were actually the husband of the beautiful Countess Prascovie Labinska. Compassionate souls would say on hearing you: Poor Octave! And you would be disowned like Balzac's Chabert who wished to prove he was not dead."

This was all so mathematically true that the discouraged count let his head fall on his breast.

"As you are at present Octave de Saville you have doubtless

searched his desk and rummaged among his papers, and you are not ignorant that for three years he has nourished for the Countess Prascovie Labinska a desperate, hopeless love, which he has tried in vain to tear from his heart, and which will only leave him with his life, unless it follows him to the tomb."

"Yes, I know it," said the count, biting his lip.

"Well, to reach her I have employed terrible means, on which a delirious passion alone would venture. Dr. Cherbonneau has attempted for me a task that would startle the thaumaturgists of the universe. After putting us both to sleep he changed the envelopes of our souls. But in vain! I will return you your body: Prascovie does not love me! Under the husband's form she recognized the lover's soul; her look was the same on the threshold of the conjugal apartment as in the garden of the Villa Salviati."

Octave's tone betrayed such true sorrow that the count had faith in his words.

"I am a lover," added Octave, smiling, "and not a thief, and as the only thing which I desired in this world cannot belong to me, I do not see why I should keep your titles, castles, lands, money, horses, and weapons. There, give me your arm; let us appear reconciled, thank our seconds, take with us Dr. Cherbonneau, and return to the magical laboratory from which we came forth transformed. The old Brahman will know how to undo his work."

"Gentlemen," said Octave, sustaining for a little longer the part of Count Olaf Labinski, "my adversary and I have exchanged confidential explications which render the continuation of the duel useless. There is nothing like crossing swords a bit to clear the minds of sensible people."

MM. Zamoieczki and de Sepulveda reëntered their carriage, and Alfred Humbert and Gustave Raimbaud regained theirs, while Count Olaf Labinski, Octave de Saville, and Dr. Cherbonneau drove at full speed towards the Rue du Regard.

XII

During the transit from the Bois de Boulogne to the Rue du Regard, Octave de Saville said to Dr. Cherbonneau—

"My dear doctor, I am about to test your science once more; you must restore our souls, each to its customary habitation. That should not be difficult for you. I hope that Count Labinski will not be angry at you for having made him change a palace for a hovel, and lodging his illustrious personality for some hours in my poor individuality. But then, you possess a power which fears nothing."

With an acquiescent gesture Dr. Balthazar Cherbonneau replied: "The operation will be much simpler this time; the imperceptible filaments which hold the soul to the body have with you been recently broken, and have not had time to be renewed, and your minds will not form that obstacle which the instinctive resistance of the magnetized opposes to the magnetizer. The count will doubtless pardon an old erudite like myself for not having been able to resist the pleasure of putting in practice an experiment for which one finds but few subjects, and particularly as this attempt has only served to brilliantly confirm a virtue which carries delicacy to divination and triumphs where every other would have succumbed. If you wish, you can look on this momentary transformation as a strange dream, and perhaps, later, you will not be sorry to have experienced the odd sensation, which few men have known, of having inhabited two bodies. Metempsychosis is not a new doctrine; but before transmigrating into another existence the souls drink the cup of forgetfulness, and every one cannot, like Pythagoras, remember to have assisted at the Trojan war."

"The benefit of being reinstalled in my own individuality," the count answered politely, "equals the unpleasantness of having been expropriated from it; this is said without ill-feeling for M. Octave de Saville, whom I still am, and whom I am about to cease to be."

Octave smiled with the lips of Count Labinski at this sentence, which could only reach him through another's envelope, and silence established itself between these three persons whose abnormal situation rendered all conversation difficult.

The unfortunate Octave thought of his vanished hope, and his reflections were not, it must be owned, precisely rose-color. Like all repulsed lovers, he still asked himself why he was not loved—as if love had a why! The only reason one can give it is the *because,* a reply logical in its obstinate laconism, and which women oppose to all embarrassing questions. Nevertheless, he recognized his defeat, and felt that the spring of life, which for an instant Dr. Cherbonneau had renovated for him, was newly broken, and rattled in his heart like that of a watch dropped on the ground. Octave would not have caused his mother the sorrow of his suicide; and he sought a spot wherein he might extinguish his unknown grief quietly under the scientific name of a plausible illness. Had he been an artist, poet, or musician, he would have crystallized his pain in masterpieces; and Prascovie, robed in white, crowned with stars, like Dante's Beatrice, would have hovered about his inspiration like an angel of light; but, as has been intimated at the beginning of this story, though well instructed and gifted, Octave was not one of those chosen spirits who imprint on this earth the trace of their passage. In his obscure sublimity he only knew how to love and die.

The carriage entered the court of the old hotel in the Rue du Regard, a court whose pavement was set in green grass through which the visitors' steps had worn a path, and which the high gray walls of the building inundated with shadow, like that which falls from a cloister's arcades; Silence and Immobility, like invisible statues, watched on the threshold protecting the meditations of the erudite.

When Octave and the count had alighted, the physician jumped from the carriage with a lighter step than one would have expected from his age, without even leaning on the arm which the footman offered to him with that politeness which servants of large establishments affect towards old or feeble persons.

As soon as the double doors had closed on them, Olaf and Octave felt themselves wrapped in the hot atmosphere which recalled to the physician that of India, and in which only he could breathe at his ease, but which almost suffocated those who had not, like him, been for thirty years torrified in tropical suns. The incarnations of Vishnu still leered in their frames, weirder by day than by lamplight; Shiva, the blue god, sneered on his pedestal; and Dourga, biting his callous lip with his wild boar's tusks, seemed to agitate his chaplet of skulls. The apartment retained its magical and mysterious appearance. Dr. Balthazar Cherbonneau led his two subjects to the room where the first transformation had taken place. He turned the glass disk of the electric machine, shook the iron rods of the mesmeric battery, opened the hot-air registers to make the temperature rise rapidly, read two or three lines from parchments so ancient that they resembled old bark ready to crumble into dust, and, when several minutes had elapsed, said to Octave and the count—

"Gentlemen, I am at your service; shall we begin?"

While the physician was making these preparations, disquieting reflections passed through the count's mind.

"When I am asleep, what is this old lugubrious-faced magician, who might be the devil himself, going to do with my soul? Will he restore it to my body, or will he carry it off to hell with him? Is not this exchange, which ought to give me back my happiness, a Machiavellian combination for some sorcery whose end escapes me? Still, my position could not be worse. Octave possesses my body, and, as he wisely remarked this morning, in reclaiming it with my present figure I should cause myself to be shut up as a lunatic. If he wished to put me definitely out of his way, he had only to drive in the point of his sword; I was disarmed, at his mercy; the justice of man could have said nothing against it; the form of the duel was perfectly regular, and it would have been done all in order. I must think of Prascovie and have no childish fears. Let me try the only way which is left me to regain her!"

And, like Octave, he grasped the rod which Dr. Balthazar Cherbonneau presented to him.

Overpowered by the metal conductors, charged to the utmost with electric fluid, the two young men sank into an unconsciousness so profound that to any one unprepared for it it would have resembled death. The physician made the passes, performed the rites, pronounced the syllables as on the first occasion, and soon two luminous stars appeared above Octave and the count. The physician led to its original abode Count Olaf Labinski's soul, which followed the electrician's gesture with an eager flight.

During this time Octave's soul moved slowly from Olaf's body, and instead of rejoining its own, rose, rose as if glad to be free, and appeared indifferent to its prison. The physician was touched with pity for the fluttering, winged Psyche, and asked himself if it were a kindness to bring it back to this vale of misery. In this momentary hesitation the soul continued to ascend. Remembering his part, M. Cherbonneau repeated with the most imperious accent the irresistible monosyllable, and made a pass pregnant with volition, but the tiny quivering spark was already out of the circle of attraction, and swiftly traversing the upper pane of the window it disappeared.

The physician ceased making efforts which he knew to be useless, and awakened the count, who, seeing himself in a mirror with his usual features, gave a cry of joy, threw a glance at Octave's immobile body to make sure that he was thoroughly clear of that envelope, and with a nod of farewell to M. Balthazar Cherbonneau rushed away.

A few seconds later the muffled roll of a carriage under the arch was heard, and Dr. Balthazar Cherbonneau was alone face to face with the corpse of Octave de Saville.

"By the trunk of Ganesa!" exclaimed the pupil of the Brahman of Elephanta when the count had gone, "this is a provoking affair. I opened the cage-door, the bird flew away, and now it is already beyond the sphere of this world, so far indeed that the Sannyâsi Brahma-Logum himself could not overtake it, and here am I with a corpse on my hands. It is true, I can dissolve it in a corrosive bath of such strength that not an appreciable atom will remain, or I can make of it in a few hours a beautiful mummy, like those inclosed in cases covered with variegated hieroglyphs; but inquiries will be started, my dwelling searched, my chests opened, myself subjected to all sorts of tiresome questions . . ." Here a bright idea crossed the physician's mind; he seized a pen and wrote rapidly a few lines on a sheet of paper, which he put in the drawer of his table.

The paper contained these words:

"Having neither relatives nor connections, I bequeath all my belongings to M. Octave de Saville, for whom I have a particular affection, on condition that he pays a legacy of one hundred thousand francs to the Brahmanic hospital of Ceylon for old, worn-out, and sick animals; that he gives twelve hundred francs yearly for life to my Indian and to my English servant; and that he sends the manuscript of the laws of Manu to the Mazarin library."

This testament made to a dead man by a living one is not the strangest thing in this story, improbable yet true; but the singularity of it will be at once explained.

The physician felt Octave de Saville's body, from which the warmth of life had not yet departed, looked in the glass, with a singularly disdainful air, at his own wrinkled face, tanned and rough like a zebra's skin, and making over his head the motion with which one throws off an old coat when the tailor brings a new one, he muttered the formula of the Sannyâsi Brahma-Logum.

Immediately, Dr. Balthazar Cherbonneau's body fell to the floor as if struck by a thunderbolt, and that of Octave de Saville rose up in full strength and activity.

Octave-Cherbonneau stood for some minutes before the thin, bony, and livid carcass, which, no longer upheld by the powerful spirit that had before animated it, at once took on a look of complete senility, and rapidly assumed a cadaverous appearance.

"Farewell, poor human remnant, miserable out-at-elbow garment, frayed at every seam, which for seventy years I have dragged about the five parts of the globe! You did me good service, and I do not leave you without regret. One gets accustomed to living so long together! but with this young envelope, which my science will soon make robust, I can study, work, and read still a few words more in the great book before Death, saying 'It is enough!' closes it at the most interesting paragraph!"

After this funeral oration, addressed to himself, Octave-Cherbonneau went forth with a tranquil step to take possession of his new existence.

Count Olaf Labinski had returned to his house and had immediately sent to ask if the countess could receive him.

He found her in the conservatory seated on a bank of moss amid a virgin forest of exotic and tropical plants. The half-raised panes of glass admitted the warm, bright air. She was reading Novalis, one of the most subtile, rarefied, and immaterial authors which German spiritualism has produced. The countess did not like books which paint existence in strong, real colors; and, from having lived in a world of elegance, love, and poetry, life appeared to her a trifle coarse.

She threw down her book and slowly lifted her eyes to the count. She feared to encounter again in her husband's dark pupils that ardent, stormy look, full of mysterious thoughts, which had troubled her so much, and which had seemed to her—foolish apprehension—the look of another!

In Olaf's eyes shone a serene joy, and a pure, chaste love burned in them with a steady fire; the stranger soul, which had so, mysteriously changed the expression of his features, was gone forever. Prascovie at once recognized her adored Olaf, and a quick blush of pleasure colored her transparent cheeks. Though she was ignorant of the transformations performed by Dr. Cherbonneau, her delicate sensitiveness had unconsciously been aware of all these changes.

"What are you reading, dear Prascovie?" said Olaf, lifting from the moss the book bound in blue morocco. "Ah! the history of Henri d'Ofterdingen—it is the same volume that I went full gallop to get you at Mohilev, one day when you had expressed a wish for it at dinner. At midnight it was on the table beside your lamp; but poor Ralph was broken-winded ever after!"

"And I told you that I would never again mention the least desire before you. You have the character of that Spanish noble who prayed his mistress not to gaze at the stars, since he could not give them to her."

"If you looked at one," replied the count, "I should try to climb to heaven and ask it of God."

While listening to her husband the countess smoothed a refractory mesh of her hair which scintillated like a flame in a ray of gold. The motion had disarranged her sleeve, and uncovered her beautiful arm encircled at the wrist by the turquoise-studded lizard which she wore on the day of her apparition in the Cascine so fatal to Octave.

"What a fright that poor little lizard once gave you!" said the count. "It was when you had, on my insistent prayer, descended to the garden for the first time, and I killed it with the stroke of a switch. I had it dipped in gold and decorated with a few stones; but even as a trinket it still appeared disagreeable to you, and it was some time before you could bring yourself to wear it."

"Oh, I am quite accustomed to it now, and it is my favorite ornament, for it recalls a very dear remembrance."

"Yes," replied the count, "on that day we agreed that on the morrow I should make your aunt an official request for your hand."

The countess recognized the look and tone of the real Olaf, and reassured also by these intimate details, she rose smiling, took his arm, and made several turns about the conservatory with him, plucking with free hand as she went some flowers whose petals she pulled off with her fresh lips, looking as she did so like that Venus of Schiavoni's who is feasting on roses.

"As you have such a good memory to-day," she said, flinging from her the flower she had been mutilating with her pearly teeth, "you ought to have recovered the use of your mother-tongue . . . which yesterday you no longer knew."

"If souls retain a human language in paradise," answered the count in Polish, "it is the one my soul will speak in heaven to tell you that I love you."

Prascovie, still moving, let her head fall gently on Olaf's shoulder.

"Dear heart," she murmured, "now you are as I love you to be. Yesterday you frightened me, and I fled as from a stranger."

The next day Octave de Saville, animated by the spirit of the old physician, received a black-edged letter which begged him to assist at the funeral service and burial of M. Balthazar Cherbonneau.

Clothed in his new aspect, the physician followed his former body to the cemetery, saw himself buried, listened with a well-assumed air of regret to the address pronounced over his grave, in which the irreparable loss to science was deplored, and then returned to the Rue Saint-Lazare and awaited the opening of the will he had made in his own favor.

That day could be read among the items of the evening papers:

"Dr. Balthazar Cherbonneau, known by his long sojourn in India, his philological knowledge, and his marvelous cures, was yesterday found dead in his laboratory. A most thorough examination of the body has banished all idea of a crime. M. Cherbonneau probably succumbed to excessive mental fatigue, or perished in some audacious experiment. It is said that a will in the testator's own handwriting leaves to the Mazarin library some extremely valuable manuscripts, and names as heir a young man belonging to a distinguished family, M. O. de S."

Jettatura

I

The *Leopold,* a splendid Tuscan steamer plying between Marseilles and Naples, had just doubled Procida Point. The passengers, cured of their sea-sickness by the sight of land, most efficacious of all remedies, were all out on deck. On the part reserved for the first-class passengers stood a number of Englishmen endeavouring to get away as far as possible from one another and to trace around themselves a circle none might venture to enter. Their splenetic faces were carefully shaven, their cravats had not a wrinkle, their shirt collars, white and stiff, looked like triangles of Bristol board, their hands were protected by brand-new suede gloves, and their new boots shone with Lord Elliot's blacking. They looked as if they had just emerged from one of the compartments of their dressing-cases, for in their correct get-up there was visible none of the little disorders of dress that are the usual consequences of travel.

There were noblemen, members of Parliament, City merchants, tailors from Regent Street, and cutlers from Sheffield, all proper, grave, motionless, and bored. Nor were ladies wanting, for Englishwomen are not sedentary like the women of other lands, and the smallest pretext suffices to justify their leaving their island. By the side of the great ladies and of the wives of commoners, somewhat ripe beauties, with blotchy faces, bloomed, their faces half concealed by their blue veils, maidens with complexions of milk and roses, with shimmering golden tresses, and long white teeth, recalling the favourite types of "Keepsakes," and proving that English engravings are not so untrue to life as is often said. These lovely creatures repeated, each in turn, with the most delightful British accent, the obligatory *"Vedi Napoli e poi mori;"* perused their Murray or wrote down their impressions of travel in their notebooks,

217

without paying the least attention to the glances of a number of would-be Don Juans from Paris who roamed about in their vicinity, while the angry mammas grumbled about French impropriety.

On the edge of the aristocratic quarter-deck, strolled, while smoking their cigars, three or four young fellows whose straw or felt hats, sack-coats with huge horn buttons, and duck trousers, made it easy to recognise them as artists, a fact confirmed by their mustaches *à la* Van Dyck, their hair curled *à la* Rubens, or cropped short *à la* Paolo Veronese. Inspired by very different motives, they also were trying, like the dandies, to catch a glimpse of the beauties whom their lack of wealth forbade their approaching more closely, and these efforts somewhat interfered with their enjoyment of the magnificent panorama outspread before them.

In the bows of the vessel, leaning against the bulwarks or seated on coils of rope, were grouped the third-class passengers, engaged in consuming the provisions uneaten on account of the seasickness, and casting not one glance upon the finest view in the world, for the feeling of nature is the privilege of cultivated minds that are not absorbed wholly by the material needs of life.

The weather was fine; the blue waves rolled broadly on with scarcely enough power to efface the ship's wake. The smoke from the funnel, forming clouds in the glorious heavens, blew away softly in cottony flakes, and the paddle-wheels, revolving in an iridescent diamond spray, churned the water with joyous activity as if aware of the proximity of the harbour.

Already the purple lines of hills that, from Posilipo to Vesuvius, encircle the wondrous gulf at the upper end of which Naples lies like a sea-nymph resting and drying herself after her bath, were becoming more distinct and stood out more plainly against the brilliant azure of the heavens. Already a few white spots, showing on the darker background of the land, indicated the presence of towns scattered along the country-side. The sails of the homeward-bound fishing-boats slipped along the smooth blue waters like swans' feathers blown by the breeze, and spoke of human activity upon the majestic solitude of the sea.

Very soon the Castle of Saint-Elmo and the Convent di San Martino came out distinctly on the crest of the mountain on which stands Naples, showing above the domes of the churches, the terraces of the hotels, the fronts of the palaces, and the verdure of the gardens, which were as yet only faintly visible through a luminous haze. Then the Castello dell'Ovo, squatting on its foam-flecked reef, seemed to approach the steamer, and the pier with its lighthouse drew near like an arm holding a torch.

At the end of the bay, Vesuvius, now nearer, changed its blue tints, due to distance, for more vigorous and solid tones; its sides were seen to be furrowed with gullies and streams of lava grown cold, and from its truncated cone, as from the holes of a perfume-burner, plainly issued little jets of white smoke that wavered in the wind.

Chiatamone, Pizzo Falcone, the hotel-bordered quay of Santa Lucia, the Palazzo Nuovo, flanked with its balconied towers, the Arsenal, and ships of all nations, mingling their masts and spars like the trees of a leafless wood, were plainly to be seen, when there emerged from a cabin a passenger who had not shown up once during the whole trip, either because seasickness had kept him in confinement, or because his reserve prevented his mingling with his fellow-travellers, or again because the prospect, new to most of them, had long been a familiar sight to him and had ceased to excite his interest.

He was a young fellow of twenty-six to twenty-eight years. At least such was the age one felt tempted to give him at the first glance, though when he was examined attentively he seemed to be either younger or older than that, so curiously mingled were weariness and youthfulness upon his enigmatical countenance. His hair, of that dark fairness called auburn by the English, shone in the sunlight with coppery, metallic sheen, and in the shade seemed almost black. His profile was clear-cut, his brow would have called forth the admiration of a phrenologist, thanks to its protuberances, his nose was nobly aquiline, his lips well formed, and his chin had that powerful roundness which recalls the medals of antiquity. Yet these various features, individually handsome, did not form an agreeable whole. They lacked the mysterious harmony that softens contours and makes them melt into one another. There is a legend of an Italian painter who, seeking to represent the rebellious archangel, composed a face of dissimilar beauties and thus attained an effect of terror far beyond what is possible by the use of horns, arched eyebrows, and unholy grin. The stranger's face produced a similar impression. His eyes, in particular, were extraordinary. The black lashes that edged them contrasted with the pale gray colour of the pupils and the auburn shade of the hair; the thinness of the nose caused them to look nearer each other than was allowed by the rules of drawing, and as for their expression it was quite undefinable. When the young man's gaze did not consciously rest upon anything, it was moist with vague melancholy and soft tenderness, but if he looked at any one or anything, his brows bent and formed a perpendicular wrinkle on his forehead; the pupils lost their gray colour and turned green, spotted with black spots and striated with yellow lines; his glance then flashed sharply, almost painfully, after which he would resume his former placidity and from a Mephistophelian individual turn into a young man of the world—a member of the Jockey Club, if you like—on his way to spend the season in Naples, and glad to step on a lava floor less mobile than the *Leopold*'s deck.

His dress was elegant and did not draw the eye by any striking details. He wore a dark blue frock-coat and a black cravat with polka-dots, which was tied in a way that avoided both carelessness and over carefulness; a waistcoat of the same pattern as the tie, a pair of light gray trousers, and neat boots. His gold watch chain was of the plainest pattern, and the cord of his eyeglasses was of silk, tressed flat. In his well-gloved hand he carried a slender cane, made of a twisted vinestem, mounted in silver.

He took a few steps along the deck, his glance wandering idly over the shore, now drawing closer, and on which one could see the carriages driving along, the people crowding and the collecting of those groups of idlers to whom the arrival of a stage-coach or a steamer is an ever interesting and ever novel sight, even though they have gazed upon it a thousand times.

Already a flotilla of boats and other craft was starting for the quay, with the intention of boarding the *Leopold*. They bore waiters, guides, facchini, and other assorted samples of the rabble that is accustomed to look on strangers as its natural prey. The various craft were rowing hard in order to be the first to reach the ship, and, as usual, the crews were exchanging insults in a loud tone of voice fit to terrify people unused to the manners and customs of the lower classes in Naples.

The auburn-haired young man had, in order to grasp more readily the details of the prospect unrolled before him, put on his eyeglasses, but his attention, distracted from the sublime prospect of the bay by the concert of yells that rose from the flotilla, was drawn to the boats. No doubt he was annoyed at the noise, for his brows bent, the wrinkle on his brow became marked, and his gray eyes turned yellowish.

An unexpected billow, running in from sea, with a fringe of foam on its crest, passed under the steamer, which it raised and let fall again heavily, broke on the quay in blinding spray, wetted the promenaders surprised by the suddenness of the douche, and with its backwash dashed the boats together so roughly that a number of facchini fell overboard. The accident had no serious consequences, for the rascals swam like fish or marine deities and reappeared a few seconds later, with the salt water running out of their mouths and their ears, their hair plastered against their temples, and assuredly as much astonished at the unexpected dive as was Telemachus, the son of Ulysses, when Minerva, under the guise of the sage Mentor, threw him into the sea from the top of a rock in order to withdraw him from the love of Eucharis.

At a respectful distance behind the strange traveller, there stood by a pile of trunks a small groom, a sort of old man of fifteen, a liveried gnome, who looked like one of the dwarfs whom the Chinese patiently bring up in porcelain jars to prevent their growing. His flat face, on which the nose scarcely showed, seemed to have been compressed in earliest childhood, and his protruding eyes had the sweetness of look that certain naturalists attribute to the toad's eye. Neither his chest nor his back was deformed, and though one would in vain have looked for a hump on him, he gave the impression of being a hunchback. In a word, he was a very proper groom, who might have ridden at Ascot or Chantilly without first going into training; his queer looks would have determined any gentleman-rider to engage him on the spot. He was repulsive, but irreproachable in his own way, like his master.

The passengers landed and, with their luggage, fell prey to the porters after the latter had exchanged insults that were more than Homeric, and proceeded to the various hotels with which Naples is abundantly provided.

The traveller with the eyeglasses and his groom went to the Hôtel de Rome, followed by a numerous company of robust facchini who pretended to groan and sweat under the burden of a hatbox or a small parcel, guilelessly expecting a heavy tip, while four or five of their comrades, who exhibited muscles as powerful as those of the "Hercules" so much admired in the Studj, pushed a handcart on which had been placed two trunks of moderate size and equally moderate weight.

When the hotel was reached and the *padron di casa* had shown the newcomer to his apartment, the porters, although they had received about three times their legal fare, indulged in the most frantic gesticulations and in speeches in which supplications and threats were mingled in the most comical fashion, all shouting at one and the same time with terrific volubility, claiming additional pay and swearing by all that was holy that they had not been sufficiently rewarded for their exertions. Paddy, who had to face them alone—for his master, heedless of the noise, had already gone upstairs—looked like a monkey surrounded by a pack of hounds. In order to still the tumult, he attempted a harangue in his mother tongue, that is, in English, but his speech proved unacceptable. Then, closing his fists and placing his arms breast-high, he assumed, to the great hilarity of the facchini, a very correct boxing attitude, and with a blow straight from the shoulder, worthy of Adams or Tom Cribb, he landed on the breadbasket of the biggest fellow in the crowd and sent him flying heels over head on the lava pavement.

This exploit put the rabble to flight; the hulking fellow picked himself up with difficulty, feeling very sore, and, without seeking to have his revenge on Paddy, went off with endless contortions, rubbing with his hand the blue-black mark that was already showing on his skin, and convinced that a devil must be hidden under the jacket of the monkey-like groom, who looked as if he were fit to ride nothing bigger than a dog and as if a breath of wind would blow him away.

The stranger, having summoned the *padron di casa,* asked him if any letters had come for Mr. Paul d'Aspremont. The hotelkeeper replied that a letter so addressed had been lying for a week in the letter-rack, and he hastened to fetch the epistle. The letter, enclosed in a thick envelope of blue cream laid paper and sealed with aventurine sealing-wax, was addressed in a sloping, angular hand with cursive strokes, denoting a high aristocratic education, and common, too uniformly perhaps, to English young ladies of good family.

The contents of the note, which Mr. d'Aspremont opened with an eagerness due apparently to something more than mere curiosity, were as follows:—

"DEAR MR. PAUL—We reached Naples two months ago, travelling by short stages. Uncle complained bitterly of the heat, the mosquitoes, the wine, the butter, the beds. He swore he must have been crazy to leave his comfortable home near London to travel on dusty roads lined with wretched inns, in which no decent English dog would consent to pass the night; but, for all his grumbling, he accompanied me and I could have taken him to the world's end. He is none the worse for his trip, and I am a great deal better. We have settled down on the seashore, in a whitewashed house hidden in a sort of virgin forest of orange, lime, myrtle, and rose laurel trees, and other exotic plants. From our terrace we have a wonderful view, and every afternoon you will find there a cup of tea or a glass of lemonade, whichever you may prefer. Uncle, whom you have fascinated, I know not how, will be delighted to see you again; and need I add that I shall not be sorry to do so either, although you did cut my fingers with your ring when you bade us good-bye on the pier at Folkstone?

"Alicia W."

II

Paul d'Aspremont, after he had dined in his room, called for a carriage. There are always plenty of them round the large hotels on the lookout for travellers, so that his wish was at once gratified. By the side of Neapolitan cab horses, Rosinante itself would seem in excellent condition; their skinny heads, their ribs showing like the hoops of a barrel, their protruding backbones, always raw, seem to implore as a kindness the knacker's knife, for the careless Southerner deems it a piece of needless attention to feed animals. The harness, usually broken, is mended with bits of cord, and when the coachman has gathered up his reins and calls on his horses to start, one feels sure that the horses will vanish into thin air and the vehicle disappear in smoke, after the manner of Cinderella's carriage when she returned from the ball after midnight, contrary to the fairy's orders. But it is not so; the poor brutes stiffen their limbs and, after a few struggles, start on a gallop which they keep up steadily. The coachman inspires them with his own ardour, and the lash of his whip brings out the last spark of life concealed within their skeleton frames. They prance, throw their heads up and down, try to look spirited, open their eyes and their nostrils, and go at a pace that the fastest English trotters could not equal. To what this phenomenon is due, and what is the mysterious power that enables dead animals to gallop at full speed, I cannot explain, but the fact is patent that this miracle is of daily occurrence in Naples and that no one is in the least surprised at it.

Mr. Paul d'Aspremont's carriage was flying through the dense crowd, shaving the citron-wreathed acquajoli shops, the open-air stalls of vendors of stews and macaroni, the fishmongers' stalls, and the heaps of watermelons ranged on the highway like piles of cannonballs in an artillery park. Scarcely did the lazzaroni, lying along the walls wrapped up in their mantles, deign to draw their legs out of the way of the equipages. From time to time a corricolo, with its great scarlet wheels, dashed past bearing a crowd of monks, nurses, facchini, and ragamuffins, and scraping the wheels of d'Aspremont's carriage in the midst of a cloud of dust and noise. Corricoli are now proscribed, and it is forbidden to build any new ones, but it is permitted to put a new body on an old pair of wheels or to fit new wheels to an old body, an ingenious method that will enable these quaint vehicles to last a long time yet, to the great delight of amateurs of local colour.

Our traveller, however, paid scant attention to the animated and picturesque sights that would certainly have attracted any tourist who had not found awaiting him at the Hôtel de Rome a note addressed to him and signed "Alicia W." He looked with inattentive gaze at the blue, limpid sea, on which could be made out, in a brilliant light, and coloured by distance with amethyst and sapphire tints, the lovely isles scattered in fan shape at the entrance of the bay: Capri, Ischia, Nisida, Procida, the harmonious names of which resound like Greek dactyls. But his soul was not there; it was flying away in the direction of Sorrento, toward the little white house nestling in the greenery, and spoken of by Alicia in her note.

At this moment d'Aspremont's face did not have the indefinably unpleasant expression it bore when some inward joy failed to harmonise its dissonant perfections. It was positively handsome and sympathetic, as the Italians are fond of saying. The corners of his mouth were not drawn down disdainfully, and his quiet eyes were filled with tender light. It was easy to understand, on seeing him thus, the feelings for him apparently indicated by the half-tender, half-mocking words on the cream laid paper. His individuality, backed up by his high breeding, must have proved attractive to a young girl brought up with much freedom in the English fashion by an old and very indulgent uncle.

Thanks to the pace at which the coachman drove his horses, Chiaja and La Marinella were soon left behind, and the carriage drove through the open country on a road now replaced by a railway line. Black dust, like triturated coal, imparts a Plutonian aspect to the whole of this shore, over which shines a dazzling sky and which is washed by a sea of the loveliest azure. It is the soot of Vesuvius, sifted by the wind, that dusts the beach and makes the houses of Portici and Torre del Greco look like Birmingham factories. But d'Aspremont did not concern himself with the contrast between the ebon earth and the sapphire heavens; he was in too great a hurry to reach his destination. The finest roads are long when a Miss Alicia is waiting for one at the end of them, and when it is six months since one parted from her on the pier at Folkestone. The sky and the sea of Naples fail to work their spell under these circumstances.

The carriage left the highway, turned down a crossroad, and drew up in front of a gate formed of two whitewashed brick pillars, surmounted with vases in terra cotta, in which bloomed aloes with leaves like tin and sharp as daggers. It was closed by an openwork green-painted swinging gate, and the wall was replaced by a hedge of cacti, the angular stems of which had inextricably interlaced their thorny fronds. Above the hedge, three or four huge fig-trees spread out their broad metallic leaves in compact masses, growing vigorously like African vegetation. A great umbrella pine waved its crown of leaves, and one could scarcely make out, through the luxuriant growth, the white façade of the house gleaming in spots behind the thick curtain of foliage.

A dark-complexioned servant, with curling hair so thick that it would have broken a comb, hastened up at the sound of the wheels, opened the gate, and, walking in front of Mr. d'Aspremont down a rose laurel walk, the blooms of which caressed his cheeks, led him to the terrace where Miss Alicia was having tea with her uncle.

Yielding to a very justifiable caprice in a young lady, tired of comfort and elegance, and perhaps also to tease her uncle, whose commonplace tastes she made fun of, Miss Alicia had chosen, in preference to a more civilised dwelling, this villa, the owners of which were travelling, and which had remained uninhabited for a number of years. She found in this abandoned garden, which had almost returned to a state of nature, a wild poetry that pleased her; in the quickening Neapolitan climate everything had grown with prodigious activity. Orange trees and myrtles, pomegranates and lime trees had thoroughly enjoyed themselves, and not having the fear of the gardener's pruning-knife before their eyes, had clasped hands across the walk from one end to the other, or penetrated familiarly into the rooms wherever there was a broken pane. The place did not have the sad look of a deserted Northern abode, but was marked by the mad joy and happy carelessness of Southern nature left to itself. In the owner's absence, the exuberant vegetation had indulged in a debauch of leaves, flowers, fruits, and scents, and re-conquered the ground man had deprived it of.

When the Commodore, for so Alicia familiarly called her uncle, saw the impenetrable thicket, through which a machete was needed to cut a way, he broke out into the liveliest remonstrances and swore his niece was crazy. But Alicia gravely promised to have cut from the entrance-door to the drawing-room and from the drawing-room to the terrace a passage wide enough for the bringing in of a butt of Malmsey wine, this being the only concession she would grant to her uncle's positivism. The Commodore had to give in, for he could never resist his niece, and at this very time he was on the terrace, seated opposite to her, sipping a big glass of rum, which he called tea.

The terrace, which had mainly attracted the young lady, was in point of fact very picturesque and merits a detailed description, for Paul d'Aspremont will often return to it, and one ought to paint the setting of the scenes one describes.

The terrace, the precipitous walls of which overhung a hollow road, was reached by steps formed of broad disjointed stones, between the interstices of which vigorous wild plants grew luxuriantly. Four broken pillars, brought from some antique ruin, their lost capitals replaced by square stones, supported a trellis of poles intertwined and covered with vines. From the parapet fell in sheets and wreaths wall plants and wild vines. At the foot of the walls Indian figs, aloes, and arbutus grew in delightful disorder, while beyond a wood topped by a palm tree and three Italian pines, the view extended over rolling ground on which were scattered white villas, embraced the violet outlines of Vesuvius, or was prolonged over the blue distance of the sea.

When Paul d'Aspremont appeared at the top of the steps, Alicia rose with an exclamation of pleasure and came forward to meet him. Paul shook hands with her in English fashion, but the young lady raised her prisoned hand to the lips of her friend with a motion full of youthful grace and ingenuous coquetry.

The Commodore tried to raise himself on his gouty legs, and managed to do so after a few grimaces due to pain, which contrasted comically with the look of delight that illumined his broad face. He approached, alertly enough for him, the two young people and grasped Paul's hand in a way to crush his fingers against one another, which is the highest outward mark of good British cordiality.

Miss Alicia Ward belonged to that class of English brunettes who realise an ideal the very conditions of which seem to be irreconcilable; that is, a skin so dazzlingly fair as to make milk, snow, lilies, alabaster, virgin wax, and whatever poets use by way of comparisons of whiteness look almost yellow by the side of it, cherry lips, and hair as black as the darkness of night on a raven's wing. The effect of this contrast is irresistible and results in a singular loveliness that has no equivalent. It may be that some Circassians, brought up in the seraglio from childhood, possess the same wonderful complexion, but on this point I have no information to go by save the exaggerations of Oriental poetry and the watercolour paintings by Lewis that represent the harems of Cairo. Alicia was assuredly the most perfect type of this style of beauty.

The long oval of her face, her incomparably pure complexion, her well-shaped, delicate, transparent nose, her dark blue eyes fringed with long lashes that fluttered on her rosy cheeks like black butterflies when she lowered her eyelids, her lips coloured with dazzling crimson, her hair falling in long, shimmering ringlets like satin ribbons on either side of her face and of her swan-like neck, testified in favour of the romantic female faces by Maclise that, at the Universal Exhibition, looked like delightful impostures.

She wore a flounced grenadine dress, the flounces themselves festooned and embroidered with red sprigs that harmonised wonderfully well with the small-grained strings of coral that formed her head-dress, her necklace, and her bracelets. Five pendants, hung from a facetted coral pearl, quivered in each of her small, delicately convoluted ears. If the reader feels like blaming this wealth of coral, let him remember that he is in Naples, where the fishermen come up out of the sea on purpose to present you with these branches that the air turns red.

I owe that reader of mine, were it but by way of contrast to the portrait of Alicia that I have just drawn, at the very least a Hogarthian caricature of her uncle.

The Commodore, who was some sixty years old, was noticeable for his uniformly crimson face, on which his white eyebrows and mutton-chop whiskers stood out, so that he looked like an old redskin tattooed with chalk. Sunstrokes, unavoidable on a trip to Italy, had added a few more layers to that ardent colouring. He was dressed from head to foot, jacket, waistcoat, trousers and gaiters, in a reddish-gray vicuna, which no doubt his tailor had assured him was the most fashionable shade and that most worn, wherein perchance he did not lie. Yet, in spite of his brilliant complexion and his eccentric dress, the Commodore looked by no means vulgar. His thorough cleanliness, his irreproachable neatness, and his fine manner pointed him out as a perfect gentleman, even though he had more than one external resemblance to the Englishmen in farces that Hoffmann and Levassor are fond of parodying. As for his character, he adored his niece and drank much port wine and Jamaica rum to keep up the humid root, after the manner of Corporal Trim.

"See how well I am now, and how lovely! Look at my colour; I am not yet up to uncle, and I hope I shall never be. But I have roses here, real roses," said Alicia, as she drew across her cheek a slender finger tipped with a nail polished as agate. "I have grown stouter, too, and those horrid salt-cellars that caused me so much trouble when I went to balls have vanished. Now, must not a woman be a coquette to part with her lover for three months, so that at the end of the time he may find her blooming and splendid!"

As she spoke this tirade in the playful and sparkling tone familiar to her, Alicia stood before Paul as if to challenge him to examine her.

"She is as robust and full of health now," added the Commodore, "as those Procida girls who carry amphora; on their heads, is she not?"

"Unquestionably, Commodore," answered Paul; "it was impossible for Alicia to be more lovely, but she is plainly in better health than when, through coquetry, as she claims, she compelled me to endure a painful separation."

As he said this, his glance rested with strange fixity upon the young girl who stood before him. Suddenly the lovely rosy flush she had boasted of having acquired faded from Alicia's cheeks as the flush of evening fades from the snowy mountain slopes when the sun sinks in the west. Trembling all over, she put her hand to her heart, and her lovely lips paled and were contracted with pain.

Paul, much alarmed, rose, as did the Commodore. Alicia's bright colour had returned, though her smile still cost her an effort.

"I promised you a cup of tea or a sherbet, and, although I am English, I advise you to have the sherbet. Snow is better than hot water in this country, so near to Africa that the sirocco comes straight from it."

The three sat down round the stone table, under the vine-leaf bower. The sun had sunk into the sea, and the azure day, called night in Naples, followed the golden day. The moon scattered silvery spots upon the terrace through the interstices of the foliage; the sea rippled with kissing sound upon the beach, and from a distance came the sound of the tambourines that accompanied the tarantella.

By and by Paul had to take his leave. Vice, the dark-complexioned, wavy-haired maid, came with a lantern to show Paul his way through the mazes of the garden. While serving the sherbet and snow water, she had fized upon the newcomer a glance in which curiosity was mingled with fear. Doubtless the result of this examination had been unfavourable to Paul, for Vice's brow, already as brown as a cigar, darkened still more, and as she accompanied the stranger she directed toward him, but so that he should not notice it, her first and fourth fingers, while the other two, folded back under the palm, met the thumb as if to form some cabalistic sign.

III

Alicia's friend returned to the Hôtel de Rome by the same road he had come. The night was incomparably beautiful; the bright, splendid moon cast upon the diaphanous blue waters a long trail of silvery spangles, the perpetual motion of which, due to the lipping of the wavelets, increased their brilliancy. In the offing, the fishing boats, each bearing in the bows an iron cradle filled with lighted tow, studded the sea with red stars and left ruddy wakes behind them. The smoke from Vesuvius, white by day, had changed into a pillar of fire and also cast its reflection upon the bay that, at this moment, had that appearance which strikes Northern eyes as improbable, and which it has in those Italian watercolours, in black frames, so widespread a few years ago, and which were more accurate than one would have supposed, judging by their crude exaggeration.

A few noctambulistic lazzaroni still mooned about the beach, unconsciously moved by the wondrous prospect, and looked out into the blue distance with their great black eyes. Others, seated on the rail of some boat hauled up on the shore, were singing the aria from *Lucia* or the then popular romance, *"Ti voglio ben' assai,"* in a voice that many a highly paid tenor would have envied. Naples sits up late, like all Southern cities, yet the lights in the windows were going out one by one, and only the lottery offices, with their coloured paper decorations, their favourite numbers, and their bright lights, remained open, ready to receive the money of capricious gamblers who, as they wended homeward, might be seized with the fancy of wagering a few carlini or a few ducats upon some number they had dreamed of.

Paul turned in, drew the gauze mosquito-netting about his bed, and speedily fell asleep. As happens to travellers after a sea trip, his couch, though motionless, seemed to him to pitch, scend, and roll, just as if the Hôtel de Rome had been the *Leopold.* This feeling caused him to dream that he was still at sea and that on the pier he saw Alicia, looking very pale by the side of her red-faced uncle, signing to him not to land. The face of the young girl expressed deep grief, and she seemed, as she motioned him back, to be obeying much against her will some imperious fatality.

The dream, to which recent images lent extraordinary reality, so troubled the sleeper that he awoke, and he was glad to find himself in his room, in which quivered the opaline reflections of a night-light that illumined a small porcelain tube round which the mosquitoes buzzed and swarmed. In order not again to have such a painful dream, Paul struggled against sleep and began to think of the beginning of his acquaintance with Alicia, going over, one after another, the innocently charming scenes of first love.

He saw again the red brick house in Richmond, covered with roses and honeysuckle, where Alicia and her uncle dwelt, and to which he had gone, on his first visit to England, with one of those letters of introduction the sole result of which is usually an invitation to dinner. He recalled the white Indian muslin dress, with a single ribbon for sole ornament, which Alicia, who had just left boarding-school, wore on that day, and the spray of jasmine that twined in the wealth of her hair like a floweret from Ophelia's wreath borne away by the stream, her velvet blue eyes and her half-opened mouth that allowed a glimpse of her pearly teeth, her slender neck that turned like that of a bird whose attention is awakened, and her sudden blush when the glance of the young French gentleman met hers.

The dark wainscotted sitting-room, hung with green cloth, and adorned with fox-hunting scenes and steeplechasing incidents, coloured in the crude English way, came up in his mind as in a camera obscura. There was the piano with its row of keys like the set of teeth of some old dowager. Under the mantelpiece, round which grew a spray of ivy, shone the black-leaded grate; he could see the oaken armchairs, covered with morocco, the carpet with its rose pattern, and Alicia, trembling like a leaf, singing in the most adorably out-of-tune voice, the romance from *Anna Bolena, "Deh, non voler costringere,"* while he, not less moved than she, accompanied her, entirely out of time, and the Commodore, dozing in slow digestion, and redder than ever, let slip to the ground a bulky *Times* and its *Supplement.*

Then the scene changed. Paul, who had been admitted to the intimacy of the family, was invited by the Commodore to spend a few days in their Lincolnshire home. An old feudal castle, with crenellated towers and Gothic windows, half-covered with ivy, but arranged internally with all modern comforts, rose at the end of a lawn, the turf of which, carefully watered and rolled, was smooth as velvet. Round the sward ran a sanded walk, which served Alicia for a riding-ground, and on which she cantered on one of the wild-maned Scottish ponies that Sir Edward Landseer loves to paint, and to which he gives an almost human glance. Paul, mounted on a bright bay lent him by the Commodore, accompanied her on her circular ride; for the physician, who found her lungs rather weak, had ordered her to take exercise.

Or again a light boat glided over the pond, brushing aside the water-lilies and sending the kingfishers scurrying away to the refuge of the silvery willows. Alicia rowed and Paul held the yoke-lines. How lovely she looked in the golden halo formed round her head by the sunbeams that shone through her straw hat! She pulled her oars well back, pressing the tip of her gray shoe against the thwart. Alicia's foot was not short and round like a smoothing iron, the Andalusian shape so much admired in Spain; she had a neatly turned ankle, a high instep, and if the sole of her shoe was a shade long, it was not two inches wide.

The Commodore remained on shore—not that his rank kept him there, but his weight, which would have proved too much for the light craft. He waited for his niece at the landing-place and carefully wrapped her in a mantle, lest she should take cold; then, the boat having been made fast to the mooring post, the trio returned to the castle to lunch. It was delightful to see Alicia, who usually ate no more than a wren, put her pearly teeth into a slice of York ham cut thin as paper and make away with a roll without leaving a single crumb for the goldfish in the basin.

How swiftly pass away happy days! Every week Paul postponed his departure; the glorious foliage in the park began to wear the russet livery of autumn, and light white mists rose in the morning from the lake. In spite of the constant raking in which the gardener indulged, the dead leaves strewed the gravel of the drive; innumerable little pearls of frost glittered upon the sward of the bowling green, and in the evening the magpies might be seen squabbling in the tops of the leafless trees.

Paul's anxious gaze saw Alicia growing paler, and her colour diminish to two little spots on her cheeks. She often felt chilly, and the hottest coal fire failed to warm her. The doctor seemed anxious, and his last prescription was to the effect that Alicia must spend the winter in Pisa and the spring in Naples.

Paul had been recalled to France by family affairs; Alicia and the

Commodore were on their way to Italy, and the party had separated at Folkestone. No word had been spoken, but Alicia looked on herself as engaged to Paul, and the Commodore had squeezed his hand in significant fashion. It is only a son-in-law's fingers that one squeezes so unmercifully.

Paul, compelled to wait six long months, which to his impatience seemed six centuries, had had the delight of finding Alicia freed from the languor from which she had been suffering, and radiant with health. The child had made way wholly to the maiden, and he thought with intoxicating happiness that the Commodore would raise no objections when he should ask for her hand.

Lulled by these pleasant thoughts, he fell asleep and slept until day. Naples was already beginning its riot of noise; the sellers of iced water were shouting their wares; the keepers of cook-shops held out to the passersby meats stuck on poles; bending from their windows, the lazy housekeepers lowered with a string their market baskets, which they drew up again laden with provisions, tomatoes, fish, and great pieces of pumpkin. The public scriveners, in rusty black coats and a pen behind their ears, sat down at their tables; the moneychangers were arranging in little piles, on their boards, grani, carlini, and ducats; the coachmen drove their skeleton horses at a gallop in quest of early customers, and the bells in every belfry were joyously ringing out the Angelus.

Paul, wrapped in his dressing-gown, leaned on the rail of the balcony. From his window he could see Santa Lucia Castello dell'Ove, and an immense stretch of sea as far as Mount Vesuvius and the blue promontory on which showed white the vast casini of Castellamare and the distant villas of Sorrento. The sky was free from clouds, save one light fleck that drew nearer the city, driven onwards by a faint breeze. Paul fixed upon it that strange glance to which I have before drawn attention. Forthwith other vapours united with the single cloudlet, and soon a dark pall of cloud stretched out over Castle Saint-Elmo. Great drops of rain pattered down upon the lava pavement and in a few minutes turned into one of the torrential rains that transform the streets of Naples into torrents and sweep dogs, and even donkeys, into the gutters. The surprised multitude of pedestrians scattered in search of shelter; the open-air stalls moved in haste, not without the loss of a part of their wares, and the rain, left in possession of the battlefield, swept in white gusts upon the deserted quay of Santa Lucia.

The huge facchino whom Paddy had smitten with such vigour, and who was leaning under a balcony, somewhat sheltered by the projection, had not joined the universal rout and gazed with deeply meditative glance upon the window whereon Paul d'Aspremont was leaning.

His thoughts found expression in words which he grumbled out with an angry look:—

"The skipper of the *Leopold* would have done better to chuck that *forestière* overboard."

And putting his hand into the opening of his coarse linen shirt, he touched the bag of amulets hung round his neck by a string.

IV

The weather speedily cleared, in a few minutes the bright sunshine had dried the last drops of the shower, and the multitude again swarmed joyously upon the quay. But Timberio, the porter, seemed not to change his opinion of the young Frenchman and prudently transported his penates beyond the range of the hotel windows. When some lazzaroni of his friends expressed surprise at his giving up a good stand in favour of one much less advantageous, he replied, shaking his head with a look of mystery:—

"Whoever wants it can have it; I know what I know."

Paul breakfasted in his room, either through reserve or disdain, for he did not care to mix with the public. Then he dressed, and while waiting until it was time for him to call on Miss Ward, he visited the Studj Museum. He admired rather inattentively the valuable collection of Campanian vases, the bronzes found in the ruins of Pompeii, the verdigrised brazen Greek helmet that still contains the head of the soldier who wore it, the piece of hardened mud that has preserved, like a mould, the imprint of the lovely torso of a young woman surprised by the eruption of Vesuvius in the country house of Arrius Diomedes, the Farnese Hercules and his wonderful muscles, the Flora, the archaic Minerva, the two Balbi, and the magnificent statue of Aristides, perhaps the most perfect work that antiquity has handed down to us. But a lover is not one to appreciate very enthusiastically the monuments of art; to him, the least glimpse of the beloved head is worth more than all the marbles of Greece and Rome.

Having managed somehow to wear out two or three hours in the Studj, he sprang into a carriage and started for the country house where Miss Ward dwelt. The coachman, with that quick perception of love which is characteristic of Southern natures, drove his Rosinantes at breakneck speed, and soon the carriage drew up in front of the pillars, surmounted by vases with aloes growing in them, that I have already described. The same servant came to open the gate; her hair still curled rebelliously, and, as before, her dress consisting simply of a coarse linen chemise with coloured thread embroideries on the sleeves and round the neck, and of a skirt of thick stuff, with transversal stripes, such as is worn by the women of Procida. Her legs, I must admit, were bare, and she trod the dust with feet that a sculptor would have admired. On her breast hung from a black cord a bundle of curiously shaped charms of horn and coral, on which, to Vice's evident satisfaction, Paul's glance rested.

Miss Alicia was on the terrace, that being her favourite spot. An Indian hammock, of red and blue cotton, ornamented with feathers, was suspended from two of the pillars that supported the vine-leaf roof, and in it was swinging the young girl, dressed in a light wrapper of écru China silk, the accordion pleats of which she was pitilessly crushing. On her feet, the tips of which showed through the netting of the hammock, she wore slippers of aloe fibre, and her lovely bare arms were crossed above her head in the attitude of the Cleopatra of antiquity, for, although it was only the beginning of May, the heat was already extreme, and innumerable crickets were singing in shrill chorus in the neighbouring bushes.

The Commodore, in planter's dress, and seated on a cane armchair, pulled with great regularity the rope that set the hammock swinging, and the group was completed by a third personage, Count d'Altavilla, a young Neapolitan dandy, whose presence caused Paul's brows to contract in the fashion that gave him an expression of diabolical wickedness.

The count, indeed, was one of those men whom one does not much care to see by the side of the woman one loves. He was of high stature and perfectly proportioned; his hair, as black as jet and clustering in thick masses, set off his smooth and well-shaped forehead; the brilliant Neapolitan sun sparkled in his eyes, and his large, strong teeth, clear as pearls, shone the brighter by contrast with his crimson lips and his olive complexion. The one objection that a person of fastidious taste could have made to the count was that he was too handsome.

As for his clothes, d'Altavilla sent to London for them, and the severest dandy would have approved of his get-up. The one Italian touch in his whole dress was his shirt studs, which were too costly and showy, betraying the Southerner's love of jewelry. It may be also that anywhere but in Naples people might have thought it in bad taste for him to be wearing a collection of bifurcated branches of coral, of hands, in Vesuvius lava, with closed fingers or brandished dagger, of dogs lying down with outstretched paws, of bits of horn, black or white, and other similar trifles suspended from his watch chain by a ring; but it needed only a turn down the Strada di Toledo (Via di Roma), or along the Villa Reale, to ascertain that the wearing of these charms was not a mark of eccentricity on the count's part.

When Paul d'Aspremont came up, the count, at Miss Ward's urgent request, was singing one of those exquisite Neapolitan popular airs whose author is nameless, and a single one of which, picked up by a composer, suffices to secure the success of an opera. Gordigiani's charming romances may give some idea of them to those who have not heard such airs sung by a lazzarone, a fisherman, or a trovatella on the Chiaja beach or on the pier. They are composed of the sigh of the breeze, a moonbeam, the scent of an orange tree, and the beating of the heart.

Alicia, with her pretty English voice, which was not quite true, hummed the melody, that she wished to remember, and nodded in friendly fashion to Paul, who, annoyed at the presence of the handsome young man, looked at her with no very amiable glance.

One of the cords of the hammock broke, and Miss Ward slipped to the ground, though without hurting herself, and six hands were simultaneously outstretched toward her. The young lady was already up, blushing rosy red, for it is "improper" to fall when men are present. Yet not one of the chaste folds of her dress was disarranged.

"I do not understand it," said the Commodore; "I tested the ropes myself, and Alicia is light as a feather."

Count d'Altavilla shook his head in a mysterious fashion, and though it was plain that he attributed the breaking of the rope to a very different cause than Miss Ward's weight, he kept silence, like the well-bred man he was, and contented himself with rattling the bunch of charms on his chain.

Like all men who turn sulky and cross when in the company of a rival they fear may prove dangerous, instead of becoming more gracious and amiable, Paul d'Aspremont, although well used to society, could not manage to conceal his ill-temper. He replied in monosyllables, let the conversation fall, and when he looked at d'Altavilla, his glance assumed its sinister expression, and the yellow streaks twisted and writhed under the gray transparency of his eyes like watersnakes in a spring.

Every time Paul looked at him in that way, the count, with a gesture apparently mechanical, plucked a flower from a jardinière that stood near him and threw it in such a way that it should cross the direction of the angry glance.

"What are you ravaging my jardinière for?" exclaimed Miss Ward, who observed his action. "What harm have my poor flowers done to you that you should behead them?"

"Nothing, Miss Ward; it is purely a nervous affection," answered the count as he nipped off a superb rose, which he sent flying after the other blooms.

"You make *me* dreadfully nervous," said Alicia, "and without knowing it, you are shocking one of my fancies. I have never picked a single flower; a bouquet inspires me with a sort of terror; the blooms of which it is composed are dead flowers, the bodies of roses, vervain, or periwinkles, and their scent has something sepulchral."

"By way of expiating the murders I have just committed," said the count with a bow, "I shall send you a hundred baskets of living flowers."

Paul had risen and was twisting the brim of his hat with a constrained look as though he intended to take leave.

"Surely you are not going already?" said Miss Ward.

"I have letters to write; important letters."

"That is a pretty thing to say," returned the young girl with a pout. "Are there any letters of importance save those you write to me?"

"Do stay, Paul," said the Commodore. "I have laid out a plan for the evening, subject to the approbation of my niece. I propose that we shall first go to drink a glass of water at the Santa Lucia fountain; it is true the water smells like rotten eggs, but it gives one an appetite. Then we shall go and eat a dozen or two of oysters, both white and red, at the fishhouse and dine in some thoroughly Neapolitan osteria, under an arbour, and drink Falernium and Lacryma Christi, winding up with a visit to Signor Pulcinello. The count could explain to us the fine points of the dialect."

Mr. D'Aspremont did not seem to be much taken with the plan, and he withdrew with a cold bow. D'Altavilla remained a few moments longer, but as Miss Ward, put out at Paul's departure, did not adopt the Commodore's proposal, he also took his leave.

Two hours later, Alicia received an immense number of pots of the rarest plants in bloom, and what surprised her much more, a huge pair of horns of the Sicilian ox, transparent as jasper and polished as agate, fully three feet in length and ending in menacing black points. They were splendidly mounted in gilded bronze, so that they could be placed, tips up, on a mantelpiece, a bracket, or a cornice.

Vice, who had helped the porters unpack both the flowers and the horns, seemed to understand the object of this curious gift and placed the superb crescents, which might have been thought to have belonged to the divine bull that bore away Europa, full in sight on the stone table and said:—

"Now we are properly protected."

"What do you mean, Vice?" asked Miss Ward.

"Nothing, except that the French signor has very queer eyes."

V

The hour for meals had long since passed, and the coal fires that during the day turned the kitchen of the Hôtel de Rome into a crater of Vesuvius were slowly dying out in glowing embers under the sheet-iron extinguishers. The stew-pans had been hung on their respective nails and glittered like a row of bucklers on the rail of a trireme. A yellow brass lamp, like those found in the ruins of Pompeii, was suspended by a triple chain to the main beam in the ceiling and, with its three wicks dipping into the oil, lighted up the centre of the great kitchen, the corners of which remained in shadow.

The luminous beams falling from above illumined, with most picturesque play of light and shade, a group of characteristic figures collected around the thick wooden table, cut and slashed in every direction with knife marks, and which stood in the centre of the great hall whose walls the smoke of the cooking had turned to the dark brown so dear to the painters of Caravaggio's school. Unquestionably neither Spagnoletto nor Salvator Rosa, with their bold love of truth, would have disdained the models collected there by chance, or, to be more accurate, by nightly custom.

First, there was the chef, Virgilio Falsacappa, a very important personage, of colossal stature and tremendous size, who, had he but worn a Roman toga instead of a white duck jacket, might have passed for one of the guests of Vitellius. His strongly marked features formed a sort of serious caricature of the types of certain medals of antiquity; his eyes, cut like those in stage masks, were topped by bushy black eyebrows sticking out half an inch; an enormous nose overshadowed a broad mouth apparently provided with three rows of teeth like a shark's. A dewlap, as deep as that of the Farnese bull, joined the chin—in which was a dimple fit to hold a fist—with a muscular neck, heavily veined and athletic-looking. Bushy whiskers, each of which would have sufficed to provide a sapper with a reasonable beard, framed the face, which was marked with violet spots. His hair was black, curly, and shiny, mingled with a few silvery threads, and clustered on his head in short curls, while his bull neck, with its three deep wrinkles, overlapped the collar of his jacket. In the lobes of his ears, pushed up by the protuberances of a pair of jaws capable of chewing up an ox in the course of a day, glittered silver rings as large as the disc of the moon. Such was Master Virgilio Falsacappa, who, with his apron pulled up on the hip and his knife stuck in a wooden sheath, looked more like a torturer than a cook.

Next came Timberio, the porter, who, thanks to the exercise necessitated by his trade and the sobriety of his regimen—consisting of a handful of half-cooked macaroni, dusted over with cacio-cavallo, a slice of watermelon, and a glass of snow water—was comparatively thin, but who, if well fed, would certainly have been as stout as Falsacappa, so truly did his huge frame seem intended to bear up an enormous bulk of flesh. His dress consisted simply of a pair of drawers, a long brown stuff vest, and a coarse cloak thrown over his shoulder.

Striking also was the appearance of Scazziga, the coachman who drove Paul d'Aspremont, and who was leaning against the table. He had a clever face, but irregular features with an expression of simplicity and craftiness combined; a feigned smile flitted on his mocking lips, and his agreeable manners showed that he was constantly serving well-bred people. His garments, purchased from a dealer in second-hand clothing, had a look of livery about them of which he was particularly proud, and which, in his opinion, placed him a long way higher up the social scale than the rough Timberio. He sprinkled his talk with English and French words that did not always fit with the meaning of his remarks, but which nonetheless excited the admiration of the kitchen maids and scullions, who were amazed at his wonderful knowledge.

Somewhat in the background stood two young maids whose features, though of course less noble, recalled the well-known type of the heads on Syracusan coins: the low forehead, the nose running straight from the brow, the somewhat thick lips, the broad, full chin. Their blackish-blue hair was dressed in bandeaux, which met behind their heads in heavy chignons, stuck with coral-headed pins, and triple necklaces of the same material were wound round their caryatid-like necks, the muscles of which were strengthened by their habit of carrying their burdens upon their heads. No doubt dandies would have looked with contempt at these poor girls in whose veins ran the untainted blood of the splendid races of fair Greece, but an artist, on seeing them, would at once have pulled out his sketch-book.

If my reader has ever seen that painting by Murillo in which angels are cooking, I need not describe the heads of the three or four curly-headed scullions who completed the group.

The company was discussing a serious question that concerned Mr. Paul d'Aspremont, the French traveller who had come in the steamer. The kitchen was sitting in judgment upon the guest.

It was Timberio, the porter, who was speaking, and he paused between each of his remarks, like a popular orator, in order to allow his hearers to grasp their full meaning, and to express assent or dissent.

"Follow me carefully," the orator was just then saying. "The *Leopold* is an honest Tuscan steamer, against which there is nothing to be said, save that it carries round too many English heretics."

"English heretics spend their money freely," put in Scazziga, whom the receipt of tips rendered more tolerant.

"No doubt; the least a heretic can do when a Christian works for him is to reward him handsomely, so as to diminish the humiliation."

"It does not humiliate me to drive a *forestière* in my carriage. I do not follow the trade of beast of burden like you."

"Am I not just as good a Christian as you?" replied the porter, frowning and clenching his fists.

"Let Timberio have his say," chorused the rest of the company, afraid of seeing the interesting account turn into a dispute.

"You will allow," continued the orator, soothed by this, "that the weather was superb when the *Leopold* entered the harbour."

"Certainly, Timberio," said the chef with majestic condescension.

"The sea was smooth as glass," continued the facchino; "yet a huge billow tossed Gennaro's boat so roughly that he fell overboard with two or three of his comrades. Is that not out of the way? For Gennaro is a seaman and could dance the tarantella on a yard without the help of a balancing-pole."

"Perhaps he had drunk a little too much Asprino," put in Scazziga, the rationalist of the company.

"He had not even had a glass of lemonade," Timberio went on. "But there was on board that steamer a gentleman who looked at him in a peculiar fashion. You take me?"

"Yes, indeed," replied the chorus, every one of them extending the first and fourth fingers together as if drilled to the business.

"Now that gentleman was no other than Mr. Paul d'Aspremont," added Timberio.

"The one in number three," asked the chef, "who has his dinner in his room?"

"The very same," replied the younger and prettier of the maids. "Never have I come across a sourer, more disagreeable, and more conceited man; he never said a word to me or even looked at me, and yet I am well worth looking at, say all the gentlemen."

"You are worth a good deal more than that, my lovely Gelsornina," said Timberio gallantly; "but it is lucky for you that the stranger did not look at you."

"You are altogether too superstitious," interjected Scazziga, whose intercourse with foreigners had made him something of a sceptic.

"And by dint of frequenting heretics, *you* will end in not believing in Saint Januarius."

"Because Gennaro happened to tumble overboard, that is no reason for attributing an evil influence to Mr. Paul d'Aspremont," went on Scazziga, standing up for his customer.

"You want more proof, do you? Well, this morning I saw him at the window, looking at a cloudlet no larger than a down-flake out of a burst pillow, when at once black clouds collected and it rained so hard that the dogs could drink standing up."

But Scazziga was not yet convinced and shook his head incredulously.

"And the servant is no better than his master," went on Timberio. "The booted monkey must be in league with the devil, or he could never have knocked me out, when I could kill him with a flip of the finger."

"I am of Timberio's opinion," said the chef, majestically. "The stranger eats little; he sent down the stuffed zucchetti, the chicken stew, and the macaroni and tomatoes that I had myself prepared for him. There must be some reason for such sobriety. Why should a rich man refuse tasty dishes and content himself with egg soup and a slice of cold meat?"

"He is red-haired," said Gelsomina, as she passed her hand through her own thick raven locks.

"And a bit goggle-eyed," added Pepita, the other maid.

"And his eyes are very close to his nose," went on Timberio.

"And the wrinkle between his eyebrows is in the shape of a horseshoe," said, by way of completing the indictment, the huge Virgilio Falsacappa. "Therefore he is—"

"Do not say the word; there is no need of it," cried the chorus, save and except the still incredulous Scazziga. "We shall be on our guard."

"And to think that I should get into trouble with the police," said Timberio, "if I were to let drop a three-hundred-pound trunk on the head of that accursed *forestière*."

"It is pretty risky in Scazziga to go about driving him," put in Gelsomina.

"I am on my box; he can see my back only, and his glance cannot cross mine at the right angle. Besides, I do not believe in the whole business."

"You are a heathen, Scazziga," said the huge Palforio, the Hercule-
an cook. "You will come to a bad end."

While the servants were thus engaged in discussing him, Paul, whose
temper had been upset by finding Count d'Altavilla with Miss Ward, had
gone for a walk at the Villa Reale, and more than once the wrinkle between his brows deepened and his glance became fixed. He thought he
caught sight of Alicia in a carriage with the count, and he hurried to the
carriage door, putting on his eyeglasses to make sure he was not mistak-
en. It was not Alicia, however, but a lady who, at a distance, resembled
her. The horses, no doubt startled by Paul's rush, bolted.

Paul sat down to eat an ice at the Café de l'Europe, on the Palace
Square. A number of people looked at him attentively and then
changed their seats, making a curious gesture at the same time.

He entered the Pulcinella Theatre, where a play *tutto da ridere* was
being performed. The actor got confused in the middle of his comic improvisation and remained dumb. He pulled himself together, however,
but in the very middle of one of his by-plays his black false nose came off
and he found it impossible to replace it. By way of excusing himself he
explained the cause of the accident by a rapid gesture, for Paul's glance,
now fixed upon him, prevented his going on. The spectators nearest
Paul vanished one after another. He rose to go out, unconscious of the
effect he was producing, and in the lobby he heard people whispering a
strange word, the meaning of which he did not understand:—

"A jettatore! A jettatore!"

VI

The day after he had sent her the horns, Count d'Altavilla paid Miss
Ward a visit. He found the young English lady drinking tea with her uncle, exactly as if she had been in a yellow brick house at Ramsgate, instead of in Naples upon a whitewashed terrace and surrounded by fig
trees, cacti, and aloes, for one of the distinguishing traits of the Anglo-
Saxon race is the persistence of its habits, however contrary to the climate they may be. The Commodore was beaming. By means of artificial ice, manufactured with the aid of a chemical apparatus—for snow
only is brought from the mountains behind Castellamare—he had suc-

ceeded in keeping the butter in a solid condition, and he was just then engaged in spreading a pat of it upon a thin slice of bread.

After the first commonplaces that form the preface of every conversation, and which resemble the preludes with which pianists try an instrument before they begin their performance, Alicia, suddenly breaking away from conventionalities, abruptly asked the young Neapolitan count:—

"What do you mean by the strange gift of a pair of horns that came with the flowers? All I could get out of my maid Vice was that they are a preservative against the *fascino.*"

"Vice is right," replied the Count d'Altavilla with a bow.

"But what is the fascino?" went on the young lady. "I am not familiar with your superstitions—your African notions, for no doubt it has to do with some popular belief."

"The fascino is the pernicious influence exercised by a person endowed, or afflicted rather, with the evil eye."

"I am pretending to understand you, so that you will not have too low an opinion of my capacity if I confess that the meaning of your words escapes me," said Alicia. "You explain the unknown by the unknown, and *evil eye* is, so far as I am concerned, as unintelligible as the expression *fascino.* Like the character in the play, I understand Latin, but please speak as if I did not."

"I shall explain myself as clearly as possible," replied d'Altavilla; "only pray do not, with British contempt, mistake me for a barbarian, and do not wonder whether under my clothes my skin is tattooed red and blue. I am a civilised man; I was educated in Paris; I speak both French and English; I have read Voltaire; I believe in steam engines, in railways, and in a double Chamber, just like Stendhal; I eat macaroni with a fork; in the morning I wear suede gloves, coloured kid in the afternoon, and straw-coloured kid in the evening."

The Commodore, who was buttering a second slice of bread, was attracted by this strange preface, and he remained with his knife in the air, gazing at d'Altavilla with his Northern blue eyes, the shade of which contrasted so amusingly with his brick-like complexion.

"Your account of yourself is quite reassuring," said Miss Ward with a smile, "and it would be very rude of me to suspect you of being a barbarian. But surely you must have something very dreadful to tell me, or else something very absurd, to indulge in such circumlocutions before coming to the point."

"You are right; it is very terrible, very absurd, and even very ridiculous, which is worse," answered the count; "and were I with you in London or Paris, I dare say I should laugh at it with you, but here in Naples—"

"You will remain serious. Is not that what you were going to say?"

"Exactly."

"Well, let us get to the fascino," said Miss Ward, impressed, in spite of herself, by the count's gravity.

"The belief is one that goes back to the farthest antiquity; it is alluded to in the Bible. Virgil mentions it as one who firmly believes in it; the bronze amulets found in Pompeii, Herculaneum, Stabiae, the protective signs drawn on the houses that have been cleared out, show how widespread that superstition was formerly." D'Altavilla slyly laid stress upon the word *superstition*. "The whole of the East still credits it today. Red or green hands are placed upon each front of Moorish houses in order to avert the evil influence. On the Gate of Judgment, in the Alhambra, there is a hand carved on the keystone, which is a proof that if the belief is not well grounded, it is at least very ancient. When an opinion has been held by millions of men for thousands of years, it is probable that it rests upon some positive facts, upon a long series of observations borne out by events. However well I may think of myself, I find it somewhat difficult to believe that so many persons, some of whom were unquestionably illustrious, enlightened, and learned, should have been so egregiously mistaken in the matter and that I alone should see it clearly."

"There is an obvious retort to your argument," broke in Miss Ward. "Was not polytheism the religion believed in by Hesiod, Homer, Aristotle, Plato, Socrates himself—as witness his sacrificing a cock to Esculapius—and numberless other men of undoubted genius?"

"That is true; but no one nowadays sacrifices bulls to Jupiter."

"They are better made into beefsteaks and rumpsteaks," sagely remarked the Commodore, who had always been shocked at the custom of burning the fat legs of victims upon coals, as related by Homer.

"Doves are no longer offered to Venus, nor peacocks to Juno, nor he-goats to Bacchus; Christianity has replaced the fair marble dreams with which Greece had filled Olympus. Truth has caused error to disappear, and yet innumerable people still fear the effects of the fascino, or, as it is popularly called, *jettatura.*"

"I can understand that the ignorant multitude should fear such an influence," said Miss Ward; "but that a man of your rank and education should share the belief is what amazes me."

"Many who claim to be strong-minded," replied the count, "hang horns in their windows, nail antlers above their door, and go about covered with amulets. For my part, I make no bones about it, and I am not ashamed to own that when I meet a jettatore, I prefer to cross over to the other side of the street, and that if I cannot avoid his glance, I do my best to conjure it by making the conventional sign; I do it just as readily as would a lazzarone, and I am the safer for it. Numerous misadventures have taught me not to disdain such precautions."

Miss Alicia Ward was a Protestant, brought up in great philosophical freedom of thought and trained to admit nothing save after examination, so that her lucid reasoning powers rebelled against whatever could not be mathematically explained. The count's remarks caused her surprise, and at first she assumed that he was merely trying to be amusing, but his calm and convinced manner showed her she was mistaken, though he failed to convince her.

"I grant you," she said, "that the prejudice exists and that it is very widespread; that you are sincerely afraid of the evil eye, and that you are not trying to play upon the credulity of a stranger. But you must give me some physical reason for the existence of this superstitious idea, for, even at the cost of being considered by you wholly devoid of poetic feeling, I am very incredulous. The fantastic, the mysterious, the occult, the inexplicable have very little hold upon me."

"You surely admit, Miss Ward," the Count went on, "the power of the human eye? The light of heaven mingles in it with the reflection of the soul; the pupil is a lens that concentrates the beams of life, and intellectual electricity flashes forth from that small opening. Does not a woman's glance pierce the hardest heart? Does not a hero's inspire a whole army? Does not the physician's look tame a madman as effectually as a cold douche? Does not a mother's glance repel lions?"

"You plead your cause eloquently," answered Miss Ward, shaking her pretty head. "But you must forgive me if I still entertain doubts."

"What of the bird, then, that, fluttering with terror and uttering pitiful cries, descends from the top of the tree whence it might fly away, to fall into the maw of the serpent that fascinates it? Is it impelled by a prejudice? Has it heard stories of jettatura told in the nests of the feathery gossips? Is not the cause of many an effect beyond the grasp of our organs? Are the miasmata of malaria, of plague, of cholera visible? No eye can see the electric fluid on the lightning rod, yet the electricity is drawn down it. Why is it absurd to suppose that from the black, blue, or gray disc called the eye there issues a beam that may be beneficent or deadly? Why should not that effluvium be fortunate or unfortunate according to the mode of its emission and the angle at which it impinges upon the object it strikes?"

"It seems to me," said the Commodore," that there is something to be said in favour of the Count's argument. For my part, I have never been able to look at a toad's yellow eyes without feeling intolerable heat in the stomach, just as if I had swallowed an emetic; yet the poor reptile had more reason to fear than I, since I could crush it with my heel."

"Ah! uncle," said Miss Ward, "if you are going to side with Count d'Altavilla, I shall have the worst of it. I am not fit to cope with the two of you. Although I might raise many an objection to that ocular electricity of which no physicist has spoken, I am willing, for the sake of argument, to admit its existence; but I do not perceive in what way the huge horns with which you have presented me can efficaciously protect one against its fatal effects."

"Just as the point of the lightning-rod diverts the lightning, so do the sharp points of the horns upon which the jettatore's glance falls divert the malevolent fluid and deprive it of its dangerous electricity. Outstretched fingers and coral amulets perform the same service."

"What you have been telling me, Count," returned Miss Ward, "is very mysterious, but so far as I can make it out, I am under the spell of a most dangerous jettatore, and you sent me the horns to protect me against him."

"I fear that is the case," replied the count, with an accent of deep conviction.

"I should just like to see one of those squinting rascals try to fascinate my niece," exclaimed the Commodore. "I am over sixty, but I have not yet forgotten how to strike straight from the shoulder."

And as he said this, he closed his fist, pressing his thumb against the folded fingers.

"Two fingers are enough, sir," said d'Altavilla, at the same time placing the Commodore's fingers in the correct position. "Jettatura is usually an unconscious act, and is exercised unwittingly by those who possess the fatal gift. Often, indeed, jettatori deplore its effects more than any one else, once they have become aware of their deadly power. They should therefore be avoided, not ill treated. Besides, their influence may be neutralised or at least attenuated, by horns, outstretched fingers, or forked branches of coral."

"Very strange, in truth," said the Commodore, impressed in spite of himself by d'Altavilla's seriousness.

"I was not aware that I was so greatly haunted by jettatori. I scarcely ever leave the terrace, save, in the evening, to drive with my uncle along the Villa Reale, and I have never noticed anything that might justify your belief," said the young lady, whose curiosity was awakened, though she was as incredulous as ever. "To whom do your suspicions point?"

"They are not suspicions, Miss Ward; I am absolutely certain," replied the Neapolitan count.

"Pray, then, reveal to us the name of the fatal being," returned Miss Ward, with a trace of mockery.

D'Altavilla remained silent.

"It is well to know whom we should be on our guard against," added the Commodore.

The young nobleman appeared to be thinking deeply; then rose, walked up to Miss Ward's uncle, bowed respectfully to him, and said:—

"Sir, I have the honour to ask for your niece's hand in marriage."

At this unexpected request, Alicia blushed rosy red and the Commodore's face turned scarlet, from red that it had been.

Undoubtedly Count d'Altavilla might be a suitor for Miss Ward's hand; he belonged to one of the oldest and noblest families in Naples; he was handsome, young, wealthy, and in favour at Court; he was thoroughly well bred and irreproachable in demeanour. His request, therefore, was entirely proper, but it came so suddenly, so strangely, it had apparently so little to do with the conversation that had been going on, that the amazement of uncle and niece was justified. Nor did d'Altavilla appear either surprised or discouraged by it, and he awaited the reply with firm mien.

"My dear Count," at last said the Commodore, when he had somewhat recovered from his surprise, "your request astonishes as well as honours me. The truth is that I do not know how to answer you; I have not consulted my niece. We were talking of fascino, jettatura, horns, amulets, open and closed hands, of all sorts of things that have nothing to do with marriage, and then all of a sudden you ask me for Alicia's hand! That is not logical, and you must not be annoyed if I am somewhat mixed. The match would certainly be quite suitable, but I fancied my niece had other intentions. It is true, on the other hand, that an old sea-dog like me is not one to read fluently a young girl's heart—"

Alicia, perceiving that her uncle was floundering about, profited by his pausing for breath to put an end to a situation that was becoming embarrassing, and said to the Neapolitan:—

"Count, when a gentleman loyally asks for an honest girl's hand, she has no right to take offence, but she may feel surprise at the strange manner in which the request is made. I was asking you to tell me the name of the jettatore whose influence, according to you, may prove fatal to me, and you suddenly prefer to my uncle a request the motive for which I do not clearly perceive."

"My reason is," answered d'Altavilla, "that a gentleman does not care to denounce another man, and that a husband alone has the right to defend his wife. But pray take some time before deciding. Until then the horns, placed in a sufficiently conspicuous place, will, I believe, avail to protect you against any unfortunate consequences."

Whereupon the count rose, bowed low, and went out.

Vice, the crinkly-haired maid, who was coming to clear away the tea things, had heard the end of the conversation as she was slowly ascending the terrace steps. She nourished against Paul d'Aspremont the fullest aversion natural in an Abruzzi peasant, scarcely tamed by two or three years of domestic service, for a *forestière* suspected of jettatura. Besides, she thought Count d'Altavilla a splendid man and could not understand that Miss Ward should prefer to him a pale, meagre fellow whom she, Vice, would not have had anything to do with, even if he had not had the fascino. Therefore, unappreciative of Count d'Altavilla's delicate methods and desiring to withdraw her mistress, whom she loved, from a hurtful influence, Vice bent to Miss Ward's ear and said to her:—

"I know the name that Count d'Altavilla will not tell you."

"And I forbid you to speak it, Vice, if you care to retain my favour," answered Alicia. "Such superstitions are positively shameful, and I shall brave them like a Christian girl who fears God alone."

VII

"Jettatore! Jettatore! These words were certainly addressed to me," said Paul d'Aspremont to himself, as he returned to his hotel. "What they mean I do not know, but they were evidently intended for an insult or a mockery. What is there strange, peculiar, or ridiculous about me that attracts such unpleasant attention? Though one is not a good judge of oneself, it seems to me that I am neither handsome nor ugly, neither tall nor short, neither stout nor thin, and that I ought to be able to go about without attracting notice. There is nothing eccentric in my dress; I am not adorned with a turban with lighted tapers, like Mr. Jourdain in the ceremonial scene in the *Bourgeois Gentilhomme;* I do not wear a jacket with a sun embroidered in gold on the back; I do not go about with a Negro in front of me playing on the cymbals. My personality, which, for the matter of that, is wholly unknown in Naples, is concealed under the ordinary dress, the domino of modern civilisation, and I am in every respect like the dandies who walk up and down the Strada di Toledo or on the Largo del Palazzo Reale, save that I have a rather quieter necktie, not so large a breastpin, a less gorgeously embroidered shirt-front, not so loud a waistcoat, not so many gold chains, and that my hair is very much less curled.

"That may be it! My hair is perhaps not curled enough. Tomorrow I shall have it done up by the hair-dresser in the hotel.

"Yet the people here are used to seeing strangers, and a few slight differences in my dress do not account for the mysterious word and the strange gesture called out by my presence. Besides, I have noticed an expression of antipathy and terror on the faces of the people who drew out of my way. What can I possibly have done to them, since I have never met them before? Everywhere a traveller—who is but a passing shadow that returns not—excites indifference only, unless he happens to come from some distant place and is of an unknown race; and every week the steamers land on the pier thousands of tourists in every respect like me. Nobody troubles about them, save the facchini, the hotel-keepers, and the guides. I have not killed my brother, for I never had one; consequently I cannot be bearing about the brand of Cain upon my brow. Yet people are startled at sight of me and move away. I do not remember having ever produced such an effect in Paris, London, Vienna, or in any of the towns where I have lived. I have been thought proud, disdainful, reserved at times. I have been told that I affected the English sneer, that I was aping Lord Byron, but everywhere I have been received as a gentleman should be, and my advances, though infrequent, have been all the more appreciated on that account. Surely the three days' trip from Marseilles to Naples cannot have altered me to the extent of having become odious or grotesque, for more than one woman has before now singled me out, and I have won the heart of Alicia Ward, a charming girl, a heavenly creature, one of Thomas Moore's angels!"

These reflections, undoubtedly quite sensible, somewhat calmed Paul d'Aspremont, and he succeeded in convincing himself that he had attached to the exaggerated pantomime of the Neapolitans, who gesticulate more than any other people, a wholly gratuitous meaning.

It was late. All the guests, save Paul, had retired to their rooms, and Gelsomina, one of the servants whose portrait I sketched in the account of the kitchen council presided over by Virgilio Falsacappa, was waiting to lock the doors as soon as Paul should have returned. Nanella, the other maid, whose turn it was to sit up, had begged her braver companion to take her place, as she herself desired to avoid the *forestière* who was suspected of jettatura. Gelsomina, therefore, was armed at all points; a huge bunch of amulets bristled on her bosom; five little coral horns hung, instead of vine leaves, from the faceted pearls in her ears; her hand, ready outstretched, extended its index and fourth fingers in a position so accurate that it would certainly have met with commendation from the reverend Father Andrea de Jorio, author of the *Mimicha degli antichi investigata nel gestire napoletano.*

The brave Gelsomina, concealing her hand behind a fold of her skirt, handed the candlestick to Mr. d'Aspremont, and fixed upon him a sharp, steady, almost provocative glance, so singular in its expression that the young man cast down his eyes, a result that appeared to give remarkable pleasure to the handsome girl. As she stood there, motionless and erect, holding out the candlestick with a statuesque gesture, her profile brought out by the light, her glance fixed and flashing, she looked like the Nemesis of antiquity overawing a criminal.

When d'Aspremont had ascended the stairs and the sound of his footsteps had died out, Gelsomina threw back her head with an air of triumph and said:—

"Well, I fairly looked him down, that ugly fellow, whom may Saint Januarius confound. I am sure no harm will come to me."

Paul had a bad night of it, and his slumbers were troubled by all sorts of strange, tormenting dreams connected with the thoughts that had filled his mind during the course of the evening. He seemed to be surrounded by monstrous, grimacing faces expressing hatred, anger, and terror; then these would vanish, and he saw himself threatened by long, lean, bony fingers, with knotty joints, that came out of the darkness, reddened by a light of Hell and making cabalistic signs. The nails on these fingers, curved like tigers' claws and vultures' talons, came closer and closer to his face and appeared to seek to tear his eyes out. By a supreme effort he managed to brush aside these hands that were winged like bats, but the hands were followed by heads of bulls, buffaloes, and stags, the whitened skulls filled with a life that was death, and which, goring him with horns or antlers, forced him to leap into the sea, where he tore his limbs upon a forest of coral with pointed or bifurcated branches. Then a billow would cast him ashore, worn out, broken, half dead; and, like Byron's Don Juan, he seemed to see, in his fainting condition, a lovely head bending down over him. It was that, not of Haidee, but of Alicia, more beautiful than the imaginary being created by the poet. The maiden strove in vain to draw up on the sand the body the sea endeavoured to snatch back, and called on Vice, the tawny maid, to help her, but the latter refused with ferocious laughter. Alicia's strength gave way, and Paul fell back into the waters.

These confused and terrifying fancies, horrible in their vagueness, and others still more vague and recalling the shapeless phantoms that half emerge from the dense shadows of Goya's aquatintas, tortured the dreamer until early dawn. His soul, freed by the exhaustion of the body, appeared to divine what his waking thought failed to understand and strove to translate its presentiments into images in the camera obscura of dreams.

Paul rose tired out, uneasy, dimly conscious of some mystery in these nightmares, but not daring to sound it. He turned round and round the fatal secret, closing his eyes in order not to see, and closing his ears in order not to hear it. Never had he felt so depressed. He even lost faith in Alicia; the count's air of satisfied conceit, the complaisant manner in which the young girl listened to him, the approving air of the Commodore, all these things recurred to him full of painful particulars, filled his heart with bitterness, and deepened his melancholy.

Day has the power to dispel troubles caused by the visions of the night. When the dawn's golden shafts flash into the room through the parted curtains, Smarra, annoyed, flees away flapping its bat-like wings. The sun was shining joyously, the sky was clear, and the blue sea sparkled with innumerable spangles. Little by little Paul grew calmer; he forgot his painful dreams and the strange impressions felt the evening before, or, when he did give a thought to them, he blamed himself for his folly in dwelling upon them.

He took a turn round Chiaja to enjoy the Neapolitan excitability. The dealers were crying their wares in queer musical phrases in a popular dialect unintelligible to Paul, who knew Italian only, and with excited gestures and a fury of pantomime unknown in the North. But every time he stopped before a shop, the dealer looked alarmed, murmured an imprecation in a low voice, and stretched out his first and fourth fingers as if he were about to stab Paul with them. The women, bolder, overwhelmed him with insults and shook their fists in his face.

VIII

On hearing himself insulted by the Chiaja people, Mr. d'Aspremont imagined that they were addressing to him the coarsely burlesque litanies to which fishwives treat well-dressed persons who happen to traverse the market, but the lively repulsion, the genuine terror visible on every face compelled him to seek some other explanation. He heard once more, but with a threatening accent, the word *jettatore,* which had already struck upon his ear at the San Carlo Theatre; he therefore slowly walked away, without letting his glance, the cause of so much trouble, rest upon anything.

As he passed along the houses trying to escape attention, he came upon a second-hand bookstall. He stopped, turned over and opened some of the books, by way of pulling himself together. He thus turned his back upon the passersby, and as he half concealed his face within the pages of the volume, he avoided insult. He had for one moment thought of using his stick upon the shoulders of the rabble, but an undefinable superstitious terror that was beginning to lay hold of him restrained him. He remembered that once, having struck an insolent driver with a light switch, he had hit him on the temple and killed him on the spot, an involuntary murder he had never got over.

Having picked up and put back a number of books in the boxes, he came upon Signor Niccolo Valetta's treatise on jettatura, the title of which seemed to flash up before him, as if the book had been placed there by the hand of Fate. He threw to the dealer, who was looking at him with a sarcastic expression of countenance, and rattling the three or four black horns that hung with other charms upon his watch-chain, the six or eight carlini he asked for the book, and hurried back to his hotel to begin the study that was to clear away the doubts that had worried him since his arrival in Naples.

Valetta's book is as widely read in Naples as the *Secrets of Albertus the Great, Etteila,* or the *Key to Dreams* in Paris. Valetta gives a definition of jettatura, shows by what means it may be recognised, and what are the methods to be resorted to for protection. He divides jettatori into several classes, in accordance with their power for evil, and discusses every point in connection with this important subject.

If d'Aspremont had come across this book in Paris, he would have glanced carelessly through it as through an old almanac stuffed full of nonsensical tales, and have laughed at the serious manner in which the author treated of such absurdities. But in his present condition, away from his usual surroundings, prepared to credulity by numberless trifling incidents, he perused it with secret horror, like some profane person spelling out of a black-letter folio formulae for the evocation of spirits and other cabalistic performances. Though he had not sought to penetrate them, the secrets of Hell were being revealed to him, and he was now aware of his fatal gift; he was a jettatore! He had to admit it to himself, for he possessed every one of the distinctive marks described by Valetta.

It sometimes happens that a man who believes himself to be enjoying the best of health opens by chance a medical work and, on reading the pathological description of some disease, perceives that he is suffering from it. Enlightened by the dread knowledge, he feels, as he notes each symptom in the tale, some hidden portion of his organs, some concealed fibre, the play of which he was ignorant of, quiver with pain, and he turns pale at the thought that death, which he had fancied far distant, is near. Paul experienced just such a feeling.

He went to the mirror and looked at himself with terrifying intensity. The dissonant perfection of features, composed of beauties not usually found together, made him more than ever like the fallen archangel and gleamed with sinister fire out of the dark depths of the mirror. The rays in his pupils writhed like vipers; his eyebrows quivered like a bow from which the deadly shaft has just been shot; the white line in his forehead recalled a cicatrice due to a thunderbolt, and flames of Hell seemed to burn in his auburn hair, while the marble pallor of his complexion brought out more startlingly still each feature of his absolutely terrifying face.

He was frightened at himself. It seemed to him that his glance, reflected by the mirror, returned to him like a poisoned arrow. Imagine Medusa looking at her own hideous, yet charming face in the ruddy reflection of a brazen shield!

It may be objected that it is difficult to believe that a young man of the world, educated in the truths of modern science, and who had lived in the very midst of a sceptical civilisation, could accept seriously a popular prejudice and fancy himself endowed with a mysterious deadly power; but to that I answer that common belief exercises an irresistible power of magnetism that masters a man in spite of himself, and with which the individual will cannot always cope successfully. A man may arrive in Naples laughing jettatura to scorn, and end by surrounding himself with horned preventives and by fleeing from every individual whose glance he suspects of evil. But Paul d'Aspremont was in a much more serious situation: he was himself possessed of the fascino, and every one avoided him or made in his presence the protective signs recommended by Signor Valetta. His common sense rebelled at the thought, yet he could not help acknowledging that he bore every mark characteristic of a jettatore. The human mind, even when most enlightened, has always some dark nook in which crouch the hideous monsters of credulity and where cling the bats of superstition. Ordinary life itself is so full of problems that cannot be solved that impossibility becomes probability. A man may deny everything or believe in everything; from a certain point of view dreams are as true as reality.

Profound melancholy overpowered Paul. He was a monster! Though endowed with a most affectionate disposition and the kindest of hearts, he nevertheless bore misfortune wherever he went. His glance, unconsciously filled with venom, was fatal to those upon whom it rested, even when he looked kindly upon them. He suffered from the horrible privilege of collecting, concentrating, and distilling the morbid miasmas, the dangerous electricity, the fatal influences of the ambient air and scattered them around. A number of incidents in his life, which until now had been unintelligible to him and which he had attributed to chance, now stood out in hideous clearness. He remembered all manner of strange misadventures, of unexplained misfortunes, of causeless catastrophes, the reasons for which he now understood. Startling coincidences occurred to his mind and confirmed the unhappy opinion he now had of himself.

He went back over his life year by year. He recalled his mother, who had died in giving him birth; the unfortunate fate of his young schoolfellows—the one he loved best had been killed by a fall from a tree while he, Paul, was watching him climb it. He recalled the boating excursion on which he had started so joyously with two of his comrades, and from which he had returned alone, after making desperate efforts to drag from the weeds the bodies of the two poor lads drowned by the up-setting of the craft; the assault at arms in which his foil, the button of which had broken off and transformed the weapon into a sword, had so dangerously wounded his opponent, a young man whom he loved dearly. Unquestionably there could be no rational explanation for these events, although Paul had hitherto believed there was. Now, however, the appar-ently fortuitous and accidental character of these events appeared to him to depend upon another cause, which he had learned since he had read Valetta's book. The deadly influence, the fascino, the jettatura had evi-dently a share in these catastrophes. Such a persistent series of misfor-tunes in connection with one and the same individual was *unnatural.*

A still more recent circumstance recurred to his memory in all its horrible details and contributed largely to strengthen his unhappy belief.

He often used to attend the performances at Her Majesty's Theatre, in London, having been struck by the grace of a young English ballet dancer. Without being more taken with her than a man is with a charm-ing figure in a painting or an engraving, he had got into the habit of fol-lowing her with his eyes in the midst of her companions in the ballet, through the wildering maze of the evolutions of the dance. He had got fond of her sad, gentle face, of her delicate pallor which the exertion of the dance never flushed, of her beautiful silky, shining fair locks, crowned, as the case might be, with stars or flowers, of her glance that lost itself in space, of her limbs that shyly lifted the clouds of gauze and shone under the silk like the marble limbs of some statue of antiquity. Every time she flashed past the footlights, he saluted her with a quiet, furtive sign of admiration or put up his glasses in order to see her better.

One night, in the circular flight of a waltz, the dancer swept closer to the dazzling line of fire that, in a theatre, separates the world of reality from the realm of fancy. Her airy sylph-like draperies fluttered like the wings of a dove about to take to flight, when a tongue of flame shot up, blue and white, and reached the light stuff. In an instant the young girl was wrapped in flames; she danced on for a second like a will-o'-the-wisp in the midst of a ruddy blaze, and then, terrified, rushed to the wings, crazed with fright and was burned alive in her blazing garments.

Paul had been deeply grieved by the accident, of which the newspapers of the day all spoke, and in which the name of the victim may be found by any one curious to know it. But his sorrow was unmixed with remorse, and he did not suppose he had in the least degree contributed to an accident that he regretted more than any one else. Now, however, he was convinced that his insistent habit of following her with his glance had had something to do with the death of the lovely girl. He looked on himself as her murderer; he felt a horror of himself and wished he had never been born.

This state of prostration was followed by a violent reaction. Paul broke into a nervous laugh, threw away Valetta's book, and exclaimed:—

"Upon my word, I am going crazy or turning into an idiot. The Naples sun must have affected my brain. What would the men at my club say if they knew that I have seriously discussed whether or not I am a jettatore?"

Paddy here knocked discreetly at the door. Paul opened, and the groom, conscientiously performing his duties, presented to him upon the shining leather of his cap, a letter from Alicia, excusing himself the while for not having a silver salver.

D'Aspremont broke the seal and read as follows:—

"Are you annoyed with me, Paul? You did not come last night, and your lemon sherbet melted sadly away on the table. I kept looking for you until nine o'clock, trying to make out the sound of your carriage wheels amid the din of the cicadas and the rumbling of the tambourines. Then I gave up hope and quarrelled with the Commodore. Are not women wonderfully just? Pulcinella's black nose, Don Limon, and Donna Pangrazia must have a wonderful attraction for you, for I know by my secret police that you spent the evening at San Carlino. You did not write a single one of those letters you said were so important. Why do you not simply confess that you were stupidly jealous of Count d'Altavilla? I thought you had more pride, and your modesty is touching. You need have no fear; Count d'Altavilla is too handsome, and I do not care for Apollos who wear watch charms. I ought to treat you with haughty disdain and inform you that I did not notice your absence, but the truth is that the time hung very heavily on my hands, that I was in a very bad temper, very nervous, and that I nearly beat Vice who was laughing as if she were crazy, though what it was at, I have not the faintest idea.

"A. W."

Paul completely recovered the feeling of real life on reading this playfully sarcastic letter. He dressed, ordered the carriage, and soon the incredulous Scazziga was cracking his whip at his horses that dashed at a gallop down the lava-paved street, through the crowd that is ever dense on the Santa Lucia quay.

"What is the matter with you, Scazziga?" asked Paul. "You will have a smash presently."

The coachman turned sharply round to reply, and Paul's angry glance fell full upon him. A stone he had not perceived forced up one of the fore wheels, and the violence of the shock caused him to fall from his box, though he managed to keep hold of the reins. He clambered back as nimbly as a monkey, with a bump the size of a hen's egg on his forehead.

"The devil take me if I turn round again when you speak to me," he grumbled low. "Timberio, Falsacappa, and Gelsomina were right. He is a jettatore. Tomorrow I shall buy a pair of horns; it can do no harm and may do good."

Paul was disturbed by the incident, for it brought him back within the magic circle he was trying to escape from. Of course the fact that a stone happens to be struck by the wheel of a carriage and that the driver tumbles off his seat, is of daily occurrence, but the *effect* had followed so closely upon the *cause,* Scazziga's fall had coincided so exactly with the *look* he had cast upon him, that all his fears returned.

"I have a great mind," he said to himself, "to leave this extravagant country tomorrow, for as long as I stay in it I feel my brain rattling around in my head like a dried nut in its shell. But if I were to acquaint Alicia with my fears, she would laugh at me, and the climate of Naples is beneficial to her. But, by the way, she was in excellent health before she made my acquaintance! Never had that swan's nest, England, floating on the waves, given birth to a fairer and rosier child. Life sparkled in her glorious eyes and bloomed upon her satiny fresh cheeks; a rich clean blood coursed in the azure veins under her transparent skin, and her beauty made itself felt under her grace and strength. But once my glance fell upon her, she grew pale, thin, and altered; her delicate hands became more slender; her brilliant eyes were circled with dark rings, and it seemed as though consumption had touched her with its bony fingers. During my absence, she quickly regained her lovely colour; her breath came freely from the lungs that the physician had sounded with anxiety. If she were freed from my fatal influence, she would live long. I believe I am killing her. The other evening, while I was there, she experienced such acute pain that her cheeks became pallid as though death had breathed upon her. I wonder whether I unknowingly cast jettatura upon her? Of course the whole thing may be explained in the most natural manner, for many English girls have a predisposition to consumption."

Paul d'Aspremont turned these thoughts over in his mind all the way. When he appeared on the terrace, where the Commodore and Alicia spent most of their time, the huge Sicilian ox-horns, given by Count d'Altavilla, outspread their jasper-like crescents in the most conspicuous place. The Commodore, observing Paul's glance fall upon them, turned blue, which was his way of blushing. Less delicately minded than his niece, he had listened to Vice's confidences.

Alicia, with a gesture of profound disdain, signed to the servant to remove the horns and cast upon Paul an adorable glance full of love, of courage, and of faith.

"Leave them where they are," said Paul to Vice. "They are very handsome."

IX

Paul's remark upon the horns presented by Count d'Altavilla appeared to give the Commodore pleasure. Vice smiled, exhibiting a row of teeth of which the canines, separate and sharp, shone with ferocious whiteness. Alicia's swift look asked of her friend a question that remained unanswered, and an awkward silence fell upon the company.

The first moments of a visit, even when it is cordial, familiar, and the repetition of a daily call, are usually embarrassing. During the time of absence, even though it be of a few hours' duration only, an invisible atmosphere has gathered about each one and bars confidence. It is like a perfectly clear pane of glass through which one can see the landscape but that a fly cannot traverse. There is apparently nothing the matter, yet an obstacle makes itself felt.

An unspoken thought kept well in the background—for all three were well-seasoned people of the world—caused each member of the party to be more preoccupied than was the wont of persons usually so much at their ease. The Commodore was mechanically twiddling his thumbs; d'Aspremont could not take his eyes off the black, polished points of the horns he had forbidden Vice to remove, studying them as though he were a naturalist seeking to classify some hitherto unknown species; Alicia was toying with the bow of the broad ribbon that she wore as a belt round her wrapper and pretended to be refastening it.

She was the first to break the ice, with the playful freedom of English girls, who are, however, so modest and reserved once they are married.

"Really, Paul, you have not been very amiable of late. Is your love a cold-house plant that can bloom only in England—one whose development the high temperature of this climate interferes with? You were so attentive, so thoughtful, so ready to forestall my least wishes when you were with us at our Lincolnshire place. You presented yourself with smiling lips, your heart on your sleeve, your hair irreproachably curled, and ready to bend the knee before the goddess of your soul; such, in a word, as lovers are depicted in the illustrations to novels."

"And I still love you, Alicia," replied d'Aspremont, in a voice full of feeling, but without removing his eyes from the horns hanging on one of the antique pillars that supported the vine-leaf roof.

"You say it in so lugubrious a tone," returned Alicia, "that it taxes my self-conceit to believe it. I fancy that what you liked in me was my pallor, my diaphaneity, my Ossianic and vaporous grace. My state of ill-health bestowed upon me a certain romantic charm that I have now lost."

"You were never lovelier, Alicia."

"Words, words, words, as Shakespeare says. I am so lovely that you do not condescend to look at me."

As a matter of fact d'Aspremont's eyes had not once rested upon the girl.

"Well," she said, with a comically exaggerated sigh, "I see plainly that I have turned into a stout, sturdy peasant girl, blooming, high-coloured, and blowzy, without a trace of breeding and unfit to appear at Almack's or in the 'Book of Beauty,' with a sheet of tissue paper between my portrait and a sonnet."

"Miss Ward, you take pleasure in gratuitously slandering yourself," said Paul with downcast glance.

"You had better own at once that you think me horrid. It is your fault, Commodore," she went on. "You have been feeding me up on chicken wings, choice chops, fillet of beef and Canary wine, and with your rides on horseback, your sea-bathing, and your gymnastic exercise, you have worked me up to a state of rude country health that has scattered to the winds Mr. d'Aspremont's poetic illusions."

"You are teasing Mr. d'Aspremont and making fun of me," said the Commodore. "It is quite certain that fillet of beef is strengthening and that Canary wine never hurt any one."

"What a disappointment it must be for you, Paul, to have parted with a nixie, an elf, a willis, and to come upon what physicians and parents call a healthy lass! But since you have not the courage to look at me, shudder with horror—I am seven ounces heavier than when I left England!"

"Eight ounces," proudly corrected the Commodore, who looked after Alicia as carefully as the most tender mother could have done.

"Is it eight ounces exactly? Oh, you dreadful uncle—you want to disenchant Mr. d'Aspremont for good."

While the young girl was thus rallying him with a coquetry she would not have permitted herself to indulge in had she not had serious reasons for doing so, d'Aspremont, a prey to his fixed notion and resolved not to harm Miss Ward with his deadly glance, kept his eyes resolutely upon the talismanic horns or let his gaze wander over the vast blue horizon visible from the terrace. He asked himself whether he was not in duty bound, even at the cost of passing for a man false to his word and to the dictates of honour, to flee from Alicia and to spend the rest of his life on some desert island where at least his jettatura would die out for lack of a human glance that could absorb it.

"I see," continued Alicia, keeping up her raillery, "what is making you so sombre and so grave. Our wedding is only a month hence, and you are startled at the thought of becoming the husband of a poor country girl who has lost all trace of elegance. I willingly give you back your plighted word, and you may marry my friend Sarah Templeton, who eats pickles and drinks vinegar in order to get thin."

And she laughed with the silvery, bright laughter of youth at the notion, Paul and the Commodore joining in heartily.

When the last burst of her nervous gaiety had spent itself, she went up to d'Aspremont, took him by the hand, led him to the piano placed in the corner of the terrace, and opening a music book on the desk, said:—

"My dear Paul, you evidently do not feel up to talking today, and what is not worth saying is sung. You shall therefore take your part in this duettino, the accompaniment of which is not difficult; it consists chiefly of chords."

Paul sat down on the stool; Alicia stood behind him in such a way as to read the song upon the score. The Commodore leaned back, stretched out his legs, and assumed a pose of anticipated beatitude, for he claimed to be something of a dilettante and affirmed that he adored music. After the sixth bar, however, he slept the sleep of the just and insisted, in spite of his niece's sarcasms, on giving the name of ecstasy to his dozing—although he not infrequently snored, which is not a usual sign of ecstasy.

The duettino was a bright and lively air set to words by Metastasio, and in the taste of Cimarosa, which I can best liken to a butterfly flitting to and fro in a sunbeam.

Music hath power to cause the evil spirits to depart. Paul had not been playing long before he forgot everything about conjuring fingers, magical horns, and coral amulets. He forgot Valetta's terrible work and all he had read about jettatura. His soul was rising joyously, borne on the accents of Alicia's voice, into a pure and harmonious atmosphere. The cicadas were silent, as if listening, and the sea breeze, which had just risen, bore the notes away with the petals of the flowers that fell from the vases on the edge of the terrace.

"Uncle is as sound asleep as the Seven Sleepers in their grotto, and if it were not his habit, it might be painful to our self-love as artists. Shall we take a turn round the garden while he is resting? I have never yet shown you my Paradise."

So saying, Alicia took down a broad-brimmed Florentine straw hat from a nail driven into one of the pillars, on which it was hung by the long ribbons.

In matters of horticulture Alicia held the most eccentric opinions; she would not allow flowers to be picked or the shrubbery to be trimmed. It was, as I have said, the wild, uncultivated appearance of the garden that had attracted her. So the two young people had to make a way for themselves through the dense bushes that immediately closed in behind them. Alicia went first and laughed to see the branches of the rose laurels that she displaced lash Paul's face; but hardly had she gone twenty steps when, as if to play a botanical practical joke, a green bough caught and lifted her hat so high that Paul was unable to recover it. Fortunately the foliage was thick and the sun cast scarcely a few golden sequins upon the sand through the interstices of the branches.

"This is my favourite retreat," said Alicia, showing Paul a picturesquely broken rock protected by a dense growth of orange trees, lime trees, lentisks, and myrtles.

She sat down on a part of the rock cut to the shape of a seat, and signed to Paul to kneel down in front of her upon the dry moss that carpeted the foot of the rock.

"Put both your hands in mine and look straight into my eyes," she said. "In another month I shall be your wife. Why does your glance avoid mine?"

Paul, indeed, again a prey to his thoughts of jettatura, had looked away.

"Are you afraid of reading in it any rebellious or guilty thought? You know my heart has been yours since the day you brought the letter of introduction to my uncle in our drawing-room at Richmond. I am one of those Englishwomen who are tender, romantic, and proud, and who love in a moment with a lifelong love, a love more than lifelong, it may be, and she who can love can die too. Look straight into my eyes; I insist upon it; do not try to look down, or I shall be compelled to believe that a gentleman who ought to fear God alone allows himself to be frightened by wretched superstitions. Fix on me your eyes, which you fancy so dangerous and which are so sweet to me, for I read your love in them. Then tell me if you still think me pretty enough to drive with me, when we are married, in an open carriage in Hyde Park."

Paul, bewildered, looked long at Alicia with a glance filled with love and enthusiasm. Suddenly the girl turned deadly pale; a sharp pain shot through her heart like an arrow; something seemed to give way in her breast, and she put her handkerchief quickly to her lips. A red drop stained the fine cambric, which Alicia swiftly concealed.

"I thank you, Paul. You have made me very happy, for I believed you had ceased to love me."

X

Alicia's gesture, as she strove to hide her handkerchief, had not, quick as it had been, escaped d'Aspremont's notice. He turned pale in his turn, for this was an unmistakable proof of his fatal power. His brain was filled with the most sinister thoughts, and for a second suicide occurred to him. Was it not, indeed, his duty to destroy himself as being a maleficent creature, and thus to remove the involuntary cause of so many misfortunes? He would willingly have endured the hardest trials and borne courageously the burden of life, but the thought of dealing death to the woman he loved best was horrible beyond expression.

The heroic girl had mastered the feeling of pain, the consequence of Paul's glance, and which coincided so strangely with the warning given her by Count d'Altavilla. A less strong-minded person might have been struck by the result, which, if not supernatural, was at least difficult of explanation; but, as I have said, Alicia was religious and not superstitious. Her faith, unshakable in matters of belief, rejected as old women's tales every story of mysterious influences, and she laughed at the most deeply rooted popular beliefs. Besides, even had she admitted the existence of jettatura, and had she recognised in Paul its evident signs, she was too tender-hearted and too proud to hesitate for a moment. Paul had done nothing to which the most delicate susceptibility could take exception, and Miss Ward would rather have fallen dead under his so-called fatal glance than have rejected a love she had accepted with her uncle's consent and which marriage was soon to crown. She resembled somewhat the chastely bold, virginly resolute heroines of Shakespeare, whose sudden love is nonetheless pure and true, and who unhesitatingly bind themselves for life. Her hand had pressed Paul's, and no other man on earth was henceforth to hold it in his. She looked upon her life as linked to his, and her maidenly modesty would have revolted at the mere thought of any other hymen.

She therefore exhibited genuine happiness, or at least so admirably simulated it that the keenest observer would have been deceived, and raising Paul, still kneeling at her feet, she led him through the flower-tangled and shrub-obstructed walks of her wild garden to a spot where the vegetation, less dense, allowed the sea to show like an azure dream of the infinite. The luminous serenity dispelled Paul's dark thoughts. Alicia leaned upon his arm as if they were already man and wife, and in this mute and pure caress, meaningless in any other woman but decisive in her case, she gave herself to him more formally still, reassured him, and gave him to understand how little she feared the dangers with which she was said to be threatened. Although she had at once imposed silence on Vice, and then on her uncle, and although Count d'Altavilla had refused to name any one, she had quickly understood that it was Paul d'Aspremont who was meant, for the mysterious remarks plainly pointed to him. She had also noticed that Paul himself, sharing the prejudice so widespread in Naples that turns into a jettatore any man whose face is somewhat out of the common, had come, through incredible weakness on his part, to believe himself a victim of the fascino, and he deliberately avoided looking at her in order not to hurt her by his glance. It was in order to react against this incipient mania that she had brought about the scene I have just described, but which had a result very different from what she had intended, since it confirmed, even more than before, Paul's sad conviction.

They returned to the terrace, where the Commodore, still under the influence of the music, was melodiously sleeping in his rattan armchair. Paul took leave, and Alicia, imitating the Neapolitan gesture of farewell, blew a kiss to him on her fingertips and said, in a voice full of suave caresses, "Goodbye till tomorrow, Paul. You will be sure to come, will you not?"

The Commodore, aroused by Paul's departure, was struck by Alicia's radiant, alarming, almost supernatural beauty. The whites of her eyes had a burnished silver tone in which her pupils flashed like luminous black stars; her cheeks were ideally rosy, and of a purity and warmth no painter ever knew; her temples, transparent as agates, were veined with a network of delicate blue lines, while her flesh seemed to be interpenetrated by sunbeams, so that her soul appeared to be breaking out of her.

"How beautiful you are today, Alicia," said the Commodore.

"You flatter me, uncle. It is not your fault if I am not the most conceited girl in the United Kingdom. Happily I do not believe flatterers, even when disinterested."

"Beautiful, dangerously beautiful," went on the Commodore, speaking to himself. "She is the living image of her poor mother, Nancy, who died at nineteen. Angels like them cannot remain on earth. A mere breath blows them away, and invisible wings seem to grow on their shoulders. They are too fair, too pure, too perfect; they lack the red, coarse blood of life, and God, who lends them to this earth for a few days, hastens to recall them to Himself. Her supreme brilliancy of beauty saddens me as though it were a farewell."

"Well, Uncle," said Miss Ward, who noted the darkening of her uncle's brow, "if I am so pretty, it is time I were married. The veil and orange wreath will become me."

"Marry! Are you in such a hurry to leave your old uncle?"

"I shall not leave you, for it is agreed with Mr. d'Aspremont that we are to live all together. You know very well that I cannot do without you."

"Mr. d'Aspremont is all very well, but he is not your husband yet."

"Your word and mine are both pledged to him, and you have never broken yours."

"He has my pledged word, there is no doubt of that," replied the Commodore, somewhat embarrassed.

"And is it not some days since the six months' delay you wished for came to an end?" said Alicia, whose rosy cheeks became rosier yet.

"So you have been counting the months, my girl. Well, there is no trusting you demure ones."

"I love Mr. d'Aspremont," replied Alicia, gravely.

"There's the rub," jerked out Sir Joshua Ward, who, filled with the notions put into his head by Vice and Count d'Altavilla, did not at all care to have a jettatore for a son-in-law.

"I have but one heart," returned Alicia, "and but one love, even if, like my mother, I were to die at nineteen."

"Die!" exclaimed the Commodore. "Pray do not utter such a horrible thing."

"Have you anything to urge against Mr. d'Aspremont?"

"Nothing whatever."

"Has he shown himself dishonourable in any way? Has he once proved cowardly, vile, untruthful, or perfidious? Has he ever insulted a woman or backed down before a man? Is there any secret stain upon his crest? Would a girl, entering society as his wife, have to blush for him or cast her eyes down?"

"Mr. Paul d'Aspremont is a perfect gentleman, and absolutely respectable."

"You may be sure, Uncle, that if he were not, I should at once give him up and bury myself in some inaccessible retreat; but I shall not break my plighted word for any other reason. You understand me?" said Miss Ward, gently but firmly.

The Commodore was twiddling his thumbs, his usual recourse when bothered.

"Why are you so cool toward Paul nowadays?" went on Miss Ward. "You used to be so fond of him; you could not do without him when we were in Lincolnshire; and when you shook hands with him and crushed his fingers in doing so, you said he was a fine fellow, to whom you would not hesitate to confide a girl's happiness."

"Yes, indeed, I was very fond of him," said the Commodore, moved by the remembrances called up by his niece. "But what is not so plain when shrouded in English fogs, is plain enough in the Neapolitan sunshine."

"What do you mean?" asked Alicia, whose bright colour suddenly faded away and who turned as white as an alabaster statue upon a tombstone, while her voice trembled.

"I mean that Paul is a jettatore."

"What, Uncle! You, Sir Joshua Ward, a Christian gentleman and a subject of Her Majesty; you, a retired naval officer, and an enlightened and civilised man, so often consulted on so many matters; you who have education and wisdom, and who daily read your Bible, you do not hesitate to accuse Paul of jettatura? Oh! I did not expect that from you."

"I may be all you say, my dear Alicia," replied the Commodore, "when your happiness is not at stake; but when a danger, even if imaginary only, threatens you, I become more superstitious than a peasant of the Abruzzi, a lazzaroni on the Mole, a Chiaja ostricajo, a maidservant of Terra di Lavoro, or even a Neapolitan count. Paul may glare at me as much as he likes with his cross look; I shall remain as cool as in front of a rapier point or a pistol barrel. Fascino can have no hold on me, who have been burned, tanned, and baked by every sun. It is only where you are concerned, my dear, that I am credulous, and I confess that I feel a cold sweat all over me when that unfortunate fellow's glance rests upon you. I know very well that he has no evil intentions and that he loves you better than his own life, but it seems to me that when he does look at you your features change, your colour goes, and you strive to hide keen pain. Then I do feel like tearing out his eyes with the count's horns."

"Poor dear uncle," said Alicia, moved by the Commodore's warmth. "Our lives are in God's hands. Not a prince dies on his state bed, not a sparrow under the slates, unless the appointed time has come. Fascino has nothing to do with it, and it is wicked to suppose that a more or less oblique glance can have any influence upon our fate. Come, Nunky," continued she, using the term of familiar endearment of the jester in *King Lear,* "you were not serious in what you said just now. Your love for me biased your judgment, usually so sound. I am sure you would never dare to say to Paul that you cannot now give him your niece's hand and that you do not want him to marry into your family because he is a jettatore."

"By Joshua, my namesake, who stopped the sun, I shall not hesitate to speak my mind to your handsome Paul," cried the Commodore. "What do I care whether I am ridiculous and absurd, or whether I break my word even, when it is a question of your health? I pledged my word to a man, not to a jettatore. I have promised, it is true, and I shall simply not keep my promise. If he is not satisfied, I am ready to give him satisfaction."

And the exasperated Commodore lunged out without thinking of the gout that tortured him.

"Sir Joshua Ward, you will not do so," said Alicia, with calm dignity.

The Commodore fell back in his armchair quite out of breath, and remained silent.

"Granting that the shameful and stupid charge were true, Uncle, is it a reason for dismissing Mr. d'Aspremont and turning his misfortune into a crime? You acknowledge yourself that the harm he may do is done unconsciously, and that no man was ever more loving, generous, and noble."

"One does not marry a vampire, however good his intentions may be," replied the Commodore.

"But that is all nonsense and extravagant superstition. The one bit of truth in the whole business is that Paul has taken it seriously and is terrified and under the spell of a hallucination. He has come to believe in his fatal power, is afraid of himself, for every slight accident, unnoticed by him formerly, confirms his belief, for he now fancies it is caused by him. Is it not my part, since I am his wife before God and soon shall be so before men, with your blessing, Uncle dear, is it not my part, I say, to calm his overexcited imagination, to drive away these vain shadows, to dispel, by apparent and real trustfulness, his haggard anxiety, twin sister of monomania, and to save, by making him happy, his troubled soul and his imperilled mind?"

"You are right, as usual, Alicia," answered the Commodore, "and I am only an old fool. I do believe Vice is a witch, who has upset me with her stories. As for Count d'Altavilla, he strikes me at present, with his horns and his cabalistic gimcracks, as being very ridiculous. No doubt it was a trick to get Paul out of the way so that he might get you himself."

"It is possible that Count d'Altavilla has acted in good faith," said Miss Ward, smiling. "But now you were of his opinion."

"Do not hit a man when he is down, my dear. Besides, I might fall away again, for I have not quite got rid of my erroneous ideas. The best thing we can do is to leave Naples by the next steamer and go quietly back to England. When Paul ceases to see around him bulls' horns,

stags' heads, pointed ringers, coral amulets, and all the rest of these diabolical inventions, he will grow calmer, and I also shall forget the nonsense that nearly led me to break my word and to act as no gentleman
should act. You shall marry Paul, since you have agreed to do so; you
shall keep for me the sitting-room and bedroom on the ground floor of
our Richmond home, and the octagonal tower in our Lincolnshire castle, and we shall live happily together. If your health requires that you
should go to a milder climate, we shall rent a country house near Tours,
or else at Cannes, where Lord Brougham has a fine property, and
where these damnable jettatura superstitions are unknown, thank God!
What say you to that, Alicia?"

"You do not need my approval; am I not the most obedient of
nieces?"

"Yes, when you have your own way, you minx," said the Commodore with a smile as he retired to his own room.

Alicia remained a few moments longer on the terrace, but, whether
the scene she had gone through had induced feverishness in her or
whether Paul really exercised over the young girl an influence such as
the Commodore dreaded, she shivered with cold as the warm evening
breeze blew upon her gauze-covered shoulders, and that night, feeling
unwell, she begged Vice to spread over her feet, cold and white as marble, one of those Harlequin rugs that are manufactured in Venice.

Meanwhile the glow-worms sparkled in the grass, the cicadas were
chirping, and the great golden moon rose in the heavens out of a haze
of heat.

XI

The next day, Alicia, who had had a bad night, scarcely touched the
drink brought her by Vice as was her daily habit, and she placed it languidly upon the table at her bedhead. She did not suffer from any pain
in particular; it was rather that she felt worn out, that she found it difficult to live; and she would have experienced some difficulty in stating
the symptoms of her trouble to a physician.

She ordered Vice to bring her a mirror, for girls are more concerned with the change in their looks due to suffering than with suffering

itself. She was extremely pale; two little spots only, like two rose leaves fallen upon a cup of milk, showed on her pallid cheeks. Her eyes shone with unaccustomed brilliancy, filled with the last flashes of fever, but her cherry lips had paled and, in order to restore their brightness, she bit them with her pearly teeth.

She rose, put on a white cashmere wrapper, twisted a gauze scarf around her head, for, in spite of the heat that kept the cicadas chirping, she felt shivery and went out on the terrace at her accustomed time in order to avoid awaking the ever-watchful solicitude of the Commodore. She barely tasted her breakfast, though she forced herself to do so, as the least symptom of illness would have been attributed by the Commodore to Paul's influence, and this Alicia desired above all things to avoid. Then, under pretext that the blinding light of day tired her, she withdrew to her room, after having several times repeated to her uncle, who was very suspicious in such matters, that she was particularly well that morning.

"Particularly well," said the Commodore to himself when she had gone; "I am not so sure of that. She had pearly tones round the eyes and a bright colour on her cheeks, exactly like her poor mother, who also used to insist that she had never felt better. What had I best do? If I were to make her break off her engagement to Paul, I should be merely killing her in another way. Best leave Nature to herself; Alicia is young yet. True, but it is the young that old Mob attacks; it is as jealous as a woman. I might send for a physician; but what can medicine do for an angel? Yet all the bad symptoms have disappeared. Ah! if it be indeed you, you cursed Paul, whose breath is withering that heavenly flower, I will strangle you with my own hands. But Nancy did not suffer from a jettatore's glance, and yet she died. Suppose Alicia were to die! No, no; it is impossible. What have I done that God should inflict such pain upon me? Long before she dies I shall be under the sod, in the shadow of the church in my native place, with *Sacred to the Memory of Sir Joshua Ward* upon my tombstone. And Alicia will come and weep upon the gray stone over the old Commodore. I do not know what is the matter with me this morning; I am as low-spirited and dull as it is possible to be."

By way of dispelling these dark thoughts, the Commodore added a little Jamaica rum to his cup of tea, now grown cold, and called for his hookah, an innocent indulgence he allowed himself only when Alicia was absent, for her sensitiveness might have suffered even from that light-scented smoke.

He had already got the perfumed water bubbling and had puffed a few bluish wreaths of smoke when Vice appeared and announced Count d'Altavilla.

"Sir Joshua," said the count, after the exchange of the ordinary civilities, "have you thought over the request I had the honour of making of you the other day?"

"I have thought it over," replied the Commodore, "but, as you are aware, I am pledged to Mr. Paul d'Aspremont."

"I am aware of the fact. Yet there are cases in which a pledge may be withdrawn. For instance, when the person to whom it has been made turns out to be different from what he was believed to be."

"Speak more plainly, Count."

"I dislike speaking ill of a rival, but after the conversation we had, you cannot help understanding me. If you were to refuse Mr. Paul d'Aspremont's suit, would you allow me to come forward?"

"For my own part I can answer in the affirmative, but it is not quite as sure that Miss Ward would approve of the change. She is very much in love with Paul, and it is somewhat my fault, for I favoured his suit myself before hearing all this nonsense. Pray forgive me, Count, for putting it in that way, but I am all upset."

"Do you want your niece to die?" said Count d'Altavilla, in a tone of deep emotion.

"Blood and thunder! My niece die!" exclaimed the Commodore, springing from his armchair and dropping the morocco tube of his hookah, for he was very sensitive on this point. "Is she dangerously ill?"

"Do not be so easily alarmed, sir. Miss Ward may live a long time yet."

"I am glad to hear that; you terrified me."

"On one condition, however," continued Count d'Altavilla—"that she shall cease to see Mr. Paul d'Aspremont."

"The jettatura again! Unfortunately, Miss Ward does not believe in it."

"Listen to me," said the count quietly. "The first time I met Miss Alicia at the Prince of Syracuse's ball and began to love her with a love as respectful as it was deep, I was struck at once by the brilliant health, the joy of life, and the bloom of strength that radiated from her. Her beauty was positively luminous and seemed to float in an atmosphere of well-being. She shone in that phosphorescence like a star; Englishwomen, Russians, and Italians paled by her side. I could look at no one but her. To her English high breeding she united the clean, strong grace of the goddesses of antiquity. Forgive my indulging in mythology, but I am descended from one of the Greek colonies."

"She was indeed splendid. Miss Edwina O'Hara, Lady Eleanor Lilly, Mrs. Jane Strangford, and Princess Vera Federeovna Bariatinski turned yellow with envy," returned the delighted Commodore.

"And now do you not notice that her beauty has become somewhat languid, that her features have acquired a morbid delicacy, that the veins on her hands show bluer than they should, and that the sound of her voice has a troubled vibration and a painful charm? The earthly in her is vanishing and making way for the angelic. She is attaining an ethereal perfection that, at the cost of your thinking me too materialistic, I must admit I do not care to see in the daughters of our earth."

The count's words corresponded so accurately with the secret preoccupation of Sir Joshua Ward that the latter remained for some moments silent and apparently sunk in deep thought.

"I have not yet done," went on the count. "Had Miss Ward's health caused you any anxiety previous to the arrival of Mr. d'Aspremont in England?"

"Never once. She was the brightest and most blooming girl in the kingdom."

"You see, then, that Mr. d'Aspremont's presence coincides with the periods of ill-health that are undermining Miss Ward's life. I do not ask you, a Northerner, to credit implicitly a belief, a prejudice, a superstition, if you please, that prevails throughout our Southern lands, but you must confess that the facts are startling and deserve attention."

"May there not be a natural cause in her case?" said the Commodore, shaken by the count's specious reasoning, but held back by his English conservatism from adopting the popular belief.

"Miss Ward is not ill; she is poisoned, as it were, by Mr. d'Aspremont's glance. If he is not a jettatore, he is at the least maleficent."

"But what can I do? She is in love with him, laughs at jettatura, and pretends that one cannot refuse an honourable man for such a reason."

"I have no right to interfere on behalf of your niece. I am neither her brother, her relative, nor her betrothed; but if I could get your consent, there is one thing I might try in order to withdraw her from that fatal influence. Do not be afraid; I shall not commit any extravagance. Young though I am, I am well aware that a woman must not be talked about. Permit me only not to reveal my plan to you and believe me when I say that it does not involve anything that the most punctiliously honourable man might not confess openly."

"You are very much in love with my niece, are you not?" said the Commodore.

"I am, and my love is hopeless. But do you grant me leave to act?"

"You are a terrible fellow, Count d'Altavilla. Well, try to save Alicia in your own way; not only do I not object, I approve."

The count rose, bowed, got into his carriage, and ordered the coachman to drive to the Hôtel de Rome.

Paul was leaning on the table, his head in his hands, plunged in the most painful reflections. He had caught sight of the two or three drops of blood on Alicia's handkerchief, and still under the spell of his conviction, he blamed himself for his deadly love and reproached himself for accepting the devotion of the lovely girl who was ready to die for him; and he was wondering what superhuman sacrifice he could accomplish that would repay such sublime unselfishness.

His groom Paddy interrupted his meditations as he brought in Count d'Altavilla's card.

"Count d'Altavilla! What can he possibly want with me?" said Paul, greatly surprised. "Show him in."

When the Neapolitan gentleman appeared at the door, d'Aspremont had already masked his astonishment with the look of cold indifference under which men of the world conceal their feelings.

"Sir," began the count, while toying with the charms on his watch chain, "what I am about to say to you is so strange, so improper, so out of place that you would be justified in throwing me out of the window. Spare yourself so brutal a proceeding, for I am ready to give you satisfaction as a gentleman."

"I am listening, sir; reserving to myself the right of availing myself of your offer later, in the event of your remarks proving unpleasant to me," replied Paul, steadfastly.

"You are a jettatore."

At these words d'Aspremont's face suddenly turned ashy green, and a red ring formed around his eyes; he bent his brows, the wrinkle in his forehead deepened, and a sulphurous light flashed from his eyes. He half rose, scoring with his nails the mahogany arms of his chair. It was so terrible that d'Altavilla, brave though he was, seized one of the tiny forked branches of coral hanging on his watch chain and instinctively directed the points of it toward Paul.

By a supreme effort of the will, d'Aspremont sat down again and said:—

"You were right, sir; I ought to throw you out of the window for your insult, but I shall have the patience to await another form of reparation."

"Believe me," the count went on, "when I say that I should not offer such an insult, which blood alone can wash out, to a gentleman were I not impelled to it by the gravest of motives."

"What is that to me?"

"It matters little to you, as you say, for you are fortunate in your love, but I, Don Felipe d'Altavilla, I forbid you to see Miss Alicia Ward again."

"I take no orders from you."

"I know that," answered the Neapolitan count, "and I do not, therefore, expect that you will obey me."

"Then what is your reason for acting as you are doing?"

"I am convinced that the fascination with which you are unfortunately endowed acts fatally upon Miss Alicia Ward. It is an absurd notion, a prejudice worthy of the Middle Ages, which no doubt strikes you as profoundly ridiculous. I do not propose to discuss that side of the question with you. Your eyes when turned upon Miss Ward cast upon her, in spite of yourself, a fatal glance that will be her death. I have no other means of preventing that sad result than picking an apparently causeless quarrel with you. In the sixteenth century I should have had you killed by one of my highland peasants, but that sort of thing is not good form nowadays. I did think of begging you to return to France, but it was too absurd. You would have laughed at a rival, who, under pretext of jettatura, requested you to depart and to leave him alone with your future bride."

While the count was speaking, Paul d'Aspremont felt himself a prey to a secret horror. He, a Christian, was then really the plaything of the powers of Hell, and the Evil One in person looked out of his eyes! Catastrophes followed in his train, and his love was deadly! For a moment his reason tottered on its throne, and madness fluttered in his brain.

"On your honour, Count, do you believe what you have just said to me?" he exclaimed after a few minutes' reflection during which the Neapolitan spoke no word.

"On my honour, I do believe it."

"Then it is true," murmured Paul, "and I am a murderer, a fiend, a vampire. I am killing that heavenly girl and driving that old man to despair."

He was on the point of promising the count not again to see Alicia, but human respect and jealousy awaking in his heart kept back the words he was about to utter.

"I will not conceal from you, Count, that I am even now going to call on Miss Ward."

"I shall not take you by the scruff of the neck to prevent your doing so. You refrained from assaulting me a moment ago, and I am grateful to you for that, but I shall be delighted to see you tomorrow, at six o'clock, in the ruins of Pompeii, let us say in the Thermae; it is a very suitable spot. What weapons do you prefer? You have the choice, as it is I who have insulted you. Shall it be rapiers, swords, or pistols?"

"We shall fight with knives, blindfolded, and separated by the length of a handkerchief of which we shall each hold one end. We must even up the chances; I am a jettatore, and I should only have to look at you to kill you, Count."

And Paul laughed stridently, threw open a door, and disappeared.

XII

Alicia had settled herself in a low room in the house, the walls of which were decorated with the landscapes in fresco that, in Italy, take the place of wallpaper. The floor was covered with Manila matting. A table, on which was thrown a Turkish cloth, whereon lay volumes of verse, Coleridge, Shelley, Tennyson, and Longfellow, a mirror in an antique frame, and a few cane chairs formed the furniture. Blinds of China reeds, adorned with pagodas, rocks, willows, storks, and dragons, fitted to the openings and, half drawn up, allowed a soft light to filter in. The branch of an orange tree, laden with flowers that the swelling fruit caused to fall, entered the room familiarly and spread like a garland above Alicia's head, scattering upon her its perfumed blooms.

The young girl, somewhat unwell, was lying upon a narrow sofa by the window, supported by two or three morocco cushions, her feet wrapped up in the Venetian rug. The book she had been reading had slipped from her hands; her eyes, under their long lashes, had a faraway look and seemed to be gazing into the world beyond. She was experiencing that almost voluptuous weariness which follows upon an attack of fever, and she was busy chewing the orange blossoms she picked up on her coverlet and whose bitter savour she enjoyed. Schiavone has painted a Venus chewing roses, and a modern artist might have made a companion piece to the old Venetian master's painting by representing Alicia biting away at the orange blossoms.

She was thinking of Paul d'Aspremont, and wondering whether she would really live long enough to become his wife; not that she believed in the influence of jettatura, but that she was, in spite of herself, a prey to the gloomiest presentiments. That very night she had had a dream whose impression had not been dispelled by her waking.

In that dream she had seen herself lying down, but awake, and looking at the door of the room with the feeling that *some one* was about to enter. After a few moments of anxious waiting, she had perceived against the dark background of the door a slender white form, which, transparent at first, and allowing the various objects to be seen through it as through a faint mist, had acquired greater consistency as it approached her.

The shade wore a muslin dress whose long folds dragged on the ground; long black curls, half undone, hung mournfully down either side of her face, on the cheekbones of which showed two bright red spots. The bosom and neck were so white that they could scarcely be distinguished from the dress, and it was impossible to say where the skin ended and where the cloth began. A very fine Venetian necklace circled the slender neck with its golden line, and in the delicate, blue-veined hand she held a tea-rose whose petals were falling to the ground like tears.

Alicia had never known her mother, who had died a year after giving birth to her, but she often gazed long at a faded miniature, whose ivory tone and almost vanished colouring, wan as the resemblance of the dead, made one think of the portrait of a shadow rather than of that of a living woman, and she understood that the woman who had entered the room was her mother, Nancy Ward. The white dress, the Venetian necklace, the flower in the hand, the black hair, the cheeks with their red spots—nothing was lacking. It was indeed the original of the miniature, taller and larger, moving in the reality of a dream.

Love and terror made Alicia's heart beat fast. She tried to hold her arms out to the shade, but they were heavy as lead and she could not raise them from the couch on which she lay. She strove to speak, but could only utter confused sounds.

Nancy, having placed the tea-rose upon the table, knelt by the bed and laid her cheek against Alicia's breast, listening to the working of the lungs and noting the beating of the heart. The shade's cold cheek felt like ice to the young girl, terrified by the silent auscultation.

The apparition rose, cast a sorrowful glance upon the maiden, and counting the petals of the rose, some of which had fallen since she had placed it on the table, said, "There is but one left." Then sleep had interposed its dark gauze between the sleeper and the shade, and night had swallowed up everything.

Had her mother's soul come to warn her and to fetch her? What was the meaning of the mysterious words that had dropped from the shadowy lips—"There is but one left"? Was the fading rose with the falling petals a symbol of her own life? The strange dream, with its graceful terrors and its awesome charm, the lovely spectre draped in muslin and counting the petals of the flower, had taken fast hold of the girl's imagination. A shadow of melancholy brooded upon her lovely brow, and the sombre wings of dread presentiments swept across her face.

Had not the orange branch that shook its blooms down upon her also a funereal meaning? Were the little virginal stars not to open under her bridal veil? Sorrowful and preoccupied, Alicia withdrew from her lips the bloom she was biting; the bloom was already yellowed and faded!

It was nearly the hour when Paul d'Aspremont would call. Alicia pulled herself together, smoothed her face, curled her ringlets, arranged the folds of her somewhat rumpled gauze scarf, and picked up her book to give herself the air of being occupied.

Paul entered and Miss Ward welcomed him with a playful glance, for she did not wish him to feel any alarm at seeing her lying down, as he would infallibly have believed himself to have caused her illness. The scene with Count d'Altavilla had left on Paul's face a look of irritation and fierceness that led Vice to make the sign of protection, but Alicia's loving smile speedily dispelled the cloud on her lover's face.

"You are not seriously ill, I trust," he said as he sat down by her.

"It is nothing; I am a little overtired; the African sirocco that was blowing yesterday wore me out, but you shall see how well I shall be when we get back to Lincolnshire. Now that I am strong again, we shall take turns in rowing upon the lake."

But even as she spoke, she could not keep back a fit of coughing. D'Aspremont turned pale and looked away, and for a few moments silence reigned in the room.

"I have never given you anything, Paul," went on Alicia, removing from her wasted finger a plain gold ring. "Take this ring and wear it in remembrance of me. I daresay it will go on your finger, for your hand is almost as small as a woman's. And now, goodbye; I feel tired and I should like to try to sleep. Be sure to come to see me tomorrow."

Paul went away broken-hearted. Alicia had in vain tried to conceal her sufferings; he loved her madly, and he was killing her. The very ring she had just given him—was it not the symbol of their betrothal in another life?

He wandered along the beach, nearly out of his senses, planning flight, bethinking himself of entering a Trappist monastery and awaiting death seated on a coffin without ever raising the cowl of his frock. He called himself a coward and an ingrate for not having the strength to sacrifice his love, and taking a mean advantage of Alicia's love; for it was plain that she knew everything, that he was a jettatore, as Count d'Altavilla had said; yet, full of angelic pity, she would not repel him.

"Yes," he said to himself, "that handsome Neapolitan, that count whom she disdains, is really in love. His love shames mine, since, in order to save Alicia, he did not fear to attack and challenge me, a jettatore—that is, as he sees it, a being as much to be dreaded as the fiend himself. While he spoke to me, he was toying with his amulets, and the glance of that famous duelist who has slain three men fell before mine."

On his return to the Hôtel de Rome, Paul wrote a few letters, drew up a will in which he left all he possessed, save a legacy to Paddy, to Miss Ward, and took the various precautions that a gentleman takes when about to engage in a duel to the death.

He opened the rosewood cases in which he kept his weapons in compartments lined with green serge, turned over the rapiers, the pistols, and the hunting-knives, and at last came upon a couple of Corsican stilettoes, absolutely identical, which he had purchased with the intention of giving them to his friends. The blades were of pure steel, stout near the hilt, and double-edged toward the point, damascened, curiously terrible, and carefully mounted. He also selected three silk handkerchiefs and made a bundle of the lot. Then he sent word to Scazziga to be ready very early in the morning for an excursion into the country.

"May the duel prove fatal to me," said he as he threw himself on the bed. "If I am only lucky enough to be killed, Alicia will live."

XIII

Pompeii, the dead city, does not awake in the morning like living cities, and although it has partially thrown back the covering of ashes that has lain over it for so many centuries, it remains asleep on its funereal couch even when the night has passed away.

At that time the tourists of all nations who visit it during the day are still in their beds, worn out by their fatiguing excursions, and dawn, as it lights up the ruins of the mummy-city, does not behold a single human face. The lizards alone, with quivering tails, crawl along the walls, skurry across the disjointed mosaics, heedless of the *Cave canem* inscribed on the threshold of the deserted houses, and joyously hail the first beams of the rising sun. They are the dwellers who have taken the places of the former inhabitants, and it seems as though Pompeii had been exhumed for their special benefit.

Strange indeed is it to see in the rose and azure light of morn the dead city that was surprised in the midst of its pleasures, its work and its civilisation, and which has not undergone the slow decay of ordinary ruins. One cannot help thinking that the owners of the houses, preserved in their smallest parts, are about to issue forth clad in their Roman or Greek dresses; that the cars will presently be tearing along the ruts in the pavement made by them of old; that the topers will in a moment enter the taverns on the counters of which the stains made by the drinking cups are still visible. One walks as in a dream amid the scenes of the past; on the street corners may be seen the red letter posters advertising the shows of the day—except that the day has passed away more than seventeen centuries ago. In the early light of morn, the dancing girls painted on the walls seem to be clinking their crotalae, and with the tip of their white feet to raise the rosy, foam-like edge of their draperies, believing no doubt that the lamps are being relighted for the orgies in the triclinium. The Venuses and the satyrs, heroic or grotesque figures, animated by a sunbeam, attempt to take the place of the vanished inhabitants and to provide the dead city with a painted population. The coloured shadows tremble along the walls, and the mind may, for a few minutes, indulge in the fancy of an evocation of antiquity.

On that day, however, to the great dismay of the lizards, the matutinal serenity of Pompeii was broken by a strange visitor. A carriage drew up at the entrance to the Street of Tombs; Paul alighted and walked on foot to the meeting-place.

He was early, and though he must have been thinking of anything but archaeology, he could not help noticing, as he went along, innumerable little details he probably would not have observed had he been in his usual frame of mind. When the brain relaxes its vigilance over the senses, these, acting for themselves, occasionally acquire singular lucidity. A man condemned to death and on his way to the scaffold will mark a little flower blooming between the cracks of the pavement, the number on the button of a soldier's uniform, a misspelt word on a sign, and many another trifling circumstance that becomes suddenly of enormous importance.

D'Aspremont passed by the Villa of Diomedes, Mamia's tomb, the funeral hemicycles, the antique gate of the city, the houses and the shops that line the Consular Way, almost without glancing at them, yet the coloured and brilliant images of these monuments reached his brain with wonderful clarity. He saw everything: the fluted pillars overlaid halfway up with red or yellow stucco, the fresco paintings, and the inscriptions traced on the walls. An advertisement of a house for rent had even engraved itself so deeply in his mind that he mechanically kept on repeating the Latin words without attaching any meaning to them.

Was it the thought of the approaching duel that thus absorbed Paul? By no means. He did not even dwell upon it; his mind was elsewhere—in the drawing-room at Richmond. He was presenting to the Commodore his letter of introduction, and Alicia was watching him. She had on a white dress and jasmine blossoms in her hair. How lovely, young, and strong she was then!

The old baths are at the end of the Consular Way, near the Street of Fortune, so that d'Aspremont had no difficulty in finding them. He entered the vaulted hall surrounded by a series of niches formed by terra-cotta Atlases, which support an architrave ornamented with foliage and figures of children. The marble overlaying, the mosaics, and the bronze tripods have disappeared. Of the former splendour nothing is left save the terra-cotta Atlases and the walls, bare as those of a tomb. A faint light, filtering through a little round window in which a disk of blue sky shows, shimmers on the broken slabs of the pavement.

Here it was that the women of Pompeii were wont to come, after the bath, to dry their lovely wet bodies, to dress their hair, to resume their tunics, and to smile at their own beauty in the burnished brass of the mirrors. A very different scene was about to take place there, and blood was about to flow on the ground formerly drenched with perfumes.

Presently Count d'Altavilla appeared, carrying a case of pistols in his hand and a couple of swords under his arm, for he had taken it for granted that d'Aspremont had not made his proposal seriously. He had merely looked upon it as a piece of Mephistophelian raillery, of infernal sarcasm.

"What do we want with those pistols and swords, Count?" said Paul when he perceived him. "Did we not agree upon another mode of fighting?"

"Certainly, but it occurred to me that you might change your mind. No one ever fought a duel in that way."

"Even if we were equally skilful, my position gives me too great an advantage over you," answered Paul, with a bitter smile. "I do not propose to avail myself of it. Here are stilettoes that I have brought with me. Examine them; they are absolutely alike. Here are handkerchiefs with which to blindfold ourselves; they are thick, as you see, and *my glance* cannot pierce through them."

Count d'Altavilla bowed in acquiescence.

"We have no seconds," went on Paul, "and one of us must not emerge alive from this vault. Let us, therefore, each write a note certifying that the fight was a fair one, and the victor shall place it on the breast of the dead."

"A good idea," replied the count with a smile, as he wrote a few lines on a leaf torn from Paul's pocketbook.

Paul did the same.

Then the two adversaries threw off their coats, blindfolded themselves, seized their stilettoes, and took hold each of one end of the handkerchief, the link between their respective hatreds.

"Are you ready?" asked d'Aspremont of Count d'Altavilla.

"Yes," replied the Neapolitan, in a perfectly cool voice.

Don Felipe d'Altavilla was a man of tried courage, who feared nothing on earth save jettatura, and this duel in the dark, which would have caused any other man to tremble with terror, did not in the least trouble him. He was simply staking his life on the issue, and he was saved the unpleasantness of seeing his opponent glare at him with his yellow eyes.

The two combatants brandished their knives, and the handkerchief that linked them in the thick darkness drew taut. Paul and the count had instinctively thrown themselves back, that being the only parry possible in so strange a duel, and their arms fell back after a useless stab in the empty air.

This obscure struggle, in which each one felt death without being able to see it approach, was horrible. Grim and silent the two adversaries retreated, twisted around, sprang aside, struck against each other at times, missing their stroke, or sending it too far. There was no sound but that of the trampling of their feet and the panting of their breasts. Once d'Altavilla felt the point of his stiletto strike something. He stopped, thinking he had slain his rival, and listened for the fall of the body; but it was the wall he had struck.

"By Jove!" he said, as he fell on guard again. "I made sure I had run you through."

"Do not speak," answered Paul; "your voice guides me."

And the duel went on as before.

Suddenly the two opponents felt the taut handkerchief fall. A stroke of Paul's stiletto had severed it.

"A truce," cried the Neapolitan. "We are loose; the handkerchief is cut."

"No matter; let us go on," replied Paul.

A dead silence fell upon the scene. Like the loyal adversaries that they were, neither d'Aspremont nor the count wished to take advantage of the knowledge of the other man's position gained by the exchange of words. They therefore took a few steps to disconcert each other, and then began to grope for each other in the darkness.

D'Aspremont stumbled on a stone. The slight sound alerted the Neapolitan, who was brandishing his knife in space the direction in which he must go. Bending low in order to spring with greater force, he leaped forward like a tiger and struck full upon d'Aspremont's stiletto.

Paul felt the point of his weapon, and felt it wet. He heard staggering steps upon the pavement; heard a deep groan, and a body falling heavily to the earth.

Horrified, he snatched off the handkerchief and beheld Count d'Altavilla, pale and motionless, stretched on his back, and a great red stain on his shirt just above the heart. The handsome Neapolitan was dead!

Paul placed upon the count's breast the note that certified to the fairness of the duel and left the baths paler in the broad daylight than is in the moonlight the criminal whom Prud'hon has represented as pursued by the avenging Erinnyes.

XIV

At about two o'clock that afternoon, a company of English tourists, in charge of a cicerone, was visiting the ruins of Pompeii. The island tribe, composed of a father, a mother, three tall girls, two small boys, and a cousin, had already traversed with dull, lacklustre eyes, in which could be read the profound weariness characteristic of the British race, the amphitheatre, the Tragic Theatre, and the Comic Theatre, so quaintly collocated, the military quarter, full of the caricatures sketched by the idle guardsmen, the Forum, destroyed while it was undergoing repairs, the Basilica, the Pantheon, the Temples of Venus and of Jupiter, and the shops which line them. They all followed silently in their "Murray" the prolix explanations of the guide, scarcely casting a look at the pillars, the fragments of statues, the mosaics, the frescoes, and the inscriptions.

They at last reached the Baths, discovered, as the guide pointed out, in 1824. "Here stood the vapour baths; here was the furnace, and there the cooling room." These details, imparted in Neapolitan dialect, mingled with a few English terminations, did not appear to be of great interest to the visitors, who had already turned around in order to go out, when Miss Ethelwina, the eldest of the young ladies, a maiden with tow-like fair hair and a very freckled complexion, started back, half-shocked, half-frightened, exclaiming:—

"There's a man!"

"No doubt some workman employed in the work of digging, who thought this was a good place in which to enjoy a siesta, as it is cool and shady in this vault," answered the guide. "You need not be afraid, Miss." And he kicked the prone body. "Here, you fellow, wake up and let their ladyships pass."

But the supposed sleeper did not budge.

"He is not sleeping, he is dead," said one of the lads, who, owing to his smaller stature, could better make out the look of the body in the darkness.

The guide bent down to examine the body and started up quickly, his face full of terror.

"The man has been murdered!" he cried.

"Oh! how shocking to come upon such a thing," exclaimed Mrs.

Bracebridge. "Come away, Ethelwina, Kitty, and Bess," she went on. "It is not proper for young ladies who have been well brought up to look at so unpleasant a sight. Is there no police in this country? Why has not the coroner removed the body?"

"Here is a paper," said the cousin, who was as tall, stiff, and awkward as the Laird of Dumbiedikes in *The Heart of Midlothian.*

"True," said the guide, picking up the note placed upon d'Altavilla's breast.

"Read it out," cried the islanders in a body, their curiosity fully awakened.

> "Let no one be sought out or prosecuted on account of my death. If this note is found on my wound, I shall have fallen in a fair duel.
>
> "Felipe, Count D'Altavilla."

"He was a man of rank. It is most sad," said Mrs. Bracebridge, impressed by the dead man's title.

"And handsome," whispered Miss Ethelwina the freckled.

"You cannot complain any longer of not meeting with anything startling on our trip," said Bess to Kitty, "for if we have not been stopped by brigands on the road from Terracina to Fondi, to come upon a young nobleman stabbed with a stiletto in the ruins of Pompeii is surely an adventure. There must have been some love affair at the bottom of it, and we shall now have something Italian, picturesque, and romantic to tell our friends. I shall make a sketch of the scene in my album, and you can add to it some mysterious stanzas in the Byronic style."

"All the same," said the guide, "the stroke was a good one, from below upwards, quite according to rule, and no mistake."

Such was the funeral discourse pronounced over the body of Count d'Altavilla.

Some workmen, summoned by the guide, proceeded to fetch the police, and poor d'Altavilla's remains were conveyed to his family seat near Salerno.

As for d'Aspremont, he had returned to his carriage with staring eyes, seeing no more than a somnambulist would have done. He looked like a statue walking along. Although the sight of the body had filled him with the religious awe inspired by death, he did not feel guilty and there was no remorse in his despair. Insulted in a way that admitted of no refusal, he had accepted the duel only in the hope of losing in it a life that was henceforth odious to him. Gifted with a deadly glance, he had insisted upon the blindfolding in order that fatality alone should bear the responsibility of the outcome. He had not even struck the blow; his foe had rushed upon the blade. He felt as sorry for d'Altavilla as if he had had nothing to do with his death.

"It was my stiletto that slew him," he said to himself. "Now, if I had looked at him in a ballroom, a chandelier would have fallen from the ceiling and broken his head. I am as innocent as the thunderbolt, the avalanche, the manchineel tree, as all destructive, unconscious forces. My will has never been maleficent, my heart is full of love and kindliness, but I know that I am a harmful being. The thunderbolt does not know that it inflicts death, but I, who am a man, an intelligent creature, have I not a hard duty to fulfil toward myself? I am bound to summon myself to the bar of my own conscience and to examine myself. Have I the right to remain on this earth where I do nothing but work woe? Would God damn me if I were to kill myself for love of my fellow-creatures? It is a terrible and difficult question I dare not solve. Yet it seems to me that suicide is excusable in a man situated as I am. But if I am mistaken? Then throughout eternity I should be deprived of the sight of Alicia, whom I could then gaze upon without hurting her, for the eyes of the soul are free from the fascino. That is a risk I shall not run."

A sudden thought flashed through the brain of the unfortunate jettatore, breaking in upon his mental monologue. His features became relaxed, and the peace that comes of a great resolution smoothed his pale brow. He had come to a supreme decision.

"Be ye condemned, ye eyes of mine, since ye are murderous. But before closing forever, saturate yourselves with light, gaze upon the sun, the blue sky, the mighty sea, the green trees, the far horizons, the palace colonnades, the fishers' huts, the distant isles in the bay, the white sails flitting over the deep, Vesuvius and its plume of smoke; gaze upon all these lovely sights that you shall never again behold, so that you may remember them. Study every form and every tint, feast on them for the last time. Today, whether ye be deadly or not, ye shall rest upon everything and intoxicate yourselves with the glorious spectacle of creation. Come! look around, for the curtain is about to fall between you and this earthly scene!"

The carriage, at this moment, was driving along the shore. The azure bay glittered in the light; the sky seemed made of a single sapphire; a splendour of beauty was on all things. Paul ordered Scazziga to pull up; he alighted, sat down upon a rock, and looked long, long, long, as though he were striving to imbibe the infinite. His eyes plunged into space and light, rolled as though in ecstasy, filled themselves with the colour, and absorbed the sunshine. The night that was about to fall upon him was to have no morrow.

Tearing himself away from his contemplation, d'Aspremont reentered his carriage and had himself driven to Miss Ward's.

He found her, as on the previous day, lying upon her narrow couch in the lower room I have already described. Paul sat down opposite her, and this time he did not keep his eyes on the ground as was his habit since he had learned he was a jettatore.

Alicia's wondrously perfect beauty had become idealised through suffering; the woman in her had almost disappeared and made way for the angel. Her flesh had become transparent, ethereal, luminous. Her soul shone through it as the flame through an alabaster lamp. Her eyes were filled with the infinity of the heavens and scintillated like stars; scarce did the mark of life show in her crimson lips.

A heavenly smile, like a sunbeam in a rose, illumined those lips when she saw her lover's glance envelop her like a long caress. She thought Paul had at last got rid of his fancies and was returning to her happy and trustful as in the early days of their love. She held out to him her little white, slender hand, and he kept it in his own.

"So you are no longer afraid of me," she said with sweet raillery to Paul, who still kept his glance fixed upon her.

"Oh! let me gaze upon you," replied d'Aspremont in a strange tone of voice as he knelt down by her. "Let me drink in your ineffable beauty."

And he eagerly contemplated Alicia's lustrous black hair, her lovely brow as pure as that of a Greek statue, her eyes dusky blue as a lovely night, her delicately modelled nose, her mouth with the pearly teeth revealed by a languorous smile, her willowy, swan-like neck, and he seemed to note each detail, each perfection as might a painter preparing to draw a portrait from memory. He was sating himself with the sight of the beloved one, making a collection of remembrances, assuring himself of the outlines, going over the contours.

Under his burning gaze, Alicia, fascinated and charmed, experienced a voluptuously painful sensation, pleasantly deadly. Her life seemed to become more intense and to be leaving her; she blushed and paled, turned hot and cold by turns. In another moment her soul would have fled.

She put her hand on Paul's eyes, but his glance traversed the transparent and frail fingers like a flame.

"Now my eyes may close forever, for in my heart I shall see her forever," said Paul to himself as he rose to his feet.

That night, after having looked at the sunset—the last he was to behold—he ordered, on his return to the Hôtel de Rome, a brazier and charcoal.

"Does he propose to asphyxiate himself?" wondered Virgilio Falsacappa, as he handed Paddy the required articles. "It is the best thing that cursed jettatore could do."

Alicia's betrothed opened the window, contrary to Falsacappa's expectation, lighted the coals, plunged the blade of a dagger into them, and waited until the steel had become red hot.

The thin blade soon showed white-hot in the burning coals. Paul, as if to bid himself farewell, leaned on the mantelpiece in front of a tall mirror that reflected the light of a candelabrum with a number of candles. He gazed with melancholy curiosity upon that sort of spectre that was himself, that envelope of his thought he was never again to see.

"Farewell," he said, "farewell, pale phantom that for so many years I have dragged through life; farewell, sinister failure in which beauty mingles with horror; mould of clay stamped on the brow with a fatal sign; contorted mask of a tender and gentle soul! Thou art about to vanish forever from my sight. Living, I plunge thee into eternal darkness, and soon I shall have forgotten thee as one forgets the dream of a night of storm. In vain shalt thou say, thou wretched body, to my inflexible will,

'Hubert, Hubert, my poor eyes!' Thou shalt not soften it. Come, let me to work, for I am both the victim and the executioner."

And he left the chimneypiece to seat himself on his bed.

He blew upon the coals in the brazier that stood on a table near by, and seized by the hilt the blade, from which flew with a crackling sound bright, white sparks.

At this crucial moment, firm as was his resolve, d'Aspremont felt himself turn faint; a cold sweat bathed his temples; but he soon overcame this purely physical weakness and put the burning steel close to his eyes.

He nearly screamed as he felt a sharp, lancinating pain. It seemed to him that two jets of molten lead were entering his eyes and penetrating to his very brain. He let fall the dagger, which rolled to the floor and charred it.

A dense, opaque darkness, in comparison with which the deepest night is as brightest day, shrouded him in its black veils. He turned his head in the direction of the mantelpiece where the tapers must have been still burning, but met only profound, impenetrable obscurity, in which did not even show the faint gleams that seeing people behold when with closed eyes they find themselves in presence of a light. His sacrifice was accomplished.

"Now," said Paul, "thou noble and charming creature, I may become thy husband without becoming a murderer. No longer shalt thou waste away under my destructive glance; thou shalt regain thy health. Alas! I shall see thee no more, but thy celestial image shall shine with immortal brilliancy in my memory; I shall behold thee with the eyes of the soul; I shall hear thy voice, more harmonious than the sweetest music; I shall feel the air displaced by thy motions; I shall notice the silken rustling of thy dress, the faint creaking of thy shoes; I shall breathe the soft scent that emanates from thee, forming an atmosphere round thee. At times thou shalt leave thy hand in mine to make me feel thy presence; thou wilt deign to guide thy poor blind lover when his steps hesitate upon their dark way; thou shalt read him the poets and tell him of the paintings and the statues. Thy speech shall restore to him the vanished universe; thou shalt be his one thought, his one dream. Freed from the distraction of things and the dazzling light, his soul shall fly to thee on unwearying wings.

"I regret nothing, since thou art saved. What have I lost, indeed? The monotonous spectacle of the seasons and the days; the more or less picturesque setting of the scenes in which the many differing acts of the sad human comedy are played, earth, heaven, waters, mountains, trees, and flowers: vain appearances, wearisome repetitions, unchanging forms. He who possesses love possesses the true sunshine, the light that never fails."

Thus did the unfortunate Paul d'Aspremont commune with himself, a prey to lyrical excitement mingled with the delirium due to pain. Little by little the acute suffering was dulled, and he fell into dark sleep, brother of death and like it a consoler.

When daylight penetrated into the room, it did not wake him. Midnight and noon were henceforth the same to him, but the bells, ringing out the Angelus with joyous peals, sounded faint through his sleep and, gradually becoming more distinct, drew him from his condition of somnolence.

He opened his eyelids, and, before his soul had recollected, experienced a horrible sensation. His eyes opened out upon the void, the darkness, the nothingness, as if, having been buried alive, he had awakened out of a trance and found himself in his coffin. He soon recovered, however, for was it not to be always thus? Was he not, day by day, to pass from the darkness of sleep to the darkness of waking?

He groped round for the bell-rope. Paddy hastened to answer his ring, and as he manifested surprise at seeing his master rise with the hesitating movements of a blind man—

"I was imprudent enough to sleep with the window open," said Paul, in order to cut short all explanations, "and I think I have got amaurosis. I shall soon be better. Lead me to my armchair and put a glass of fresh water by my side."

Paddy, with true English discretion, made no comment, carried out his master's orders, and withdrew.

Left alone, Paul dipped his handkerchief in the cold water and held it to his eyes to deaden the inflammation due to the burning.

But let me leave d'Aspremont in his painful immobility, and let me turn to the other characters in my story.

The strange news of Count d'Altavilla's death had quickly spread through Naples and furnished food for innumerable conjectures, each more absurd than the others. The count was famed for his skill as a swordsman; he had the reputation of being one of the most expert fencers of the Neapolitan school, so dangerous on the dueling-ground. He had killed three men and had grievously wounded five or six. His reputation in this respect was so well known that he was no longer called out; the most insolent duelists saluted him respectfully and, if he happened to look insultingly at them, avoided treading on his toes. Had one of these swashbucklers slain d'Altavilla, he would not have failed to brag of the victory.

There remained the possibility of murder, but that was removed by the paper found on the dead man's breast. The authenticity of the note was at first called in question, but the count's handwriting was vouched for by persons who had received many letters from him. The fact that he had been blindfolded, for the body was found with a handkerchief fastened round the head, proved an insurmountable difficulty. Besides the stiletto driven into the count's breast, a second one was found, which no doubt had fallen from his hand. On the other hand, if the duel had been fought with knives, what was the purpose of the swords and pistols that were recognised as having been the count's property? The coachman, on being questioned, stated that he had driven his master to Pompeii and had been ordered to return home if the latter did not reappear within an hour. The mystery could not be solved.

The report of the death speedily reached the cars of Vice, who informed Sir Joshua Ward. The Commodore, who at once recollected his mysterious conversation with d'Altavilla about Alicia, suspected that some dark attempt, some horrible and desperate struggle had taken place between him and d'Aspremont, with or without the consent of the latter. As for Vice, she did not hesitate to attribute the death of the handsome count to the atrocious jettatore, her hatred of the latter acting as second sight. Yet Mr. d'Aspremont had paid his visit to Miss Ward at the usual time, and his countenance did not betray the least sign of emotion after a terrible drama; indeed, he appeared calmer than usual.

The fact of the death was concealed from Miss Ward, whose condition had become critical, though the English physician summoned by

Sir Joshua could not perceive that she was suffering from any definite malady. Her life seemed to be ebbing away; her soul seemed to be fluttering its wings in an attempt to escape; she appeared to be suffocating, like a bird in a vacuum, rather than to be attacked by a real disease, capable of being treated by ordinary means. She looked like an angel kept back on earth and dying of homesickness of heaven—her loveliness so suave, so delicate, so diaphanous, so immaterial, that the coarse atmosphere of earth could no longer sustain her. One could only imagine her soaring in the golden light of Paradise, and the little lace pillow that supported her head shone like an aureole. As she lay on her bed, she resembled Schoorel's dainty Virgin, the most delicate gem of Gothic art.

Mr. d'Aspremont did not call that day. In order to conceal his sacrifice, he had resolved not to appear with his eyelids inflamed, reserving to himself to explain his blindness by some other cause. But the next morning, the pain having ceased, he entered his carriage, guided by his groom Paddy.

The carriage drew up as usual at the open-work gate. The self-blinded man pushed it open and, feeling the ground with his foot, entered the well-known walk. Vice had not, as was her custom, hastened up on hearing the bell that was rung by the opening of the gate. None of the innumerable joyous sounds that form, as it were, the breathing of an inhabited house reached Paul's attentive ear. A gloomy, deep, terrifying silence reigned in the dwelling, which might have been thought abandoned. This silence, sinister even to a seeing person, became still more dread in the darkness that surrounded the new-made blind man.

The branches, which he could no longer perceive, seemed to try to hold him back like the arms of suppliants and to prevent his going farther. The laurels barred his way; the rose-bushes caught at his clothing; the creepers clung to his limbs; the garden said to him in its mute voice: "Unfortunate man, what doest thou here? Do not force the obstacles that I oppose to thee; return, return!" But Paul did not listen, and tormented by dreadful presentiments, lurched into the foliage, pushed back the clumps of verdure, broke the branches, and kept on toward the house.

Torn and bruised by the angry shrubs, he at last reached the end of the walk. A gust of free air struck him on the face, and he continued on his way with outstretched hands. He came up against the wall, and found the door by groping for it.

He entered. No friendly voice welcomed him. Hearing no sound by which he might guide himself, he hesitated for a moment upon the threshold. A smell of ether, the perfume of aromatics, the odour of burning wax, all the faint scents of a room of death came to the blind man breathless with terror. A dreadful idea came into his mind, and he entered the room.

He had scarcely proceeded a few steps when he knocked up against something that fell with much noise. He bent down and recognised by the feel a metal candlestick like those in churches, and fitted with a tall candle.

Bewildered, he went on his way through the darkness. He thought he heard a voice repeating prayers in a low tone. He took another step forward and his hands touched the edge of a couch. He bent over it, and his trembling fingers first came in contact with a motionless body lying stiff and stark under a fine tunic; then they felt a wreath of roses and a face as pure and cold as marble.

It was Alicia lying on her deathbed.

"Dead!" shrieked Paul in a choking voice. "Dead! And I have killed her!"

The horror-stricken Commodore had seen the blind phantom stagger in, grope his way about, and stumble against Alicia's deathbed. He had understood at once, and the grandeur of the sacrifice, unfortunately useless, brought the tears to the reddened eyes of the old gentleman who had believed himself incapable of weeping again.

Paul threw himself on his knees by the bedside and covered Alicia's ice-cold hand with kisses, while convulsive sobs shook his frame. His grief softened the fierce Vice herself, as she stood silent and sombre by the wall, watching over her mistress' last sleep.

When his adieux were over, d'Aspremont rose and walked to the door, stiffly, like an automaton moved by springs. His sightless eyes, wide open and staring, had a supernatural expression, and though they were blinded they seemed still endowed with vision. He traversed the garden with the heavy tread of a marble statue, went out into the country, and walked on straight ahead, stumbling against the stones, staggering at times, listening intently as if to catch a distant sound, but ever advancing.

The sea's great voice sounded more and more distinct. The billows, lashed by a storm wind, broke on the shore with mighty sobs, expressing unknown griefs, and under the foam fringe swelled their despairing breasts; millions of bitter tears streamed upon the rocks, and the restless gulls uttered plaintive cries.

Presently Paul reached the edge of an overhanging rock. The roar of the waves, the salt spray torn from the billows by the gusts of wind and which lashed his face, should have warned him of his danger, but he heeded it not. A strange smile flitted over his blanched lips and he kept on his sinister walk, although he felt the void beneath his lifted foot.

He fell; a huge billow seized him, rolled him over and over for a moment, and then swallowed him up.

Then the storm broke out in its fury; the waves swept up the shore in serried files, like soldiers storming a fort, and threw the spray of their crests fifty feet into the air. The black clouds were torn open as though they were the walls of Hell, and through the fissures showed the burning furnace of the lightnings; sulphurous, blinding flashes illumined space; the summit of Vesuvius glowed, and its sable plume of smoke, beaten down by the wind, curled around the volcano's brow. The vessels at anchor collided with lugubrious sounds, and the tautened rigging moaned dolorously. Then the rain came down, its drops like driven bolts, and it seemed as though chaos were striving to reassert its supremacy over Nature and once again to confound the elements.

All the efforts set on foot by the Commodore failed to bring about the recovery of Paul d'Aspremont's body.

A silver-mounted, satin-lined, ebony casket, like the one concerning which Clarissa Harlowe wrote so touchingly to Master Undertaker, was shipped on board a yacht under the Commodore's superintendence and subsequently deposited in the family vault in the Lincolnshire seat. It contained the mortal remains of Alicia Ward, lovely even in death.

As for the Commodore, a great change has taken place in him. He is no longer stout, puts no rum in his tea, eats very little, talks less, and has lost his crimson and white look—for he has become pale.

Spirite: A Fantastic Tale

I

Guy de Malivert was stretched out, almost resting upon his shoulders, in a very comfortable armchair by his fireside, in which blazed a good fire. He appeared to have settled down with the intention of spending at home one of those quiet evenings that fashionable young men occasionally enjoy as a relief from the gaieties of society. His dress, at once comfortable and elegant, consisted of a black velvet, braided boating-coat, a silk shirt, red flannel trousers, and morocco slippers, in which his strong, well-turned feet were quite at ease. His body freed from any disagreeable pressure, comfortable in his soft and yielding garments, Guy de Malivert, who had enjoyed at home a simple but refined meal, washed down with a few glasses of claret that had gone to India and back, was in a condition of physical beatitude due to the perfect harmony of his organs. He was happy, though nothing specially fortunate had happened to him.

Near him a lamp, placed in a stand of old crackled celadon, shed through its ground-glass globe a soft, milky light, like moonbeams through a mist. The light fell upon a book that Guy held with careless hand, and which was none other than Longfellow's *Evangeline*.

No doubt Guy was admiring the work of the greatest poet young America has yet produced, but he was in that lazy state of mind in which absence of thought is preferable to the finest thought expressed in sublime terms. He had read a few verses, then, without dropping his book, had let his head rest upon the soft upholstering of the armchair, covered with a piece of lace, and was enjoying to the full the temporary stoppage of the working of his brain. The warm air of the room enfolded him like a suave caress. All around was rest, comfort, discreet silence, absolute repose. The only sound perceptible was an occasional rush of gas from

299

a log and the ticking of the clock, the pendulum of which rhythmically and softly marked the flight of time.

It was winter; the new-fallen snow deadened the distant roll of carriages, infrequent enough in this peaceful quarter, for Guy lived in one of the quietest streets of the Faubourg Saint-Germain. Ten o'clock had just struck, and the lazy fellow was congratulating himself upon not being in evening dress, stuck in a window recess at some ambassadorial ball, with no other prospect than the angular shoulders of some old dowager whose dress was cut too low. Although the temperature of the room was that of a hothouse, it was evident by the brisk burning of the fire and the deep silence in the streets that it was cold outside. The splendid Angora cat, Malivert's companion on this evening of idleness, had drawn so close to the fire as to scorch its lovely fur, and but for the gilded fender it would have curled itself up on the hot ashes.

The room in which Guy de Malivert was revelling in such peaceful joy was partly a studio and partly a library. It was a large, high-ceiled room on the top floor of the building, which was situated between a great court and a garden in which grew trees so old as to be worthy of a royal forest, and which are nowadays found only in the aristocratic faubourg; for it takes time to grow a tree, and the newly rich cannot improvise them to shade the mansions they build with fortunes that seem to fear bankruptcy.

The walls were hung with tawny-coloured leather, and the ceiling was a maze of old oaken beams, framing in compartments of Norway pine, of the natural colour of the wood. The sober brown tints set off the paintings, sketches, and watercolours hung on the walls of this sort of gallery in which Malivert had collected his artistic curiosities and fancies. Oak bookshelves, low enough not to interfere with the paintings, formed a wainscotting round the room, broken only by a single door. An observer would have been struck by the contrast offered by the books placed on the shelves: they appeared to be a mingling of the library of an artist and of a scholar. By the side of the classical poets of every age and every country—Homer, Hesiod, Vergil, Dante, Ariosto, Ronsard, Shakespeare, Milton, Goethe, Schiller, Byron, Victor Hugo, Sainte-Beuve, Alfred de Musset, Edgar Poe—stood Creuzer's *Symbolism,* Laplace's *Celestial Mechanics,* Arago's *Astronomy,* Burdach's

Physiology, Humboldt's *Cosmos,* the works of Claude Bernard and Berthelot, and others on pure science. Yet Guy de Malivert had no pretensions to scholarship. He knew not much more than one learns at college, but after he had refreshed his literary education it seemed to him that he ought not to remain ignorant of all the fine discoveries that are the glory of our age. He had made himself acquainted with them to the best of his ability and could talk astronomy, cosmogony, electricity, steam, photography, chemistry, micrography, spontaneous generation; he understood these matters and sometimes astonished his interlocutor by his novel and ingenious remarks.

Such was Guy de Malivert at the age of twenty-eight or twenty-nine. His hair had thinned a little on the brow; he had a pleasant, frank, and open expression; his nose, if not as regular as a Greek nose, was nevertheless handsome and parted two brown eyes, the glance of which was firm; his mouth, with its somewhat full lips, betokened sympathetic kindliness. His hair, of a rich brown, was massed in thick, close curls that needed not the hairdresser's irons, and a golden auburn moustache shaded his upper lip. In a word, Malivert was what is called a handsome fellow, and when he had made his entrance into society he had met with many unsought successes. Mothers provided with marriageable daughters were most attentive to him, for he had an income of forty thousand a year and a sickly multi-millionaire uncle, who had made him his heir. An enviable lot! Yet Guy had not married. He was satisfied with nodding approvingly at the sonatas young ladies performed for his benefit; he politely led his partners to their seats after the waltz, but his conversation with them during the intervals of the dance was confined to such commonplaces as "It is very hot in this room"—an aphorism from which it was impossible to deduce any matrimonial intentions. It was not that Guy lacked wit; on the contrary, he could have readily found something less commonplace had he not feared to become entangled in the web more tenuous than cobwebs, woven in society round maidens whose marriage portion is small. If he found himself made too welcome in a house he ceased to call there or started on a long trip; on his return he noted with satisfaction that he was entirely forgotten. Perhaps it will be supposed that Guy, like many young men of today, formed in shady society temporary morganatic unions that enabled him to dispense with a

more regular marriage, but it was not so. Without being more of a rigor-
ist than became him at his age, Malivert had no liking for the made-up
beauties who dressed their hair like that of poodles and wore exaggerated crinolines. It was a mere matter of taste. Like everybody else, he had
had one or two love affairs. Two or three misunderstood women, more
or less separated from their husbands, had proclaimed him their ideal,
whereunto he had replied, "You are very kind," not daring to tell them
that they were in no wise *his* ideal. Malivert was a well-bred young gentleman. A little supernumerary at the Delassements-Comiques, whom
he had presented with a few louis and a velvet mantle, had attempted to
asphyxiate herself in his honour; but in spite of these stirring adventures,
Guy de Malivert, entirely frank toward himself, perceived that having
reached the solemn age of twenty-nine, when a young man turns into a
mature man, he was ignorant of love—such, at least, as it is depicted in
novels, dramas, and poems, and even as described by his companions
when in a confidential or a boastful mood. He consoled himself easily for
this, however, by reflecting upon the troubles, calamities, and disasters
due to that passion, and he patiently awaited the coming of the day when
chance would bring to him the woman destined to fix his affections.

Yet, as the world is very apt to dispose of you as best it fancies and
as best suits it, it had been decided in the society which Guy de Malivert
most frequented, that he was in love with Mme. d'Ymbercourt, a young
widow whom he visited very often. Mme. d'Ymbercourt's estates
marched with those of Guy; she had about sixty thousand francs a year
and was only twenty-two years of age. She had suitably mourned for M.
d'Ymbercourt, a crusty old fellow, and she was now in a position to take
a young and handsome husband, of birth and fortune on a par with her
own. So the world had married them on its own authority, reflecting that
they would have a pleasant home, a neutral ground where people might
meet. Mme. d'Ymbercourt tacitly accepted the match and looked upon
herself as already somewhat Guy's wife, though he made no haste to declare himself, thinking rather of ceasing his calls upon the young widow,
whose airs of anticipated proprietorship palled upon him.

That very evening he was to have taken tea at Mme. d'Ymbercourt's, but laziness had mastered him after dinner. He had felt so comfortable in his own apartments that he had rebelled at the thought of

dressing and driving out with the thermometer at ten or twelve above zero, in spite of his having a fur coat, and a hot-water bottle in his carriage. He satisfied himself with the excuse that his horse's shoes had not been sharpened for frost, and that the animal might slip on the frozen snow and hurt himself. Besides, he did not care to keep standing for two or three hours, exposed to the cold north wind in front of a door, a horse that Cremieux, the famous dealer of the Champs-Elysées, had charged him five thousand francs for. From this it will be seen that Guy was not very much in love, and that Mme. d'Ymbercourt would have to wait a good deal longer for the ceremony that would enable her to change her name.

As Malivert, feeling sleepy in the warm temperature of the room, in which floated the blue, fragrant smoke of two or three cabanas, the ashes of which filled a small antique Chinese bronze cup on a stand of eaglewood, placed near him on the table that bore the lamp—as Malivert was beginning to feel in his eyes the golden dust of sleep, the door opened gently and a servant entered, bearing upon a silver salver a dainty letter, scented and sealed with a seal well known to Guy, for his face immediately clouded. The odour of musk exhaled by the note seemed also to produce a disagreeable impression upon him. It was a note from Mme. d'Ymbercourt, reminding him of his promise to come and drink a cup of tea with her.

"The devil take her!" he exclaimed most ungallantly, "and her wearisome notes too! Much fun there is in driving across the city merely to drink a cup of hot water in which have been soaked a few leaves coated with Prussian blue and verdigris, while I have here in that lacquered Coromandel caddy caravan tea, genuine tea, still bearing the seal of the Kiatka custom-house, the uttermost Russian post on the Chinese frontier. Most assuredly I shall not go."

His habits of courtesy made him change his mind nevertheless, and he ordered his valet to bring him his clothes; but when he saw the trousers' legs hanging pitifully on the back of the armchair, the shirt as stiff and white as a sheet of porcelain, the black coat with its limp sleeves, the patent-leather shoes with their brilliant reflections, the gloves stretched like hands that have been passed through a rolling-mill, he was seized with sudden desperation and plunged fiercely back into his armchair.

"I shall stay at home after all, Jack; get my bed ready."

As I have already mentioned, Guy was a well-bred young fellow and kind-hearted besides. Feeling some slight remorse, he hesitated on the threshold of his bedroom, every comfort in which smiled invitingly upon him, and said to himself that ordinary decency required that he should send a few words of apology to Mme. d'Ymbercourt, pleading a headache, important business, an unexpected obstacle, in order to explain, with some show of politeness, his not having called upon her. But Malivert, entirely capable as he was, though not a literary man, of writing a tale or an account of a trip for the *Revue des Deux Mondes,* detested writing letters, and especially merely formal, ceremonious notes, such as women dash off by the score on the corner of their toilet-table while their maid is busy attiring them. He would much sooner have wrought out a sonnet with rare and difficult rhymes. His incapacity in this respect was complete, and he would walk from one end of Paris to the other rather than scribble a couple of lines. The thought of having to reply to Mme. d'Ymbercourt suggested to him the desperate expedient of going to see her himself. He went to the window, pulled the curtains aside, and through the damp panes saw the darkness of night, full of densely falling flakes of snow that spotted it like a guinea-hen's back. This led him to think of Grimalkin, shaking off the snow heaped up on his shining harness. He reflected upon the unpleasant passage from his coupe to the vestibule; of the draft in the stairs unchecked by the warmth of the stove, and he especially thought of Mme. d'Ymbercourt standing by the mantelpiece, in a very low-necked dress, recalling that character in Dickens that was always known by the name of "The Bosom," and whose white form advertised the wealth of a banker. He saw her superb teeth set off by a fixed smile; her eyebrows, which might have been drawn with Indian ink, so perfectly arched were they, yet which owed nothing to art; her beautiful eyes; her nose, so perfect in shape and modelling that it might have been reproduced as a model in a student's textbook; her figure, which all dressmakers declared perfect; her arms as round as if turned, and laden with over massive bracelets. The remembrance of all these charms that the world had assigned to him, by marrying him, little as he cared for her, to the young widow, filled him with such intense melancholy that he went to his desk, resolved, in spite of the horror of it, to write ten lines rather than go and drink tea with that lovely woman.

He took out a sheet of paper embossed with a quaintly interlaced "G" and "M," dipped in the ink a fine steel pen in a porcupine holder, and wrote, well down the page in order to have the less to say, the word "Madam." Then he paused and leaned his cheek on his hand, for his inspiration failed him. He remained for some time thus, his wrist in place, his fingers grasping the pen, and his brain unconsciously filled with thoughts wholly foreign to the subject of his note. Then, as if Malivert's body were tired of waiting for the words that did not come, his hand, nervous and impatient, seemed inclined to fulfil its task without further orders. His fingers extended and contracted as if tracing letters, and Guy was presently much amazed at having written, quite unconsciously, nine or ten lines which he read and which were about as follows:—

"You are beautiful enough and surrounded by lovers enough for me to tell you, without giving you cause for offence, that I do not love you. It is not creditable to my taste that I should make this confession—that is all. Why, then, keep up an intercourse that must end in linking two souls so little intended to be brought together and involve them in eternal unhappiness? Forgive me; I am going away, and you will not find it difficult to forget me."

"What is this?" exclaimed Malivert, when he had read his letter over. "Am I crazy or a somnambulist? What a strange note! It is like those drawings of Gavarni's that exhibit at one and the same time in the subscription the real and the expressed thought, the true and the false. Only, in this case the words do tell the truth. My hand, instead of telling the pretty fib I meant it to write, has refused to do so, and, contrary to custom, my real meaning is expressed in my letter."

Guy looked carefully at the note and it struck him that the character of the handwriting was not quite like his usual hand.

"It is an autograph that would be contested by experts," he said, "if my correspondence were worth the trouble. How the devil did this curious transformation take place? I have neither smoked opium nor eaten hashish, and the two or three glasses of claret I drank cannot have gone to my head. I carry my liquor better than that. What will become of me if the truth takes to running off my pen without my being aware of it? It is fortunate that I re-read my note, never being quite sure of my spelling in the evening. What would have been the effect of these too truthful lines? And how indignant and amazed would Mme. d'Ymbercourt have been had she read them! After all, it might have been better had the letter gone such as it is. I should have gained the character of being a monster, a tattooed savage, unworthy of wearing a white necktie, but at least that wearisome engagement would have been broken off short. If I were superstitious, I might easily see in this a warning from heaven instead of a most improper forgetfulness."

After a pause Guy came to a sudden decision. "I shall go to Mme. d'Ymbercourt, for I am incapable of rewriting the note."

And he dressed in a very bad temper.

As he was about to leave his room, he thought he heard a sigh, but so faint, so soft, so airy that but for the deep silence of night he would not have noticed it.

Malivert stopped short on the threshold of his room, for that sigh affected him as the supernatural affects the bravest of men. There was nothing very terrifying in the faint, inarticulate, plaintive sound, and yet Guy was more deeply moved than he cared to confess even to himself.

"Nonsense," said he; "it must have been the cat complaining in its sleep." And taking from his valet a fur coat in which he wrapped himself with a skill that testified to long trips in Russia, he descended, very much out of sorts, the steps at the foot of which his carriage awaited him.

II

Leaning back in the corner of his coupé, his feet on the hot-water bottle, his fur coat drawn close round him, Malivert gazed, without noticing them, upon the strange effects of light and shade produced upon the carriage window, slightly obscured by the frost, by the sudden blaze of light from a shop brilliantly lighted with gas and still open, late though the hour was, and at the prospect of the streets dotted with brilliant points of light.

The carriage soon crossed the Pont de la Concorde, under which flowed the dark waters of the Seine in which, amid the sombre gleams, were reflected the lights of the lamps. As he drove on Malivert could not help recalling the mysterious sigh he had heard or thought he had heard as he left his room. He explained it by means of all the commonsense reasons with which sceptics explain the incomprehensible. No doubt it had been due to the wind in the chimney, to some noise from outside altered by an echo, to the low vibration of one of the piano-strings responding to the passage of some heavy dray, or after all it was but a sound uttered by his angora cat dreaming by the fireside, as he had at first believed. This was the most probable explanation, the most reasonable. Yet Malivert, while recognising the logical soundness of these views, was inwardly dissatisfied with them; a secret instinct told him that the sigh was not due to any of the causes to which his scientific prudence attributed it; he felt that the soft moan had been uttered by a soul and was no mere vague sound of matter. There was at once breath and grief in it. Whence, then, did it come? Guy dwelt on it with that sort of questioning uneasiness experienced by the strongest minds when they find themselves face to face with the unknown. There had been no one in the room, save Jack, a by no means sentimental person. The softly modulated, harmonious, tender sigh, softer than the soughing of the breeze in the branches of the trembling aspen, was unquestionably feminine—it was impossible to deny it.

Another thing puzzled Malivert—the letter that had, so to speak, written itself, as if a will independent of his own had guided his hand. He could not seriously explain this away, as he had at first endeavoured to do, by attributing it to absentmindedness. The feelings of the soul are controlled by the mind before they show on the paper; and besides, they do not write themselves down while the mind is elsewhere. Some influence he could not define must have mastered him and acted in his stead while he was dreaming, for now that he thought of it he was quite certain he had not fallen asleep even for an instant. He had certainly felt lazy, somnolent, comfortably stupid the whole evening, but at that particular moment he had unquestionably been wide awake. The unpleasant alternative of going to Mme. d'Ymbercourt's or writing her a note of apology had even somewhat feverishly excited him. The lines that expressed his real feelings more accurately and forcibly than he had yet confessed even to himself were due to an intervention that he felt compelled to consider supernatural until it was explained away by investigation or another name were found for it.

While Guy de Malivert revolved these thoughts in his mind, the carriage was traversing streets more deserted, owing to the frost and snow, than was usual in those rich and fashionable quarters in which the day does not end until very late in the night. The Place de la Concorde, the rue de Rivoli, the Place Vendôme had been quickly left behind, and the coupé, turning into the boulevard, entered the rue de la Chaussée-d'Antin where Mme. d'Ymbercourt lived.

As he entered the courtyard Guy experienced a disagreeable shock: two files of carriages, the coachmen muffled up in furs, occupied the sanded space in the centre, and the restive horses, shaking their bits, cast the foam from their mouths on to the snow on the ground.

"This is what she calls a quiet, informal evening; tea by the fireside. That is always the way with her. All Paris is here and I have not put on a white tie," grumbled Malivert. "I ought to have gone to bed, but I tried to play the diplomat like Talleyrand, and did not follow my first impulse just because it was the right one."

He slowly ascended the steps and, after throwing off his fur coat, walked up to the drawing room, the doors of which were opened for him with a sort of obsequious and confidential deference by a lackey, as for one who would soon be the master of the house and in whose service he desired to remain.

"There!" said Guy de Malivert to himself, as he noticed the man's servility was more marked than usual; "the very servants dispose of my liberty and marry me on their own authority to Mme. d'Ymbercourt! Yet the banns have not been published!"

Mme. d'Ymbercourt, on perceiving Guy advancing toward her with rounded back—the modern way of bowing to ladies—uttered a slight exclamation of pleasure, which she endeavoured to make up for by assuming an air of coldness and dissatisfaction. But her ever smiling lips, accustomed to exhibit teeth of irreproachable pearliness, could not form the pout called for, and the lady, observing in the mirror that her attempt was a failure, made up her mind to show herself good-natured, like an indulgent woman who knows that nowadays masculine gallantry must not be overtaxed.

"You are very late, Mr. Guy," said she, holding out a hand gloved with such a small glove that it felt like wood when pressed; "no doubt you remained at your club smoking and playing cards. Well, you have been punished for your remissness by not hearing the great German pianist Kreisler play Liszt's 'Grand Galop Chromatique,' and the charming Countess Salvarosa sing Desdemona's air better than ever Malibran did."

Guy, in a few well-chosen words, expressed the regret—not very deep, to tell the truth—he felt at having missed the galop by the virtuoso and the aria by the society leader, and as he felt rather awkward, among all those people dressed up to the nines, at having on a black silk tie instead of a white lawn one, he tried to escape and to gain some less brilliantly lighted spot where his involuntary solecism in dress might more easily be concealed in relative shadow. He had much difficulty in doing so, for Mme. d'Ymbercourt kept recalling him to her side by a glance or a remark that required a reply, brief though Guy strove to make it.

At last, however, he managed to gain the recess of a door leading from the great drawing room to a smaller one, arranged like a hothouse, with trellises covered with camellias.

Mme. d'Ymbercourt's drawing room was furnished in white and gold, and hung with crimson Indian damask. The chairs, armchairs, and sofas were easy, comfortable, and well upholstered. The chandelier with its gilded branches was filled with tapers in rock-crystal foliage. Lamps, vases, and a tall clock, all evidently the work of Barbedienne, adorned the white marble mantelpiece. A handsome carpet, the pile of which was soft and thick like sward, lay underfoot. Superb, full curtains draped the windows, and on the wall smiled, even more than the original, a magnificently framed portrait of the Countess painted by Winterhalter.

There was no objection to be made to this drawing room filled with rare and costly articles, the like of which, however, any one rich enough not to fear the bills of an architect or a house-furnisher could easily obtain. The commonplace luxury of the room was entirely suitable, but it lacked distinctiveness. Not a single thing indicated the individuality of the owner, and if the Countess had been absent, the room might as well have been that of a banker, a lawyer, or an American making a short stay in the capital. Soul and individuality were wanting. So Guy, naturally artistic, considered the luxury exceedingly vulgar and disagreeable, though it was exactly the background best suited to Mme. d'Ymbercourt, whose beauty was composed merely of commonplace perfections.

In the centre of the room, on a circular divan surmounted by a great China vase in which bloomed a rare exotic plant—of whose name Mme. d'Ymbercourt had not even the least idea, and which had been put there by her gardener—were seated, in dresses of gauze, tulle, lace, satin, and velvet, the swelling folds of which surged to their shoulders, ladies, most of them young and beautiful, whose fancifully extravagant gowns testified to the inexhaustible and costly powers of invention of Worth. On their brown, golden, red, and even powdered hair, so abundant that even the least sarcastic could not help thinking art had been called in to beauty's aid, diamonds sparkled, feathers waved, dewy leaves showed green, natural or imaginary flowers bloomed, strings of sequins rustled, darts, daggers, pins with double balls gleamed bright, ornaments of scarabeus wings glistened, golden bands were crossed, ribbons of red velvet wound in and out, stars of gems quivered on the end of springs, and in general there could be seen whatever may be piled upon the head of a fashionable woman—to say nothing of the grapes, the currants, and the brightly coloured berries that Pomona lends to Flora to complete an evening head-dress.

Leaning against the door-post, Guy watched the satiny shoulders covered with rice powder, the necks on which curled stray threads of hair, the white bosoms occasionally betrayed by the too low epaulet of the bodice, small misfortunes to which a woman sure of her charms easily reconciles herself. Besides, the motion of drawing up the sleeve is uncommonly graceful, and the act of adjusting the opening of the dress on the bosom so that it shall have a satisfactory contour affords opportunities for attractive poses. My hero was indulging in this interesting study, which he preferred to wearisome conversation; for, in his opinion, it was the most profitable thing one could do at a ball or a reception. He glanced with careless eye at these living Books of Beauty, at these animated Keepsakes which society scatters in drawing rooms just as it places stereoscopes, albums, and papers on the tables for the benefit of shy people who do not know which way to turn. He enjoyed his pleasure in greater security because, the report of his approaching marriage with Mme. d'Ymbercourt having gone abroad, he was not obliged to be careful of his glances, formerly closely watched by mothers desirous of settling their daughters in life. Nothing was expected of him now. He had ceased to be a prey. He was settled and done for, and although more than one woman thought to herself that he might have done better, the fact was accepted. He might even, without running any risk, have spoken two or three phrases running to a young girl, for was he not already as good as married to Mme. d'Ymbercourt?

At the same door where stood Guy de Malivert stood also a young gentleman whom he often met at his club, and whose somewhat eccentric Northern mode of thought he rather liked. It was the Baron de Feroë, a Swede, a fellow-countryman of Swedenborg's, bending like him over the abyss of mysticism, and as fully taken up with the other world as with this. He had a strange and characteristic head. His fair hair, falling almost straight, was fairer even than his skin, and his moustache was of so pale a gold that it looked like silver. His gray-blue eyes were filled with an indescribable expression, and his glance, usually half veiled by long pale lashes, flamed sharply out and seemed to reach beyond the ken of human vision. But the Baron de Feroë was too thorough a gentleman to affect the least eccentricity; his manners, cold and even, were as correct as an Englishman's, and he did not pose in front of mirrors as a seer. That evening, as he was going to the Austrian ambassador's ball on leaving Mme. d'Ymbercourt's reception, he was in full dress; on the breast of his coat, half concealed by the facing, suspended from a fine golden chain, shone the stars of the Elephant and of the Dannebrog, the Prussian Order of Merit, the order of Saint Alexander Nevsky, and other decorations from Northern sovereigns which testified to his diplomatic services.

He was really an extraordinary man, but the fact did not at once strike the beholder, so well was it concealed by diplomatic phlegmatism. He went out into society a great deal and was to be met with at the club and the Opéra, but under his outward appearance of a fashionable man he lived in a mysterious fashion. He had neither intimate friends nor companions. In his admirably kept house, no visitor had ever got beyond the outer drawing room, and the door that led to the other apartments opened to no one. Like the Turks, he devoted to outer life but a single room that he plainly did not live in. Once his visitor was gone, he

withdrew within his apartment. What did he busy himself with? No one
knew. Occasionally he remained invisible for a considerable time, and
those who noted his absence attributed it to a secret mission, or to a trip
to Sweden, the home of his family; but any one who had happened to
pass, at a late hour, through the unfrequented street where the baron
lived might have seen a light in his window or the baron himself leaning
on the balcony, his gaze lost amid the stars. No one, however, was interested in spying upon Baron de Feroë; he rendered exactly to society
what was society's, and the world asks no more of any man. With wom-
en, though scrupulously polite, he never trespassed beyond certain limits, even when he might safely have done so. In spite of his coldness he
was considered rather attractive. The classical purity of his features recalled the Greco-Scandinavian work of Thorwaldsen. "He is a frozen
Apollo," said of him the lovely Duchess of C., who, if gossip were to be
believed, had tried to melt the frost.

Like Malivert, Baron de Feroë was looking at a beautiful snow-white
neck and back, seen in a slightly bending attitude, that imparted an exquisite curve to the lines, and which occasionally shivered at the tickling
of a spray of green leaves that had become partially detached from the
head-dress.

"A lovely girl," said the Baron to Guy, whose glance he had followed. "What a pity she has no soul. The man who falls in love with her
will share the fate of the student Nathaniel, in Hoffmann's tale; he will
run the risk of pressing a lay-figure in his arms at the ball, and that is a
deathly sort of dance for a man of feeling."

"You need not fear for me, my dear baron," laughingly replied Guy
de Malivert. "I do not feel the least desire to fall in love with the fair
owner of these beautiful shoulders, though beautiful shoulders are in
themselves nowise to be disdained. At the present time, to my shame be
it spoken, I do not feel the faintest approach to love for any one whom-
soever."

"What! Not even for Mme. d'Ymbercourt, whom people say you
are going to marry?" replied the baron with an air of ironical incredulity.

"There are people in this world," returned Malivert, quoting Molière, "who would marry the Grand Turk to the Republic of Venice; but
for my part I hope I shall remain a bachelor."

"And you will do right," affirmed the Baron, in a tone that passed suddenly from friendly familiarity to mysterious solemnity. "Do not bind yourself with earthly ties. Remain free for the love that will perchance come to you. The spirits are watching over you, and in the next world you might have cause to regret eternally a mistake committed in this."

As the young Swedish baron uttered these strange words, his steel-blue eyes flashed singularly and his glance seemed to burn into Guy de Malivert's breast. Coming after the curious events of the evening, he received the advice with less incredulity than he would have felt the day before. He turned on the Swede a look full of wonder and questioning, as if to beg him to speak more clearly, but de Feroë, glancing at his watch, said, "I shall be late at the Embassy," pressed Malivert's hand earnestly, and made his way to the door without rumpling a single gown, treading upon a single train, damaging a single flounce, with a delicate skill that proved he was well used to society.

"Well, Guy, are you not coming for a cup of tea?" said Mme. d'Ymbercourt, who had at last discovered her supposed admirer leaning thoughtfully against the door of the smaller drawing room. Malivert had to follow the mistress of the house to the table whereon smoked the tea in a silver urn surrounded with porcelain cups.

The Real was trying to win its prey back from the Ideal.

III

The singular words spoken by Baron de Feroë and his almost sudden disappearance after he had uttered them gave Guy food for thought as he returned to the Faubourg Saint-Germain, carried along at Grimalkin's fastest trot; for the horse, though a thoroughbred, did not need any urging to speed, the cold north wind making the return to his warm loose-box with its comfortable litter pleasant indeed.

"What can he have meant by his solemn riddles spoken in so mysterious a tone?" thought Guy de Malivert, as Jack assisted him to undress. "De Feroë has been brought up in the least romantic of civilisations; he is sharp, clean, and cutting like an English razor, and his manners, for all their perfect courtesy, are colder than the Arctic. I cannot suppose that he was trifling with me. People do not fail in that way to Guy de Malivert, even when they are as brave as the white-eyebrowed Swede. Besides, what would be the object of such a joke? He certainly did not stay to enjoy it, for he disappeared at once like a man who is determined to say no more. Well, let me dismiss all this nonsense from my mind. I shall see the baron at the club tomorrow, and no doubt he will then be more explicit. Let me to bed and try to sleep, whether the spirits are watching me or no."

Guy did go to bed, but sleep did not come to his call, though he courted it by reading the most soporific pamphlets, perusing them with infinite mechanical attention. In spite of himself he was watching for those faint sounds which are perceptible even in the deepest silence. The rattle of the clock ere the hour or the half-hour struck, the crackling of the sparks in the embers, the creaking of the wainscotting under the influence of the heat of the room, the sound of the dropping oil in the lamp, the draft of air attracted by the hearth and moaning softly through the chinks of the door in spite of the weather-strips, the unexpected fall of a newspaper from his bed to the floor—made him start, as at the sudden explosion of a firearm, so excited were his nerves. His hearing was so tense that he could hear the pulsations of his arteries and the beating of his heart. But amid all these confused murmurs he did not manage to distinguish anything resembling a sigh.

His eyes, which he closed from time to time in hopes of inducing sleep, would forthwith reopen and examine the recesses of the room with a curiosity not unmixed with apprehension. He strongly desired to see something and yet dreaded to do so. Occasionally his dilated pupils seemed to perceive dim shapes in the corners, which the light of the lamp, covered with a green shade, left in partial darkness; the folds of the curtains assumed the aspect of feminine garments and appeared to move as though they clothed a living body, but it was all imagination. Blooms, luminous points, changing patterns, butterflies, waving vermiculated lines undulated, danced, swarmed, swelled, and sank before his weary eyes without his being able to make out anything definite.

More agitated than I can express, and feeling, though he neither saw nor heard anything, an unknown presence in his room, he rose, drew on a camel's-hair dressing-gown he had brought back from Cairo, threw two or three logs on the fire, and sat down by the chimney in a great armchair more comfortable for a sleepless man than the bed upset by his wakefulness. Near the armchair he saw lying on the carpet a crumpled paper. It was the note he had written to Mme. d'Ymbercourt under the spell of that mysterious impulse he could not yet account for. He picked it up, smoothed it out, and noticed, on examining it carefully, that the writing was not quite like his own. It seemed to be the work of an impatient hand, incapable of controlling itself, attempting, in the production of a facsimile, to copy the model exactly, but inserting, among the characters of the original, loops and strokes of its own. The aspect of the writing was more elegant, more slender, and more feminine than Guy's.

As he noted these details, Guy thought of Edgar Poe's "Gold Bug" and of the wonderful skill with which William Legrand manages to decipher the meaning of the cryptogram used by Captain Kidd to indicate enigmatically the exact spot where he had concealed his treasure. He longed to possess the deep intuition that can guess so boldly and so accurately, which fills up blanks and restores connections. But in this case not even Legrand himself, even assisted by C. Auguste Dupin, of "The Purloined Letter" and "The Murders in the Rue Morgue," could have managed to guess at the secret power that had controlled Malivert's hand.

Guy, however, at last fell into the heavy, troubled sleep that, on the approach of dawn, follows a night of insomnia. He woke when Jack entered to relight the fire and to assist his master to dress. Guy felt chilly and uncomfortable; he yawned, stretched his limbs, took a cold bath, and, refreshed by his tonic ablutions, was soon himself again. Gray-eyed morn, as Shakespeare hath it, walking, not o'er the dew of a high eastern hill, but down the slope of the snow-covered roofs, glided into the room, the shutters and curtains having been opened by Jack, and restored to every object its real aspect as it drove away the dreams of the night. There is nothing so reassuring as the sunlight, even if it be but the pale beams of a winter sun such as just then streamed in through the frost-flowers on the window-panes.

Having recovered the ordinary feelings of life, Guy felt amazed at his agitation of the past night and said to himself, "I did not know I was so nervous." Then he tore open the wrappers of the newspapers that had just been brought up, cast a glance at the articles they contained, read the news of the town, took up the copy of *Evangeline* he had been reading the previous evening, smoked a cigar, and having thus whiled away the time until eleven o'clock, dressed, and, by way of exercise, resolved to walk to the Cafe Bignon, where he proposed to breakfast. The frost of the early morning had hardened the snow that had fallen during the night, and as he traversed the Tuileries Malivert enjoyed looking at the mythological statues powdered with the white snow and the great chestnut-trees covered with a silvery mantle. He breakfasted on choice and carefully selected dishes, like a man seeking to repair the fatigue due to a sleepless night, and chatted gaily with pleasant companions, the very flower of Parisian wits and sceptics, who had adopted as a motto the Greek maxim: "Do not forget not to believe." Yet, when the jokes became rather too free, Guy smiled somewhat constrainedly. He did not share unresistingly in the paradoxes of incredulity and the boastfulness of cynicism. The words of Baron de Feroë, "The spirits are watching you," involuntarily recurred to him, and he felt as though a mysterious witness stood close behind him. He rose, waved an adieu to his friends, and took a turn or two on that boulevard along which more wit travels in one day than in a whole year in the rest of the world, and finding it rather deserted on account of the cold and the early hour, he mechanically turned into the Rue de Chaussée-d'Antin. He was soon at the house of Mme. d'Ymbercourt. As he was about to ring he thought he felt a breath sweep by his ear and that he heard these words whispered very softly but very distinctly: "Do not go in." He turned round quickly, but saw no one.

"What is the matter with me?" said Malivert to himself. "Am I going mad? Am I suffering from hallucinations in broad daylight? Shall I or shall I not obey the injunction?"

But when turning abruptly he had let go the bell-handle; the bell had rung and the door opened. The porter, standing in front of his lodge, looked at Malivert, who hesitated about entering. He did so, however, although he did not feel much like it after the supernatural incident that had just occurred. Mme. d'Ymbercourt received him in the small drawing room, decorated in buttercup yellow and blue ornaments, in which she received her morning callers. That particular shade of yellow was especially unpleasant to Guy. "Yellow is the favourite colour of brunettes," had replied the Countess to Malivert, who had more than once allowed himself to ask for the removal of the odious colour.

Mme. d'Ymbercourt wore a skirt of black taffeta with a jacket of brilliant colour braided and covered with more jet and embroidery than a *maja* going to a bullfight or a *feria* ever put on her bodice. The Countess, although a woman of the world, was foolish enough to allow dressmakers to clothe her in costumes worn only by the rosy-cheeked and small-mouthed dolls of fashion-plates.

Contrary to her habit, Mme. d'Ymbercourt seemed to be serious; a shade of annoyance darkened her usually serene brow, while the corners of her mouth were drawn down. One of her kind friends had just left her and had asked her, with the feigned naturalness of women on such occasions, when her marriage to Guy de Malivert was to take place. The Countess had blushed, stammered, and replied evasively that it would soon come off, though Guy, whom every one destined to be her husband, had never asked for her hand or even formally declared himself—a fact attributed by Mme. d'Ymbercourt to respectful timidity and partly perhaps to that feeling of uncertainty which every young man experiences when on the point of giving up bachelor life. But she felt quite sure that he would speak ere long, and she looked upon herself already as his bride; so much so that she had determined upon the changes that the entrance of a husband into her mansion would necessitate. More than once she had said to herself, as she looked at certain rooms: "This shall be Guy's room; this his study, and this his smoking room."

Although he did not much care for her, Guy could not help acknowledging that Mme. d'Ymbercourt was endowed with regular beauty, enjoyed an umblemished character, and was possessed of a considerable fortune. He had let himself drift, without being particularly attracted, and like all people who are heart-whole, into frequenting this house where he was received more cordially than anywhere else, and he returned to it because, if he were absent for a few days, an engagingly amiable note compelled him to do so.

Besides, there was no reason why he should not return to it. Mme. d'Ymbercourt received the best of society and he occasionally met there friends whom it would not have been quite so convenient to seek out in the busy life of Paris.

"You seem a little out of sorts," said Malivert to the Countess; "did your green tea give you a sleepless night?"

"No, indeed. I put so much cream into it that it loses all its strength. Besides, I am the Mithridates of tea; it has ceased to affect me. The truth is, I am annoyed."

"Have I come at the wrong time, or have I upset some of your plans? In that case I hasten to withdraw, and we can take it that finding you were out I left my card at your lodge-gate."

"You are not the least in the way, and you know very well that it is always a pleasure to me to see you," answered the Countess. "Your visits, though I ought not to say it, even seem to me rather infrequent, though others are not of the same opinion."

"Yet you are unencumbered with troublesome relatives, talkative uncles, and chaperon aunts who embroider in the window recess. Kind nature has relieved you of the collection of disagreeable relatives who too often surround a pretty woman, and has left you their inheritances only. You may receive whom you please, for you are not dependent on any one."

"That is true," replied Mme. d'Ymbercourt. "I do not depend on any one, yet I am responsible to every one. A woman is never wholly or really free, even when a widow and apparently mistress of her actions. A whole police force of interested people surrounds and watches her and interferes in her affairs. So, my dear Guy, you compromise me."

"I?—compromise you?" exclaimed Malivert with sincere surprise that betokened a modesty quite uncommon in young men not over twenty-eight years of age, who have their clothes made by Renouard and send to England for their trousers. "Why should I compromise you, rather than d'Aversac, Beaumont, Janowski, and de Feroë, each and all of whom are exceedingly attentive to you?"

"That is more than I can tell you," replied the Countess. "Perhaps without knowing it you are a dangerous man, or society has perceived in you some power of which you are yourself ignorant. None of the names you have mentioned have been connected with mine; people seem to think it quite natural that these gentlemen should call on me on my day at home, that they should call every now and then between five and six on their return from the Bois, and should drop in on me in my box at the Bouffes or the Opéra. But these very actions, innocent in themselves, assume, it appears, when performed by you, a tremendous meaning."

"And yet I am the steadiest fellow in the world, and have never given cause for gossip. I do not wear a blue frock coat like Werther, nor a slashed doublet like Don Juan. No one has ever surprised me playing the guitar under a balcony; I never go to the races in a four-in-hand with questionable women in loud dresses, and never, at any evening party, do I discuss sentimental questions in the presence of pretty women for the purpose of drawing attention to the purity and delicacy of my feelings. I am never seen posing against a pillar, one hand in my vest, gazing in silence, with a sombre, woebegone look, at some fair girl with long ringlets, like Alfred de Vigny's Kitty Bell. Nor do I wear hair rings, or a sachet round my neck in which I preserve Parma violets given me by 'her.' My most secret drawers might be searched without a single portrait of a fair or a dark beauty being found in them; nor even a bundle of scented notes tied with ribbon or a rubber band; not even an embroidered slipper, a mask edged with lace, or any of the trifles that compose the secret collections of lovers. Frankly, do I look like a lady-killer?"

"You are very modest," replied Mme. d'Ymbercourt, "or else you are trying to make out that you are very artless. Unfortunately, everybody does not agree with you. Objection is raised to the attentions you pay me, although for my part I see nothing to object to in them."

"In that case," returned Malivert, "I shall call less frequently. I shall not come more than once a fortnight or once a month, and then I shall start on a trip. But positively I do not know where to go. I have been to Spain, Italy, Russia, Germany. Well, I might go to Greece, for it is considered sinful not to have seen Athens, the Acropolis, and the Parthenon. I could go by way of Marseilles or board an Austrian Lloyds' steamer at Trieste. They call at Corfu, and on the way one sees Ithaca *soli occidenti bene objacentem,* basking in the setting sun now as in the days of Homer. They go to the head of the Gulf of Lepanto. Then you cross the Isthmus, and you can see the remains of Corinth, which not every one was allowed to enter. You get on board another steamer and in a few hours you reach the Piraeus. Beaumont told me all about it. He started as a fanatical romanticist, but he got metope on the brain there and will not hear of cathedrals now. He has turned into a confirmed classicist and maintains that since the days of the Greeks humanity has gone back to barbarism and that our boasted civilisation is but a form of decadence."

Mme. d'Ymbercourt did not feel particularly flattered by this lyrical outburst of geographical knowledge, and thought Malivert was much too ready to avoid compromising her. She did not desire him to care for her reputation by running away.

"No one wants you to go to Greece," she said. And, with a faint blush and an imperceptible trembling of the voice, "Is there not a simpler way of putting an end to all this gossip than leaving your friends and venturing into a country that is by no means safe, if we are to believe Edmond About's 'King of the Mountains'?"

Fearing lest she had spoken too plainly, the Countess flushed more deeply than before. Her breath came quick and short, and made the jet ornaments on her bodice glitter and rustle; regaining her courage, she looked at Malivert with eyes that a touch of emotion made absolutely beautiful. She loved Guy, her silent admirer, as much as it was in her nature to love any one. She liked the neat yet careless way in which he tied his cravat, and with the deep logic of women, a logic the deductions of which are often unintelligible to the subtlest of philosophers, she had inferred from that tie that Malivert possessed all the qualities needed in an excellent husband. The trouble was that the intended husband was strolling very slowly indeed toward the altar and seemed in no hurry to light the hymeneal torches.

Guy perfectly understood Mme. d'Ymbercourt's meaning, but he more than ever dreaded uttering imprudent words that might bind him, so he answered: "No doubt, no doubt; a trip breaks off matters completely, and when one returns it is easier to see what should be done."

On hearing this cold and indefinite reply the Countess allowed a gesture of annoyance to escape her and bit her lips. Guy, very much embarrassed, kept silence, and the situation was becoming unbearable when the footman relieved the strain by announcing Baron de Feroë.

IV

On seeing the Swedish baron enter, Malivert uttered an irrepressible sigh of content and cast a look of gratitude at M. de Feroë, for he had never been so glad to see any one. But for this opportune interruption Guy would have found himself in a most awkward position. He was bound to answer Mme. d'Ymbercourt plainly, and yet he hated nothing so much as formal explanations; he always preferred to act rather than promise, and even in matters of little moment he was very wary of pledging himself in any way. The glance that Mme. d'Ymbercourt cast upon the visitor was not as kindly as Malivert's, and—if good breeding had not taught dissimulation—reproach, impatience, and anger might easily have been read in her look. The Baron's unseasonable intrusion deprived her of an opportunity that would not soon recur and that her self-respect would scarcely allow her to bring about, for it was certain that Guy would not seek it and, indeed, would carefully avoid it. Although on most occasions Guy was a man of resolution and courage, he dreaded any step that might settle his life in any way. He was talented enough to succeed in any career, but he had deliberately avoided making any choice lest it should prove to be the wrong one. He was not known to entertain any attachment for any woman, though the habit he had got into of calling frequently on the Countess had led to the supposition that the pair were thinking of marriage. He mistrusted any kind of bond or obligation, and it seemed as though, urged by a secret instinct, he was trying to keep himself free for some future event.

After having exchanged a few preliminary commonplaces, chords forming a prelude to conversation, like those struck on the piano before beginning a piece, Baron de Feroë, by a transition of the kind that in a couple of sentences make you pass from the fall of Nineveh to the last win of "Gladiator," entered upon an aesthetic and transcendental dissertation on Wagner's most abstruse operas—*The Flying Dutchman, Lohengrin, Tristan and Isolde.* Mme. d'Ymbercourt, although a remarkable pianist, did not understand music and especially such deep, mysterious, complex music as Wagner's, whose *Tannhäuser* gave rise to such fierce discussions in France. While working at a strip of embroidery she had taken from a basket placed near the armchair she usually occupied, she replied from time to time to the enthusiastic analyses of the Baron, urging the commonplace objections always brought up against any new form of music, and which were once made to Rossini's compositions as well as to Wagner's, such as lack of rhythm and melody, obscurity, excessive use of brass instruments, inextricably complicated orchestration, deafening noise, and finally the material impossibility of performing the compositions.

"Your discussion is too deep for me, as I am simply an ignoramus in the matter of music. I am moved by what strikes me as beautiful; I admire Beethoven and even Verdi, though it is no longer fashionable to do so, now that one has to be a partisan, as in the days of the rivalry between Gluck and Piccini, when one had to elect to side with the king or with the queen. So I shall leave you two to fight it out, for I cannot throw any light on the question, and at most I can put in a hem! hem! like the Minorite whom Molière and Chapelle chose for arbiter in a discussion on a point in philosophy."

With these words Guy de Malivert rose to take leave and shook hands with Mme. d'Ymbercourt, whose glance said, as plainly as feminine reserve permitted, "Stay," and followed him to the door with a sadness that would no doubt have touched him had he seen it; but Guy's attention was engrossed by the quietly imperious expression of the Swede, which seemed to say: "Do not again expose yourself to the peril from which I have rescued you."

When he found himself in the street, he thought, with some feeling of dread, of the supernatural warning he had received as he was about to enter Mme. d'Ymbercourt's house, and of the call made by Baron de Feroë, a call that coincided in the most singular way with Guy's disregard of the mysterious warning. The baron seemed to have been sent to his assistance by the occult powers of whose presence around him he was vaguely conscious. Although Guy de Malivert was not systematically incredulous or sceptical, he found it hard to bring himself to believe in spirit influences, and he had never indulged in the fantasies of table-turning and spirit-rapping. He felt indeed a sort of repulsion for experiments intended to exploit the marvellous, and he had refused to go to see the famous Home, whom all Paris went crazy over for a season. Until the previous evening he had led a careless bachelor life, fairly satisfied on the whole with being alive and feeling that he was cutting by no means a bad figure in the world; thinking of material things only and not troubling to ascertain whether or not the earth carried with it, in its daily circling round the sun, a world peopled with invisible and impalpable beings. But he was compelled to own to himself that a change had come over his life; that a new element, unsought by him, was seeking to enter into his hitherto peaceful existence, from which he had carefully excluded all possible disturbing causes. So far it was not much: a sigh as soft as the breathing of an Æolian harp, a thought substituted for his own in a letter written mechanically, a word or two whispered in his ear, his meeting with a solemn, mysterious-looking Swedenborgian baron. It was plain, nevertheless, that a spirit was circling round him *quarens quem devoret,* as the eternal wisdom of the Bible has it.

While thus ruminating Guy de Malivert had reached the great open space in the Champs-Elysées without having in the least intended to go in that direction rather than in any other. His body had borne him thither, and he had allowed it to have its way. There were not many people there. A few of those obstinate persons who insist—for hygienic reasons—on exercising at all times of the year, and who cut holes in the ice in order to get their bath, were returning from the Bois de Boulogne, their noses blue and their cheeks purple with cold, riding horses with kneecaps. Two or three of them waved a greeting to Guy, and he even received, though he was on foot, a gracious smile from a lady in an open carriage, and wrapped in costly Russian furs.

"As I happen to be the whole of the public, my attention and admiration are worth having," thought Malivert. "In summer I should not have received such a bow. But what am I doing here? This is not the time of year to dine in an arbour with some lively girl, and besides I do not feel particularly gay. All the same, the sun is setting behind the Arc de l'Étoile, and it is time to think of satisfying the inner man."

Malivert was right. The great arch of the Arc de Triomphe was framed in a mass of clouds heaped up in strange fashion, their edges brilliant with a foam of light. The evening breeze, as it set them in motion, imparted to them a sort of life, and it would have been easy to make out figures and groups in the dark mass of vapours through which flashed the sunbeams, just as in those drawings of Doré's where the fancies that fill the minds of the characters are reflected on the clouds, making the Wandering Jew see Christ toiling up Calvary, and Don Quixote behold knights tilting with enchanters. Malivert thought he saw angels with great wings of flame soaring over a swarming multitude of indistinct beings that moved to and fro on a bank of black clouds, like a sombre promontory jutting out into a phosphorescent sea. Occasionally one of the lower figures broke away from its companions and rose toward the lighted regions, traversing the red disk of the sun. On reaching the higher spheres, it flew for a moment by the side of one of the angels and then melted into the universal glow. No doubt fancy had much to do with the ever-changing combinations, and of a cloud-picture it may be said, in the words of Hamlet to Polonius: "Do you see yonder cloud that's almost in shape of a camel? . . . Or like a whale?" And in either case one may answer affirmatively, without necessarily being an imbecile courtier.

Night coming on put an end to the vaporous fancifulness, and the gas lamps, as they were lighted, soon traced, from the Place de la Concorde to the Arc de l'Étoile, the two lines of fire, so magical in effect, which delight the wondering strangers who enter Paris at night by that triumphal avenue. Guy hailed a passing cab, on the lookout for a fare, and had himself driven to the rue de Choiseul, where his club was situated. Leaving his overcoat to the care of the liveried servants in the vestibule, he glanced over the book in which members put down their names for dinner, and noted with satisfaction that it contained Baron de Feroë's. He wrote his own below, traversed the billiard room, where the marker was sadly waiting until it should please some one to indulge in a game, and several other high-ceiled rooms, spacious and furnished with every modern comfort—the temperature kept at an even warmth by a huge furnace, though great logs blazed on the monumental andirons within the vast fireplaces. Four or five members were idling on the divans or leaning on the green reading-table and glancing through the papers and reviews, arranged methodically and continually being disarranged. Two or three were writing love letters or business notes on the club stationery.

It was near the dinner hour, and the guests were chatting together until the butler should announce that the meal was served. Guy began to fear that Baron de Feroë was not coming, but as he passed into the dining room the baron arrived and sat down by him. The dinner, served with a wealth of glassware and silver plate, was distinctly good, and each man washed it down with his own particular tipple, some with claret, others with champagne, others again with pale ale, according to individual habit or caprice. A few, of English tastes, called for a glass of sherry or port, which tall waiters in knee breeches brought ceremoniously upon silver salvers, marked with the club monogram. Every man drank to his liking, without troubling about his neighbour, for at the club every man is at home.

Contrary to his custom, Guy did not do honour to the dinner. He left the dishes scarcely tasted, and the bottle of Chateau-Margaux in front of him was being very slowly emptied.

"The white angel could not say to you," remarked Baron de Feroë, "as he did one day to Swedenborg, 'You are eating too much,' for you are uncommonly abstemious tonight, and it might be thought that you are trying to attain to the spiritual state by fasting."

"I do not know whether a few mouthfuls more or less would free my soul from its material envelope," answered Guy, "and tend to make more diaphanous the veils that separate the visible from the invisible; but whatever the reason, I do not feel much appetite. Certain circumstances you appear to be acquainted with have, I confess, astonished me somewhat since yesterday and caused me to be more absentminded than is my wont. Normally I am not usually preoccupied at meals, but today other thoughts master me in spite of myself. Have you any engagements this evening, Baron? If you have nothing better to do, I propose that we smoke together after dinner in the music room, where we shall not be disturbed, unless the fancy strikes some of our fellow-members to pound on the piano—which is not at all likely, for our musical friends are all away tonight at the dress rehearsal of the new opera."

Baron de Feroë courteously agreed to Malivert's suggestion and politely replied that no better way could be devised of passing the time. So the two gentlemen settled themselves on the couch and started to puff clouds of smoke from excellent cigars of *la Vuelta de Abajo,* each of them mentally thinking of the curious conversation that could not be put off long. After a few remarks on the quality of the cigars they were smoking, and on the respective merits of strong and mild, the Swedish baron himself opened the subject that Malivert was dying to enter upon.

"First," he said, "I must apologise for the liberty I took in warning you in mysterious fashion the other evening at Mme. d'Ymbercourt's, for as you had not confided in me it was in a way indiscreet of me to penetrate your thoughts before you had spoken. You may be sure I should not have done so—for it is not my habit to abandon my part as a man of the world and to take up that of wizard—had you not inspired me with a lively interest, and had I not been made aware, by signs perceptible to adepts alone, that you had recently been visited by a spirit, or at least that the invisible world was seeking to enter into relations with you."

Guy hastened to say that he had not been in the least offended by the baron, and that, indeed, in the novel situation in which he found himself, he was only too glad to have found a guide apparently so well informed in matters supernatural, and whose seriousness of disposition was so well known to him.

"You readily understand," said the baron, with a slight bow by way of thanks, "that I do not easily break through my reserve, but you have perhaps seen enough no longer to believe that our senses suffice to inform us of everything, and I do not fear, therefore, that you will take me, if our conversation should turn upon such mysterious subjects, for a visionary or one of the *illuminati.* My position is a guarantee that I am not a charlatan, and, besides, the world knows my outer life only. I do not ask you to tell me what has happened in your case, but I perceive that in the sphere beyond that of ordinary life an interest is being taken in you."

"Yes," answered Guy de Malivert, "there is something indefinable floating around me, and I do not think I am indiscreet, as far as the spirits—with which you appear to be on an excellent footing—are concerned, if I tell you in detail what your superhuman intuition has enabled you to divine."

Thereupon Guy related to the Baron the extraordinary events that had marked the previous evening.

The Swedish nobleman, twisting his blond moustache the while, listened to him with extreme attention, but without manifesting the least surprise. He remained silent for a time and seemed buried in thought.

Then, as if the words summed up a series of reflections, he suddenly said to Guy:—

"M. de Malivert, did a young girl ever break her heart on your account?"

"Neither girl nor woman ever did, so far as I am aware at least," replied Malivert. "I am not conceited enough to suppose myself capable of inspiring so great a passion. My love affairs, if a kiss carelessly given and carelessly received may be dignified by such a name, have been of the most peaceful and least romantic character, and ended as easily as they began. Indeed, in order to avoid pathetic scenes, of which I have a horror, I have always so managed matters as to be betrayed and abandoned, my self-love being very ready to make that sacrifice to my repose of mind. So I fancy I have not left behind me in life many disconsolate Ariadnes; in our Parisian mythology, the arrival of Bacchus invariably precedes the departure of Theseus. Besides, even at the risk of giving you but a poor opinion of my power of loving, I must admit that I have never felt for any one that mad, exclusive, all-absorbing passion of which everybody speaks without perhaps having experienced it. No woman has ever inspired me with the desire to attach her to myself by an indissoluble bond or made me dream of two lives blended into one, or wish to flee with her to that paradise of azure, light, and beauty which love, it is said, can create even in a hut or an attic."

"It does not follow, my dear Guy, that you are unable to feel passionate love. There are many varieties of love, and, no doubt, in the place where the fate of souls is settled upon, you have been reserved to higher destinies. But you have still time, for spirits have no power over us save by our free consent. You are standing on the threshold of a boundless, deep, mysterious world, full of illusions and shadows, wherein contend influences for good or evil that a man must learn to distinguish. In that world are to be seen wonders and terrors fit to upset human reason. No one ever returns from its depths without bearing on his brow a pallor that time can never efface; the carnal eye cannot behold with impunity the things reserved for spiritual sight alone; these excursions beyond the material world are paid for by inexpressible fatigue and inspire at the same time desperate nostalgia. Stay your feet at that dread bourne; do not pass from this world into the other, and do not yield to the call that seeks to draw you beyond the bounds of material life. The enchanter is safe within the circle he traces around him and which the spirits cannot cross. Let reality be to you as that circle; do not overpass it, or you will lose your power. You see that, though I am a hierophant, I do not indulge in proselytism."

"Do you mean," said Malivert, "that I should run the risk of perilous adventures in that invisible world by which we are surrounded, and which reveals its existence to but a small number of privileged beings?"

"By no means," replied the Baron de Feroë. "Nothing that the eye of the flesh can note will happen to you, but your soul may remain forever deeply troubled."

"Is, then, the spirit that does me the honour to concern itself with me of a dangerous character?"

"It is sympathetic, kindly, and loving. I have met it in the radiance of light. But heaven causes vertigo as much as the abyss does. Remember the story of the shepherd that loved a star."

"Yet," replied Malivert, "what you said to me at Mme. d'Ymbercourt's seemed to be a warning against any terrestrial entanglement."

"I was bound to warn you," returned the Baron de Feroë, "in the event of your answering the manifestations of that spirit, but since you have not as yet done so, you are still your own master. Perhaps it would be best for you to remain in that condition and to lead your old life."

"And marry Mme. d'Ymbercourt," put in Guy de Malivert with an ironical smile.

"Why not?" said the Baron de Feroë. "She is young, beautiful, and loves you; I read in her glance the genuine grief your veiled refusal caused her. She might possibly acquire a soul."

"That is a risk I do not choose to run. Pray do not endeavour, dear Baron, through a kindly feeling which I quite understand, to tie me down to material life. I am more detached from it than may appear at first sight. The fact that I have ordered my days in pleasant and convenient fashion does not involve sensuality on my part. At bottom, comfort is a matter of indifference to me. If I have thought it best to appear careless and joyous rather than to affect a romantic melancholy, which is in very bad taste, it does not follow that the world as I find it delights and satisfies me. It is quite true that I do not maunder, in drawing rooms, and in presence of an assembly of pretentious women, about my heart, or the ideal, or the passion of love, but I have kept my soul true and unstained, unspotted by any vulgar love, in the expectation of the coming of the unknown deity."

While Malivert spoke thus, with more earnestness than men of the world usually display, the eyes of Baron de Feroë lighted up and his face assumed an expression of enthusiasm which he generally concealed under a mask of icy indifference.

He was pleased to see that Guy resisted prosaic temptation and maintained his spiritual will.

"Since you have made up your mind, my dear Guy, return home, and you will no doubt receive some new communications. I have to stay; I won a hundred louis yesterday from d'Aversac, and I am going to give him his revenge."

"The rehearsal must be over, for I hear our friends returning and humming, very much out of tune, the airs they have failed to catch."

"Away with you, then; the discord would throw your soul out of harmony."

Guy shook hands with the baron and entered his carriage, which was waiting for him at the door of the clubhouse.

V

Guy de Malivert returned home, his mind made up to run the venture. Though he did not appear to be romantic, nevertheless he was so; but his proud, shy reserve led him to conceal his feelings, and he did not expect of others more than he was willing to give himself. His relations with society were pleasantly indifferent and in no way binding upon him; they were bonds that he could easily cast off at any moment, but it can be readily understood that he dreamed of a happiness that until now he had never experienced.

Acting upon what Baron de Feroë had told him at the club about the need of exercising his will in order to summon the spirits from the vasty deep to the confines of our own world, Malivert concentrated all his powers within himself and mentally formulated his desire to enter into more direct communication with the mysterious spirit that he felt around him and that would not, in all likelihood, prove very restive, since it had of its own accord attempted to manifest itself.

Having done this, Malivert, who was in the room, half studio, half drawing room, in which he was sitting at the beginning of this story, applied himself to listen and watch with the utmost attention. At first he neither saw nor heard anything, though the furniture, the statuettes, the pictures, the old carved dressers, the exotic curiosities, and the trophies of weapons struck him as having an unusual and extraordinary aspect, and a sort of fantastic lifelike appearance due to the lights and shadows cast upon them by the lamp. A Chinese grotesque of jade stone seemed to grin to the ears like an old man in his dotage, and a copy of the Venus of Milo, her pointed breasts standing out strongly in the light that fell on them against a dark background, assumed a disdainful look as she swelled her nostrils and drew down the corners of her mouth. Both the Chinese god and the Greek goddess disapproved of Malivert's undertaking, or at least the expression on the two lighted faces might have led him to believe this. Unconsciously Malivert's eyes, as if urged by a mental impulse, turned toward a Venetian mirror suspended on the Cordova leather tapestry.

It was an eighteenth-century mirror, like those commonly seen in Loughi's "Lady at Her Toilet" and "Leaving for the Ball," subjects often painted by that decadent Watteau, and like those to be found in the shops of second-hand dealers in the Ghetto. The glass itself was bevelled; the frame was composed of ornaments in cut glass, surmounted by a mass of scrolls and flowers in the same material, which, against the uniform tint of the background, sometimes resembled mat silver, sometimes flashed prismatic rays from their facets. Amid this sparkling and blazing, the glass itself, of small size like all Venetian mirrors, showed a deep bluish-black and resembled an opening into a void full of ideal darkness.

Curiously enough, none of the objects opposite the mirror were reflected in it, and it looked like one of the stage mirrors that the scene painter washes over with faint neutral tints to avoid the reflection of the auditorium.

A vague instinct led Malivert to feel that if any revelation was to be made to him, the mirror would prove to be the medium employed. He was fascinated by it, although as a rule he never looked at it, and it attracted his glance irresistibly. Yet, though he gazed at it intently, he could make out nothing but the black colour, made more intensely mysterious by the cut-glass framework. At last he thought he perceived on its surface a faint, milky whiteness, like a distant trembling light that appeared to be drawing nearer. He turned round to see what article in the room caused this reflection, but saw nothing. Brave though Malivert was, and he had proved his courage on more than one occasion, he felt the hair of his flesh stand up and the fear and trembling of which Job speaks. This time he was about to cross, knowingly and of his own free will, the dread threshold. He was about to step outside the circle that Nature has traced around man. Henceforth he might be thrown out of his orbit and revolve around some unknown point. Unbelievers may laugh at it, yet never was a step fraught with more serious consequences, and Guy fully realised its importance. An irresistible attraction impelled him on, however, and he continued to stare into the Venetian mirror. What was he about to see? Under what form would the spirit present itself so as to become appreciable to his human perception? Would it be a sweet or a terrible figure? Would it cause joy or terror? Although the luminosity within the glass had not yet assumed any definite form, Guy was convinced that it would prove to be a feminine spirit. It could not be otherwise, he thought, as he recollected the sigh of the evening before that still sounded softly in his heart. Had that spirit belonged to this earth, or had it come from a distant planet or a higher region? That he could not tell. However, judging by what Baron de Feroë had said, he judged that it must be a soul that had lived on earth, and which, drawn by reasons he would probably learn later, was returning to its former abode.

The luminosity in the mirror began to assume a more distinct form and faint colours, immaterial, so to speak, which would have dulled the pigments on the brightest of palettes. It was rather a suggestion of colour than colour itself; a vapour flushed with light and of such delicate tints that human words are incapable of rendering it. Guy stared on, a prey to nervous, intense emotion. The image became plainer and plainer, without, nevertheless, acquiring the hard precision of reality, and Guy de Malivert at last discerned, enclosed within the border of the mirror as within a frame, the head of a young woman, or of a young girl rather, by the side of whose loveliness earthly beauty was but as a shadow.

A faint, rosy flush gave colour to the head, on which light and shade were scarcely noticeable, and which did not need, as do earthly faces, the contrast of chiaroscuro to bring out the modelling, for it was illuminated by another light than ours. The hair, halo-like, softly outlined the brow like a golden vapour. The eyes, half cast down, were of a dark blue, infinitely sweet, recalling the spaces of heaven that at sunset are flushed with violet tints. The fine, small nose was ideally delicate; a smile such as Leonardo da Vinci gave to his female faces, but more tender and less ironical, curved the lips adorably; the willowy neck, bending somewhat under the weight of the head, was bowed forward and blended into a silvery half-tint that might have served for light to another figure.

This slight sketch, necessarily written with words intended to describe earthly things, can give but a most imperfect idea of the apparition that Guy de Malivert beheld in the Venetian mirror. And was it with the eye of the flesh or the eye of the soul that he beheld it? Did the image really exist, and could it have been seen by any one not under the same nervous influence as Guy? That is a difficult question to answer. This much may be said, that what he saw, though it was *like* the face of a beautiful woman, in no respect *resembled* what, on this earth, is called a beautiful female face. The features were similar, but they were purer, transfigured, idealised, and rendered perceptible by an immaterial substance, so to speak, only just dense enough to be visible in the gross earthly atmosphere by eyes not yet freed from the veils that covered them. No doubt the spirit or the soul that was entering into communication with Guy de Malivert had borrowed the form of its former perishable body, but such as it must have become in a more subtile, more ethereal region where the ghosts of things alone and not things themselves can exist. The vision was an ineffable delight to Guy; the feeling of fear that he had initially experienced had vanished, and he gave himself up unreservedly to the strangeness of the situation, discussing nothing, admitting everything, and resolved to think the supernatural natural.

He drew nearer the mirror, in the hope of noting the features more clearly; the image remained as it had at first appeared to him, very close and yet very distant, resembling the projection, upon the inner surface of a crystal, of a figure placed at a distance beyond the power of man to measure. The reality of what he saw, if the expression may be allowed in this connection, was evidently elsewhere, in deep, distant, mysterious regions inaccessible to mortals, on the outskirts of which even the boldest thinker scarce dares venture. In vain did Guy try to connect the face with some of his earthly memories; it was wholly new to him, and yet he seemed to recognise it. Where had he seen it? Assuredly not in this sublunar, terraqueous world.

This, then, was the form under which *Spirite* desired to show herself. Malivert, seeking for a name by which to call to himself the apparition he had beheld in the mirror, had given her this appellation until he could ascertain what name would suit her better. Presently it seemed to him that the image was growing fainter and vanishing within the depths of the mirror. It now showed only as the light vapour of a breath, and even that vapour disappeared in its turn. The passing of the vision was marked by the sudden reflection of a gilded frame suspended on the wall opposite the mirror, which had regained its usual power of reflection.

When he could no longer doubt that the apparition would not return, on that evening at least, Guy threw himself into an armchair, and although the clock had just struck two in the morning, its silvery sound advising him to retire, he could not make up his mind to go to bed. He felt fatigued, it is true; the novel emotions, the first step into an unknown world had brought on the wakeful fatigue that prevents sleep. Besides, he feared to miss another manifestation of Spirite if he should fall asleep.

His feet stretched out on the fender before the fire that had burned up again by itself, Guy thought over the events that had just taken place and the very possibility of which he would have denied a couple of days before. He thought of the lovely head recalling, as if to cause them to be forgotten like vain shadows, the beauties revealed in dreams by the imagination of poets or the genius of painters. He discovered in it infinite, inexpressible suavity, innumerable charms that neither Nature nor art could unite in one and the same face; and he augured well, from the sample he had beheld, of the looks of the inhabitants of the world beyond. Then he asked himself by what strange sympathy, by what mysterious and hitherto unconfessed affinity that angel, that sylph, that soul, that spirit, of whose nature he was as yet ignorant, and which he was unable to connect with any immaterial order, could have been drawn toward him from the infinite depths. He dared not flatter himself with having inspired love in a being of a higher nature, for conceit was no trait of Malivert; yet he could not help owning that Spirite seemed to experience for him, Guy de Malivert, a mere mortal, a sentiment entirely feminine in its character and that in this world would have been called jealousy. The sigh she had uttered, the letter whose wording she had changed, the warning whispered at Mme. d'Ymbercourt's door, and the remark suggested by her, no doubt, to the Swedish baron proved it. What Guy did understand quite plainly and at once was that he himself was madly, desperately, hopelessly in love; a prey all of a sudden to a passion that eternity itself could not satiate.

From that moment every woman he had ever known was totally forgotten by him. On the appearance of Spirite, he had forgotten earthly loves, just as Romeo forgot Rosalind when he beheld Juliet. Had he been Don Juan in person, the three thousand lovely names would have vanished by themselves from his book. He did experience a sense of terror on feeling himself a prey to that sudden flame that swept away thought, will, and resistance and left nothing alive in his soul but passion. It was too late, however, and he no longer belonged to himself. Baron de Feroë was right, and Guy had found how dangerous it is for a mortal man to overstep the bounds of life and to venture, in material form, among the spirits if he bears not the golden branch to which all spirits bow.

A fearful thought occurred to Malivert. How was he to bring Spirite back if she did not choose to reappear? If there were no means of doing so, how would he be able to bear with the darkness of the sun after having contemplated real light for a moment? He was filled with a sense of utter misfortune and sank into deep despondency; he passed through an instant, as long as eternity itself, of hideous despair. The mere possibility, unconfirmed by any indication of its truth, brought the tears to his eyes, and try as he might to restrain them, ashamed as he felt at the exhibition of such weakness, they overflowed and slowly rolled down his cheeks. As he wept, he felt, with delight and surprise, a veil more tenuous than the finest of stuffs, like woven air, being passed over his face, absorbing, drying in its caress the bitter drops he had shed. The touch of a butterfly's wing could not have been softer, yet it was no illusion, for he thrice felt it, and when his tears had been dried, Malivert thought he perceived a diaphanous white flake vanishing in the shadows, like a cloudlet in the heavens.

This attentive and tender sympathy convinced Malivert that Spirite, who seemed to be ever fluttering around him, would answer his call and find, thanks to her higher intelligence as a superior being, the means of communicating easily with him. Spirite could enter the world in which he lived—to the extent, at least, that a soul can mingle with the living—while he, a mortal, was prevented from following her into the ideal region in which she moved, by the obstacle of his carnal body. It will surprise no one that Malivert passed from the deepest despair to the truest joy. If a mere mortal woman can, ten times in the course of a day, plunge you into the lowest depths or transport you to the highest heavens, inspire you with the desire of blowing your brains out or of purchasing on the shores of Lake Como a villa in which to shelter your loves forever, it may easily be understood that the feelings awakened by a spirit are infinitely deeper.

Guy's love for Spirite may, it is true, appear rather sudden, but it should be remembered that love is often called out by a single glance, and that a woman seen through a pair of opera glasses at the theatre does not differ very greatly from the reflection of a soul seen in a mirror; that many serious cases of passionate love have begun in a manner precisely similar, and that besides, though he himself was not aware of the fact, Guy's love was far less sudden than it seemed to be. Spirite had for a long time been haunting him, preparing his unconscious soul for supernatural communications, suggesting to him, in the midst of his worldly frivolity, thoughts deeper than vain appearances, inspiring him with the nostalgia of the ideal by vague remembrances of higher spheres, drawing him away from idle loves, and making him foresee a happiness that earth could not give. She it was who had broken the threads spun around Guy; who had torn away the webs in which he was to be caught; who had shown him the ridiculous side or the perfidy of a mistress of a day, and until now had kept him free from any lasting tie. She had stopped him on the very brink of the irrevocable, for, though nothing had happened to Guy that was appreciably significant from the human point of view, he had come to a crucial point in his life; his fate was hanging in the mysterious scales: this it was that had made Spirite resolve to issue from the shadow in which her occult protection of him was concealed, and to reveal herself to him, since he could no longer be directed by secret influences alone. Why did she interest herself thus in him? Did she yield to an impulse of her own, or did she obey an order emanating from that radiant sphere where, as Dante says, one *can* what one *wills?* She alone could tell, and the time was perhaps near when she would do so.

Malivert at last went to bed and soon fell asleep. His slumbers were light, bright, and full of a wondrous brilliancy that resembled visions rather than dreams. Vast azure spaces, in which the long trails of light formed endless perspectives of silvern and golden vales, opened before his closed eyes; then the picture would vanish, leaving visible in even greater depths streams of blinding phosphorescence, like unto a cascade of molten suns falling from eternity into the infinite; in its turn the cascade disappeared, and in its place was outspread a heaven of that intense, luminous whiteness that of yore clothed the three transfigured figures on Mount Tabor. From its depths, which seemed the very paroxysm of splendour, flashed here and there bursts of stars, brighter gleams, still more vivid scintillations. There was in that light, against which the most brilliant stars would have shown black, something like the swelling and surging of an incessant *becoming*. From time to time, as birds pass across the sun's disk, spirits visible sped across that vast irradiation, not through the shadow they cast, but through a different kind of light. Among them Guy thought he recognised Spirite; nor was he mistaken, though she seemed to be but a brilliant point in space, but a globule in the incandescent brightness. Spirite had desired to show herself to her lover, by means of the dream she evoked, in her real home. The soul, freed during the hours of sleep from the bonds of the flesh, lent itself to the vision, and for a few moments Guy was enabled to see with the inner sight, not the outer world itself, the contemplation of which is permitted only to souls wholly freed, but a ray filtering under the imperfectly closed door of the unknown, as from a darkened street one sees under the door of a palace lighted within a beam of brilliant light that suggests the splendour of the feast.

Spirite, not wishing to fatigue Guy's yet too human organ, dispelled the visions and wafted him from ecstasy into ordinary sleep. He felt, as he fell back into the night of common dreams, that he was being caught, as though he were a shellfish, in a matrix of black marble, in a darkness of deepest intensity. Then all passed away, even that sensation, and for two hours Guy rested in the non-existence whence life arises more youthful and refreshed.

He slept until ten in the morning, and Jack, who had been awaiting his awakening, seeing that his eyes were fully opened, pushed open the door that he had held ajar, entered the room, drew back the window curtains, and, directing his steps toward Malivert's bed, handed him on a silver salver two letters that had just been delivered. The one was from Mme. d'Ymbercourt, the other from Baron de Feroë. It was the latter that Guy opened first.

VI

The baron's note contained these words merely: "Has Caesar crossed the Rubicon?" Mme. d'Ymbercourt's, much less brief, insinuated, in cleverly turned phrases, that indefinite gossip should not be taken seriously, and that to break off suddenly visits that had become habitual would perhaps be more compromising than to make them more frequent. The note closed with a remark about Adelina Patti, the purpose of which appeared to be that a seat would be kept for him in box 22 at the Opéra. Guy certainly admired the young diva greatly, but in his present state of mind he preferred to hear her some other evening and determined he would find a way to avoid the appointment.

The human mind has a tendency to doubt that extraordinary events have taken place when the environment in which these have occurred has resumed its normal appearance. So Malivert, on looking into the Venetian mirror by daylight, asked himself, as he gazed at its silvery surface framed in by the cut-glass border, and as he saw in it the reflection of his own face only, whether it was true that that piece of polished glass had actually shown him, only a few hours since, the loveliest face the eye of man had ever beheld. In vain did his reason attempt to explain the celestial vision as the effect of a dream, of a vain fancy; his heart gave his reason the lie. Difficult as it is to appreciate the reality of the supernatural, he felt that it was all true and that behind the outwardly calm appearances surged a whole world of mystery. Yet nothing was changed in the apartment, and a visitor would not have noticed anything peculiar in it; as far as Guy was concerned, however, the door of every dresser, of every cupboard, might prove to be one opening into the infinite. The least noises, which he took for warnings, made him start.

In order to get rid of his nervous condition of excitement, he resolved to take a long drive. He had a fancy that Spirite would appear at night only; besides, if she wished to communicate with him, her fantastic ubiquity enabled her to find him and to manifest herself to him wherever he might be. In this affair, if such vague, frail, aerial, impalpable relations may be called an affair, Malivert's role was necessarily passive. His ideal mistress could enter his world at any time she chose, but he was unable to follow her in the mysterious spaces wherein she dwelt.

It had been snowing two nights before, and—a rare thing in Paris—the white carpet had not melted, under the influence of a soft wind, into that cold slush worse even than the black slush of the old pavements or the yellow mud of the new asphalt. It had been hardened by a sharp frost and crunched under the foot like crushed glass under carriage wheels. Grimalkin was a capital trotter, and Malivert had brought back from St. Petersburg a sleigh and a complete set of Russian harness. Opportunities for enjoying sleighing are infrequent in our temperate climate, and sportsmen seize on them with avidity. Guy was very proud of his sleigh, unquestionably the best turned-out in Paris, and which might have figured advantageously in the races on the Neva Place. He rather enjoyed the idea of a rapid drive in the bracing icy air. He had learned, during the winter he had spent in Russia, to enjoy the arctic delights of snow and cold; he loved to glide over the white carpet scarce rayed by the steel of the skates, driving a fast horse with both hands, like an izvostchick. He had the sleigh brought round and soon reached the Place de la Concorde and the Champs-Elysées. The road had not been cared for and improved as on the Neva Place, but the snow was deep enough to allow the sleigh to glide along without bumping too much. A Parisian winter cannot be expected to be as perfect as a Russian one. At the Bois de Boulogne he might have thought he was in the Islands, so even and white did the snow lie, especially in the side drives where fewer horsemen and carriages are met with. Guy de Malivert turned down a road leading through a wood of firs, the dark limbs of which, laden with snow that the wind had not shaken off, recalled to him his drives in Russia. He had plenty of furs, and the northern blast seemed to him but a zephyr by comparison with the cold gales he had faced in that country.

The approaches to the lake were crowded, and the number of carriages as large as on fine days in autumn or spring, when all sorts and conditions of men are attracted to Longchamp by the races in which celebrities of the turf are involved. In carriages hung on easy springs were to be seen ladies belonging to the great world, warmly covered with huge bear-skin robes edged with scarlet, and pressing against their fur-lined satin cloaks warm zibeline sable muffs. On the box-seats, covered with heavily embroidered hammercloths, coachmen of great houses, seated majestically, their shoulders protected by fur capes, looked as disdainfully as did their mistresses at the women not in society who were driving themselves in extravagant and pretentious vehicles drawn by ponies. There were also numerous closed carriages, for the idea of driving in an open carriage with the thermometer only twelve or thirteen degrees above zero strikes Parisians as far too arctic. A certain number of sleighs were to be seen among the many wheeled carriages, for the snow had evidently not been anticipated; Malivert's sleigh, however, easily surpassed all others. Some Russian noblemen, idling around as happy as reindeer in snow, condescended to approve of the elegant curves of the *douga* and of the correct way in which the harness straps were fastened to it.

It was about three o'clock; the lower portion of the sky was veiled by a soft haze, and against the delicate gray background stood out the slender twigs of the leafless trees, which, with their slender branches stripped of foliage, looked like skeleton leaves. A rayless sun, resembling a great red seal, was sinking through the haze. The lake was covered with skaters, three or four days of frost having made the ice thick enough to bear the weight of the crowd. The snow, swept off the surface and heaped up on the edges of the shore, showed the dark, polished surface rayed in every direction by the blades of the skates, like the mirrors in restaurants on which lovers scratch their names with a diamond. On the banks stood people hiring skates to *bourgeois* amateurs, whose tumbles formed the comic intermedes of the winter festival, like the ballet in the *Prophète* on a large scale. In the centre of the lake the more famous skaters, dressed in neat costumes, indulged in fancy feats. They flew like the wind, swung abruptly around, avoided collisions, stopped short by digging in the heel of their skates, cut curves, grapevines, figures of eight, letters, like Arab horsemen who, with the rowels of their spurs, write the name of Allah on the flanks of their steeds. Others pushed around, in light hand-sledges quaintly ornamented, handsome ladies wrapped in furs, who leaned back and smiled at them, excited by the speed and the cold air. Some guided by the hand elegant young women, wearing Russian or Hungarian fur caps, jackets frogged and braided, and trimmed with blue fox, bright-coloured skirts, looped up with clasps, and pretty patent-leather boots, crossed, like cothurns, by the straps of the skates. Others again, racing each other, flew along on one foot, heading forward like the Hippomenes and the Atalanta under the chestnut trees in one of the parterres of the Tuileries. The best way to win the race, now as formerly, might well have been to drop a golden apple or two in front of these Atalantas dressed by Worth; but there were those among them of such rank that even a diamond brooch would not have stopped them for an instant. The constant passing and repassing of so many people dressed with such strange elegance and rich originality, making a sort of fancy-dress ball on the ice, formed a graceful, charming, animated spectacle worthy of the brush of Watteau, Lancret, or Baron. Some of the groups recalled the paintings placed above the doors in old chateaux representing the Four Seasons, and in which Winter is personified by gallants pushing, in swan-necked sledges, marchionesses wearing velvet masks, who turn their fur muffs into receptacles for love letters. In the present case, it is true, the pretty faces, made rosier by the cold, lacked the masks, but the veils embroidered with steel beads or fringed with jet made a fair substitute for them.

Malivert pulled up by the lake shore and watched the entertaining and picturesque scene, the chief performers in which he was acquainted with. He was enough of a society man to follow the loves, intrigues, and flirtations that agitated the select few whom one soon learns to distinguish from the vulgar herd, the troop of supernumeraries that surrounds, without understanding it, every performance, and whose use is to prevent the action from standing out too clearly and too bare. But he looked on without any interest in the scene, and he even saw pass by a very charming lady, who had formerly favoured him, and who was now leaning in loving, familiar fashion upon the arm of a handsome skater, without feeling the least trace of jealousy.

Grimalkin was impatiently pawing the snow-covered ground, and presently Guy gave him his head, turned in the direction of the city, and drove along the Lake Avenue, up and down which carriages were constantly coming and going, to the great delight of the foot passengers who appeared to enjoy seeing for the tenth or twelfth time in the course of an hour the same yellow-bodied coach with a solemn dowager in it, and the same little dark-green coupe, with a Havana poodle at the window, and inside a light o' love with her hair dressed like a poodle's coat.

Guy, as he drove homewards, checked the speed of his horse, to avoid running over any one in the crowded road; and besides, it is not good form to drive fast on that fashionable thoroughfare. He saw advancing in his direction a carriage he would rather not have met. Mme. d'Ymbercourt was a chilly person, and Guy had not supposed that she would come out in such cold weather, which merely went to show how little he knew women; for no known cold would keep a woman from going to a fashionable drive and showing herself where she should do so. Now, in that particular winter, the correct thing was to go to the Bois de Boulogne and to take a turn on the frozen lake, the meeting-place, between three and five in the afternoon, of all the celebrities, in one way or another, that all Paris can manage to collect in one spot. A woman of any standing would never forgive herself if her name failed to appear among those of the beauties of the day in the columns of some well-informed newspaper. Now Mme. d'Ymbercourt was beautiful enough, rich enough, and fashionable enough to consider herself bound to conform to the requirements of fashion, and therefore, though shivering a little under the furs in which she was wrapped up, she was performing her pilgrimage to the lake. Malivert was tempted to let Grimalkin, who would not have objected, swing into his fastest trot, but Mme. d'Ymbercourt had caught sight of him and he was forced to drive alongside her carriage.

He chatted on various indifferent subjects, in an uninterested way, putting forward as a pretext for not accepting her invitation to the Opéra that he had to go to a dinner, when a sleigh passed so close as almost to touch his own. This sleigh was drawn by a superb horse of the Orloff breed; it was iron-gray, with a white mane and a tail every hair of which gleamed like silver. Held in by a Russian coachman with a long beard, green cloth caftan, and fur-bordered velvet cap, the horse champed its bit and stepped along throwing up its head and occasionally touching his knees with it. The beauty of the equipage, the correct get-up of the coachman, and the handsome horse attracted Guy's attention; but great was his amazement when in the lady seated in the sleigh, and whom he had at first assumed to be one of those Russian princesses who come to Paris for a season or two to dazzle the capital by their eccentric display of wealth—supposing that Paris can be dazzled by anything—he recognised, or thought he recognised, a likeness to a face he had had only a glimpse of, but which was now forever ineffaceably imprinted on his memory, though he certainly did not expect to meet with it in the Bois de Boulogne, after having seen it appear, as Helen to Faust, in a sort of magic mirror. At the sight of her he started so suddenly that Grimalkin, feeling the nervous thrill, plunged forward. Guy, casting a word of apology to Mme. d'Ymbercourt to the effect that he could not hold in his horse, followed the sleigh, which increased its pace.

As if surprised at being followed, the lady looked half round to see who was so bold as to do so, and although she showed only a small portion of her profile, Guy made out under the black net veiling wavy golden hair, deep blue eyes, and an ideal complexion, such as only the snow on lofty mountaintops, flushed by the beams of the setting sun, can give any idea of. She wore turquoise earrings, and on the part of the neck showing between the collar of her fur pelisse and her hat, curled a stray lock of hair, light as down and fine as a child's hair. It was, indeed, the face that had appeared to him the night before, with the added reality

needed by a phantom in broad daylight and close to the lake in the Bois
de Boulogne. How did Spirite happen to be there in so charmingly human a form, visible, no doubt, to others as well as to himself? For it was
difficult to admit that, even were the apparition itself impalpable, the
coachman, the horse, and the sleigh were likewise unsubstantial shadows. Guy did not waste his time trying to solve the problem; for, in order to make sure that he had not been deceived by a likeness of the sort
that disappears when it is examined closely, he endeavoured to pass the
sleigh so as to have a good look at the mysterious face. He allowed
Grimalkin to step out at his best gait, whereupon the good horse went
off like an arrow, his breath steaming for a few moments upon the back
of the sleigh Guy was pursuing. Nevertheless, although Grimalkin was a
very fast horse, he was no match for the Russian stepper, perhaps the
finest of his breed that Malivert had ever seen. The caftan-clad coachman clicked his tongue, and the iron-gray in a few bounds put enough
space between the two sleighs to reassure his mistress, if she happened
to be disturbed by the proximity of Guy.

No doubt the object of the lady who bore such a startling resemblance to Spirite was not to discourage Malivert's pursuit, for her sleigh
was again driven at a more moderate pace. The race had taken the pair
into the Fir Avenue, at this moment empty of carriages, and the chase
settled down in earnest. Yet Grimalkin did not once manage to get
alongside of the Orloff stepper; the best he could do was to prevent the
distance between the sleighs from increasing. The hoofs of the horses
sent lumps of white snow flying against the dashboards, where they
broke into frosty dust, and the two noble animals were enveloped in
clouds of steam as in classic clouds. For one moment, at the end of the
drive, barred by the file of carriages driving down the main avenue, the
two sleighs were side by side, and Guy was able to see for a second or
two the face of the supposed Russian lady, whose veil was blown aside
by the wind. A celestially arch smile played upon her lips, the curve of
which recalled that of Mona Lisa. Her eyes were starry and blue like
sapphires, and a rosier flush warmed her velvety cheeks. Spirite—for it
was she—drew down her veil, the coachman urged on his horse, and the
animal dashed forward furiously. A cry of terror escaped Guy, for at
that very instant a carriage was crossing the drive; and, forgetting that

Spirite, as a disembodied spirit, was safe from all earthly accidents, he feared a dreadful collision; but the horse, the coachman, and the sleigh passed through the carriage as through a mist, and were speedily out of Malivert's sight. Grimalkin seemed terrified; nervous shudders ran all over his limbs, usually so firm, as if he were puzzled by the disappearance of the sleigh. Animals have a wonderfully deep instinct and often see what escapes man's careless glance. Many of them seem endowed with a sense of the supernatural. But Grimalkin soon calmed down on joining the procession of undoubted carriages along the lake shore.

As he drove down the Avenue de l'Impératrice, Guy met Baron de Feroë, who was also returning from the Bois in a light droshky. After asking Malivert for a light for his cigar, the baron said to him, half mysteriously, half quizzically: "Mme. d'Ymbercourt will not be very well pleased, and you will be scolded in rare fashion at the Opéra tonight, if you are imprudent enough to go. I fancy that sleigh race can scarcely have been to her taste. Meanwhile you had better tell Jack to throw a blanket over Grimalkin, if you do not want him to catch his death of cold."

Guy was past being amazed at strange things. It had not appeared to him at all out of the ordinary that a sleigh should pass through a carriage. This facility in traversing obstacles against which terrestrial vehicles would have been smashed showed that it was indeed a mysterious equipage come from the spheres of the impossible, and which could contain Spirite only. Unquestionably Spirite was jealous, or at least—for all her actions proved it—she desired to keep Malivert and Mme. d'Ymbercourt apart; and evidently she had gone about doing so in the right way, for as he turned into the open space of the Arc de l'Étoile, Guy saw the countess in her carriage appearing to listen very attentively to the doubtless gallant conversation of M. d'Aversac, who was bending elegantly over his horse's withers as he walked it by her side.

"That is to pay me for the sleigh," said Malivert to himself; "but I am not the kind of fellow to be egged on in that way. D'Aversac is a sham clever fellow, just as Mme. d'Ymbercourt is a sham beauty. They are an excellent match for each other. I can judge them in the most disinterested fashion, since affairs of this sort have ceased to concern me. They will be a well assorted pair, as the song says."

Such was the net result of Mme. d'Ymbercourt's manoeuvres. On perceiving Guy she had bent forward, perhaps a little more than was proper, to reply to the sweet sayings of M. d'Aversac. The poor woman thought she might recall her lukewarm adorer by touching his self-love. She had had a glimpse of Spirite, and she had guessed that she had a formidable rival in her. The eagerness displayed by Guy, usually so cool, in pursuing the mysterious sleigh and the woman whom no one had ever met at the Bois, had stung her to the quick, for she had easily seen through the excuse so hurriedly given and did not believe that Grimalkin had run away. D'Aversac, who was swelling with satisfaction, for he was not in the habit of being so well treated, modestly attributed to his own merit what he would have been wiser to ascribe to feminine annoyance. He even magnanimously pitied poor Malivert, who had reckoned too surely on possessing Mme. d'Ymbercourt's affections. All the projects that the gentleman's conceit, helped by appearances, immediately proceeded to build up on this slight event may easily be imagined.

On that day Guy was engaged to dinner to people with whom it would be difficult to fail in keeping an appointment made long before. Fortunately there were many guests, and his absentmindedness was not noticed. The dinner over, he exchanged a few words with the mistress of the house, and having thus sufficiently made plain that he had come, he performed a masterly retreat toward the second drawing-room, where he shook hands with men of distinction with whom he was acquainted and who had withdrawn there to talk more freely of important or secret matters; then he vanished and went to his club, where he expected to meet Baron de Feroë. He did find him seated in front of a small card table, playing écarté with the radiant d'Aversac, of whom it is only just to say that he endeavoured to repress his joy in order to avoid humiliating Malivert. Contrary to the proverb, "Fortunate at cards, unfortunate in love," d'Aversac was winning, and if he had been at all superstitious he might have felt some doubt as to the soundness of his hopes. The game having come to an end, the baron, as he was the loser, could rise, pretending fatigue, and simply refuse the revenge offered by his adversary. Feroë and Guy de Malivert went out together and walked up and down the Boulevard near the club.

"What will the frequenters of that drawing-room called the Bois," said Guy to the baron, "think of the lady and the sleigh, the horse and the coachman, all so very striking and yet unknown to every one?"

"The vision manifested itself but to you, to the countess, on whom Spirite desired to act, and to me, who, as one of the initiated, can see what is invisible to other men. You may be sure that if Mme. d'Ymbercourt speaks of the handsome Russian princess and the splendid stepper, nobody will know what she is talking about."

"Do you think," Malivert asked the baron, "that I shall soon see Spirite again?"

"You may expect an early visit," replied de Feroë. "The communications I receive from the other world inform me that much interest is taken in you there."

"Shall it be tonight or tomorrow?—in my rooms or in a place where I do not expect to see her, as happened today?" cried Malivert, as impatient as a passionate lover or a neophyte eager to penetrate a mystery.

"I cannot quite tell you that," replied the Swedish baron. "The spirits, for whom time does not exist or has ceased to exist, do not reckon hours, since they live in eternity. As far as Spirite is concerned, if she saw you tonight or in a thousand years, it would be exactly the same thing. But spirits that deign to enter into communication with us poor mortals remember the brevity of our life, the imperfection and fragility of our organs; they know that between one apparition and another, if measured by the eternal dial, the perishable envelope of man has time to dissolve into dust a hundred times over; it is probable, therefore, that Spirite will not keep you waiting. She has descended to our sphere and appears to have made up her mind to go back to her own only after carrying out her project."

"What is that project?" said Malivert. "You, to whom nothing is closed in that supernatural world, must know the motive that directs this pure spirit toward a being yet subjected to material conditions."

"On that point, my dear Guy," replied Baron de Feroë, "my lips are sealed. I may not repeat the secrets of the spirits. I was warned to put you on your guard against any terrestrial entanglement and to prevent your entering into bonds that might perhaps chain your soul to a place

in which it would suffer from the eternal regret of having lost its freedom. My mission does not go beyond that."

Thus chatting, Malivert and the baron, followed by their carriages,
which were being driven along the pavement, reached the Madeleine,
the Greek columns of which, silvered by the pale beams of a winter
moon, looked at the end of the broad Rue Royale something like the
Parthenon, a resemblance that disappears with daylight. On arriving
there the two friends separated and got into their respective coupés.

On reaching home, Malivert threw himself into his armchair and,
his elbow leaning on the table, began to think. Spirite's apparition in the
mirror had inspired him with immaterial desire, the winged volition to
which the sight of an angel gives birth, but her presence on the lake
shore, under a more real feminine form, had lighted in his heart the fire
of human love. He felt himself suffused with burning effluvia and possessed by that absolute love which even eternal possession does not satisfy. As he was thinking, his hand outstretched on the table covered with
papers, he saw against the dark background of the Turkish table cover
the outlines of another hand, slender, of a perfection unequalled by art
and that nature would in vain attempt to reach; a tenuous hand with
long fingers, polished onyx-like nails; on the back of the hand showed a
few veins of azure like the polished reflections that colour the milky
opal, and it was lighted by a light that was certainly not from the lamp.
The rosy freshness of the tone and the ideal delicacy of the form proved
conclusively that it could only be Spirite's hand. The small, clean, well-
turned, high-bred wrist ended in a mist of soft lace. As if to mark plainly
that the hand was there only as a sign, the arm and the body were lacking. While Guy gazed at it with eyes no longer amazed at anything extraordinary, the fingers of the hand stretched out on one of the sheets of
writing paper thrown confusedly on the table and began to simulate the
movements of some one writing. They seemed to trace lines, and when
they had gone over the whole page with the rapidity of an actor writing a
letter in a play, Guy caught hold of the paper, expecting to find on it
written sentences, known or unknown signs. The paper was perfectly
white. Guy looked at the sheet with considerable disappointment. He
put it nearer the lamp, examined it in every way, made the light fall upon it in every possible manner without discovering the least trace of writ-

ing, and yet the hand was continuing upon another sheet the same imaginary work, apparently producing no result.

"What does this mean?" asked Malivert himself. "Can Spirite have written with sympathetic ink that one must heat in order to bring out the letters? But her mysterious fingers hold neither pen nor shadow of a pen. What does it mean? Am I to serve myself as secretary to this spirit, to be my own medium—to use the consecrated term? The spirits, it is said, who can produce illusions and appearances and call up in the brain of those whom they haunt fearful or superb spectacles are incapable of acting upon material reality and of displacing even a straw."

He remembered the impulse that had led him to write the note to Mme. d'Ymbercourt, and it occurred to him that by nervous influence Spirite might perhaps succeed in dictating to him inwardly what she wished to say to him. All he had to do was to let his hand go and to still his own thoughts as much as he could, so that they should not mingle with those of the spirit. Collecting himself and abstracting himself from the external world, Guy calmed his overexcited brain, turned up a little the wick of the lamp, took the pen, dipped it in the ink, placed his hand on the paper, and, his heart beating with timid hope, waited

Very soon he experienced a curious sensation. It seemed to him that he was losing the sense of his own personality, that his individual remembrances were vanishing like those of a confused dream, that his thoughts were disappearing like birds in the heavens. Although his body was still near the table, preserving the same attitude, Guy was inwardly absent; he had vanished, disappeared. Another soul, or at least another mind had taken the place of his own and was directing those servants who, to act, were awaiting the unknown master. The nerves of his fingers trembled and began to execute movements of which he was unconscious; the pen began to move on the paper, tracing rapid signs in Guy's handwriting, slightly modified by the external impulse. This is what Spirite dictated to her medium. This confession of the outer world was found among Malivert's papers, and I have been permitted to transcribe it.

SPIRITE'S DICTATION

"First, you must know the being, undefinable by you, who has entered into your life. However penetrating you may be, you cannot succeed in making out its true nature, and as in a badly written tragedy, in which the hero states his names, titles, and references, I am obliged to explain myself; but I have this excuse—that no one else can do it for me. Your intrepid heart, which did not hesitate to confront at my call the mysterious terrors of the unknown, does not need to be reassured. Besides, even if danger existed, it would not prevent your pursuing the adventure. The invisible world, of which this world is but the veil, has its pitfalls and abysses, but you shall not fall into any of them. Spirits of falsehood and evil traverse it; there are angels of darkness as there are angels of light, revolted powers and submissive powers, beneficent and harmful forces. The lower portion of the mystic ladder, the summit of which is lost in eternal light, is shrouded in darkness. I hope that, with my help, you will ascend the luminous rounds. I am neither angel nor demon, nor one of the intermediary spirits who bear through space the Divine Will as the nervous fluid communicates the human will to the limbs of the body. I am merely a soul still awaiting judgment and allowed by divine goodness to anticipate a favourable sentence. I, too, have dwelt on your earth, and I could repeat the melancholy epitaph of the shepherd in Poussin's picture, *'Et in Arcadia ego.'*

"Do not, because I quote Latin, mistake me for the soul of a literary woman. In the place where I am everything is known intuitively, and the various languages spoken by humankind before and after the confusion of tongues are equally familiar to us. Words are but the shadows of ideas, and we possess the idea itself in its essential state. If age could exist in a place where time is not, I should be very young in my new country. It is only a few days since, freed by death, I left the atmosphere that you breathe and to which I am recalled by a feeling that the passage from one world to another has not effaced. My terrestrial life, or rather, my last apparition on your planet, was very short, but it was sufficient to give me time to learn how deeply a loving soul may suffer. When Baron de Feroë sought to ascertain the nature of the spirit whose vague manifestations troubled you, and when he asked you if a woman or a girl had ever died of a broken heart on your account, he was nearer the truth than he believed; and although you can recall nothing of the kind, since you were unaware of it, the remark deeply troubled you and your confusion was ill concealed under a playfully sceptical denial.

"You never knew it, yet my life touched yours. Your eyes looked elsewhere, and as far as you were concerned I was lost in the shadow.

"The first time I saw you was in the parlour of the Convent of the Birds, where you went to visit your sister, who was boarding there as I was. She was in a more advanced class, for I was then only thirteen or fourteen at most, and I seemed younger, for I was very frail, dainty, and fair. You paid no attention then to the little chit, to the child who, while busy eating the chocolate creams that her mother had brought her, glanced timidly at you. You were then about twenty or twenty-two. In my childish simplicity I thought you very handsome. The air of kindness and affection with which you spoke to your sister touched and attracted me, and I wished I had a brother like you. My childish imagination went no further.

"As Mlle. de Malivert had finished her education, she left the convent, and you not did come again. But your image was never effaced from my remembrance; it remained on the white parchment of my soul like those light outlines traced in pencil by a skilled hand which are found again long afterwards, almost invisible but persisting, the only traces at times of a vanished hand. The idea that so great a personage could ever notice me, who was still in the youngest class and treated somewhat disdainfully by the older boarders, would have been much too ambitious and did not even occur to me, at least at that time. But I very often thought of you, and in those chaste romances woven by the most innocent imaginations it was you who always played the part of Prince Charming, who delivered me from fancied perils, who carried me off through underground ways, who put to flight corsairs and brigands and brought me back to the king my father. For such a hero as you were must have at least an infanta or a princess, and I modestly assumed that rank. At other times the romance changed into a pastoral; you were a shepherd and I was a shepherdess, and our flocks mingled in tender green meadows.

"Without suspecting it, you formed a very considerable part of my life, and you lorded over it. It was to you that I ascribed all my little successes at school, and I worked with all my strength to deserve your approbation. I said: 'He does not know that I have won a prize, but he will know it and he will be pleased'; and although naturally idle, I set to work again with renewed energy. Was it not curious that my child's soul should have given itself to you secretly and acknowledged itself the vassal of a lord of its own choice who did not even suspect this homage? Is it not stranger still that that first impression should never have been effaced?—for it lasted all my life, alas! a very short one, and is prolonged even beyond it. At sight of you, something indefinable and mysterious moved in me whose meaning I understood only when my eyes, as they closed, were opened forever. My condition as an impalpable being, as a pure spirit, permits me now to tell you those things which a daughter of earth would no doubt hide. But the immaculate innocence of a soul cannot blush; celestial modesty may confess love.

"Two years thus went by. I had grown out of childhood into maidenhood, and my dreams began to become less puerile, while still remaining innocent. There was rather less rose and azure in them and they did not always end in the blaze of an apotheosis. I often went to the end of the garden, sat down on a bench far from my companions busy with their games or whispered conversations, and murmured the syllables of your name like a litany. Sometimes I was even bold enough to think that that name might become my own in consequence of chances or adventures as entangled as those of a comedy of cloak and sword, the plot of which I arranged to suit my own fancy.

"I belonged to a family the equal of your own, and my parents enjoyed a fortune and a rank that made the distant project of marriage that I formed almost timidly, in the most secret corner of my heart, seem anything but a chimera or a foolish vision. It would have been most natural that we should meet someday in the society in which we both moved. But would I take your fancy? would you think me pretty? That was a question that my small boarding-school mirror did not answer in the negative, as you may now judge by the reflection I sent to your Venetian mirror, and by my appearance in the Bois de Boulogne. Supposing, however, you were to pay as little attention to the young lady as to the child in the convent? When I thought of that, I was filled with the deepest discouragement. But youth never despairs very long, and I would soon indulge in brighter fancies. It seemed impossible to me that when you saw me you should not recognise that I was yours, that my soul was marked with your seal, that I had adored you from childhood—in a word, that I was the one woman created purposely for you. I did not say these things to myself so plainly, for I did not then understand the emotions of my heart as I do now, when I can see the two sides of life, but it was the deep instinct of blind faith and irresistible feeling.

"In spite of my virginal ignorance and a candour that has perhaps never been surpassed, my soul was filled with a passion that was to destroy me, and which today has been revealed for the first time. I had no bosom friend at the convent, and I lived alone with my thoughts of you. Jealous of my secret, I dreaded confidences, and every friendship that would have drawn me away from my one idea was repellent to me. I was called serious, and the teachers used to propose me as a model. I awaited the time when I was to leave the convent with less impatience than might be supposed. It was a moment of respite between thought and action. As long as I was shut up within the convent walls, I had the right to lose myself indolently in my dream without any self-reproach, but once I had flown forth from the cage, I should have to direct my own flight, to tend to my aim, to ascend toward my star; and customs, manners, conventionalities, infinite modesty, the numerous veils with which civilisation surrounds her, forbid a young girl to take the initiative in a matter of love. She cannot take any step to reveal herself to her own ideal; a proper pride is opposed to her offering what must be priceless. Her eyes must be cast down, her lips closed, her bosom motionless; no flush, no pallor must betray her when she finds herself in the presence of the man she secretly loves, and who often goes away believing her disdainful or indifferent. How many souls created one for the other have, for lack of a word, a glance, a smile, gone different ways that separated them more and more and made their meeting forever impossible? How many lives deplorably wrecked owe their misfortune to such a cause unperceived by all, and at times unknown even to themselves? I had often thought over these things, and they recurred more strongly to my mind at the moment when I was about to leave the convent to enter into the world. Yet I held to my resolution. The time of my departure came, my mother sent for me, and I bade farewell to my companions with only slight marks of feeling. I left no friendship and no remembrance within those walls, where several years of my life had been spent. The thought of you alone formed my treasure.

VIII

"It was with a lively feeling of pleasure that I entered the room, or rather the small apartment that my mother had prepared for me on my leaving the convent. It consisted of a bedroom, a large dressing-room, and a sitting-room, the windows of which looked out on a garden prolonged by a view over the neighbouring gardens. A low wall covered with a thick mantle of ivy formed the boundary line, but the stone showed nowhere, and nothing was visible except a procession of gigantic old chestnut trees, which gave the gardens the appearance of a vast park. Scarcely at the very extremity did the glance rest, between the more distant masses of foliage, upon the corner of a roof or the elbow of a chimney-pot, a signature that Paris places upon every one of its horizons. It was a rare satisfaction, possible only to wealth, to have before me, in the very centre of the great city, a broad, free, empty place with air, sky, sunshine, and verdure. Is it not disagreeable to feel other lives, passions, vices, misfortunes too close to oneself, and isn't the delicate modesty of the soul somewhat depressed by such close proximity?

"I therefore felt genuine joy as I gazed out of my windows upon that oasis of coolness, silence, and solitude. It was August, for I had finished my last school year in the convent, and the foliage was still intensely green, but with the warmer tone that the passing of summer imparts to vegetation. In the centre of the flower garden under my windows a bed of geraniums in full bloom dazzled the eyes with its scarlet blaze. The sward surrounding this flower-bed, a carpet of green velvet of English rye grass, brought out by its emerald tint a red more ardent than fire. On the finely sanded walk marked like a ribbon by the teeth of the rakes, the birds were hopping about trustfully and seemed perfectly at home. I promised myself that I should share their excursions without making them fly away.

"My room was hung with white cashmere trimmed with blue silk cords. This was also the colour of the furniture and the window curtains. In my small sitting-room, decorated in the same way, a magnificent Érard piano offered its keyboard to my hands, and I at once tried its soft sonority. A bookcase of rosewood placed opposite the piano contained the pure books, the chaste poets whom a maiden may read, and the lower shelves contained the scores of the great composers; Bach elbowed Haydn, Mozart was side by side with Beethoven, like Raphael and Michelangelo, and Meyerbeer leaned upon Weber. My mother had brought together the masters I admired, those who were my favourites. An elegant jardinière full of sweet-scented flowers bloomed in the centre of the room like a great nosegay. I was being treated like a spoiled child. I was the only daughter, and the whole affection of my parents was naturally concentrated upon me.

"I was to make my entrance into society at the beginning of the season—that is, two or three months later, at the time that puts an end to country life, to travel, to sojourns in watering-places and gambling-places, to country-house parties, to hunting, racing, and all that society invents to pass the time that it is not proper for well bred people to spend in Paris, where my parents had been detained by business. I greatly preferred remaining in town to staying in the old and rather gloomy chateau in the very depths of Brittany to which I had gone regularly for every vacation. Besides, I fancied I should have a chance of meeting you, of hearing you spoken of, or of coming across people acquainted with you; but I learned indirectly that you had been gone for some time on a trip to Spain that would last a few months longer. Your friends, to whom you rarely wrote, did not expect you back before winter. It was said that your fancy had been caught by a mantilla-wearing Spanish girl. That troubled me little, for in spite of my modesty, I was conceited enough to think that my golden hair could rival the jet tresses of Andalusia.

"I learned also that you wrote in reviews under the Latinised pseudonym of one of your given names, known only to your intimate friends, and that the well-bred gentleman in you concealed a distinguished writer. With a curiosity you can easily understand, I sought in the files of newspapers all the articles marked by that sign. To read a writer is to place yourself in communication with his mind, for is not a book a confidence addressed to an ideal friend, a conversation from which the interlocutor is absent? One must not always take literally what the author says; one must allow for philosophical or literary systems, for fashionable affectations of the day, for necessary reticence, for the style that imposes itself on him, for admiring imitations, and whatever may modify the exterior form of a writer; but under all these disguises the true attitude of the soul at last reveals itself to the real reader, the genuine thought is often to be seen between the lines, and the poet's secret, which he does not choose to tell to the crowd, is at least to be guessed. One after another the veils fall and the answers to the riddles are learned.

"In order to get an idea of you, I studied with great attention your accounts of travel, your articles on philosophy and criticism, your tales and the pieces of verse scattered here and there at rather long intervals, and which marked the various phases of your mind. It is less difficult to learn to know a subjective author than an objective one. The former expresses his own feelings, exposes his ideas, and judges society and creation in virtue of an ideal. The second presents objects such as they are in nature; he proceeds by images, by description; he brings things under the reader's eyes; he draws, dresses up, colours his personages accurately, puts in their mouths what they ought to have said, and keeps his own opinion to himself. That is your way of doing. At first sight you might have been accused of a certain disdainful impartiality that did not see much difference between a lizard and a man, between the glow of a sunset and the glow of a conflagration; but by reading more closely and judging by certain sudden outbreaks, swift rushes at once checked, I could divine that you were possessed of deep feeling maintained by a haughty reserve, which did not care to allow your emotions to be seen.

"This judgment of you as a writer harmonised with the instinctive judgment of my heart, and now that nothing is concealed from me I know how true it was. All sentimental trifling and hypocritically virtuous magniloquence you held in horror, and in your opinion the worst of crimes was to deceive the soul. That made you excessively shy of expressing tender or passionate feelings; you preferred silence to falsehood or exaggeration in such sacred matters, even though fools considered you insensible, hard, and even cruel. I at once perceived this, and not for a moment did I doubt that you were kind-hearted. As to the nobility of your mind, there could be not the least uncertainty. Your proud disdain of vulgarity, commonplaceness, envy, and all moral ugliness amply proved it. By dint of reading you, I learned to know you, whom I had seen but once, as well as if I had met you intimately every day. I penetrated the intimate recesses of your thought and knew your starting-point, your motives, sympathies, antipathies, what you desired, what you disliked—in a word, your whole mental being—and from it I deduced what your character must be. Sometimes when reading, struck by a passage that was a revelation to me, I would rise and go to the piano and play, as a comment on your sentences, motives analogous in colour and sentiment that prolonged the passage in sonorous or melancholy vibrations. I enjoyed hearing in another way the echo of your thought. Perhaps these relations were imaginary and could have been seized by none but myself, but unquestionably some of them were real. I know it now that I dwell in the eternal source of inspiration, and that I see it fall like luminous sparks upon the head of genius.

"While reading those of your works which I could procure—for the range of action of a young girl is so narrow that the smallest step is difficult for her—the season was advancing, the trees were turning yellow with the golden tints of late autumn, the leaves, one after another, fell from the branches, and the gardener, in spite of his care, could not prevent the sward and the gravel from being thickly covered with them. Sometimes, when I wandered in the garden under the chestnut trees, a chestnut falling on my head like a ball or rolling at my feet out of its broken husk interrupted my reverie and made me involuntarily start. The delicate plants and shrubs were being taken into the hothouse, the birds had the uneasy look they have at the approach of winter, and at evening I could hear them quarrelling on the bare branches. The season was about to begin; society was returning to Paris from every point of the horizon. On the Champs-Elysées were again to be seen carriages with coats of arms on the panels driven slowly up toward the Arc de l'Étoile to enjoy the last rays of the sun; the Théâtre-Italien published its list of singers and its repertoire, and announced the forthcoming opening. I rejoiced at the thought that this general movement of return would bring you back from Spain and that, weary of the gloomy sierras, you would enjoy coming to receptions, parties, and balls, where I hoped I might meet you.

"Once, while driving in the Bois de Boulogne with my mother, I saw you ride by our carriage, but so swiftly that I had scarcely time to recognise you. It was the first time that I had seen you since your visit to the convent. My blood rushed to my heart and I felt a sort of electric shock. Under pretext of feeling the cold, I lowered my veil to conceal the change in my face and sank silently back into the corner of the carriage. My mother pulled up the window and said: 'It is not warm. A mist is coming up and we had better return, unless you wish to drive on.' I nodded assent. I had learned what I wished to learn; I knew that you were in Paris.

"We used to go to the Opéra once a week. It was a great treat to me to hear the singers of whom I had heard so much, but whom I did not know. Another hope also stirred my heart; I need not tell you what it was. Our day came. Patti was to sing 'La Sonnambula.' My mother had had made for me a simple, pretty dress suited to my age: an underskirt of white taffeta with an overskirt of tarlatan, and bows of blue velvet and pearls. My hair was dressed with a band of velvet of the same colour, with pearls twisted around it and the ends falling down on my shoulders. As I looked in my mirror while my maid was putting on the last touches, I asked myself, 'Is he fond of blue?' In Alfred de Musset's 'Caprice,' Mme. de Léry says it is a stupid colour. And yet I could not help thinking that the blue ribbon looked very well with my golden hair. If you had seen me, I think you would have loved me. Clotilde, my maid, as she arranged the folds of the dress and the bows on my bodice, said that I was very pretty that evening.

"The carriage deposited my mother and myself in front of the peristyle—my father was to join us later—and we began slowly to ascend the great, red-carpeted staircase. The warm atmosphere was perfumed with cuscus and patchouli; ladies in full dress, their gowns still concealed by the mantles, pelisses, burnouses, scarfs, and opera cloaks that they were presently to hand to their lackeys, were ascending the stairs, their long trains of watered silk, satin, and velvet trailing behind them, and resting their hands on the arms of grave men in white neckties, whose black coats had in their buttonholes strings of orders, which meant that they intended, after the opera, to proceed to some official or diplomatic reception.

Tall, slender young fellows, their hair parted in the middle, most correctly and elegantly dressed, followed close behind, drawn to a group by a smile.

"All this is no novelty to you, and you would paint the picture better than I, but the sight was new to a little boarding-school girl making her entrance into society. Life is always the same. It is like a play in which the spectators alone change; but one who has not seen the performance is interested in it as if it were made purposely for him and were being given for the first time. I was happy. I felt I was beautiful; approving glances had been cast upon me; some women had looked around after having examined me with a rapid glance, and found nothing to blame either in my dress or my coiffure.

"I had a secret presentiment that I should see you that evening. This hope imparted a slight animation to my features and flushed my cheeks more brilliantly than usual. We sat down in our box, and soon glasses were turned upon me. Mine was a new face, and new faces are quickly noted at the Opéra, which is like a great drawing-room where everybody knows everybody else. My mother's presence told people who I was, and I understood from the way they bent toward each other that I was being talked about in several boxes, favourably no doubt, for kindly smiles followed the whispered sentences. I felt somewhat awkward at being the observed of all observers; wearing a low-necked dress for the first time, I felt my shoulders shiver under the gauze that covered them with its semi-transparency.

"The rise of the curtain—for the overture had been little listened to—made every one look toward the stage and put an end to my embarrassment. Undoubtedly the aspect of that beautiful hall starred with diamonds and bouquets, with its gilding, its footlights, its white caryatids, awoke in me both surprise and admiration, and Bellini's music performed by artists of the first rank carried me away into a world of enchantment; yet the real interest of the evening did not lie there so far as I was concerned. While my ears listened to the suave melodies of the Sicilian composer, my eyes were timidly examining every box, roaming over the balcony, and examining the orchestra stalls in order to discover you. The first act was nearly ended before you came, and when the curtain was rung down you turned half round toward the auditorium, looking rather bored and gazing at the boxes indifferently without letting your glance rest on any one in particular. Your complexion was browned by six months' travel in Spain, and there was on your face a certain expression of nostalgia, as if you regretted the country you had left. My heart beat loudly while you were making this rapid inspection, and for a moment I thought your glance had noted me, but I was mistaken.

"I saw you leave your seat and reappear shortly afterwards in a box opposite our own. It was occupied by a pretty woman very splendidly dressed, whose black hair shone like satin. Her pale rose-coloured dress was almost undistinguishable from the flesh tones of her bosom; diamonds sparkled in her hair, in her ears, on her neck and her arms. On the velvet-covered rail by the side of her opera-glasses bloomed a great bouquet of Parma violets and camellias. At the back, in the shadow, I could make out an old, bald-headed, obese person, the lapel of whose coat half concealed the star of some foreign order. The lady spoke to you with unmistakable pleasure and you replied to her in a careless, easy way, without seeming to be particularly taken with her more than friendly manner. My disappointment at not having been noticed by you was compensated for by the joy of feeling that you did not love that bold-eyed woman with the alluring smile and the dazzling toilet.

"A few minutes later, as the musicians began to tune up for the second act, you took leave of the lady with the diamonds and the old gentleman with the foreign order and returned to your seat. The performance ended without your turning your head once, and in my soul I felt annoyed with you. I wondered that you could not guess that a young girl in a white dress with blue bows wanted very much to be looked at by the man she had secretly chosen. I had so long wished to find myself in the same place as you; my wish was granted, and you did not even suspect that I was present. You ought to have felt, it seemed to me, a sympathetic thrill; you ought to have turned around and looked slowly through the hall impelled by a secret emotion; your glance should have stopped on the box I was in, and you should have put your hand to your heart and fallen into an ecstasy. The hero of a novel would not have failed to do so. But you were not the hero of a novel.

"My father, who had had to go to a state dinner, came only in the middle of the second act and, seeing you in the orchestra stalls, said, 'Why! there is Guy de Malivert! I did not know he had returned from Spain. His trip means for us endless bullfights in the Review, for Guy is a bit of a barbarian.' I delighted in hearing your name spoken by my father's lips. You were not unknown to my family; we might therefore meet. It would be easy indeed to do so. I was thus somewhat consoled for the lack of success I had encountered that evening. The performance closed without any other incident than showers of bouquets, recalls, and ovations to Patti. While waiting in the vestibule until our footman announced our carriage, I saw you pass with a friend and draw a cigar from a case of fine Manila esparto. The desire to smoke made you careless, I am bound to say, of the exhibition of beauties and ugly women, who were ranged upon the lower steps of the staircase. You made your way through the mass of dresses, caring little whether or not you rumpled them, and you soon reached the door with your friend following in your wake.

"On returning home, happy and dissatisfied, I went to bed after having tried with no great success some of the melodies of 'La Sonnambula,' as if to prolong the vibrations of the evening; and then I went to sleep, thinking of you.

IX

"One often finds, when after a certain time the remembrance and the image are compared, that imagination has worked like a painter, who goes on with a portrait in the absence of his model, softening the surfaces, graduating the tints, making the contours melt one into another, and bringing back, in spite of himself, the portrait to his own particular ideal. I had not seen you for more than three years, but my heart had accurately preserved the memory of your face. But you had changed somewhat; your features had become firmer and more accentuated, and the sunburn of travel had imparted to your complexion a warmer and more vigorous colour. The man showed more in the young man, and you had that air of tranquil authority and assured force which appeals to women perhaps more than beauty. Nonetheless I preserved carefully within my soul the first drawing, the slight sketch of the being who was to have so much influence over me, just as one preserves a miniature of the youth by the side of the portrait of later days. My dreams had not harmed you, and I was not obliged, when I saw you again, to strip you of a mantle of fancied perfections. I thought of all this, curled up in my bed and watching the gleam of the night-light trembling on the blue roses of the carpet, while awaiting sleep that did not come, but which toward morning closed my eyes, mingling vague harmonies with disconnected dreams.

"A few weeks later we received an invitation to a great ball given by the Duchess de C——. For a young girl her first ball is an event. This one was the more interesting to me in that it was likely you would be at it, the duchess being a great friend of yours. Balls are our battles that we win or lose. It is there that the young girl, issuing from the shadows of the women's quarters, shines in all her splendour. Custom grants her during this short space of time, under the pretext of dancing, a sort of relative freedom, and the ball is to her like the foyer of the Opéra where dominoes walk with uncovered faces. She may be approached with an invitation to dance a quadrille or a mazurka, and during the figures of a country-dance she may even be spoken to; but very often the long list on her engagement card does not contain the one name that she really has longed for.

"I had to think of my dress, for a ball dress is a poem, and that of a young girl is a very difficult thing to make up. It has to be both simple and rich; that is to say, it must possess contrary characteristics. A light dress entirely white would not have been the thing; so I made up my mind, after a good deal of hesitation, to have a skirt and overskirt of gauze worked with silver, caught up with bouquets of forget-me-nots, the blue of which matched admirably the turquoise set that my father had purchased for me. Clusters of turquoises, imitating the flowers scattered over my dress, formed my head-dress. Thus attired, I fancied myself capable of showing not too disadvantageously among the splendid toilettes and the famous beauties. Indeed, for a mere child of earth, I looked rather well.

"The Duchess de C—— inhabited one of those vast mansions in the Faubourg Saint-Germain built for the splendid lives of other days, mansions that modern life finds it difficult to fill. It takes the crowd and splendour of a feast to animate them as of yore. From the outside no one would have suspected the extent of this princely mansion. A high wall between two houses with a monumental carriage-gate, over which, in gilt letters upon a tablet of green marble, was written 'Hôtel de C——,' was all that could be seen from the street. A long avenue of old lime trees, trimmed in the shape of an arch after the old French fashion and which winter had stripped of their leaves, led to a vast court at the back of which rose the mansion, built in the pure Louis XIV style, with high windows and columns half engaged and mansard attics, like the architecture of Versailles. A red and white awning, supported by carved uprights, projected over the red-carpeted steps. I had time to examine all these details by the light given out by the clusters of lamps, for the guests, though select, were numerous, and we had to fall in line just as at a great reception. The carriage drew up before the steps, and we handed our pelisses to our footman. By a glass door, the leaves of which he opened and shut, stood a gigantic porter with splendid broad shoulders. In the vestibule we passed between two lines of footmen in full livery and powdered; every one of them tall, motionless, and perfectly serious. They looked like domestic caryatids, and seemed to feel that it was an honour to be lackeys in such a house. The whole of the staircase, in which a small palace of today could easily have been put, was lined with huge camellias. At every landing great mirrors allowed the ladies to repair, as they went up, the slight disorder caused in a ball toilette by mantles, light as they may be, and which was shown by the brilliant blaze of a chandelier that hung, sustained by a golden cord, from a cupola where in azure and clouds the brush of some pupil of Lebrun or Mignard had painted a boldly foreshortened mythological allegory in the taste of his day.

"Between the windows were landscapes, oblong in shape, severe in style, and dark in colour, which might have been attributed to Poussin, or at least to Gaspard Dughet; so, at least, thought a famous painter who was going up the stairs by our side, and who had put his glass to his eye to examine them more closely. At the turn of the stairs, upon the steps of the balustrade, which was a marvel of ironwork, were statues of marble by Lepautre and Théodon, bearing candelabra the brilliancy of which equalled that of the chandelier, so that the feast, thanks to the splendour of the light, began even on the staircase. At the door of the antechamber, hung with Gobelins tapestries after cartoons by Oudry and wainscotted in old oak, stood an usher dressed in black with a silver chain around his neck, who in a voice more or less loud according to the importance of the title called out into the first drawing-room the names of the guests.

"The duke, tall, thin, made up of long lines like a thoroughbred greyhound, had a distinguished, aristocratic air and, in spite of his age, preserved traces of his former elegance. Even in the street, no one could have mistaken his rank. Standing a short distance from the door, he received the invited guests with a gracious word, a hand-shake, a bow, a nod, a smile, with a sure appreciation of what was due to each, and with such perfect grace that every one was satisfied and believed himself specially favoured. He bowed to my mother in a respectful, friendly way, and as it was the first time he had seen me, he spoke in a few words a semi-paternal, semi-gallant madrigal that smacked of the old Court. Near the mantelpiece stood the duchess, rouged with utter care-lessness of illusion, plainly wearing a wig and exhibiting historical dia-monds upon her thin bosom intrepidly low-necked. She was an uncommonly witty woman, and under her broad brown eyelids her eyes still shone with extraordinary brilliancy. She wore a dress of dark-garnet velvet with great flounces of English point-lace, and a row of diamonds at her bodice. With a careless hand she fanned herself with a large fan painted by Watteau, while she spoke to the persons who came to pay their respects. She looked uncommonly aristocratic. She exchanged a few words with my mother, who presented me to her, and as I bowed she touched my brow with her cold lips and said, 'Go, dear, and be sure not to miss a single dance.'

"This ceremony over, we entered the next drawing-room, which led to the ballroom. On the red damask hangings, in magnificent frames contemporary with the paintings themselves, hung family portraits that were not put there through aristocratic pride, but simply as masterpieces of art. They were by Clouet, Porbus, Van Dyck, Philippe de Cham-pagne and de Largillière, and every one was worthy of being placed in the Tribune of a museum. What I enjoyed about the luxury in this house was that nothing was recent. The paintings, the gilding, the dam-asks, the brocades, though not faded, were dulled and did not annoy the eye by the loud brilliancy of newness. One felt that the wealth was of long standing, and that things had always been so.

"The ballroom was of a size now scarcely met with save in palaces. Numerous standing-lamps and bracket-lamps placed in the bays between the windows formed with their thousands of tapers a sort of luminous conflagration through which the azure paintings of the ceiling with their wreaths of nymphs and cupids showed as through a rosy vapour. In spite of the brilliant light the room was so large that there was no lack of air and one breathed comfortably. The orchestra was placed in a sort of gallery at the end of the room in a grove of rare plants. On velvet benches arranged in semicircles were rows of ladies dazzlingly dressed if not dazzlingly beautiful, though there were some very pretty ones. The sight was superb. We happened to come in exactly between two dances and, seated near my mother on the end of a bench which happened to be free, I gazed on this spectacle, new to me, with astonishment and curiosity. The gentlemen, having taken their partners back to their seats, were walking about in the centre of the room looking to right and left, as if reviewing the women before making their choice. It was the youthful time of the ball, for mature men do not now dance. There were young attachés of embassies, secretaries of legations, auditors of the Council of State in expectation, beardless masters of requests, officers who had gone through their first campaign, clubmen diplomatically serious, youthful sportsmen thinking of keeping a stud, dandies whose whiskers were not much more than down, and eldest sons with the precocious authority of a great name and of a great fortune. Among these young people were a few serious personages covered with orders, whose polished heads shone like ivory in the light of the lustres or were concealed under wigs either too dark or too fair. As they passed by, they addressed polite remarks to the dowagers contemporary with their own youth, then turning aside, they would examine like experts and disinterested connoisseurs the feminine harem outspread before their eyes and their glasses. The first strains of the orchestra made them retreat as quickly as their gouty feet allowed toward quieter drawing-rooms, where at tables lighted by tapers covered with green shades they played at bouillotte or écarté.

"You will readily believe that I did not lack dancers. A young Hungarian in his magnate's dress, braided, embroidered, studded with buttons of precious stones, bowed gracefully to me and asked me for a mazurka. His features were regular, romantically pale, with great, black, somewhat shy eyes, and mustaches as sharp as needles. An Englishman of twenty-two or twenty-three who resembled Lord Byron except that he was not lame, the attaché of a Northern court, and some others wrote their names at once on my card. Although the old dancing master at the convent used to boast of me as being one of his best and most graceful pupils and praised my lightness and my feeling for time, I was not, I confess, entirely at my ease; I felt, as the papers say, the emotions inseparable from a debut. It seemed to me, as shy people always fancy, that all eyes were fixed upon me. Fortunately my Hungarian partner was an excellent dancer who helped out my first attempts, and soon, carried away by the music, intoxicated by the motion, I regained assurance and allowed myself to be spun into the whirlpool of floating skirts with a sort of pleasurable excitement.

"Yet I never forgot my usual thought and my object in coming to the ball. As I passed by the dancers, with a rapid glance I tried to see if you were in the other rooms. I at last caught sight of you in the recess of a window, talking with a dark-faced, long-nosed, black-bearded man wearing a red fez, in the uniform of the Nizam, with the Medjidieh order on his breast, no doubt either a bey or a pacha. When the whirl of the dance brought me back, there you were still speaking with animation to your orientally placid Turk, not deigning to cast a glance at the pretty faces that passed before you, flushed by the dance, in the shimmer of light.

"Nevertheless I did not lose hope, and for the time I was satisfied to know that you were there. Besides, the evening was not over, and some fortunate chance might bring us together. My partner took me back to my seat, and again the men began to walk up and down the space circumscribed by the benches. You took a turn with your Turk through the moving multitude, looking at the ladies and the toilettes, but with no more interest than you might have looked at pictures or statues. From time to time you made a remark to your friend the pacha, who smiled gravely. I could see you doing all this through my fan, which I closed, I confess, when you approached the place where we were seated. My heart beat high and I felt myself blush to the shoulders. It was impossible this time that I should escape your notice, for you walked as close to the benches as the dazzling fringe of overflowing gauze, lace, and flounces allowed you to do; but unfortunately two or three friends of my mother's stopped before us and paid her compliments, some of which were addressed to me. This screen of black coats masked me entirely. You had to go around the group and I remained invisible, though I did bend my head somewhat in the hope that you might see me. But you could not guess that those black coats, respectfully inclined, concealed from you a rather pretty girl who thought of no one but you and who had come to the ball on your account alone. I saw you leave the room by the other end, the Turk's red cap being the mark by which I followed you in the maze of dark coats that answer for a festival as well as for mourning.

"My enjoyment vanished, and I seemed dreadfully discouraged. Ironical Fate seemed to enjoy teasing me and taking you away from me. I danced the dances I was engaged for, and pretending to be somewhat tired, I refused other invitations. The play had lost its charm for me, the dresses seemed faded, and the lights turning dim. My father, who was playing cards in another room and who had lost some hundred louis to an old gentleman, came in to take us around the apartments and show us the hothouse into which the last room led, which was reputed to be marvellous; indeed, nothing could be more magnificent. It was like a virgin forest, so vigorously did the banana trees, the shaddocks, the palms, and other tropical plants grow in the warm atmosphere saturated with exquisite perfumes. At the end of the hothouse a white marble naiad poured out the waters of her urn into a gigantic shell of the Southern Seas surrounded by a mass of waterplants. There I caught sight of you again. You had your sister on your arm, but you were ahead of us and we could not meet you, for we followed in the same direction the narrow path, covered with yellow sand and bordered with verdure, that wound around the clumps of shrubs, flowers, and plants.

"We walked two or three times through the drawing-rooms, where the crowd had somewhat diminished, for the dancers had gone to restore their strength at the buffet, served with elegant profusion in a gallery wainscotted with ebony and gilding and adorned with paintings by

Desportes, representing flowers, fruits, and game, of splendid colouring, which time had simply made richer. All these details, which I glanced at carelessly, remained in my memory, and I recall them even in this world where life seems only the dream of a shadow. They are connected for me with feelings so deep that they compel me to return to earth. I returned to my home as sad as I had left it joyous, and attributed my mournful look to a slight headache. As I exchanged for a night wrapper the ball toilette that had been useless to me, since I desired to be beautiful for you alone, I said with a sigh, 'Why didn't he ask me to dance, as the Hungarian, the Englishman, and the other men did, although I cared nothing for them? It was a very easy matter. It was the most natural thing at a ball. But everybody looked at me except the one being whose attention I desired to attract. There is no doubt that my unfortunate love is very unlucky.' I went to bed, and a few tears rolled from my eyelids to my pillow."

Here stopped Spirite's dictation. The lamp had long since gone out for lack of oil, and Malivert, like somnambulists who need no exterior light, was still writing. Page followed page without Guy being conscious of it. Suddenly the impulse that guided his hand stopped, and his own thought, suspended by that of Spirite, returned to him. The faint light of dawn was filtering through the curtains of his room. He pulled them aside, and the pallid light of a winter morning showed him on the table many pages covered with feverish, rapid writing, the work of the night. Although he had written them with his own hand, he did not know their contents. With ardent curiosity, with deep emotion, he read the artless and chaste confidences of the lovely soul, of the adorable being, whose executioner he had been; innocently, it is needless to add. This tardy confession of love coming from the other world, breathed by a shadow, inspired him with desperate regret and powerless rage against himself. How could he have been stupid enough, blind enough to pass thus by the side of happiness without perceiving it? But he grew calm at last. Happening to look up at the Venetian mirror, he saw the reflection of Spirite smiling upon him.

X

A strange experience it is to receive a revelation of retrospective happiness that has passed close to you without being perceived, and which you have lost through your own fault. Never can regret for the irreparable be more bitter. One would like to live over again one's past days. Wonderful plans are made, and after the event one indulges in the most amazing perspicacity; but life cannot be turned over like an hourglass; the grain of sand once fallen will never ascend again. Guy de Malivert reproached himself in vain for not having found out the charming creature, who was neither buried in a Constantinople harem nor hidden behind the gratings of an Italian or Spanish convent, nor guarded like Rosina by a jealous guardian, but who had been of his own world, whom he could have seen every day, and from whom no insuperable obstacle separated him. She loved him; he could have asked her in marriage, he would have obtained her hand, and he would have enjoyed the supreme and rare felicity of being united even in this life to the soul destined to his soul. From the way in which he adored her shadow he understood what a passion the girl herself would have inspired in him. But soon his thoughts took another course; he ceased to reproach himself and regretted his commonplace grief. What had he lost, since, after all, Spirite had preserved her love beyond the tomb and had come from the depths of the Infinite to descend to the sphere he inhabited? Was not the passion he felt nobler, more poetic, more ethereal, more like eternal love, since it was thus rid of terrestrial contingencies and had for its object a being idealised by death? Has not the most perfect human union its weariness, its satiety, its lassitude? The most dazzled eyes see, after a few years, the charms they first adored turn pale; the soul is less visible through the worn flesh and love seeks in amazement its vanished ideal.

These reflections and the ordinary course of life with its exigencies, which even the most enthusiastic dreamers cannot escape, led on Malivert until the evening, which he so impatiently awaited. When he had shut himself up in his room and seated himself by the table as the night before, prepared to write, the little white, slender, blue-veined hand reappeared, signing to Malivert to take the pen. He obeyed and his fingers began to move of themselves without his brain dictating anything. Spirite's thought had taken the place of his own.

SPIRITE'S DICTATION

"I do not intend to weary you in posthumous fashion by telling you of all my disappointments. One day, however, I did feel a lively joy, and I thought that imperious fate, which seemed to enjoy concealing me from your glance, was about to cease troubling me. We were to dine the following Saturday at Mme. de L——'s. That alone would have been very indifferent to me, had I not learned during the week through Baron de Feroë, who sometimes came to see us, that you were to be one of the guests at this half-worldly, half-literary feast, for M. de L—— enjoyed entertaining artists and writers. He was a man of taste, a connoisseur of books and paintings, and possessed a library and a very fine collection of paintings. You occasionally went to his receptions, as did also several famous authors, and others who were becoming famous. M. de L—— prided himself on his ability to discover talent, and he was not of those who believe in settled reputations only. I said to myself, in my childish exultation, 'At last I have got hold of that fugitive, of that unapproachable man. This time he cannot escape me. When we shall be seated at the same table, perhaps side by side, lighted by fifty tapers, careless though he may be, he will have to see me—unless, however, there happens to be between us a mass of flowers or a centre-piece which may conceal me.' The days that still separated me from the happy Saturday seemed dreadfully long, as long as study hours at the convent. They went by, however, and the three of us, my father, my mother, and myself, reached M. de L——'s some thirty minutes before the dinner hour. The guests, grouped about the drawing-room, were chatting with each other, coming and going, looking at the pictures, glancing at the pamphlets on the tables, or telling stage news to some ladies seated on a divan near the mistress of the house. Among them were two or three illustrious writers whose names my father told me, but whose faces did not seem to me in harmony with their works. You had not yet arrived. The guests were all there, and M. de L—— was beginning to complain of your lack of punctuality, when a tall footman entered, bringing on a silver salver, on which was a pencil to sign and to mark the hour of delivery, a telegram from you, sent from Chantilly and containing these words only, in telegraphic style: 'Missed my train. Don't wait. Awfully sorry.'

"Cruel was my disappointment. The whole week I had caressed this hope, which vanished at the moment it was about to be fulfilled. I was filled with a sadness I had great difficulty concealing, and the flush that animation had imparted to my cheeks vanished. Fortunately the doors of the dining-room were opened, and the butler announced dinner. The movement that took place among the guests prevented my emotion being noticed. When everybody was seated, a chair remained empty on my right. It was yours; I could not be mistaken, for your name was written in fine writing upon a card with pretty coloured arabesques placed near your glasses. So the irony of fate was complete. But for this commonplace railway difficulty I should have had you near me during the whole meal, touching my dress, your hand touching mine when paying those innumerable little attentions that at table the least gallant man feels himself bound to render to a woman. A few commonplace words to begin with, like every overture to a dialogue, would have been exchanged between us, then, the ice having been broken, our conversation would have become more intimate, and your soul, your mind would soon have understood my heart. Perchance I might not have displeased you, and although fresh from Spain, you might have forgiven the rosy fairness of my complexion, the pale gold of my hair. If you had come to that dinner, your life and mine would unquestionably have moved in another direction; you would no longer be a bachelor, and I should be alive and not reduced to tell you my love from the other world. The love you feel for my shadow leads me to believe, without being too conceited, that you would not have been insensible to my terrestrial charms. But it was not to be. The unoccupied chair that isolated me from the other guests seemed to me a symbol of my fate—it betokened vain expectation and solitude in the midst of the crowd. The sinister omen has been too well fulfilled. My neighbour on the left was, as I learned later, a very amiable and very learned academician. He tried several times to make me talk, but I answered in monosyllables only, and even these were so ill fitted to the questions that my neighbour naturally took me for a little idiot, left me to myself, and chatted with his other partner.

"I scarcely touched the food; my heart was so heavy that I could not eat. At last the dinner ended and we went to the drawing-room, where the guests formed groups according to their preferences. In one, rather close to the armchair in which I was seated, so that I could hear what was being said, your name, spoken by M. d'Aversac, excited my curiosity. 'That chap Malivert,' said d'Aversac, 'is cracked about his pacha. On the other hand, the pacha is crazy about Malivert. They are never apart. Mohammed or Mustapha—I do not remember what his name is—wants to take Guy to Egypt and talks of giving him a steamer to take him to the first cataract; but Guy, who is as barbaric as the Turk is civilised, would prefer a dahabheah. He rather likes the plan, for he thinks it is very cold in Paris. He has a fancy for spending the winter in Cairo and continuing the study of Arab architecture that he commenced in the Alhambra; but if he does go, I am afraid we shall never see him again, and that he will turn Moslem like Hassan, the hero of "Namouna."'

"'He is quite capable of it,' answered a young fellow who was in the group; 'he has never greatly liked Western civilisation.'

"'Nonsense!' replied another. 'Once he has worn a few genuine costumes, taken a dozen vapour baths, purchased from the Djellabs one or two slaves whom he will sell at a discount, gazed on the Pyramids, sketched the broken-nosed profile of the Sphinx, he will calmly come back to tramp the asphalt of the Boulevard des Italiens, which is, after all, the only inhabitable place in the world.'

"This conversation filled me with deep anxiety. You were about to leave and for how long nobody knew. Would I have the chance of meeting you before your departure and leaving you at least my image to carry away with you? That was a piece of happiness I dared no longer believe in after so many disappointments.

"On returning home, after having reassured my mother, who fancied I must be ill, so pale was I, for she could not suspect what was going on in my heart, I thought deeply over my position. I asked myself whether the obstinacy of circumstances to separate us was not a secret warning of Fate that it would be dangerous to disobey. Perhaps you would be fatal to me, and it was wrong to insist on throwing myself in your way. My reason alone spoke, for my heart repelled the idea and meant to incur to the very last the risk of its love. I felt myself irresistibly drawn to you, and the bond, frail though it seemed, was more solid than a diamond chain. Unfortunately I was the only one bound. 'How painful is the fate of woman!' I said to myself. 'Doomed to expectation, to inaction, to solitude, she cannot, without failing in modesty, manifest her feelings. She must yield to the love she inspires, but she must not declare that which she feels. From the moment my heart awoke, one sentiment alone filled it—a pure, absolute, eternal sentiment—and the being who is the object of it will perhaps never know it. How can I let him know that a young girl whom he no doubt would love if he could suspect such a secret lives and breathes for him alone?'

"For a moment I thought of writing you one of those letters such as authors, I am told, receive at times, in which, under the veil of admiration, crop out feelings of another sort, and which solicit a rendezvous, in no way compromising," at the theatre or at the promenade; but my feminine modesty revolted at the employment of such means, and I feared lest you should take me for a bluestocking seeking your assistance to have a novel accepted by the *Revue des Deux Mondes.*

"D'Aversac had spoken the truth: the next week you had started for Cairo with your pacha. Your departure, which postponed my hopes to an uncertain time, filled me with a melancholy I found it difficult to conceal. I had lost interest in life. I cared nothing for dress; when I went into society, I let my maid select my toilettes. What was the use of being beautiful, since you were not there? And yet I was still beautiful enough to be surrounded like Penelope with a whole crowd of suitors. Little by little our drawing-room, frequented by my father's friends, serious and somewhat mature men, was filled with younger men, who came very assiduously to our Fridays. In the recesses of the doors I could see handsome dark fellows, correctly curled, whose cravats had cost them much meditation before they tied them, and who cast on me passionate and fascinating glances; others, during the figures of a quadrille, when we danced to the accompaniment of the piano, uttered sighs that, without being the least touched, I attributed to their being breathless; others, bolder, risked a few moral and poetic phrases about the happiness of a suitable marriage and claimed to be created purposely for legitimate happiness. They were all brave, irreproachable, well-dressed, ideally delicate; the scent on their hair came from Houbigant, their clothes were made by Renard. What more could an exacting, romantic imagination ask for? Therefore those handsome young fellows seemed somewhat surprised at the slight impression they produced on me; those who were most annoyed even suspected me, I believe, of being poetical. I had some serious offers; my hand was more than once asked of my parents, but on my being consulted I always replied in the negative, managing to find excellent objections. My parents did not insist. I was so young that there was no need of hurrying and later repenting a precipitate choice. Believing that I had some secret preference, my mother questioned me, and I was on the point of revealing the truth to her, but an invincible modesty kept me back. The love I alone felt, and which you were ignorant of, seemed to be a secret that I had no right to tell without your consent. It did not belong to me alone; you had a share in it. So I kept silence; and besides, I could never confess, even to the most indulgent of mothers, my mad passion—for thus it might well seem—born from an impression of childhood in the convent parlour, obstinately maintained in my soul, and justified by nothing from a human point of view. Had I spoken, my mother, seeing that my choice was in no way blameworthy or impossible of realisation, would no doubt have sought to bring us together and used, to make you declare yourself, some of those subterfuges which, on similar occasions, the most honest and virtuous women manage to invent. But this was repugnant to my virginal probity. I would have no intermediary between you and me. You alone were to notice me and find me out. In that way alone could I be happy and forgive myself for having been the first to love you. My maidenly modesty needed this consolation and this excuse. It was neither pride nor coquetry, but a genuine feeling of feminine dignity.

"Time passed and you returned from Egypt. I began to hear of your attentions to Mme. d'Ymbercourt, with whom you were said to be very much in love. My heart took fright and I wished to see my rival. She was shown to me in her box at the opera. I tried to judge her impartially, and I thought her handsome, but without charm or refinement. She was like a copy of a classical statue made by a mediocre sculptor. She united in herself everything that goes to make up the ideal of dolts, and I wondered that you could have the least fancy for such an idol. Mme. d'Ymbercourt's face, so regular at first sight, lacked distinguishing traits, original grace, unexpected charms. Such as she appeared to me on that evening, such she must always be. In spite of what I heard, I was conceited enough not to be jealous of her. Yet the reports of your marriage became more and more numerous, and as ill news always reaches those whom it interests, I was informed of everything that went on between you and Mme. d'Ymbercourt. At one time I was told that the banns had been called; at another the exact day of the wedding was named. I had no means of ascertaining the accuracy or falseness of these reports. The whole thing appeared to every one settled and most delightful in every respect, and so I had to believe it; yet the secret voice of my heart assured me that you did not love Mme. d'Ymbercourt. But very often people marry without love, to have an establishment, a settled position in society, or because they feel the need of repose after the heat and excitement of youth.

"I was filled with deep despair and saw my life drawing to a close. My chaste dream, caressed so long, vanished forever. I dared not even think of you in the most mysterious recesses of my soul, for as you now belonged to another before God and men, my thoughts of you, hitherto innocent, became culpable. In my passion as a girl nothing had occurred to make my guardian angel blush. Once I met you in the Bois de Boulogne, riding by Mme. d'Ymbercourt's carriage, and I threw myself back in my own, taking as much care to conceal myself as I formerly would have taken to be seen by you. That rapid glimpse was the last I had of you.

"I was scarcely seventeen. What was going to become of me? What would be the end of a life secretly destroyed at its very beginning? Should I accept one of the suitors approved by my parents in their wisdom? That is what, on such occasions, many young girls separated as I was from their ideal by some obscure fatality have done. But my sense of loyalty revolted from such a course, for I believed that, my first and only thought of love having been for you, I could belong to no one but you in this world; any other union would have struck me as almost adulterous. My heart held but a single page; you had written your name on it unwittingly, and no other was to take its place. Your own marriage would not free me from being faithful to you. Unconscious of my love, you were free, but I was bound. The idea of being the wife of another man filled me with insurmountable horror, and after having refused several suitors, knowing well how difficult a position in society is that of an old maid, I made up my mind to leave the world and become a nun. God alone could shelter my grief and perhaps console me.

XI

"I entered as a novice the convent of the Sisters of Mercy in spite of my parents' remonstrances, which moved me, but did not shake my courage. Firm though one's resolve may be, the moment of the final separation is terrible. At the end of a long passage a grating marks the limit between the world and the cloister. The family may accompany to that threshold, not to be crossed by the profane, the maiden who gives herself to God. After the last embrace, the end of which is awaited by gloomy, veiled figures with an impassible air, the grating opens just wide enough to allow the passage of the novice, whom shadowy arms seem to carry away, and it closes with a rattle of iron that echoes down the long corridors like distant thunder. The sound of the closing of a coffin is not more lugubrious and does not strike the heart more painfully. I felt myself grow pale, and an icy chill seized me. I had taken my first step out of earthly life, henceforth closed to me; I was penetrating into that cold region where passions die, where remembrance vanishes, and which the rumours of the world no longer reach. There exists nothing but the thought of God. It suffices to fill the frightful void and the silence that weighs on this place, a silence as deep as that of the tomb. I may tell you all this, now that I am dead.

"My piety, though tender and fervent, did not go to the length of mystical exaltation; it was a human motive rather than an imperious vocation that had caused me to seek peace in the solitary cloister. I was a shipwrecked soul, cast upon an unknown reef, and my dream, invisible to all, had ended tragically. At the beginning, therefore, I suffered what in the devout life is called dryness of heart, weariness, longing for the world, vague despair—the last temptations of the spirit of the day, trying to seize his prey; but soon the tumult was appeased, the habit of prayer and of religious practices the regularity of the offices and the monotony of a rule intended to overcome the rebellion of the soul and of the body, turned toward heaven thoughts that yet too often recalled the earth. Your image still lived in my heart, but I succeeded in loving you only in and through God.

"The Convent of the Sisters of Mercy is not one of those romantic cloisters such as worldly people imagine might shelter a despairing life. There were no Gothic arcades, no columns festooned with ivy, no moonbeams entering through the trefoil of a broken rose window and casting their light upon the inscription of a tomb; no chapel, with stained-glass windows, slender pillars, and traceried vaultings, forming excellent motives for a decoration or a panorama. The religious feeling that seeks to understand Christianity by its picturesque and poetic side would find in it no theme for descriptions after the manner of Chateaubriand. The building is modern and has not the smallest obscure corner in which to lodge a legend. Nothing satisfies the eyes, no ornaments, no fancy of art, no paintings, no sculptures; everywhere bare, straight lines. A white light illumines like a winter's day the pallor of the long corridors and the walls, cut by the symmetrical doors of the cells, and glazes with rippling beams the shining floors: everywhere gloomy severity, heedless of beauty, and careless of clothing the idea with a form.

"This dull architecture has the advantage of not distracting souls that must lose themselves in the contemplation of God. The windows are placed very high and are grated; between the black bars one can get but a glimpse of the blue or gray sky outside. It is like a fortress built as a defence against the ambushes of the world. Solidity is sufficient; beauty would be superfluous. The chapel itself is but half opened to the devotions of the faithful outside. A huge screen rising from the ground to the vaulting and provided with thick green curtains intervenes like the portcullis of a fortress between the nave and the choir reserved for the nuns. Wooden stalls with sober mouldings polished by wear run on either side; at the back, in the centre, are placed three seats for the Mother Superior and her two assistants. There the nuns come to hear divine service, their veils down, their long black dresses on which shows a broad strip of white stuff like the cross of a pall from which the arms have been cut, trailing behind them. From the trellised gallery of the novices I watched the nuns bow to the Mother Superior and to the altar, kneel down, prostrate themselves, and vanish into their stalls changed into prie-dieu. At the elevation of the Host, the centre of the curtain opens somewhat and allows a glimpse of the priest performing the Holy Sacrifice at the altar, placed opposite the choir. The fervour of the worship edified me and confirmed my resolution to break with the world to which I could not have returned. In this atmosphere of ecstasy and incense, in the trembling light of the tapers casting pale gleams upon these prostrate brows, my heart felt it was becoming winged, and tended more and more to rise to ethereal regions. The ceiling of the chapel turned azure and gold and in an opening of the heaven I seemed to see in a luminous cloud, the smiling angels bending toward me and signing to me to come to them. I saw no longer the ugly tint of the whitewash, the mediocre taste of the chandelier, and the meanness of the black-framed paintings.

"The time for the taking of my vows approaching, I was overwhelmed with the flattering encouragement, the delicate attentions, the mystic caresses, the hopes of perfect felicity lavished in convents upon young novices about to consummate their sacrifice and to give themselves forever to God. I did not need these aids; I could walk to the altar with a firm step. Forced—or so I thought—to give you up, I regretted nothing in the world save the affection of my parents, and my resolve never to re-enter it was unchangeable.

"I had passed the tests, and the solemn day arrived. The convent, usually so peaceful, was filled with an agitation that the severe monastic discipline repressed. The sisters came and went in the corridors, sometimes forgetting the phantom-like walk ordered by the rule; for the coming in of a new sister is a great event, and the entrance of a new lamb into the flock throws the whole fold into commotion. The worldly dress that the novice puts on for the last time is a subject of curiosity, joy, and astonishment; the satin, lace, pearls, and gems intended to represent the pomps of Satan are admired somewhat fearfully. Thus adorned, I was led to the choir. The Mother Superior and her assistants were in their places, and in the stalls the nuns were praying on bended knee. I spoke the sacred words that separated me forever from the living, and as the ritual of the ceremony requires it, I pushed aside with my foot the rich velvet carpet on which I had to kneel at certain moments. I took off my necklace and bracelets and undid my ornaments in token of my renunciation of vanity and luxury. I abjured the coquetry of women, which was not a difficult thing for me to do, since I had not had the joy to please you and to be beautiful in your eyes.

"Then came the most lugubrious and the most dreaded scene of the religious drama—the moment when the new nun's hair is cut off as a vanity henceforth useless. It recalls the dressing of the condemned, except that the victim is innocent, or at least purified by repentance. Although I had sincerely and from my heart given up all human bonds, I became pale as death when the scissors began cutting my long, fair hair, held up by one of the sisters. The golden curls fell in thick quantities upon the flags of the sacristy into which I had been led, and I gazed at them with dry eyes as they fell around me. I was terrified and felt a secret horror; the cold of the scissors, as they touched my neck, made me start nervously as if I felt the touch of the axe; my teeth chattered, and the prayer I strove to utter could not pass my lips. Ice-cold sweat, as that of one in agony, bathed my temples; my sight grew dim, and the lamp suspended before the altar of the Virgin seemed to be vanishing in a mist; my knees sank under me, and I had only time to say, as I stretched out my arms as if clinging to emptiness, 'I am dying.'

"They made me breathe salts, and when I had regained my senses, amazed, like one emerging from the tomb, at the brightness of the day, I found myself in the arms of the sisters, who supported me placidly, accustomed as they were to such scenes.

"'It does not amount to anything,' said the youngest of the nuns with an air of sympathy. 'The most trying part is over. Recommend yourself to the Blessed Virgin, and all will be well. The same thing happened to me when I took the vows. It is the last effort of Satan.'

"Two sisters put on me the black dress of the order and the white stole, took me back to the choir, and cast over my head the veil, the symbolical shroud that made me dead to the world and left me visible to God alone. A pious legend I had heard stated that if one asked of Heaven a favour when under the folds of the funereal veil, it would be granted. When the veil was cast over me, I implored of the divine goodness to allow me to reveal my love to you. It seemed to me, as I felt a sudden inward joy, that my prayer was granted, and I was greatly relieved; for that was my secret pain, that was the dagger in my heart, the thorn in my flesh that made me suffer night and day. I had given you up in this world, but my soul could not consent to keep its secret forever.

"Shall I tell you of my life in the convent? There day follows day exactly alike, every hour with its devotion, its task; life moves on with equal step toward eternity, glad to approach the end. Yet the apparent calm often conceals much languor, sadness, and depression. Thoughts, although tamed by prayer and meditation, will wander off in reverie; the nostalgia of the world seizes upon you; you regret your liberty, your family, and nature; you dream of the great horizons filled with light, of the meadows diapered with flowers, of the swelling, wooded hills, of the blue smoke that rises in the evening over the fields, of the road traversed by carriages, of the river with its boats, of life, of motion, of joyous sounds, of incessant variety of objects. You would like to go out, to run, to fly; you wish you had wings like a bird; you turn in your tomb; in imagination you cross the high walls of the convent, and your thoughts return to the pleasant places, to the scenes of your childhood and your youth, which live again with magical vivacity of detail. You form useless plans for happiness, forgetting that the bolts of the irrevocable have been drawn upon you. The most religious souls are exposed to these temptations, remembrances, mirages, which the will represses, which prayer tries to dispel, but which nevertheless rise again in the silence and solitude of the cell with its four white walls, whose sole decoration is a black wooden crucifix.

"The thought of you, put away at first in my early fervour, returned, more frequent and more tender; the regret of lost happiness oppressed me painfully, and often silent tears streamed down my pale cheeks. At night I would weep in my dreams and in the morning find my coarse pillow wetted with bitter tears. In happier visions I found myself on the steps of a villa, after a drive, walking with you up a wide staircase on which the great neighbouring trees cast bluish shadows. I was your wife, and your caressing and protecting glance rested on me. Every obstacle that had come between us had disappeared. My soul did not consent to these fair imaginings, which it strove against as if they were sinful. I confessed them, I did penance for them. I sat up in prayer and I struggled against sleep to avoid these guilty illusions, but they ever returned. The struggle impaired my strength, which soon began to abandon me.

Without being sickly, I was delicate; the harsh life of the cloister, its fasts, its abstinences, its macerations, the fatigue of the night services, the sepulchral chill of the church, the rigours of the long winter, against which I was ill protected by the thin serge dress, and above all the struggle in my soul, the alternate exaltation and despair, doubt and fervour, the fear of delivering to my divine spouse a heart distracted by human attachments, and of suffering celestial vengeance—for God is jealous; and perhaps also the jealousy inspired in me by Mme. d'Ymbercourt—all these causes acted disastrously upon me.

"My complexion had become of a mat, waxy tint; my eyes, showing larger in my wasted face, shone with the light of fever in their dark orbits; the veins of my temples stood out in a network of darker azure; my lips had lost their fresh, rosy colour; my hands had become slender and transparent like the hands of a shadow. Death is not dreaded in the convent as it is in the world. In the convent it is joyfully welcomed, for it is the deliverer of the soul, the door opening into heaven, the end of the trials, and the beginning of beatitude. God withdraws to Himself earlier than others those He prefers, those He loves, and shortens their passage through the vale of sorrow and tears. Prayers full of hope in their funereal psalmody surround the deathbed of the dying nun, whom the sacraments purify of every terrestrial stain and on whom beams the splendour of the other world. She is to her sisters an object of envy, and not of terror.

"I saw the fatal day approaching without fear. I hoped that God would forgive me my only love, so chaste, so pure, and so involuntary, and which I had endeavoured to forget as soon as it had appeared culpable in my own eyes. I hoped that He would receive me in His grace. Soon I became so weak that I would swoon away at prayers and remain as if dead under my veil, with my face to the ground. My immobility was respected, for it was mistaken for ecstasy. Then, when it was seen that I did not rise, two sisters, bending toward me, would make me sit up like an inert body, and, their hands under my arms, would lead me, or rather carry me back to my cell, which before long I was unable to leave. I would remain for long hours on my bed, dressed, counting my beads with my thin fingers, lost in some vague meditation, and asking myself if my hope would be fulfilled after death. My strength was visibly ebbing, and the remedies proposed for my illness diminished my sufferings, but did not cure me. Nor did I wish to be cured, for beyond this life I had a hope long caressed, the possible realisation of which inspired me with a sort of curiosity to enter the other world.

"My passage from this world to the other was most gentle. All the bonds between mind and matter had been broken except one, more tenuous a thousand times than the light cobwebs that float in the air of a fine autumn day; it alone held back my soul ready to open its wings in the breath of the Infinite. Alternations of light and shade, like the intermittent light of a night-light before it goes out, palpitated before my already dim eyes; the prayers murmured near me by the kneeling sisters, and which I tried to join in mentally, reached me only as a confused buzzing, as a vague, distant rumour. My deadened senses had ceased to perceive anything earthly; my thoughts, abandoning my brain, fluttered uncertain in a strange dream halfway between the material and the immaterial world, no longer belonging to the one and not yet pertaining to the other, while mechanically my fingers, pale as ivory, were rumpling and drawing up the folds of the sheet.

"At last my agony began, and I was stretched on the ground, a bag of ashes under my head, to die in the humble attitude that becomes a poor servant of God, giving back her dust to the dust. Breathing became more and more difficult; I stifled; a feeling of fearful anguish racked my breast; it was the instinct of nature in me still fighting against destruction. But soon the useless struggle ceased, and with a faint sigh my soul was exhaled from my lips.

XII

"Human words cannot render the sensation of a soul that, freed from its earthly bonds, passes from this life into the next, from time into eternity, from the finite into infinity. My motionless body, already white with a mat whiteness, the livery of death, lay upon the funeral couch surrounded by the nuns in prayer; but I was as thoroughly freed from it as the butterfly is from its chrysalis, an empty shell, a shapeless form, which it abandons to open its young wings to the unknown light suddenly revealed to it. An interval of deepest darkness had been followed by dazzling splendour, by the broadening of the horizon, by the disappearance of every limit and every obstacle, and by the intoxication of inexpressible joy. The sudden accession of new sensations made me understand mysteries closed to terrestrial thought and organs. Freed from the frame of clay, no longer subject to the law of gravity, which but a moment before still fettered me, I sprang with delighted eagerness into the unfathomable ether. Distance had ceased to exist for me, and my mere wish enabled me to be wherever I wished to be. More swiftly than light I soared in great circles through the illimitable azure of space, as if to take possession of immensity; crossing and recrossing on my way swarms of souls and spirits.

"The atmosphere was formed of an ever-burning light shining like diamond-dust, and I soon perceived that every grain of the dazzling powder was a soul. It was full of currents, eddies, billows, shimmerings like the fine dust that is spread over a sounding-board in order to study sonorous vibrations, and all these movements caused increased brilliancy in the splendour. The numbers that mathematics can furnish to calculators who venture into the depths of the infinite cannot, with their millions of zeros adding their tremendous power to the initial number, give even an approximate idea of the tremendous multitude of souls that compose this effulgence, differing from the material light as much as day differs from night.

"To the souls that, since the creation of our world and of other spheres, had already passed through the trials of life were joined expectant or virgin souls, awaiting their turn to be incarnated in a body on a planet belonging to some system or another. There were enough of them to people for thousands and thousands of years all these worlds, the breath of God, which He will re-absorb by drawing back to Himself His own breath when He becomes weary of His work. These souls, though differing in essence and aspect according to the globe they were to inhabit, recalled, every one of them, in spite of the infinite variety of their types, the divine type, and were made in the image of their Maker. Their constituent monad was the celestial spark. Some were white as the diamond; others were of the colour of rubies, emeralds, sapphires, topazes, and amethysts. For lack of terms intelligible to you, I make use of these names of gems, mere pebbles, opaque crystals black as ink, the most brilliant of which make but a dark spot against that background of living splendour.

"Sometimes there swept by a great angel, bearing an order of God to the very ends of the infinite and making the universe oscillate by the beating of its vast wings. The Milky Way was poured out over the heavens in a great stream of glowing suns. The stars, which I beheld in their real form and size, so enormous that the imagination of man cannot possibly conceive it, flamed with vast, terrific fulguration. Behind these and between them, at depths more and more vertiginous, I saw others and still others, so that nowhere was the end of the firmament visible, and I might well have believed myself enclosed in the centre of a prodigious sphere constellated internally with stars. Their light, white, yellow, blue, green, red, was of such intensity and brightness as to make the light of our own sun seem black, but the eyes of my soul stood it without the least difficulty. I came and went, ascended and descended, traversed in a second millions of leagues through the light of rainbow-like reflections, golden and silver irradiations, diamond-like phosphorescence, stellar outbursts, amid all the magnificence, all the beatitudes, all the ravishments of the divine life.

"I heard the music of the spheres, the echo of which struck the ear of Pythagoras; a mysterious harmony, the pivot of the universe, marked the rhythm. With a harmonious sound, as tremendous as thunder and as soft as the flute, our own world, borne away by its central sun, moved slowly through space, and with one glance I beheld the planets, from Mercury to Neptune, describing their ellipses, accompanied by their satellites. A rapid intuition revealed to me the names by which they are known in heaven, acquainted me with their structure, with the thought and purpose of their creation; no secret of that prodigious life was concealed from me. I read as in an open book the poem of God, the lines of which were formed of suns. Would it were permissible for me to explain some of its pages to you! But you are still living in inferior darkness, and your eyes would be blinded by the dazzling effulgence.

"In spite of the ineffable beauty of this wondrous spectacle, I had not forgotten earth, the poor habitation I had just left. My love, triumphant over death, followed me beyond the tomb, and I saw with divine voluptuousness, with radiant felicity, that you loved no one, that your soul was free, and that you might be mine forever. Then I knew what I had dimly felt before. We were predestined one for the other; our souls formed one of those celestial pairs that, when they unite, form an angel. But these two halves of the supreme whole, in order to meet in immortality, must have sought each other in life, divined each other under the veil of the flesh, through trials, obstacles, and distractions. I alone had felt the presence of my sister soul and had hastened toward it, urged on by an unerring instinct. Your perception, not so clear, had merely put you on your guard against vulgar bonds and loves. You had understood that none of the souls around you were intended for you, and passionate, though apparently cold, you had reserved yourself for a higher ideal. Thanks to the favour shown me, I could make you know the love that you had ignored during my life, and I hoped to inspire you with the desire to follow me within the sphere in which I dwell. I felt no regret, for what could the best of human ties be compared with the happiness of two souls in the eternal kiss of divine love? Until the supreme moment arrived, my task consisted in preventing the world from engaging you in its ways and separating you from me forever. Marriage binds in this world and the next, but you did not love Madame d'Ymbercourt. As a spirit I could read within your heart, and I had nothing to fear on this account; yet, not meeting the ideal you dreamed of, you might have become tired and, through fatigue, indolence, discouragement, or the need of changing your state of life, you might have allowed yourself to be drawn into that commonplace union.

"Leaving the fount of light, I flew earthward, where I saw your globe rolling beneath me in its foggy atmosphere and its strata of clouds. I found you easily, and I watched over your life, an invisible witness, reading your thoughts and influencing them without your being conscious of it. Through my presence, which you did not even suspect, I drove away the ideas and caprices that might have turned you from the aim toward which I directed you. Little by little I detached your soul from every earthly bond; to keep you more safely, I cast over your home a mysterious spell that made you love it. When there, you felt around you a sort of faint, impalpable caress and experienced inexpressible comfort. It seemed to you, though you could not account for it, that your happiness lay within the walls that I filled with life. The lover who, on a stormy night, reads his favourite poet by a bright fire, while his sleeping mistress lies, her head on her arm, in the deep alcove, lost in pleasant dreams, feels just such deep happiness in the solitude of love. Nothing could induce him to leave; for his whole world is contained within that room. I had to prepare you gradually to behold me and mysteriously establish relations with you. Between a spirit and an uninitiated living being communications are difficult. A deep gulf separates this world from the other. I had crossed it, but it was not enough; I still had to make myself visible to your eyes, which were yet covered with a bandage and unable to perceive the immaterial through the opacity of matter.

"Mme. d'Ymbercourt, bent upon marrying you, attracted you to her home and wearied you with her eagerness. Substituting my will for your sleeping thought, I made you write that reply to the lady's note in which your secret sentiments betrayed themselves and which caused you so much surprise. The idea of the supernatural awoke in you and, having become more attentive, you understood that a mysterious power had entered into your life. The sigh I uttered when, in spite of my warning, you made up your mind to go out, faint and soft though it was, like the vibration of an Æolian harp, troubled you deeply and awoke hidden sympathy in your soul. You had recognised in it the note of feminine suffering. I could not then manifest myself to you in plainer fashion, for you were not sufficiently free from the bonds of matter. I therefore appeared to the Baron de Feroë, a disciple of Swedenborg and a seer, to beg him to speak to you the mysterious words that put you on your guard against the peril you were running and inspired you with the desire to penetrate into the world of spirits to which my love called you. You know the rest. Now am I to return to the regions above, or am I to remain here below, and will the shadow be happier than was the woman?"

Here the impulse that had driven Malivert's pen over the paper stopped, and Guy's power of thought, suspended for a time by the influence of Spirite, resumed possession of his brain. He read what he had just unconsciously written and was strengthened in the resolve to love till death the charming soul who had suffered for him during her short stay upon earth.

"But what shall our relations be?" he said to himself. "Will Spirite take me away with her into the regions where she dwells, or will she hover around me, visible to me alone? Will she answer me if I speak to her? and how, in that case, shall I understand her?" These questions were not easy to answer, so Malivert, after having turned them over in his mind, gave up the effort and remained plunged in a deep reverie, from which Jack roused him by announcing the Baron de Feroë.

The two friends shook hands heartily, and the Swede with the pale golden moustache threw himself into an armchair.

"Guy, I have come very unceremoniously to breakfast with you," he said, stretching out his feet on the fender. "I went out early this morning, and on passing your house I was seized with a fancy to pay you a visit almost as early as if I were an officer of the law."

"You were right—it was a happy thought on your part," replied Malivert, ringing for Jack, to whom he gave orders to serve breakfast.

"My dear Guy, you look as if you had not gone to bed," said the baron, as he saw the tapers that had burned down to their paper frills, and the sheets of writing spread out on the table. "You have been working during the night. Is it a novel or a poem? Shall you publish it soon?"

"It may be called a poem," replied Malivert, "but it is not of my own composition. I simply held the pen, led by an inspiration superior to my own."

"I understand," went on the baron; "Apollo dictated and Homer wrote. Such verses are the best."

"The poem, if it be one, is not in verse, and it was no mythological god who dictated it to me."

"I beg your pardon. I forgot that you are a romanticist, and that with you Apollo and the Muses must be left to Chompre's Dictionary or the 'Letters to Emily'!"

"Since you have been in some sort my mystagogue and my initiator into things supernatural, dear Baron, there is no reason why I should conceal from you that the writing you take for 'copy,' to use the printer's expression, was dictated to me last night and the preceding night by the spirit who is interested in me and who appears to have known you on earth, for you are named in the story."

"You served as your own medium because relations are not yet well established between you and the spirit that visits you," replied Baron de Feroë; "but very soon you will be able to dispense with these slow and coarse means of communication. Your souls will know each other by thought and desire, without any external sign."

Jack now announced that breakfast was served. Malivert, quite upset by his strange adventure, by his love affair from beyond the tomb, which Don Juan would have envied, scarcely ate the food placed before him; Baron de Feroë did eat, but with Swedenborgian sobriety, for whoever desires to live in communion with spirits must make the share of matter as small as possible.

"That is excellent tea you have, Guy," said the baron. "It is the white-tipped, green-leafed tea plucked after the first spring rains, which Mandarins drink without sugar, steeping it in cups set in filigree holders to avoid burning their fingers. It is the drink, *par excellence,* of dreamers, for the intoxication it produces is purely intellectual. Nothing more quickly dispels human grossness and better predisposes to the vision of things hidden from the vulgar herd. Since you are now going to live in an immaterial sphere, I recommend you to drink this tea. But you are not listening to me, and I can easily understand your inattention. So novel a situation must strike you as very strange."

"Yes, I confess it," replied Malivert; "I am somewhat dazed, and constantly asking myself whether I am not a prey to hallucinations."

"Drive away these thoughts, for they would cause the spirit to fly forever. Do not seek to explain the inexplicable, but yield with absolute faith and submission to your guiding influence. The least doubt would cause a break and entail eternal regret on your part. By special favour, but rarely accorded, souls that have not met in life may meet in heaven. Profit by the chance given you and show yourself worthy of such happiness."

"I shall indeed, and I shall not again inflict on Spirite the pain of which I was the innocent cause while she still dwelt in this world. But now that I think of it, in the story she dictated to me, that adorable soul has not told me the name she bore upon earth."

"Would you like to know it? Go to Père-Lachaise, climb the hill, and near the chapel you will see a white marble tomb on which is carved a cross laid flat; at the intersection of the arms of the cross there is a wreath of roses with delicate marble leaves, a masterpiece by a famous sculptor. In the medallion formed by the wreath a brief inscription will tell you what I am not formally authorised to impart to you.

The mute language of the tomb shall speak in my place, although, in my opinion, your curiosity is vain. What matters a terrestrial name when an eternal love is at stake? But you are not yet quite detached from human ideas, and I can understand it, for it is not so long since you stepped outside the circle that bounds ordinary life."

Baron de Feroë took leave. Guy dressed, had his carriage brought round, and hastened to the shops of the most famous florists to purchase a quantity of white lilac. As it was winter, he found it difficult to obtain, but in Paris there is no such thing as impossibility when a man is willing to pay; so he bought his white lilac and ascended the hill with a beating heart and eyes full of tears.

A few flakes of snow, still unmelted, shone like silver tears upon the dark leaves of the yew trees, the cypresses, the firs, and the ivy, and brought out with white touches the mouldings of the tombs, the tops and the arms of the funereal crosses. The sky was lowering, of a yellowish grey, heavy as lead, the right kind of a sky to hang over a cemetery, and the sharp wind moaned as it swept through the lines of monuments, made for the dead and exactly proportionate to human nothingness. Maliveit soon reached the chapel, and not far off, within a border of Irish ivy, he saw a white tomb made whiter still by the light layer of snow. He bent over the railing and read the inscription engraved within the wreath of roses: "Lavinia d'Aufideni, in religion Sister Philomena, died at the age of eighteen."

He stretched his arm over the railing, threw the lilacs over the inscription, and, although sure of having been forgiven, remained for a few moments by the tomb in a dreamy contemplation, his heart big with remorse; for was he not the murderer of that fair dove, who had so soon returned to heaven? While he was thus leaning on the railing of the monument, letting fall his hot tears upon the cold snow, which formed the second shroud of the virginal tomb, there was a break in the thick curtain of grey clouds. Like light shining through successive thicknesses of gauze that are gradually removed, the orb of the sun appeared less indistinct, of a pale white, more like the moon than the orb of day, the right sort of sun to light the dead. Little by little the opening grew larger and from it streamed a long sunbeam; it showed against the dark background of cloud and lighted up and caused to sparkle under the mica of the snow, as under a winter dew, the mass of white lilacs and the marble wreath of roses.

In the luminous tremulousness of the sunbeam in which played icy dust, Malivert thought he made out, like a vapour from a silver perfume-burner, a slender white form rising from the tomb, enveloped in the floating folds of a gauze shroud like the robes of an angel. The form made a friendly gesture to him with its hand, a cloud passed across the sun, and the vision disappeared.

Guy de Malivert withdrew whispering the name of Lavinia d'Aufideni to himself, re-entered his carriage, and drove back into Paris, which is filled everywhere with the living who do not even suspect that they are dead, for they lack the inner life.

XIII

From that day Malivert's life was divided into two distinct portions, the one real, the other spiritual. There was apparently no change in him. He went to the club and into society, he appeared in the Bois de Boulogne and on the Boulevard. If any interesting performance took place, he was present at it, and to see him dressed in good taste, with neat shoes and well fitting gloves, walking about through human life, no one would have suspected that the young man was in constant communication with spirits, or that, when he left the Opéra, he gazed into the mysterious depths of the invisible universe. Yet on being examined more closely, he would have been observed to be more serious, paler, thinner, and spiritualised as it were. The expression of his face was no longer the same; unless he was drawn out of himself by others, it exhibited a sort of disdainful beatitude. Fortunately society never observes unless its interest requires it to do so, and Malivert's secret was not suspected.

The evening after his first visit to the cemetery where he had learned Spirite's terrestrial name, and while waiting for a manifestation he desired with all the strength of his will, he heard, like drops of water falling within a silver basin, the sound of the notes of the piano. There was no one in the room; but prodigies no longer astonished Malivert. A few chords were struck in such a way as to command attention and awaken his curiosity. Guy looked toward the piano, and little by little there appeared in a luminous mist the lovely form of a young girl. At first the image was so transparent that objects behind it were visible through its contours, just as the bottom of a lake is visible through its limpid waters. Without becoming in the least material, it gradually condensed enough to look like a living figure, but filled with such light, impalpable, aerial life that it resembled rather the reflection of a body in a mirror than the body itself. Certain sketches of Prud'hon, scarcely rubbed in with thin, vague contours, bathed in chiaroscuro and surrounded, as it were, with violet vapour, the white draperies seeming to be made of moonbeams, may give a faint idea of the graceful apparition then seated before Malivert's piano. The pale fingers, faintly flushed, glided over the ivory keys like white butterflies, merely touching the keys but bringing out the sound, although the gentle contact would not have bowed the feather of a pen. The notes, without having to be struck, flashed out of themselves when the luminous hands fluttered above them. A long white dress of an ideal muslin infinitely finer than the Indian tissues that can be drawn through a ring fell in abundant folds around her and foamed over her feet like snow. Her head, bent slightly forward as if a score were open upon the piano, enabled the neck to be seen with its curling, golden, shimmering, fine hair, as well as the upper portion of pearly, opaline shoulders, the whiteness of which melted into the whiteness of the dress. Between the bandeaux, which rose and fell as if lifted by the wind, shone a narrow starry band, the ends of which were fastened on the chignon. From where Malivert sat, one ear and a portion of the cheek showed, blooming, rosy, velvety, of a tone that would have made the colour of a peach look earthy. It was Lavinia, or Spirite, to call her by the name she has hitherto borne in this story. She looked around rapidly, to make sure that Guy was attentive and that she might begin. Her blue eyes shone with a tender light that penetrated his soul; there was still something of the maiden in that angelic look.

The piece that she played was the work of a great master, one of those inspirations in which human genius seems to foresee the infinite, and which now express so powerfully the secret desires of the soul, and again recall the remembrance of the heavens and the paradise from which it has been driven. It was full of ineffable melancholy, of ardent prayer, of low murmurs, last revolts of pride dashed from light into darkness. Spirite interpreted all these feelings with a *maestria* that made one forget Chopin, Liszt, Thalberg, those wizards of the piano. Guy seemed to be hearing music for the first time. A new art was being revealed to him. Innumerable new thoughts awoke within his soul; the notes stirred in him such deep, divine, interior vibrations that he felt he must have heard them in a former life that he had since forgotten. Spirite not only rendered all the intentions of the master, she expressed the ideal he had dreamed of, but which human infirmity had not allowed him to attain. She fulfilled his genius, she made perfection perfect, she added to the absolute.

Guy had unconsciously arisen and walked to the piano like a somnambulist. He remained standing, leaning his elbow upon the corner of the instrument, his eyes gazing ardently at those of Spirite.

Her expression was truly sublime. Her head, uplifted and somewhat thrown back, showed her face illumined by the splendours of ecstasy. Inspiration and love shone with supernatural brilliancy in her eyes, the azure of which almost disappeared under the upper eyelid; her half-opened lips gleamed like pearls, and her neck, bathed in bluish transparencies like those of the heads in Guido's ceilings, swelled like the neck of a mystic dove. The woman was diminishing in her, the angel augmenting; and the intensity of light she shed around her was so brilliant that Malivert was constrained to turn away his eyes.

Spirite noticed this, and in a voice more harmonious and sweeter than the music she was playing she whispered, "Poor friend! I forgot that you are still confined within your terrestrial prison and that your eyes cannot bear the faintest ray of true light. Later I shall show myself to you such as I am, in the sphere whither you will follow me. Meanwhile the shadow of my mortal form suffices to manifest my presence to you, and you can contemplate me thus without peril."

By invisible gradations she returned from supernatural beauty to natural beauty; the wings of Psyche that had for a moment fluttered on her shoulders disappeared again; her material appearance became somewhat more condensed, and a milky cloud spread about her suave contours, bringing them out more plainly, as water in which a drop of essence is thrown shows more clearly the lines of the crystal that contains it. Lavinia was reappearing through Spirite, somewhat vaporous, no doubt, but sufficiently real to cause an illusion.

She had ceased to play and was looking at Malivert, who stood before her—a faint smile playing on her lips, a smile of celestial irony, of divine archness, which mocked human debility while consoling it, while her eyes, purposely dimmed, still expressed the tenderest love, but such love as a chaste maiden might allow to be seen on earth by the man to whom she was engaged. Malivert might indulge in the belief that he was with the Lavinia who had sought him so earnestly while alive, and from whom he had always been separated by ironical fate. Carried away, fascinated, palpitating with love, forgetting that he had before him but a shadow, he advanced and by an instinctive motion sought to take one of Spirite's hands, still resting on the piano, and bear it to his lips; but his fingers closed on hers without touching anything, as if they had passed through a mist. Although she had nothing to fear, Spirite withdrew with a gesture of offended maidenliness; soon, however, her angelic smile reappeared, and she raised to Guy's lips, who felt a soft freshness and a faint, delicious perfume, her hand made of transparent, rosy light.

"I forgot," she said in a voice that was not formulated into words, but which Guy heard within his heart, "that I am no longer a girl, but a soul, a shadow, an impalpable vapour with nothing of human sense; so what Lavinia might perhaps have refused, Spirite grants, not as a pleasure, but as a sign of pure love and eternal union." And she left for a few seconds her hand under the imaginary kiss of Guy.

Soon she returned to the piano and played an air of incomparable power and sweetness, in which Guy recognised one of his poems—his favourite one—transposed from the language of verse into the language of music. It was an inspiration in which, disdaining vulgar joys, he soared eagerly toward the higher spheres in which the poet's desire is at last to be satisfied. Spirite, with marvellous intuition, rendered the unuttered words, the unphrased human speech, the unsaid in the best written verse, the mysteriousness, the depth, the secrecy of things, the unavowed aspirations, the indescribable, the inexpressible, the desideratum of thought incapable of greater effort—all the softness, the grace, the suavity that overflow the too dry contours of words. To the fluttering wings that rose in air with such desperate rush, she opened the paradise of realised dreams, of fulfilled hopes. She stood on the luminous threshold, in a scintillation before which the suns turn pale, divinely beautiful and yet humanly tender, opening her arms to the soul thirsting for the ideal, which is the end and the recompense, the starry crown and the cup of love—a Beatrix revealed beyond the tomb. In a phrase filled with purest passion she told, with divine reticence and celestial modesty, that she herself, in the leisure of eternity and the splendour of the infinite, would satisfy all his unfulfilled desires. She promised to his genius happiness and love such as the imagination of man, even when in communion with a spirit, cannot conceive.

While playing the finale, she had risen, her hands no longer even pretending to touch the keys; yet the melodies escaped from the piano in visible coloured vibrations, spreading through the atmosphere of the room in luminous undulations like those that vary the flamboyant radiance of the aurora borealis. Lavinia had disappeared and Spirite reappeared, but taller, more majestic, enshrined in a brilliant light. Long wings fluttered on her shoulders; she had already, though plainly she desired to remain, left the floor of the room; the folds of her dress floated in space; an all-compelling breath bore her away, and Malivert found himself alone in a state of agitation easy to understand. But little by little he grew calm, and delightful languor followed upon the feverish excitement. He felt the satisfaction so rarely experienced by poets and, it is said, by philosophers, at having been understood in the most delicate and the deepest parts of his imagination. How brilliantly and radiantly Spirite had commented on that poem, the meaning and force of which he had never yet so well understood! How thoroughly her soul identified itself with his own, and her thought penetrated his!

The next day he made up his mind to work. His inspiration, which had abandoned him for a long time, was returning, ideas crowded in his brain, unlimited horizons, endless perspectives opened before his eyes, a world of new sensations surged within his breast, and to express them he asked of speech more than it is able to do. The old forms, the worn-out moulds burst asunder, and sometimes the molten phrase broke forth and overflowed in splendid splashes like rays of broken stars. Never had he risen to such heights, and the greatest poets would willingly have signed what he wrote on that day.

As, having finished a stanza, he was thinking of the next, he allowed his glance to roam around the room and saw Spirite half lying on the divan, her chin resting on her hand, her elbow sunk in the pillow, her slender fingers playing in the golden waves of her hair. She was watching him with a loving, contemplative look. She seemed to have been there a long time, but had not cared to reveal her presence lest she should break in upon his work. As Malivert rose from his armchair to draw nearer to her, she signed to him not to move, and in a voice softer than any music she repeated, stanza by stanza, line by line, the poem he had been writing. By a mysterious sympathy she felt her lover's thought, followed it in its flight, and even outstripped it, for not only did she see, but she foresaw, and she said in full the unfinished stanza the end of which he was still seeking.

The poem, as will be readily understood, was addressed to Spirite. On what other subject could Malivert have written? Carried away by his love for her, he scarcely remembered earth and plunged into the heavens as high and as far as wings attached to human shoulders could bear him.

"That is beautiful," said Spirite, whose voice Malivert heard within his breast, for it did not reach his ear like ordinary sounds "It is beautiful, even for a spirit. Genius is truly divine; it invents the ideal. It sees higher beauty and eternal light. Whither can it not ascend when it has the wings of faith and love? But descend again, come back to the regions the air of which may be breathed by mortal lungs. Your nerves are trembling still like the cords of a lyre, your brow smokes like a censer, a feverish light burns in your eyes. Beware of madness, for ecstasy is akin to it. Calm yourself, and if you love me, live still your human life, for it is my wish."

In order to obey her, Malivert went out, and although people seemed to him only like distant shadows, like phantoms with whom he had nothing in common, he tried to mingle with them, endeavoured to interest himself in the news and rumours of the day, and smiled at the description of the wonderful costume worn by Mlle. —— at the last ball. He even agreed to play whist with the old Duchess de C——. Everything was equally indifferent to him.

But in spite of his efforts to cling to life, an amorous attraction drew him beyond the terrestrial sphere. He desired to walk and felt himself rise; he was a prey to irresistible desire. The apparitions of Spirite no longer sufficed him; his soul hastened after her when she disappeared, as if seeking to leave his body. Love, excited by impossibility and burning yet with something of an earthly flame, devoured him and clung to his flesh as the poisoned tunic of Nessus clung to the flesh of Hercules. In his rapid contact with Spirite, he had been unable to throw off the old Adam entirely. He could not hold in his arms the aerial phantom of Spirite, but that phantom represented the image of Lavinia with an illusion of beauty that sufficed to blind his passion and to make him forget that the adorable form, the loving eyes, the sweetly smiling mouth, were, after all, but a shadow and a reflection.

At all hours of the day and night Guy beheld before him the *alma adorata,* sometimes as a pure ideal in the splendour of Spirite, sometimes in the more humanly feminine appearance of Lavinia. Now she soared above his head with the dazzling flight of an angel, again she seemed seated in the great armchair, lying on the divan, or leaning on the table. She appeared to look at the papers scattered on his desk, to breathe the scent of the flowers in the jardinière, to open the books, to move the rings in the onyx cup placed on the mantelpiece, and to give herself up to the puerilities of passion allowable to a young girl who has entered by chance the room of her betrothed. Spirite enjoyed showing herself to Guy such as Lavinia would have been had fate favoured her love. She was living again, after death, and chapter by chapter, her chaste boarding-school girl romance. With a little coloured vapour she reproduced her dresses of old, placed in her hair the same flower, or the same ribbon; her shadow assumed once more the same grace, the same attitude, and the poses of her maidenly body. She had wished, moved by a coquetry that proved the woman had not wholly disappeared in the angel, that Malivert should love her not only with the posthumous love addressed to Spirite, but as she had been during her life on earth, when at the Opéra, in ballrooms, in society, she sought the ever missed opportunity of meeting him.

Had not his lips touched but a void when, carried away by desire, mad with love, drunk with passion, he indulged in some useless caress, he might have believed that he, Guy de Malivert, had really married Lavinia d'Aufideni, so clear, coloured, and living did the vision become at times. In a perfectly consonant sympathy he heard internally, but as in a real conversation, the voice of Lavinia with its youthful, fresh, silvery timbre, answering his burning confessions by chaste and modest caresses.

It was indeed the torture of Tantalus; the cup full of ice-water was held to his burning lips by a loving hand, but he could not even touch the edge; the perfumed grapes, the colour of amber and rubies, hung over his head, but vanished as they evaded an impossible touch. The short intervals during which Spirite left him, recalled no doubt by some invincible order pronounced in that place where one can what one wills, had become unbearable to him, and when she disappeared he felt like dashing out his brains against the wall that closed upon her.

One evening he said to himself: "Since Spirite cannot put on an earthly frame and mingle in my life otherwise than as a vision, what if I were to cast off this troublesome mortal coil, this gross, heavy shape, which prevents my rising with the adored soul into the spheres where spirits dwell?"

The idea struck him as sound. He rose and selected from a trophy of barbaric weapons hanging from the wall—tomahawks, assegais, boarding cutlasses—an arrow feathered with parrot feathers and tipped with a sharp head of fishbone. The arrow had been dipped in curare, that terrible poison whose secret South American Indians alone possess, and which kills the victim without any antidote being able to save him.

He was holding the arrow close to his hand and was about to prick himself with it, when suddenly Spirite appeared to him, terrified, horror-struck, and supplicating, casting around his neck her shadowy arms with a movement of mad passion, pressing him to her phantom heart, covering him with impalpable kisses. The woman had forgotten that she was only a spirit.

"Unfortunate Guy!" she cried. "Do not do that! Do not kill yourself to join me! Your death thus brought about would separate us hopelessly, and would open between us abysses that millions of years would not enable us to cross. Recover yourself! Bear with life, the longest term of which does not last more than a grain of sand. In order to endure the time, think of the eternity during which we can ever love each other, and forgive my coquetry. The woman wished to be loved as the spirit was; Lavinia was jealous of Spirite, and I nearly lost you forever."

Resuming her angelic form, she stretched out her hands above Malivert's head, who felt celestial calm and coolness descending upon him.

XIV

Mme. d'Ymbercourt was surprised at the little effect that her flirtation with M. d'Aversac had had upon Guy de Malivert. Her lack of success entirely upset all her ideas of feminine strategy. She believed that nothing could revive love so well as a touch of jealousy, but she forgot that love first had to exist. She had taken it for granted that a young fellow who had called pretty regularly on her Wednesdays for the past three years, who sometimes brought her a bouquet on opera nights and remained awake at the back of her box, must necessarily be somewhat in love with her. Was she not beautiful, elegant, and rich? Did she not play the piano like a prize-winner at the Conservatory? Did she not pour out tea as correctly as Lady Penelope herself? Did she not write her morning notes in an English hand, long, sloping, angular, and thoroughly aristocratic? What objection could be made to her carriages purchased from Binder, her horses bought from and warranted by Crémieux? Were her footmen not handsome fellows, and did they not bear the appearance of aristocratic lackeys? Did not her dinners deserve to be approved by experts? It seemed to her that all these things formed a very comfortable ideal.

Nevertheless, the lady in the sleigh whom she had caught sight of at the Bois de Boulogne bothered her considerably, and several times she had driven around the lake with the idea of meeting her and seeing whether she was followed by Malivert. The lady, however, did not reappear, and Mme. d'Ymbercourt's jealousy had nothing to work on. Besides, no one knew her or had seen her. Was Guy in love with her, or had he simply yielded to curiosity when he drove Grimalkin in pursuit of the stepper? Mme. d'Ymbercourt could not make it out; so she concluded that she had frightened away Guy by her suggestion that he was compromising her. She now regretted having uttered the remark, which she had made only to induce him to declare himself formally, for Guy, much too faithful to his orders, and, besides, taken up with Spirite, had refrained from calling on her. His complete obedience piqued the countess, who would have preferred to have him less submissive. Although her suspicions had no other foundation than the brief vision in the Bois de Boulogne, she felt that there was some love concealed behind this excessive care for her reputation. Yet apparently nothing was changed in Guy's life, and Jack, secretly questioned by Mme. d'Ymbercourt's maid, had assured her that he had not for a long time heard the faintest rustle of silk on the private stairs of his master, who, besides, went out very little, saw scarcely any one but Baron de Feroë, lived like a hermit, and spent the greater part of his nights in writing.

D'Aversac increased his attentions, and Mme. d'Ymbercourt accepted them with the tacit gratitude of a woman who feels somewhat abandoned and needs to be reassured as to the effect of her charms by new worship. She was not in love with d'Aversac, but she was grateful to him for prizing what Guy seemed to disdain; so on the Tuesday at the performance of *La Traviata* it was noticed that Malivert's seat was occupied by d'Aversac in white gloves and white necktie, a camellia in his buttonhole, curled and pomaded like a lady-killer who still has hair of his own, and radiant with self-satisfaction. He had long nourished the hope of making an impression upon Mme. d'Ymbercourt, but the marked preference she accorded to Guy de Malivert had thrown him into the background among the indifferent adorers who crowd more or less round a pretty woman waiting for an opportunity, a break, or a fit of annoyance that never occurs. He was full of smiling attentions. He held out to her her glasses or her program, smiled at her least remarks, bowed mysteriously in answer, and when Mme. d'Ymbercourt brought together the tips of her white gloves to approve some note sung by the diva, he applauded heartily, raising his hands as high as his head. In a word, he publicly took possession of his office of attendant lover.

In some of the boxes people were already beginning to say, "Is the marriage of Malivert and Mme. d'Ymbercourt off?" There was a slight manifestation of curiosity when Guy showed at the entrance of the orchestra stalls after the first act, and when he was seen, as he inspected the hall, to glance at the Countess's box. D'Aversac, who had also caught sight of him, felt a little uneasy, but the most perspicacious examination failed to notice the least sign of contrariety on Malivert's face. He neither blushed nor turned pale; his brows did not bend, not a muscle of his face moved; he did not have the terribly grim aspect of a jealous lover at the sight of his fair courted by another; he looked perfectly calm and utterly serene. The expression of his face was that which comes from the radiancy of a secret joy, and on his lips fluttered, as the poet says—

"The mysterious smile of inward delight."

"If Guy were loved by a fairy or a princess, he could not look more triumphant," said an old habitué of the balcony, a Don Juan emeritus. "If Mme. d'Ymbercourt cares for him, she may as well give him up, for she will never call herself Mme. de Malivert."

Between the acts Guy paid a short visit to the Countess's box to bid her farewell, for he was about to start on a trip to Greece. He was naturally polite to d'Aversac, without any trace of exaggeration, nor did he have the coldly ceremonious look that people assume when they are vexed. He shook hands very quietly with Mme. d'Ymbercourt, whose face betrayed her emotion, great as was the effort which she made to appear indifferent. The blush that suffused her cheeks when Guy left his box to come to her stall had been replaced by a pallor of which rice powder was wholly innocent. She had looked for annoyance, anger, a movement of passion, a mark of jealousy, perhaps even a quarrel. His genuine coolness upset her and caught her unprepared. She had believed that Malivert loved her, and now she saw that she had been mistaken. This discovery wounded at once her pride and her heart. Guy had inspired her with a livelier affection than she knew, and she felt unhappy. The comedy she had been playing, now that it was proved useless, wearied and bored her. When Malivert had gone, she leaned upon the edge of the box and replied only in monosyllables to the compliments addressed to her by d'Aversac, who was very much put out by her silence and her coolness. He did not understand how it was that winter had succeeded spring; the sudden frost withered the roses. "Have I said or done anything foolish?" asked of himself the poor fellow who a moment ago was so well received. "Can it be that she is making fun of me? Guy's ease of manner just now was affected, and the countess seemed very much moved. I wonder if she still loves Malivert."

However, as d'Aversac knew that he was being watched by a certain number of glasses, he went on playing his part and bent toward the countess, whispering in her ear with an intimate and mysterious air commonplaces that anybody might have listened to.

The old habitué, who was very much amused by this little drama, followed the incidents of it out of the corner of his eye. "D'Aversac is putting a good face on his ill luck, but he is not the man for such a game. However, he is a fool, and fools are sometimes lucky with women. Cupid gets along very well with folly, and Laridon succeeds Caesar, especially when Caesar does not care for his empire. But who can be Guy's new mistress?" Such were the reflections of the veteran Cytherean, as well up in theory as he had been in practice, while he followed Malivert's glances to see whether they rested upon any of the beautiful women who shone in the boxes like jewels in a case. Could it be that vaporous blonde with the wreath of silver leaves, the water-green dress, and opal ornaments, who seemed to have touched up her complexion with a moonbeam like a wraith or a nixie, and who gazed sentimentally at the chandelier as if it were the orb of night? Or was it the brunette with hair darker than night, with a profile carved out of marble, eyes like black diamonds, red lips, so living under her warm pallor, so passionate under her statuesque calm, and who might be taken for the daughter of the Venus of Milo, if that divine masterpiece deigned to have children? No, it was neither of them, neither the moon nor the sun. The Russian princess in the stage-box yonder, with her extraordinary dress, her exotic beauty, and her extravagant grace, might have some chance, for Guy was rather fond of eccentricity, and his travels had inspired him with rather barbaric tastes. Yet it was not her either; Guy had just looked at her as coldly as if he were examining a malachite coffer. Why might it not be the Parisian in the open box, dressed in perfect taste, clever, witty, pretty, whose every motion seemed to follow the sound of a flute and to raise a foam of lace, as if she were dancing on a panel in Herculaneum? Balzac would have devoted thirty pages to the description of such a woman, and it would have been style used to good purpose. She was

worth it. But Guy was not civilised enough to taste the charm which se-
duced, even more than did beauty, the author of the *Comédie Hu-
maine*. "Well, I shall have to give up fathoming this mystery today,"
said the old beau, as he put back into his case a pair of glasses that
looked like siege guns. "The lady that occupies Malivert's thoughts is
undoubtedly not here."

As people left the house d'Aversac was standing under the balustrade in as elegant an attitude as can be assumed by a gentleman
wrapped up in a greatcoat. He was by the side of Mme. d'Ymbercourt,
who had thrown over her dress a pelisse of satin edged with swan's-down,
the hood of which fell back on her shoulders and left her head bare. The
countess was pale, and that evening she was really beautiful. The pain she
felt imparted to her face, usually coldly regular, an expression and a feeling of life it had lacked hitherto. For the rest, she seemed to have wholly
forgotten her escort, who remained within a couple of paces of her with
a set gravity that sought to dissimulate and to express much.

"What is the matter with Mme. d'Ymbercourt tonight?" said a young
man who stood in the vestibule to watch the procession of beauties. "She
seems to have acquired a new beauty. D'Aversac is a lucky fellow."

"Not so very lucky, after all," said a young man with a clever, intelligent face, who looked like a portrait of Van Dyck taken from its frame.
"It is not he who has given to the countess's face, usually as inexpressive
as a wax mask moulded on a Venus by Canova, the animation and the
accent you notice. The spark comes from elsewhere. D'Aversac is not
the Prometheus of this Pandora; wood cannot give life to marble."

"Never mind," replied another; "I wonder at Malivert giving up the
countess just at this time. She deserves rather better than d'Aversac to
avenge her. I do not know if Guy can find a handsomer woman, and he
may have cause to repent his disdain."

"It would be a mistake in him to do so," replied the Van Dyck portrait. "Pray follow me. Mme. d'Ymbercourt is handsomer today than
usual because she is moved. Now, if Malivert had not given her up, she
would not feel any emotion, and her classical features would remain insignificant. The phenomenon that surprises you would, therefore, not
have taken place; so Malivert is right to go off to Greece, as he said last
night at the club he would do. I have spoken."

The footman announcing the countess's carriage put an end to this conversation, and more than one young fellow committed the sin of envy on seeing d'Aversac get into the coupé with Mme. d'Ymbercourt. The door was closed by the lackey, who climbed to the box in a twinkling, and the carriage went off at full speed. D'Aversac, half hidden in the folds of satin, close to his partner, breathing in the vague scent she gave out, tried to profit by the short tête-à-tête and to say a few tenderly gallant words to the countess. He had to find at once something decisive and passionate, for there was no great distance from the Place Ventadour to the Rue de la Chaussée d'Antin; but Guy's rival was not good at improvisation, and besides, it must be confessed that he received scant encouragement from Mme. d'Ymbercourt, who, silent and nestling in the corner of the coupé, was biting the corner of her lace handkerchief. While d'Aversac was laboriously trying to work out a loving phrase, Mme. d'Ymbercourt, who had not listened to a single word of it, busy as she was following out her own thoughts, caught him suddenly by the arm and said to him sharply, "Do you know who is the new mistress of M. de Malivert?"

This unexpected and astonishing question greatly shocked d'Aversac. It was not wholly proper, and it proved that the countess had not thought of him for a moment. The castle in Spain of his hopes fell in ruins before this breath of passion.

"I do not know," stammered d'Aversac; "but if I did, discretion—and politeness—would prevent— Any well-bred man on such occasions knows what is his duty—"

"Yes, yes," answered the countess, in short, sharp accents. "Men stand by one another even when they are rivals. I shall not learn anything." Then, after a short silence, partly mastering herself, she said, "I beg your pardon, my dear M. d'Aversac. I am terribly nervous tonight, and I feel that I am saying absurd things. Do not be angry with me, and come to see me tomorrow—I shall be quieter. Here I am at home," she said, holding out her hand to him. "Where is my coachman to take you?" And with a rapid step she got out of the coupé and ascended the stairs without allowing d'Aversac to assist her.

So it may be seen that it is not always as pleasant as naive young fellows imagine to take home a beautiful lady, and even to ride in her carriage from the Opéra to the Chaussée d'Antin. D'Aversac, rather sat upon, had himself driven to the club in the Rue de Choiseul where his own carriage was awaiting him. He played and lost some hundred louis, which did not help to improve his temper. As he returned home, he said to himself, "How the devil does Malivert manage to make all the women fall in love with him?"

Mme. d'Ymbercourt, after giving herself up to the care of her maid, who undressed her and made her ready for the night, put on a wrapper of white cashmere and leaned on a desk, her hand plunged in her hair. She remained thus for some time, her eyes fixed on the paper, turning her pen in her fingers. She wished to write to Guy, but it was a difficult matter. Her thoughts, which crowded in her brain, disappeared when she tried to express them in a phrase. She scribbled five or six notes, crossed, interlined, illegible, in spite of her beautiful English hand, without managing to satisfy herself. She said either too much or too little, and did not succeed in expressing the feelings in her heart. She tore up and threw into the fire every note, and finally managed to produce this:—

"Do not be angry, dear Guy, at my coquettish impulse, a very innocent one, I assure you, for my sole object was to make you a little bit jealous and to bring you back to me. You know very well that I love you, although you do not love me very much. Your cold, quiet look froze my very heart. Forget what I have said to you. It was a wicked friend who made me speak. Are you really going off to Greece? Do you really need to flee from me, who have no other thought than to please you? Do not go; your absence would make me too wretched."

The countess signed the note "Cecilia d'Ymbercourt," sealed it with her arms, and wished to send it at once, but as she rose to summon her attendant, the clock struck two. It was too late to send a man to the very end of the Faubourg Saint-Germain, where Guy lived. "Never mind," she said, "I will send my note very early and Guy shall have it when he wakes, if only he is not then gone."

She went to bed tired and worn out, closing her eyes in vain. She thought of the lady in the sleigh and said that Malivert loved her, and jealousy drove its sharp fangs into her heart. At last she fell asleep, but her sleep was agitated; she constantly started awake, worse than the night before. A little lamp hung from the ceiling by her, the night-light fixed in a globe of blue ground-glass cast in the room an azure light like that of the moon, and lighted with soft, mysterious beam the head of the countess, whose loosened hair spread out in great black ringlets on the white pillow, concealing one of her arms hanging out of the bed.

At the bed-head, little by little a faint, transparent, bluish vapour like the smoke from a perfume-burner gradually condensed, assumed more decided contours, and soon showed as a young girl of celestial beauty, whose golden hair formed a luminous aureole around her. Spirite, for it was she, watched the sleeping woman with the air of melancholy pity that angels must wear on beholding human suffering. Bending toward her like the shadow of a dream, she let fall upon her brow two or three drops of a sombre liquor contained in a little flagon like the lacrymatory urns found in the tombs of antiquity, whispering meanwhile: "Since you are no longer a danger to him whom I love and can no longer separate his soul from mine, I take pity on you, for you are suffering on his account, and I bring you the divine nepenthe. Forget and be happy, O you who caused my death!"

The vision disappeared. The features of the lovely sleeper softened as if a pleasant dream had succeeded to a painful nightmare. A faint smile fluttered over her lips, by an unconscious movement she drew back under the clothes her beautiful arm, which was as cold and white as marble, and covered herself up under the light eiderdown quilt. Her tranquil and restorative sleep lasted until morning, and when she awoke, the first thing she noticed was her letter upon the table.

"Shall I have this letter taken?" said Aglae, who had just entered the room to open the curtains and saw her mistress's glance rest upon the note.

"Oh, no!" cried Mme. d'Ymbercourt, quickly. "Throw it into the fire." Then she added to herself, "What was I thinking of to write such a letter? I must have been crazy."

XV

The steamer from Marseilles to Athens was off Cape Malia, the last dentellation of the mulberry leaf that forms the point of Greece and has given it its modern name. Fog and cloud had been left behind. It was a passing from night to light, from cold to warmth. The gray tints of the western skies had been succeeded by the azure of the Oriental heavens, and the sea, of a deep blue, rose and fell softly under a favouring wind, which the steamer turned to advantage by setting its smoke-blackened jibs, like the sombre-coloured sails that Theseus hoisted by mistake when he returned from the isle of Crete, where he had slain the Minotaur. It was near the end of February, and already the approach of spring, so late with us, was felt in that happy clime beloved of the sun. The air was so balmy that most of the passengers, who had already got over seasickness, remained on deck watching the coast, a glimpse of which they caught through the blue haze of evening. Above the darker zone rose a mountain still visible, on whose snowy summit yet gleamed a ray of light. It was Taygetus; which enabled the travelling bachelors of arts who knew a few lines of Latin to quote with satisfied pedantry the well-known verses of Virgil. A Frenchman who quotes correctly—which is rare—a Latin line is very nearly as perfectly happy as it is possible for him to be. As regards Greek lines, that is a happiness reserved for Germans and Englishmen fresh from Jena or Oxford.

On the slatted benches and camp-stools that encumbered the stern of the ship were young ladies wearing overcoats with huge buttons, small hats with blue veils, their abundant brown hair enclosed in nets, their travelling-bags hung about their neck by a strap. They were looking at the coast shrouded in the evening shadows, with glasses strong enough to make out the satellites of Jupiter. Some, bolder and better sailors, were walking the deck with the stride that drill-sergeants and teachers of walking teach to British girls. Others were talking with gentlemen irreproachably dressed and of perfect manners. There were also Frenchmen, pupils of the School of Athens, painters, architects, who had won the prize of Rome and who were going for inspiration to the sources of true beauty. These, with all the enthusiasm of youth, when it has hope before it and a small sum in its pocket, were joking, laughing noisily, smoking cigars and indulging in heated discussions on aesthetics. The reputations of the great masters of ancient and modern times were discussed, ridiculed or lauded; everything was admirable or absurd, sublime or stupid, for young men always go to extremes and know no middle way. They would never marry King *Modus* to Queen *Ratio;* that union takes place much later in life.

In this animated group was a young man draped in his mantle like a philosopher of the Portico, and who was neither a painter, a sculptor, nor an architect, but whom the travelling artists called in as arbitrator when a discussion ended in obstinate negation on either side. It was Guy de Malivert. His judicious and clever remarks proved that he was a true connoisseur, an art critic worthy of the name; and these very disdainful young fellows, who sneered at any one who had not handled the brush, the chisel, or the drawing-pen, as a *bourgeois,* listened to him with deference and sometimes even adopted his views. The conversation ended, for everything ends, even a discussion on the ideal and the real, and the disputants, their throats rather dry, descended to the saloon to wet their whistles with a glass of grog or other warm and restorative drinks.

Malivert remained alone on the bridge. Night had fallen, and it was now quite dark. In the deep azure sky, the stars shone with a vivacity and a brilliancy no one can imagine unless he has seen the sky of Greece. Their reflections were lengthened in the water, making long wakes, just as if they were lights placed upon the bank. The foam, beaten up by the paddle-wheels, flashed like innumerable diamonds, which gleamed for an instant and then vanished in a bluish phosphorescence. The black steamer seemed to proceed through a sea of light. It was a sight that would have excited the admiration of the most obtuse Philistine, and as Malivert was not a Philistine, he enjoyed it to the full. It did not even occur to him to go down to the saloon, which is always sickeningly hot and peculiarly objectionable when one leaves the fresh air; and he continued walking up and down the deck, moving around the Levantines installed on carpets or thin mattresses along the rail in the bows and among the coils of chains and ropes; sometimes he caused a woman, believing herself unnoticed, to lower the veil she had drawn aside to enjoy the cool air of night.

Guy was keeping the promise he had made not to compromise Mme. d'Ymbercourt.

He leaned on the bulwarks and let himself float away into a reverie full of sweetness. No doubt, since Spirite's love had freed him from earthly curiosity, the trip to Greece had ceased to inspire him with as much enthusiasm as formerly; he would have liked to have started on another voyage; but he no longer thought of hastening his departure from the world into which his thought already reached. He was now aware of the consequences of suicide, and waited, not too impatiently, until the hour should come when he might fly away with the angel who visited him. Secure in his future happiness, he allowed himself to indulge in the sensation of the present and enjoyed, like the poet he was, the superb spectacle of night. Like Lord Byron he loved the sea. Its eternal restlessness and its incessant plaint, even in hours of deepest calm, its sudden anger and its mad fury against the immovable obstacle had always struck his imagination, which saw in this vast turbulence a secret analogy with useless human effort. What he particularly loved in the sea was its immense isolation, the unchanging, yet ever-changing circle of the horizon, the solemn monotony and the absence of any sign of civilisation. The same billow that uplifted the steamer on its broad back had laved the hollow-sided vessels of which Homer speaks, yet no trace of the contact was left; the water had exactly the same tone that coloured it when it was traversed by the fleet of the Greeks. The proud sea does not preserve, like the earth, the marks of man's passage. It is vague, immense, and deep, like the infinite. Never, therefore, did Malivert feel happier, freer, and more self-possessed than when, standing in the bows of a ship, pitching and scending, he sailed into the unknown. Soaked by the foam that flew over the decks, his hair salt with the breath of the sea, it seemed to him as though he were walking upon the waters; and just as a horseman becomes identified with the speed of his steed, so he attributed to himself the swiftness of the vessel, and his thought hurried on to meet the unknown.

Spirite had silently descended like thistledown or snowflake close to Malivert, and her hand rested on the young man's shoulder. Although she was invisible to every one, it is possible to imagine the charming group formed by Malivert and his aerial friend. The moon had risen broad and bright, making the stars pale, and the night had turned into a sort of blue day absolutely magical in tone, like the light in an azure grotto. One of her beams fell in the bows of the ship upon that Love and that Psyche, effulgent in the diamond scintillation of the foam, like two young gods on the prow of an antique trireme. Over the waters, with a perpetual luminous sparkling, spread a broad wake of silvery spangles, the reflection of the orb risen above the horizon and slowly ascending into the heavens. Sometimes the swart back of a dolphin, a descendant, perhaps, of the one that bore Arion, flashed through the shining wake and suddenly disappeared in the shadow, or else, in the distance, like a quivering red dot, appeared the light of a vessel. From time to time the shore of an island, showing off a deeper violet and soon passed, loomed for a moment.

"Undoubtedly," said Spirite, "this is a marvellous spectacle, one of the finest, if not the very finest, that the human eye can gaze upon; but it is nothing by the side of the wonderful prospects of the world that I leave to visit you, and where soon we shall fly side by side, 'like doves called by the same desire.' This sea, which seems so vast to you, is but a drop in the cup of the infinite, and the pale orb that lights it, an imperceptible silver globule, is lost in the terrific immensity, like the meanest grain of sidereal dust. Oh! how I would have admired this sight with you, when I still inhabited the earth and was called Lavinia. But do not think that I am insensible to it, for I understand its beauty through your own feeling."

"You make me impatient to be in your world, Spirite," answered Malivert. "Eagerly I spring toward those spheres, of a dazzling splendour beyond imagination or speech, which we are to traverse together and where never again we shall be separated."

"Yes, you shall see them, you shall know their magnificence, their delight, if you love me, if you are faithful to me, if your thought never turns to anything lower, if you allow the impure and coarse human mud to fall within you as within still water. On that condition we shall be allowed to enjoy eternal union, the peaceful intoxication of divine love, of unintermittent love without weakness, without weariness, the ardour of which would melt suns like grains of myrrh cast on a fire; we shall be unity in duality, the ego in the non-ego, motion in rest, desire in fulfilment, freshness in flame. To deserve these supreme felicities, think of Spirite who is in heaven, and do not think too much of Lavinia who sleeps yonder under her carved wreath of white roses."

"Do I not love you madly?" said Malivert—"with all the purity and ardour of which a soul still held to this earth is capable?"

"My darling," replied Spirite, "I am satisfied with you."

And as she spoke the words, her sapphire eyes were starred full of amorous promises, and a voluptuously chaste smile parted her adorable lips.

The conversation between the living man and the shadow was prolonged until the first gleam of dawn mingled its rosy tints with the violet beams of the moon, the orb of which was slowly paling. Soon a segment of the sun appeared above the horizon, and day came with a splendid rush. Spirite, an angel of light, had nothing to dread from the sun and remained for a few moments in the bows of the vessel, radiant in the rosy light and fires of morning that played like golden butterflies in her hair, lifted by the breeze of the Archipelago. If she chose night by preference to appear to Malivert, it was because, the movements of common human life being then suspended, Guy was freer, less noticed, and did not run the risk of being thought crazy on account of actions unavoidably eccentric in appearance.

As she saw Malivert pale and shiver in the chill of dawn, she said to him in a sweetly scolding way: "Go, you dear creature of clay—do not struggle against nature. It is cold, the sea dew is falling on the deck and clinging to the rigging. Return to your cabin and sleep." And then she added, with a purely feminine grace: "Even sleep cannot separate us. I shall be with you in all your dreams, and take you whither you cannot go during your waking hours."

And as she had promised, Guy's sleep was filled with azure, radiant, supernatural dreams, in which he flew side by side with Spirite through an Elysian paradise, a mingling of light, of ideal vegetation and architecture, of which no words in our poor, scanty, heavy, imperfect speech can suggest even the remotest idea.

There is no need to describe in detail Malivert's impressions of travel; they have nothing to do with this story, and besides, Guy, filled with his love and drawn by an inexorable desire, paid less attention than formerly to material things. Nature now appeared to him only in a vague, misty, splendid distance that served as a background to his fixed thought. The world was for him only the landscape of Spirite, and he thought even the finest prospects unworthy of this function. Nevertheless, the next day at dawn he could not repress a cry of admiration and surprise when, as the steamer entered the roads of the Piraeus, he beheld the marvellous view lighted up by the rays of morn; Parnassus and Hymettus formed with their amethyst-coloured slopes the wings of the splendid setting of which Lycabetus, with its curious outline, and Pentelicus formed the background. In the centre, like a golden tripod upon a marble altar, rose on the Acropolis the Parthenon, illumined by the golden light of morn. The bluish tint of the distance, showing through the interstices of the fallen columns, made the noble form of the temple still more aerial and ideal. Malivert felt that shiver which comes from the feeling of beauty, and he understood then what, until that moment, had seemed obscure to him: the whole of Greek art was suddenly revealed to him, a romanticist, in that rapid vision—that is, the perfect proportion of the ensemble, the absolute purity of the lines, the incomparable suavity of the colour formed of whiteness, azure, and light.

No sooner had he landed than, without troubling about his luggage, which he left in Jack's hands, he jumped into one of the coupés that, to the shame of modern civilisation, bear, in the place of the cars of antiquity, the travellers from the Piraeus to Athens, along a road white with dust and bordered here and there by a few dust-covered olive-trees. Malivert's vehicle, broken-down and rattling, was carried along at a gallop by two small, thin, dapple-grey horses with hog manes, which looked like the skeletons, or rather, like clay models of the marble horses that prance on the metopes of the Parthenon. No doubt their ancestors had posed for Phidias. They were roundly lashed by a youth wearing a Palikar costume, who, driving a more brilliant team, might perhaps have carried off the prize for cars at the Olympic games.

Leaving the other travellers to invade the Hôtel d'Angleterre, Guy had himself driven to the foot of the sacred hill on which humankind, in the flower of youth, poetry, and love, heaped up its purest masterpieces, as if to present them to the admiration of the gods. He ascended the old Street of Tripods, buried under shapeless huts, and trod with respectful feet the marble dust, coming at last to that staircase of the Propylaea, some of the steps of which have been set up as tombstones. He climbed through that strange cemetery made of a maze of uplifted stones, between the substructures, on one of which stands the small temple of the Wingless Victory, while the other serves as a pedestal to the equestrian

statue of Cimon, and as a platform for the Pinacothek, where were preserved the masterpieces of Zeuxis, Apelles, Timanthes, and Protogenes.

He crossed the Propylaea of Mnesicles, a masterpiece worthy to
serve as an entrance to the masterpiece of Ictinus and Phidias. He was
filled with the sentiment of religious admiration. He was almost
ashamed that he, a Western barbarian, should tread with his boots that
sacred soil. Soon he found himself before the Parthenon, the Temple
of the Virgin, the sanctuary of Pallas Athene, the noblest conception of
polytheism. The edifice rose in the serene blue air superbly placid and
suavely majestic. Divine harmony ruled its lines, which sung the hymn
of beauty on a secret rhythm. All sweetly tended to an unknown ideal,
converged to a mysterious point, without effort, without violence, sure
of attaining it. Above the temple one felt soaring the thought to which
the angles of the pediments, the entablatures, the columns aspired and
seemed to wish to rise, imparting imperceptible curves to the horizontal
and the perpendicular lines. The exquisite Doric columns, draped in
the folds of their flutings and leaning somewhat back, made one think of
chaste virgins languorously feeling vague desires. An atmosphere of
warm, golden colour bathed the facade, and the marble, kissed by time,
had assumed a creamy tint and something of a modest blush.

On the steps of the temple, between the two pillars behind which
opens the door of the pronaos, Spirite stood in the pure Greek brightness so unfavourable to apparitions, on the very threshold of the clear,
perfect, luminously beautiful Parthenon. A long white dress pleated in
little folds like the tunics of the *canephorae,* fell from her shoulders to
the tips of her little white, bare feet. A crown of violets—those violets
whose scent Aristophanes celebrates in one of his parabases—was placed
upon the wavy bandeaux of her golden hair. Thus dressed, Spirite resembled one of the virgins of the Panathenaeon, come down from her
frieze. But in her blue eyes shone a light never seen in eyes of white
marble; to her radiant, plastic beauty she added the beauty of the soul.

Malivert ascended the steps and approached Spirite, who held out
her hand to him. Then in a dazzling vision he beheld the Parthenon as
it was in the days of its splendour. The fallen pillars were in their places,
the marbles of the pediment, carried away by Lord Elgin or broken by
the Venetian shells, were grouped again, pure and intact, in their human

and divine attitudes. At the door of the cella Malivert saw, seated upon its pedestal, the statue of gold and ivory, the celestial, the virgin, the immaculate Pallas Athene. But he cast only a rapid glance upon these wonders, and his eyes immediately turned to seek Spirite's eyes. Seeing itself disdained, the retrospective vision vanished.

"Oh!" murmured Spirite, "art is forgotten for love! His soul is becoming more and more detached from this earth. He is burning, he is being consumed! Soon, dear soul, your wish shall be fulfilled."

And the heart of the maid, still beating within the breast of the spirit, caused her white peplos to rise and fall.

XVI

A few days after his visit to the Parthenon, Guy de Malivert resolved to visit the beautiful mountains he saw from his windows. He engaged a guide and a couple of horses, leaving Jack at the hotel, as useless and likely even to be in the way. Jack was one of those servants who are more difficult to satisfy than their masters, and whose disagreeable traits come out on a voyage. He had as many fads as an old maid and considered everything abominable—the rooms, the beds, the dishes, the wines; and exasperated by the wretched waiting, he would cry, "Ah, the barbarians!" Besides, if he did admit that Malivert had some literary talent, he considered him in his own mind incapable of taking care of himself, and rather crazy, especially for some time past; he had therefore undertaken to watch over him. True, if Malivert frowned, he immediately resumed his old place, and Mentor, with a marvellous facility of metamorphosis, resumed the part of valet.

Guy put a sum of money in gold coins in a leather belt he wore under his clothes and a couple of pistols in his holsters; and when he left did not name any definite day for his return, wishing to allow himself the freedom of the unforeseen, of adventure, of wandering as he pleased. He knew that Jack, accustomed to his disappearances, would not be alarmed, even if he were several days or even several weeks late; he would be quite happy as soon as he had taught the hotel cook to prepare a beefsteak to his taste—that is, brown outside and underdone inside, in the English fashion.

Guy's excursion, unless he changed his purpose, was not to take him beyond Parnassus, and not to last more than five or six days, but a month had gone by and neither Malivert nor his guide had reappeared; no letter had reached the hotel announcing a change of plans or a prolongation of the trip; the money he had taken with him must have been nearly expended, and his silence began to cause uneasiness.

"My master has not sent for funds," said Jack to himself one morning, as he ate a beefsteak cooked at last as he wanted it, and which he washed down with white wine of Santorin, very pleasant in spite of its slightly resinous flavour. "It is strange—something must have happened to him. If he were continuing his trip he would have informed me of the town to which I was to send money, since I have his purse. I hope he has not broken his neck down some precipice. It is an absurd idea of his to go riding all the time through dirty, ill-paved countries, queer places where one starves, instead of remaining in Paris, comfortably installed in a pleasant home free from insects, mosquitoes, and other abominable creatures that blister one all over. I do not mind during the fine season; I can understand a man going to Ville-d'Avray, Celles, Saint-Cloud, Fontainebleau—no, not to Fontainebleau, there are too many painters; even then, I prefer Paris. People may say what they like, the country is made for peasants, and travelling for commercial travellers, because that is their business. But it gets to be pretty wearisome to be stuck in an inn to grow young again in a city where there is nothing but ruins to look at. What can our masters see in old stones? As if new, well-kept buildings were not a hundred times more pleasant to look at! There is no mistake about it, my master is very impolite to me. It is true I am his servant, and it is my duty to attend him, but he has no right to make me die of weariness in the Hôtel d'Angleterre. Suppose some misfortune has happened to that dear master of mine—after all, he is a kind master—I should never get over it unless I found a better situation. I have a good mind to set out to look for him—but in what direction? Who knows whither his fancy has taken him? No doubt into the most extravagant and most improbable spots, into breakneck places that he calls picturesque and of which he makes sketches as if they were worth looking at. Well, I will give him three days more to return home; after that time I shall have him drummed and posted at every street corner like a lost dog, with a promise of a handsome reward to whoever brings him back."

Acting up to his office of sceptical modern servant who makes great fun of the devoted and faithful old-fashioned valet, the worthy Jack was trying to blind himself to his very genuine anxiety. At bottom he loved Guy de Malivert and was greatly attached to him. Although he was aware that his master had put him down in his will for a very handsome sum that would secure him a comfortable home, he did not wish for Guy's death.

The hotelkeeper also began to be anxious, not concerning Malivert, whose bill was paid, but concerning the two horses he had furnished for the expedition. As he mourned over the problematical fate of these two peerless animals, so sure-footed, so easy in their gait, so tender-mouthed, and which could be driven with a silk thread, Jack said to him impatiently, with an air of supreme disdain: "Well, if your two hacks are dead, you will be paid for them"—an assurance which restored the serenity of the worthy Diamantopoulos.

Every evening the guide's wife, a handsome and robust matron who might well have taken the place of the caryatid removed from the Pandrasion, and for which has been substituted a terra cotta reproduction, came to inquire if Stavros, her husband, had returned, either with or without the traveller. On hearing the reply, which was invariably in the negative, she would sit down on a stone at a little distance from the hotel, undo the false tress of fair hair that bound her black hair, shake it out, put her hands to her face as if she were going to scratch herself, utter sighs like a ventriloquist, and engage in all the theatrical demonstrations of antique grief. At bottom she was really not very sorry, for Stavros was not much of a man, and a great deal of a drunkard, who beat her when he was tipsy and gave her very little money, although he earned quite a sum by acting as guide; but she owed it to fashion to manifest proper despair. Gossip—which was not slander in this case—charged her with being consoled in her intermittent widowhood by a handsome, wasp-waisted Palikar with a bell-like fustanella that held at least sixty yards of fine pleated stuff, and a red fez with a blue silk tassel falling down to the middle of his back. Her grief, genuine or affected, expressed in hoarse sobs that recalled the barking of Hecuba, greatly bothered the worthy Jack, who although incredulous, was somewhat superstitious. "I do not like," he would say, "that woman who howls over her absent husband like a dog that scents death." And the three days which he had set as the extreme limit of Malivert's return having passed, he went to a magistrate and made his statement.

The most active search was undertaken in the direction probably followed by Malivert and his guide. The mountain was traversed in every direction, and in a hollow road was found the carcass of a horse lying on its side stripped of its harness, and already half devoured by the crows. The horse's shoulder had been broken by a ball, and the steed had no doubt fallen with its rider. Around the dead animal the ground seemed to have been trampled as if in a struggle, but too many days had elapsed since the probable time of the attack, which had no doubt taken place several weeks before. There was little to be learned from the vestiges half-effaced by rain and wind. In a lentisk bush near the road a branch had been cut by a projectile; the upper part was hanging withered. The ball, which was that of a pistol, was found farther off in a field. The person assailed seemed to have defended himself. What had been the outcome of the fight? Probably fatal, since neither Malivert nor his guide had reappeared. The horse was recognised as one of the two hired by Diamantopoulos to the young French traveller. But for lack of clearer indications, the inquiry naturally came to a stop. Every trace of the aggressors and of the victim—or rather, victims, for there must have been two—was lost. The thread was broken at the very outset.

A detailed description of Malivert and Stavros was sent to every possible place where the direction of the roads might have taken them, but they had not been seen anywhere. Their voyage had ended there. Perhaps the brigands had taken Malivert to some inaccessible cavern in the mountains in the hope of getting a ransom out of him; but on examination this theory proved absurd. The brigands would certainly have sent one of their number in disguise to the city to find means of handing to Jack a letter stating the conditions of the ransom, with a threat of mutilation in case of delay, and of death in case of refusal, as is the way in that sort of business. But nothing of the kind had occurred; no message had come from the mountains to Athens, and the brigands' post office had not been utilised.

Jack, who was greatly worried at the idea of returning to France without his master, whom he might be supposed to have murdered, although he had never left the Hôtel d'Angleterre, did not know which way to turn, and more than ever cursed the mania for travelling that leads well-dressed men to gloomy places, where robbers in carnival costumes shoot them down like hares.

A few days after the search Stavros reappeared at the hotel, in a most pitiable condition—wan, thin, worn, with a terrified, crazed look, like a spectre rising from the tomb without having shaken off the dust of the grave. His rich and picturesque costume, which he was so proud of and which produced so marked an effect upon travellers in love with local colour, had been taken from him and replaced by filthy rags covered with the mud of the camping-places. A greasy sheepskin was drawn over his shoulders, and no one would have recognised him as the tourists' favourite guide. His unexpected return was at once reported to the magistrates, and he was temporarily arrested, for though well known in Athens and comparatively honest, he had left with a traveller and was returning alone—a circumstance that judges are not apt to think quite natural. Nevertheless, Stavros succeeded in proving his innocence. His occupation of guide naturally would not admit of his destroying travellers by whom he profited; and besides, he did not need to murder them to rob them. Why should he have waited by the edge of a road for victims when they followed him on the high road most willingly, and shared a sufficient quantity of their gold with him?

But the story he told of Malivert's death was most strange and very difficult to believe. According to him, while they were peaceably riding along the hollow way at the place where the carcass of the horse had been found, an explosion of firearms was heard, followed almost immediately by another. The first shot had knocked over the horse ridden by M. de Malivert, and the second had struck the traveller himself, who by an instinctive movement had put his hand to his holster and fired a pistol-shot at random. Three or four bandits had sprung over the bushes to strip Malivert, and two others had made Stavros get off his horse, although he did not attempt resistance, knowing it to be useless.

So far the account was not very different from the usual highwayman stories, but the continuation was much less credible, although the guide swore to its truth. He claimed to have seen by Malivert, dying, whose face, far from expressing anguish or agony, beamed on the contrary with celestial joy, a figure of dazzling whiteness and marvellous beauty, which must have been the Panagia, and which placed upon the traveller's wound, as if to still his sufferings, a hand of light. The bandits, terrified by the apparition, had fled to a distance, and then the lovely lady had taken the dead man's soul and flown away to heaven with it.

Every effort to shake his account failed. The body of the traveller had been hidden under a rock on the bank of one of the torrents always dry in summer, the bed of which was filled with rose-laurels. As for him, as he was a poor devil not worth killing, he had been first stripped of his handsome clothes, and then taken a long way into the mountains to prevent his revealing the murder, and had escaped only with the greatest difficulty. Stavros was set free, for if he had been guilty it would have been very easy for him to have reached the islands or the Asiatic coast with Malivert's money. His return to Athens, therefore, proved his innocence.

The account of Malivert's death was sent to Mme. de Marillac, his sister, very much as it had been told by Stavros; even Spirite's apparition was mentioned, but as an hallucination of the terrified guide, whose brain did not seem sound.

Just about the time when the murder was being committed on Mount Parnassus, Baron de Feroë had withdrawn according to custom into his inaccessible rooms and was busy reading that strange and mysterious work of Swedenborg entitled *Marriage in the Other Life.* While he was reading he felt a peculiar sensation, as when he was warned of a revelation. The thought of Malivert crossed his brain, although it was not brought by any natural transition. A light showed in his room, the walls of which became transparent and opened like a hypaetral temple, showing at an immense depth, not the sky beheld by human eyes, but the heavens that are beheld by seers. In the centre of a glory of light that seemed to issue from the depths of the infinite, two points of still greater intensity of splendour, like diamonds in a flame, scintillated, palpitated, and drew near, assuming the appearance of Malivert and Spirite. They floated side by side in a celestial, radiant joy, caressing each other with their wings and toying with divine endearments. Soon they drew closer and closer, and then, like two drops of dew rolling on the same lily leaf, they finally formed a single pearl.

"There they are, happy forever, their united souls forming an angel of love," said Baron de Feroë, with a melancholy smile. "But how long have I still to wait?"

About S. T. Joshi

S. T. JOSHI is the author of *The Weird Tale* (1990), *H. P. Lovecraft: The Decline of the West* (1990), and *Unutterable Horror: A History of Supernatural Fiction* (2012). He has prepared corrected editions of H. P. Lovecraft's work for Arkham House and annotated editions of Lovecraft's stories for Penguin Classics. He has also prepared editions of Lovecraft's collected essays and poetry. His exhaustive biography, *H. P. Lovecraft: A Life* (1996), was expanded as *I Am Providence: The Life and Times of H. P. Lovecraft* (2010). He is the editor of the anthologies *American Supernatural Tales* (Penguin, 2007), Black Wings I-II-III (PS Publishing, 2010, 2012, 2013), *A Mountain Walked: Great Tales of the Cthulhu Mythos* (Centipede Press, 2014), *The Madness of Cthulhu* (Titan Books, 2014–15), and *Searchers After Horror: New Tales of the Weird and Fantastic* (Fedogan & Bremer, 2014). He is the editor of the *Lovecraft Annual* (Hippocampus Press), the *Weird Fiction Review* (Centipede Press), and the *American Rationalist* (Center for Inquiry). His Lovecraftian novel *The Assaults of Chaos* appeared in 2013.